THE RISE OF THE RED EMPIRE

"This book is fantastic and the best read
in the series so far. Full of surprises
and action other than warfare. Every
chapter end is a cliff hanger.
Brilliant!"

"I think that people of my age will thoroughly
enjoy reading this epic."

Scott Griffiths aged 13

Dedication by the author

This book is for my kids.
Sorry I blew two of you up at the end of book 1.

THE RISE OF THE RED EMPIRE

Colin Foreman

Edited by Lillian King

As Scotland descends into bloody civil war, the High Table divides and clan fights against clan.

Prince Ranald fulfils his promise and Alistair of Cadbol turns to a friend, and an old enemy, to defend the Younger's legacy.

South of the land of the Franks, a descendant of kings fights his way home and Myroy's prediction about the union of the royal houses, of Elder and Donald, begins to come true.

A new Long Peace is a while away yet, but the first seeds of hope take root.

In our time, Odin holds the stone and most of the planet kneels to his authority. His forces invade the free world and the Valkyrie enslave the peoples of Europe.

Helped by a spy, a cuckoo in the nest, Peter, Bernard and the Winged Guardian lead the resistance in the Orange Band, but the very existence of the Keepers and the Realm of the Dead comes under threat.

Myroy watches helplessly, as the world he defended for centuries is torn apart. All of his fears become real and he tries to discover how to destroy the old magic, and free mankind from the curse of the Ancient Ones.

The Rise of the Red Empire is the fourth part of a five book series titled, *Keepers and Seekers*.

A catalogue record for this book is available from the British Library

Printed and bound in Poland EU, produced by Polskabook

Published by Myroy Books Limited

ISBN – 978-0-9548949-3-1

Acknowledgements

I would like to thank the following people.

Lillian King (Magnificent editing)

Wayne Reynolds (Drop dead gorgeous cover paintings)

Fiona Campbell (Cool black and white illustrations)

Rosie Crawford (Spot on proof reading)

Ian Donaldson, Royal Bank of Scotland, Kinross
(An even bigger overdraft)

John Webb (Design, support and a bill for a laptop)

Robert Snuggs at Bounce (Boundless raw energy)

Craig Brown (Everything to do with getting the
book ready for the printer – the hard bit!)

Abi, Jonny and Scott (Rave reviews)

CONTENTS

ABOUT BOOK ONE

Ten thousand years ago, as the great ice sheets begin to thaw across Scotland, four brothers, Odin, Thor, Tirani and Myroy, survive a terrible accident to become Ancient Ones. The key to their eternal lives and extraordinary powers is a living ruby.

Fearing his brother's cruel ambitions, Myroy steals the stone from Thor and destroys his invasion fleet. Odin, who is driven by anger and greed, swears vengeance for Thor's death and vows to recover the ruby, and use its power to destroy the free peoples of Scotland.

There follows a cat-and-mouse game, through the long centuries. Myroy chooses the Donald family and their descendants to live a quiet life, and hide the stone from Odin and his followers, the Seekers.

In our time, three children visit their grandparents in Scotland and get lost in a snowstorm. When they take shelter in a cottage, Myroy tells them a story about a Celtic shepherd who lived centuries ago.

Dougie of Dunfermline faces the challenges of Mountain, Island and Castle to become the first Stone Keeper. Even though Dougie survives these challenges he knows little about the stone's power, or the danger it holds for his family. Certainly, he does not know that Gora and the souls of everyone who has ever tried to steal Amera's stone, remain trapped inside the ruby, waiting for someone to give the stone away, break Thor's curse, and release them.

Storm clouds gather for Dougie's king, Malcolm the Younger, and for his people, who are surrounded by enemies intent on their destruction. Norse warriors, led by Thorgood Firebrand, invade the north of the kingdom to escape famine in their own lands. At the same time, Tella the Mac Mar, eager for revenge after his defeat on Carn Liath, forges a secret and terrible alliance with the Welsh and the Angles.

When the old man's story is told, Peter Donald realises that he is to become the next Stone Keeper. The ruby is passed on to him, but he loses it, and not to Odin's Seekers, but to Smith, a descendant of Tella the Mac Mar. Smith tricks Peter's sister into giving him the ruby and he uses its fantastic power to invade London. During the battle of Pinner High School, Peter recaptures the stone, but at an awful price, and he flees with his grandmother to Corfu.

ABOUT BOOK TWO

Denbara the Scribe travelled the length and breadth of the Scottish Kingdom, recording the fast ways to travel, and lonely places where armies might hide. Tella the Mac Mar cements his alliance with the Angles and the Welsh by gifting them a copy of this map. Worse still, Tella discovers how to make a new and stronger type of iron that will tip the balance of power in his favour.

As his evil Alliance grows in power, Alistair of Cadbol is imprisoned in the bowels of Berwick Castle, under sentence of death. His friends, Dougie, Donald and Hamish, pull off a daring rescue, which changes a number of lives. Hamish of Tain falls in love with a gypsy girl. Dougie of Dunfermline is made a member of the Younger's High Table, and Gora's spirit is finally freed from Amera's stone.

Malcolm the Younger sends the High Table to search his kingdom for clues about who is making the new light iron. Alistair suspects that the Picts are using the port of Stranraer to smuggle weapons to their allies and the search leads Dougie of Dunfermline into a vicious battle in a fort on the island of Man. The slaves of the foundry defeat the Black Kilts, but Tella escapes the island and sends his envoys to Mountjoy, to win the support of the Irish King, Patrick Three Eggs.

At the same time, the Younger realises he will face the three armies of Tella's alliance alone, and he sends Alistair and Dougie on another mission, to offer Patrick Three Eggs a gift; the hand of Murdoch's daughter Margaret. But Margaret has other ideas and falls in love with Patrick's son, Seamus.

Tella's envoys, Borak and Tumora, fear the Scots and the good relations they enjoy at the Irish court. In a bid to destroy a possible Scottish and Irish alliance, they trick Seamus into believing that Alistair and Dougie poisoned his father. They are now imprisoned and face death.

During the Second World War, Bernard recruits Peter's grandfather, Duncan Donald, into the Long Range Desert Group. But Duncan loses the stone and its incredible power threatens to turn the war in North Africa against the Eighth Army.

With luck and a brilliant idea from Private Chalk, the friends escape from a prisoner of war camp, travel across the desert and steal back the stone from General Georg Grau. The General's convoy of fuel is destroyed, before it can re-supply the German tanks west of El Alemein, and the Allied forces secure a famous victory.

In our time, Odin's forces hunt Peter down on the island of Corfu. Thorgood Firebrand captures Kylie and uses her to trap Peter. Odin takes Amera's stone and the world becomes divided.

ABOUT BOOK THREE

Ancevo, the Younger's secret rider, faces danger on his mission to Mountjoy. The message he carries is a lie, worded by Myroy and Malcolm to force anger into a shepherd's heart. Dougie's anger draws upon the power of Amera's stone and he defeats the Pict, Borak, in a duel which secures the Irish as allies in the coming war. That alliance is strengthened further by the marriage of Seamus and Margaret, but in terrible circumstances. Seamus's father has been murdered by a killer in the dark, and Margaret's father, Murdoch, has fallen in battle as the Picts take the Outer Islands, Oban and the High Glens.

Ancevo sails east to bring Gawain of Man into the war, and together with Hamish and Donald they search the Great Sea to destroy the Welsh and Pictish fleets. At the same time, Seamus places his new bride under the protection of Columba and O'Mara, and they sail for the safe haven of Iona. But the Pictish fleet is moored across Iona Sound at Fionnphort, under the control of Borak One Hand, and he takes them hostage in a bid to lure Seamus to Deros and avenge the death of his brother, Tumora. However, Borak does spare Matina and the little girl is abandoned, alone, on the island.

In our time, on a concrete slipway, Peter is consumed by grief at the death of his girlfriend. Myroy deliberately ignores his grief and continues to tell him about the history of the stone. As Peter is physically forced to listen, he learns that when Murdoch and Malcolm were children, Odin lied to them to hold his ruby again. When the Ancient One tried to use its power, the stone returned to its last place of hiding.

At the end of this part of the story, Myroy reunites Peter with his family and girlfriend, but anger, the same deadly anger forced into every Keeper's heart, is now a part of him, ready to be called upon in the final battle with Odin.

Back in Celtic times, mighty armies gather at Stirling and Cuthbert's Angles take the castle after desperate fighting and a brave defence. The Younger knows he needs more warriors and he convinces Morag McCreedy and the clans of the Great Plain to help him for the first time. As he senses Morag's hatred of Benita the gypsy, and her coldness towards men, Morag remembers the plans she has made with Prince Ranald to divide the High Table and overthrow the king. When the Scots and Irish arrive at Stirling, they see the massive Welsh army. Llewellyn holds Amera's stone and knows he is invincible. Malcolm fears him more than anyone and he pays Benita to smuggle Alistair and Dougie into the Welsh war camp. Using a simple magic trick, the gypsy leader steals back the brooch. As Benita secretly replaces it with a copy, Thorfinn and Thorgood Firebrand see Llewellyn hold what they think is their master's stone, and so Odin is also fooled. The god orders his people to seek out the stone in the land of the Welsh and, for generations, the Keepers were safe on Scottish soil.

As war rages, the lands around Stirling become littered with the dead, but Tella's army is nowhere to be seen. As instructed by Myroy, Alistair and the Younger lie again to Dougie, about the death of his family. The shepherd's devastating anger is unleashed on the Angles. Before Stirling Castle is completely destroyed, by the power which exists in the land, Belus kills Cuthbert and avenges the murder of his children.

At last, the Black Kilts arrive, confident that the Scots and Irish are weakened after the long battle. But the Welsh and Angles had been defeated with little loss and the Younger traps the Picts between his riders, spearmen and foot-soldiers. Tella and Gath flee the slaughter along their planned escape route, but are pursued by the High Table. Alistair hunts the Mac Mar down and they fight to the death inside the church on Iona.

Dougie of Dunfermline returns home, dreading what he might find there. Sadness grips him like a vice and he dreams of being with his twin, Alec, once more. As he sobs beside Dog's bones and rebuilds his cottage, his friends and family are returned to him, but like Peter, he will never be the same again.

In our time, Peter and Kylie visit Grandma in Scotland and have anything but a normal day. The last Keeper reads *Early Celtic Writings and their Meanings*, in a chamber hidden under the sea, and learns about the Realm of the Dead and Grandpa's adventures on Corfu during the Second World War.

With the help of a Winged Guardian, the SKEPERE team at MI5 and an ancient folded page left deliberately in a rucksack, Odin is tricked again. He now knows Peter of the line of Donald is the Keeper and believes he is in Australia, and sends his Seekers to search there for him. For the first time in a long time, Peter feels safe and free from the burden he carries. As he swims in Bernard's pool on the slopes of Pantokrator, he looks forward to taking Kylie to the Realm of the Dead to meet the Twelve, the Keepers who have hidden Amera's stone through the long centuries.

In this book, Scotland descends into bloody civil war and the High Table divides as clan fights against clan. Prince Ranald fulfils his promise and Alistair of Cadbol turns to a friend, and an old enemy, to defend the Younger's legacy.

South of the land of the Franks, a descendant of kings fights his way home and Myroy's prediction about the union of the royal houses, of Elder and Donald, begins to come true. A new Long Peace is a while away yet, but the first seeds of hope take root.

In our time, Odin holds the stone and most of the planet kneels to his authority. His forces invade the free world and the Valkyrie enslave the peoples of Europe. Helped by a spy, a cuckoo in the nest, Peter, Bernard and the Winged Guardian lead the resistance in the Orange Band, but the very existence of the Keepers and the Realm of the Dead comes under threat.

Myroy watches helplessly, as the world he defended for centuries is torn apart. All of his fears become real and he tries to discover how to destroy the old magic, and free mankind from the curse of the Ancient Ones.

PROLOGUE

THE BIRDS IN THE SKY
AND THE FISH IN THE SEA

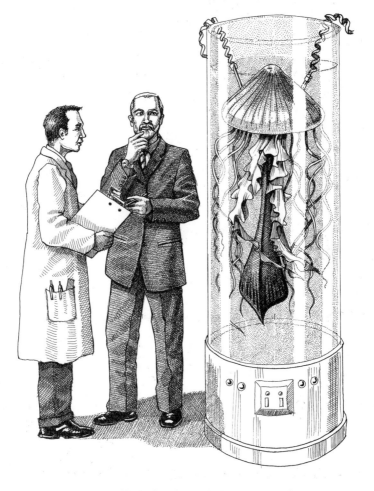

Holly Anderson sipped her coffee and walked across to the huge picture of the moon in the SKEPERE office, on lower level five of the MI5 building in Vauxhall.

"Screen on."

The picture changed to become a television screen.

"Switch to High Security."

A red dot appeared in the bottom right hand corner. Holly pulled a chair over from beside the wall and sat down, sipping more coffee.

"This is the SKEPERE team in London calling Sri Lanka."

At the words, "Sri Lanka" a small red clock appeared on the screen, showing 5.00 a.m. A woman's smiling face appeared too, the scene of a busy office behind her.

"Good morning, Pushpa. How are you today?"

"I am well. You are working late, must be twelve thirty in the UK."

Holly sighed.

"Oh, you know, things need to be done. Weekly report?"

"Position green. No problems."

"Thank you. By the way, I meant to ask you last week, does *Pushpa* mean anything in Sinhalese?"

The girl beamed.

"In Sri Lanka it means flower."

"That's lovely."

"And *Holly*?"

"Um, wish you hadn't asked. Prickly tree. Speak to you next week."

The screen went blank and Holly spoke in a tired voice.

"This is the SKEPERE team in London calling Australia."

A man's face this time and another busy office behind him, people looking at computer screens and walking around with coffee cups in their hands. The red clock showed 9.30 a.m.

"Good morning, Bob. How are you?"

The man replied in a cheery Aussie accent.

"Bloody hot, Holly, and I don't mean the weather."

"Better give me your report."

"No change from last week. Position red. Seekers are crawling all over Melbourne and they haven't found a thing. Thought I might leave a bit of a trail and send them off to Western Australia. They can't do much harm out there."

"OK, Bob. Keep up the good work. Call me if you need anything."

"How about dinner one night? I know this great seafood restaurant overlooking Sydney harbour."

Holly frowned.

"Let's just keep this to business, shall we."

Bob grinned and shrugged his shoulders.

"I'll speak to you next week then."

The TV went blank.

"This is the SKEPERE team in London calling Norway."

Nothing changed on the screen and Holly checked her watch.

"Right time for the update."

Miss Dickson joined her in the office and pulled up a chair.

"It's been a long day. Think I'll go home. Coming?"

"Yes. Let me just try Bjorn again, there must be a problem with the line. This is the SKEPERE team from London calling Norway. Bjorn, are you there?"

The screen remained blank.

"Computer. Check line to Oslo."

Words appeared –

No Fault on the Line

"Activate the automatic line-on system."

The web-cam in the Oslo office came alive. Seekers were everywhere, firing guns, handcuffing prisoners, kicking over desks and destroying equipment. Olaf Adanson's face filled the screen.

"Death to the Keepers," he said.

The television went blank.

Thorgood Firebrand and Doctor Van Heussen walked quickly along a brightly lit corridor towards the entrance to the Cloning Research Centre, deep below the O.A.S.V. offices in Oslo.

"You are the world's leading authority on genetic engineering. Give me an honest answer. Can we fulfil our master's ambition?"

The doctor glanced at him.

"Yes. There are many unanswered questions, but progress is being made. We are meeting the deadlines on the current schedule. Come, see."

They approached a circular door, that looked as though it could survive a nuclear explosion, and stopped. The floor, from their toes to the door and from the base of the walls on both sides, lit up and Odin's face stared up at them.

"Master, we wish to enter and evaluate the progress made in the experiment."

Odin's eyes flashed and the god knew that Thorgood's words were true. The floor became a floor again and the circular door swung open on a single giant hinge. As they walked across, Van Heussen shuddered. If he was an intruder, then this would be as far as he would get. Here the floor would disappear and plunge a victim into a furnace and then into the experimental rock chamber. If you survived the fall or the fire, there was only death down there. The creatures would see to that.

They walked side by side, passing glass cylinders which ran from floor to ceiling and grew wider and wider. Each cylinder showed a stage of the doctor's experiments. The first held a mosquito, hardly visible in the clear gel that preserved its body. The next cylinder contained a bird-sized creature, like a mosquito, but redder in colour and more hideous. They walked past three more cylinders and came to the last clone. Van Heussen tapped the glass.

"The Mark Six *Bird* has a wingspan of over two metres. As you can see, this specimen has evolved from the mosquito in some interesting ways. Please observe the long sting that hangs down from the body. Quite deadly to humans. The creature is fast and highly manoeuvrable, and completely without fear. Three metres from top to tail. We hold sixty creatures in the rock chamber and watch closely their speed of reproduction. I particularly like their bright red wings. Very colourful."

Another row of cylinders and the doctor nodded at the first.

"Codename, *Fish*. The original specimen. This one," he tapped the glass again, "is the Portuguese Man of War, a jelly fish that can kill. Excellent raw material."

They moved past seven cylinders that got wider and each contained more deadly creatures, which became redder, bigger and uglier. They stared through the gel of the last glass case.

"The Mark Eight *Fish*. It's a bit like a crimson umbrella. Do you see the suckers and spines that cover the tail? I am analyzing the poison as it is quite unlike anything we have encountered before."

"Deadly?" asked Thorgood.

"Oh yes."

"Kill time?"

"Less than a minute for a healthy, fully grown male."

"What about ships?"

"On their own, little impact. But imagine a long chain, a red oil slick of the creatures, that will destroy anything."

"How?"

"You see the slime on the body. It can eat through metal. A fascinating feature. I'm having that analysed too."

"And the tail?"

"Yes, elegant and powerful. The normal 'suck-in and blow-out' propulsion system was just too slow. This long tail can drive the Mark Eight forward at a good speed. The motion is modelled on a dolphin's tail."

"Anything else?"

The doctor pointed at the specimen.

"You have to imagine thousands of these creatures. They will terrify the enemy and form an impenetrable barrier, hundreds of miles long, to ships and men."

Thorgood nodded.

"Are they programmed to only attack Keepers?"

"You mean Keeper sensitive?"

"You know what I mean."

"They will attack anyone who is not protected by the stone."

"The creatures must be able to penetrate the Orange Band and attack the enemy beyond it."

"That is one of the unanswered questions. I think they will, but I have no evidence to support that view."

"We will find out when war comes. Is everything ready for the demonstration?"

"Yes."

"You are sure?"

"Yes."

"Any comments?"

"I am particularly pleased with the way the Birds have evolved. Still think the Fish are a bit slow."

"Then speed them up."

"I obey."

They walked through the rest of the cloning laboratory, strands of DNA spiraling around on computer screens, body parts floating in glass tanks with flashing probes sticking out of them and everywhere men in white coats holding clip-boards and checking things. Thorgood and Van Heussen left through another solid round door, identical to the first one, and entered a lift. Five floors down, they stepped onto the highly polished floor of a long observation room with four seats in front of a reinforced glass window that ran the entire length of the room. Olaf Adanson sat on one of the seats and behind him a tall fountain splashed and tinkled.

"The preparation here is complete."

Thorgood nodded at Olaf and spoke to Odin in his mind.

"Master, the demonstration is ready."

The waters of the fountain widened and turned red, and Odin walked out, bone dry, in an immaculate Italian suit.

"Begin."

They took their seats and the doctor picked up a remote control, and began his eager introduction.

"As you know, this demonstration has to be conducted in strictly controlled conditions and …."

Odin's eyes flashed, blue, and Olaf sensed his master's agitation.

"Doctor. We do not need a speech. Let the enemy join the fallen."

Van Heussen pushed a button on the remote control and a steel door, below the observers and to their right, rose up. Thorgood stared down at the massive rock chamber, at the field of barley and a pine wood, like an island in the barley. On the opposite side to the door was a lake, its waters grey with red strings across it. A railway line joined the two sides of the cavern, but it was the rising steel door and the honeycomb of small round caves above it that held everyone's attention.

"Audio," said Odin.

The doctor pushed another button, but the chamber was quiet. Six men, who had been taken prisoner during the raid on the Keeper's office in Oslo, stepped tentatively through the door, glancing around and one pointing at the field of barley ahead of them. They stood in silence, fearing a trick, until one spoke. His words came through the speakers as though he was in the observation chamber too.

"We can't stay here."

"But where, Bjorn?"

"There. Come on."

The man and his followers walked through the barley, their steps leaving a trail of flattened stalks behind them, and heading in single file towards the island of trees, still glancing around nervously. A low humming noise came out of the speakers as the line of men entered the pines. It grew louder, higher pitched like a scream and more menacing. The Keepers left the trees and marched on across the barley towards the lake. Thorgood watched a single spear-like spine emerge from each cave. A red body followed, legs like sticks around it, holding the body in the centre of the tunnel and shuffling the creature forward. The red birds shot out of their caves like an enraged swarm of giant bees, the whine from their wing beats making the hunted men turn. More clear voices.

"What the devil are they?"

"Who cares. Run to the trees."

The swarm dived and flashed into the pines on the other side to the runners. The screams of terrified men filled the observation room. Three men broke cover and sprinted towards the lake, one red bird chasing them.

"Why do the other clones not pursue them?" asked Odin.

"Feeding," replied the doctor.

The creature dived, its deadly tail curved forward, ready to kill. Seconds later, the slowest Keeper was stung by a weapon the size of a spear and he fell face down, the attacker flapping its wings, biting and trying to drink blood. The other two men dived into the lake and their splashes earned an instant response. Red circles appeared all around them and Thorgood witnessed another feeding frenzy. Gradually, the screams faded away and Olaf spoke to Odin.

"Master. How many do you desire?"

"One million of each creature."

The doctor gasped.

"We can achieve that number, but *when* depends on how fast they breed in captivity."

"Find out."

"I obey, Master."

Odin stared down at the red bird feeding on the Keeper and listened to the sucking noise that came from the speakers. He looked at the doctor and made his point without saying a word. Van Heussen knew exactly what would happen to him if he did not produce two million creatures. The sucking noise of his

9

creations was imprinted on his mind. Thorgood broke the tense silence.

"The human cloning experiment. Will it be ready for the bi-annual meeting?"

The doctor's voice was shaky.

"Yes. It will be ready."

Odin stood and turned to face Thorgood.

"Send Bernard a parcel."

"I obey, Master."

As the god walked into the red fountain, he called back.

"Death to the Keepers."

"Death to the Keepers," repeated everyone.

✱✱✱

Holly Anderson stared at a square brown box and lifted her mobile phone.

"Bernard, we have received a third parcel."

"From Thorgood Firebrand?"

"We have him on CCTV, rising up out of the Thames and placing it in front of the MI5 building."

"Please describe the package."

"Thirty centimetres square, light, wrapped in brown paper, no message visible."

"Has it been scanned?"

"Yes. No danger. It's some kind of tube. Paper probably."

"Please open it."

Holly used scissors to cut through the wrapping and pulled the lid off.

"A toilet roll."

"Please read the message."

"It is written in Thorgood's own hand and says, 'Bernard, my dear enemy. You are going to need this. Look for the birds in the sky and the fish in the sea.'"

"I see," said Bernard slowly.

"Do you know what it means?"

10

"No. I couldn't guess what the other messages meant either, not until things actually happened. That's the point, isn't it? Scare us. Keep us guessing until something happens."

"But this time you think something big, something terrible, is going to happen, don't you."

"Thorgood delivered it personally. It wasn't posted like the others. I am sure of it, Holly. I'm absolutely sure of it."

CHAPTER ONE

ALEC OF DUNFERMLINE : LATE AUTUMN 677 AD

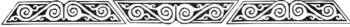

Perpigno the Tongue Speaker picked up his goatskin water carrier and walked along the deck, which was covered with barrels of wine. He stopped in front of a sleeping figure, wrapped in a brightly coloured blanket.

"Good morning, Brown Eyes."

From under the blanket a mop of long brown hair slowly appeared, followed by a sincere, tanned face with eyes squinting in the dawn sun.

"Water?" Perpigno asked.

Alec took the water carrier and drank thirstily.

"I had the saddest dream."

Perpigno smiled.

"From the way you were rolling about on the deck, I would say it was more of an adventure than a dream."

"It was all so real. I was talking to my brother, my twin, through floating bones and strange firelight. I think Dougie has lost his family. He grieves terribly."

"*Lost* his family?"

"There is war in my homeland. He believes them to be dead."

"In my village there is an old woman who can tell you what your dreams mean." Perpigno took back his goatskin carrier. "But even she would struggle with that dream."

"I think I know what it means," said Alec.

"That you fear for the safety of your brother?"

"No. I think it's time to take one last voyage."

"Where to?"

Alec smiled.

"To the land of the Scots."

At high sun, under gorgeous clear blue skies, the trader lost speed as the winds eased, and Danjou the Gaul worked hard with Alec to raise as much sail as the mast could take. Danjou said something in his native tongue and the Scotsman shrugged his shoulders, not understanding. The Gaul pointed at a tented area, just in front of the tiller, which meant he was asking how the Shipmaster was. Alec called out to Perpigno who was washing his face in a bucket of water.

"Any news of the Master?"

Perpigno stopped scooping water and rubbing it onto his cheeks.

"He said he didn't want to be disturbed. Scart took him food and he waved it away. I think he must be *very* sick."

"Can you tell Danjou that?"

Perpigno spoke to the Gaul in their native Gallic tongue, before calling back to Alec again.

"Did you hear the Master last night? He was with the fever and talking strangely."

"Will he be alright?"

Perpigno grinned.

"He is a tough man. A little fever will not stop him ordering his crew around for very long."

Alec nodded and thought about their passage to Melillia on the other side of the ocean. They had traded there many times and would stay in the small port for just two nights, before returning north to Almeria with fruits, nuts, spices, cloth and ivory. Despite the fact that their Shipmaster refused to trade in slaves, a more profitable cargo, they had all done well and Alec had more coins than Dougie could have saved in a lifetime. He wondered how his twin was and if his dream was real.

"Scart looks as though he has burned the bread again," said Perpigno.

Alec and Danjou stopped pulling on a rope and secured it. Scart waved his arms and shouted.

Instantly, Perpigno's face changed. He yelled at Danjou who ran back along the deck, between the barrels, beckoning to Alec to follow him. Outside the tent, Perpigno comforted Scart, and Danjou pulled back the flap and went inside, Alec close behind him. On deck it had been hot, but inside, the tent was like an evil-smelling oven. They stood like statues, looking at the Master's staring eyes, whilst Danjou knelt and placed the flat of his hand

15

across the open mouth, feeling for breath. There was none. He glanced back at Alec, and shook his head.

Fearing the spread of the fever, they quickly lifted the Master's body and carried it outside.

"Are you sure he has joined the fallen?" asked Perpigno.

"Quite sure," said Alec.

Perpigno asked Danjou the same question. The Gaul nodded.

"Then let him join the sea that he loved," said Perpigno.

Alec and Danjou balanced the body on the ship's rail, before pushing it overboard. They pulled down the tent, bundled it up and threw that overboard too. The Master's cushions and blankets followed. In less than the time it had taken Perpigno to wash his face, it was as though the Shipmaster had never walked upon the earth.

"Did he have any family?" asked Alec.

Perpigno shrugged his shoulders.

"I do not know. He never talked to me about them."

At sunset, the crew sat together near the prow, on the small part of the deck which was not covered in barrels. The tiller was lashed over, their boat becalmed on a smooth ocean. Scart struggled with a heavy black cauldron and placed it before them, before going back to his cooking area to fetch a tray piled with round, flat loaves. Danjou took a loaf, broke off a piece, folded it in two and used it to scoop out some of Scart's fish stew. It was good and he smiled at the young cook, and tried to guess his age. Ten summers, maybe twelve, he thought.

"The Master would have liked this stew," said Perpigno.

"Och, he just loved food," said Alec.

Danjou mumbled something, his mouth full of bread. Scart nodded.

"What did he say?" asked Alec.

"He said that some of the Shipmasters he has sailed with were cruel. We were lucky to have ours."

"Did he have a name?"

"We only ever knew him as the Master. The traders in Almeria and Melillia knew him only as that. Even his ship doesn't have a name."

"How long did you know him?"

"Eight summers. The Master heard about me and came to my father's shipyard. He needed a Tongue Speaker to help him win good terms with the Moors in North Africa. Said he would pay me well, which he did." Perpigno smiled. "I remember being so excited at going to sea, and I imagined all the ports along the edge of the ocean that I had only heard of in stories. But we never visited any of them, only Almeria and Melillia. Backwards and forwards between Almeria and Melillia all the time. I think he avoided going further east."

"Why?"

"Corsairs. They are a danger to traders throughout these waters, but they rarely troubled us."

Alec's eyes opened wide "You have seen them?"

"They have the biggest ships you have ever seen. Long, narrow, fast. They have a battering ram at the prow that could rip our ship in half as though it were made of parchment."

"How many sails?"

"Oh, just the one. Their speed comes from their slaves. I was once told they can hold as many as eighty slaves who pull on forty oars."

"How did you escape them?"

"We were lucky. We followed another trader and the Corsairs attacked them, and left us alone."

Scart had shivered at the word *Corsair*. He remembered the stories told to him by the village elders. Cruel and gruesome stories, which gave him sleepless nights for a long while afterwards.

He spoke to Perpigno, who translated for Alec's benefit.

"Scart says that he is very afraid of them, and he is right to be. The Corsairs work their slaves to death and then get new ones. Few ever escape to talk about it, but those who do say the pirates show their slaves no mercy. They are just beasts of burden to them."

Danjou interrupted and spoke to Perpigno for some time, whilst Alec and Scart took turns to dip their bread into the stew. As the conversation went on, Scart grinned at Alec, who smiled back and wondered what was going on. The ship rose and fell only very gently, and an orange glow marked the west as the last burning tip of the sun disappeared below the horizon. Danjou and Perpigno stopped talking.

"What was that all about?" asked Alec.

Perpigno ignored him and held a flat hand out above the iron cauldron. Danjou held his flat hand out too and said something to Scart, who did the same.

"It seems we have a new Shipmaster," said Perpigno.

"Who?" asked Alec.

Danjou rose and slapped him on the back.

At the end of the meal, Perpigno left them and returned with a small wooden casket. He placed it carefully beside the cauldron, sat down and crossed his legs.

"Your first test as the Master," he said.

Alec opened the lid. Inside were many silver coins of different shapes and sizes. One or two coins were gold. He looked at them for a while. They all looked at them.

"All the Master's possessions are yours now, although most of them are with the fishes," said Perpigno.

Alec thought about his dream and about Dougie's sadness.

"Will you ask Danjou and Scart something for me?"

"Of course, that is what I am paid for."

"Ask them this. For these coins, the ship and its cargo, will they, will you, Perpigno, be my crew for one long voyage? I want to see the hills around my home again."

The crew talked for a long time and, at last, Perpigno told Alec about their decision.

"I have never been that far north before. We can sell the wine, barrel by barrel, at different ports along the way and buy food. It sounds like an adventure."

At dawn, the wind picked up and they sailed west, their sail cracking each time they tacked. By nightfall, the wind was fully on their backs and their speed increased as they passed the low, shadowy outline of Isla Alboria. It looked like a lonely island, as though it had been abandoned long ago and made to rest in one of the remotest parts of the ocean. The island was soon behind them. At the tiller, under bright stars, Danjou stood with Alec. Perpigno and Scart slept peacefully, in bright-coloured blankets, in between the barrels.

"At this speed we will reach the narrow sea, between the two great oceans, in two days," said Alec.

Danjou looked at him quizzically and adjusted the tiller. There was silence for a long while and Alec thought about home. In his dream, as bones floated before his eyes, Dougie had told him of Lissy's death after he had left home and he prayed it was not so. He thought about the far hills again and how he had imagined them rising up into the sky like giant stone towers, and how the Season of Storms dusted them with a cold white blanket. A warm breeze lifted his long brown hair and he felt a long way from the farm he had known as a child. Danjou grabbed his arm and pointed at two pinpricks of light off to their left. There was no land anywhere near and they stared at the lights, guessing if they were lanterns, or fires burning in iron braziers, at the prow and stern of a ship.

"It must be a very long ship," said Alec.

Danjou's hurried, anxious voice broke in.

"Perpigno, Perpigno."

Alec put a reassuring hand on his friend's shoulder and went to wake the Tongue Speaker. Back at the tiller, they stared at the shadowy outline of the mystery ship.

"It could be anything," said Perpigno.

"It is sailing straight towards us," warned Alec.

"It could be a trader like ours. The nearer we get to the channel between the two great seas, the more ships we will see."

Alec tried to guess the distance between the two lights.

"It is big for a trader."

"Anyhow, you are the Master now. You must decide."

"I decide on caution. Tell Danjou to get us as far away from that ship as he can."

Perpigno gave Danjou the order.

"Shall I wake Scart?"

Alec looked at their small cook, sleeping, unaware of the possible danger. He smiled at him.

"No. Leave him be, laddie."

Danjou's keen ears were the first to pick up the distant sound of a deep, rhythmic drum. Now they knew. These were not traders. The menacing beat grew quicker, louder, and every bit of sail cloth was already open to the wind and no matter how Danjou steered, the two boats became closer and closer.

"Who are they?" asked Alec.

Perpigno shook his head.

"Corsican pirates, Corsairs, Moors from North Africa. Who knows? But they are all as bad as each other."

"What shall we do with Scart?"

"What can we do?"

"Is there nowhere to hide him?"

Perpigno glanced around the trader.

"A barrel?"

"A barrel," repeated Alec.

They manhandled one up onto the ship's rail and Alec used his dirk to prise open the lid. It flew off and he caught it as a cascade of red wine joined the sea. Perpigno called out in Gallic.

"Scart. Wake now."

Nothing.

"Scart. Wake now and come to me quickly."

A sleepy cook joined them.

"I had a bad dream."

Perpigno pointed at the two lights.

"You are about to have a nightmare."

He lifted Scart and lowered the boy inside the barrel, whilst Alec took a cork bung out of the lid.

20

It didn't seem big enough to provide anyone with enough air and so he took his dirk and punched more holes into the lid. Scart said something

"He says the barrel stinks and makes his head swim," said Perpigno.

Alec pushed the boy's head down and fixed the lid.

"He will just have to live with it."

They carried the barrel back with the others.

"They will see the holes," warned Alec.

Perpigno ran to his belongings and brought back a cloth, and laid it over the lid. The wind lifted its edge and Alec grabbed a coil of rope and unwound it across the tops of the barrels, holding the cloth down on Scart's barrel.

"It will have to do," he said.

Danjou shouted at them, fear in his voice. Back by the tiller, they watched two banks of oars strike the water on each side of the pirate ship. The drum beat quickened.

"What a speed they are doing," said Alec, "we cannot outrun them."

"Shall we fight?" asked Perpigno.

"What is their measure?"

"I do not know. Fifty, a hundred men?"

"So, three men against many. Tell Danjou to turn us around, then help me lower the sail."

The Corsairs turned their galley to come alongside the trader. Someone shouted and all the oars disappeared inside its hull.

"Let me do the talking," said Perpigno.

Alec smiled weakly.

"It's what you are paid for."

The sun was still below the horizon, but its growing orange glow gave them their first sense of the size of the enemy ship. It dwarfed them. Ropes were thrown at them by tough looking men, wearing brightly coloured silk waistcoats, white half-trousers and large, flat, round hats like wheels made of cloth. The crew of the trader obediently caught the ropes and secured them, and the ships were pulled together. About twenty Corsairs jumped aboard, holding long, curved swords.

"Kneel," whispered Perpigno.

They knelt down and Danjou copied them.

A huge, muscular, black Arab came to stand in front of them. He said something and Perpigno answered him, and pointed at the barrels and crew. Then he ran off and came back with the casket of coins which he laid on the deck in front of the pirate, before kneeling once more. The big man barked angry words at Perpigno.

"We must give them everything," Perpigno told Danjou and Alec.

They all got up and came back with the small bags of coins they had saved on their voyages, and knelt down again. The big Corsair took the bags and tossed them to another pirate. He barked out new orders and Perpigno jumped up immediately and prised open the lid of a barrel. He pointed inside and smiled. The big man joined him and stuck his finger into the wine and tasted it. He nodded and more Corsairs boarded and began to take the barrels back to their ship. Alec watched, holding his breath, as two of them brushed the cloth aside and lifted Scart's barrel. One of the men said something and they roughly put it back down. They broke the lid open and pulled Scart out by his hair. Danjou ran at them and punched one. Too quick for the eye, a sword flashed and severed Danjou's head. Alec jumped up, and the big Corsair smashed a fist into his face.

***

Alec woke in complete darkness, his nostrils attacked by the putrid smell of sweat and human waste. He was lying across a wooden pole and he tried to pull himself up, but his feet remained fixed to the floor. Chains rattled.

"Don't move," came a soft voice beside him. "Only whisper."

"Perpigno. Is that you?"

"It is."

"Where are we?"

"Aboard the Corsair's galley. Below deck, with the other slaves."

"How long have I been asleep?"

"All day and part of the night. Konini the Slave Master has a powerful punch."

Alec felt his chin. It still hurt. He moved his tongue around his gums. His teeth were all there.

"The big man?"

"The big man."

"Who are they?"

"Pirates from the east."

"What about Scart?"

There was silence for a while and Alec heard the sadness in his friend's words

"They didn't need a boy. He had no value. Just another mouth to feed."

"Oh, no."

More silence.

Alec felt his ankles. They were in strong iron rings, fixed to a chain that ran to the rings around Perpigno's ankles. After that, the tight chain disappeared off into blackness.

"Have you tried getting them off?"

"We all have."

"How many slaves are here?"

"One hundred and twenty here below deck, sitting in pairs, and one hundred and twenty above deck, so two hundred and forty slaves in all. It's a huge ship."

"How do we know where we are?"

Perpigno leant across, took Alec's hand and placed it into a round hole cut into the hull

"That is where the oar goes. It is our only window on the world."

"This smell is awful."

"At nightfall, some of the slaves at the front are unchained

23

by Konini. They are allowed up on deck to fetch buckets and wash out the floor. There are drain holes by your feet, where everything gets washed out to sea."

"*Everything* except the smell."

"If you obey Konini the Slave Master absolutely, you get moved forward, bench by bench, and eventually your reward is to feel the wind on your face again. For a short time, at least."

"So we eat here, sleep here, relieve ourselves here."

"And row here. I already hate the sound of the drum." His back flinched as he remembered the searing pain. "If you don't row, they whip you. I got whipped many times today because I couldn't wake you, and you lay across our oar."

"But what happens if the galley sinks?"

Perpigno leant down and rattled his chains. He didn't need to say anything.

"What about our ship?" asked Alec

"I don't know, but my guess is some of the Corsairs sailed her behind the galley. We did stop for a while yesterday and they probably sold her, and came back on board."

"We have got to get out of here."

"The only way is to be a good slave, move forward and when the deck gets cleaned, get away, somehow."

A slave behind them said something in a threatening voice.

"We stop talking now," said Perpigno. "We all need to rest and be ready for the dawn tide."

"My first day as a slave."

Perpigno rested his arms and chest onto their oar, and his breathing slowed.

"Welcome to hell," he whispered.

CHAPTER TWO

THE BEAT OF THE DRUM

As the sun burst above the horizon, horizontal beams of bright light shone through the oar holes and cut across the lower deck of the Corsair galley like golden-yellow fingers. Slaves began to stir, trying anything to put some life back into their tired limbs. Konini the Slave Master walked down the wide central aisle, pairs of slaves on either side of him, checking the chains and the condition of his prisoners. He went across to Alec of Dunfermline, grabbed his hair and stared into his eyes to see if his new arrival was awake and able to provide muscle to his oar. To the Corsairs, speed was everything. It meant an easy hunt or a successful escape. He spat in Alec's face. This new slave was not a Frank, a Gaul or an Arab. He was from northern lands, like the Celtic traders he had first met as a child in North Africa. He jerked Alec's head back viciously and spoke to Perpigno, and carried on down the aisle towards the front of the ship.

Alec watched him go, watched him pull two pegs up from holes in the floor, and the slaves in the front rows pull the long chains through their ankle irons. Then the slaves quickly grabbed buckets and climbed the stairs to the deck

"Same thing every morning," said Perpigno. "They fetch water and bread for us."

"No meat?"

"No meat."

"What did the Slave Master say?"

"That he watches you. If you disobey him, he will kill you."

Alec shuddered

"He looks powerful."

Lit from below, by a single beam on his chest, the dark outline of Perpigno's head nodded in agreement

"Do not even think of getting into a sword fight with him. He's tough.

Some of the slaves saw him fight aboard their ships. He is said to be the finest swordsman amongst the pirates. Even Spalda treats him with respect."

"Spalda?"

"The master of the galley. Corsican I think."

A slave, one of Konini's chosen helpers, passed Alec a wooden mug filled with water, and a long, thin loaf of bread. A hand shot forward from behind Alec, trying to grab the bread. The Scotsman held it away, out of range of the hungry man behind him.

"He tried the same with me on my first day," said Perpigno. "I do not blame him for trying either. Eat all of it, even if you don't like it. You won't be getting anything else until sunrise tomorrow."

The slaves in front of them began to eat noisily and Alec bit into his bread. It wasn't bad. It wasn't fresh either and was probably left over from a pirate feast the day before. The water tasted of dirt.

After a very short time, the slaves returned down the aisle, taking back the wooden mugs, and Perpigno and Alec gulped down their last drops of water. As Konini shouted at his helpers to return to their benches, Alec watched the Slave Master carefully check that their chains were pulled right through their ankle irons, that the chain was pulled tight to the centre of the aisle and the holding pegs pushed firmly back in place. Konini gave each of them two loaves, before disappearing up a ladder. A solid-looking metal grid banged shut behind him. The sound of two bolts being snapped into place followed. The slaves breathed a sigh of relief and slowly ate their bread, grateful that they had not been beaten, or denied food.

As the day wore on, Alec's legs went numb and he rubbed them hard, and wiggled his feet to help the blood circulate inside his toes.

"When will they tell us to row?"

Perpigno pointed up at the deck, his hand slicing through the oval beam of light from their oar hole.

"We rowed all day yesterday, from the dawn tide until you woke up. They did well from our capture. Wine is a valuable commodity and, of course, they took our coins. Maybe they celebrated last night and are in no mood to sail today."

"Any idea where we are?"

"No. Moored off the coast somewhere. The slaves on the landward side might know."

Perpigno asked a question in his native tongue and no one answered. He asked it again in the language of the Moors and the man behind him replied.

"He says we might be heading for the pirate village. It is two days' sail, east of Melillia. There is a river there and the village is hidden somewhere on its banks," said Perpigno.

"How long has he been a prisoner here?" asked Alec.

Perpigno asked the Moor the question and Alec listened as the man's words tumbled out, as though he needed someone to share his misery with.

"Three hundred and ten nights, so almost a year. He has survived longer than almost any of the slaves on the lower deck and certainly much longer than those chained above us."

"Do the slaves on deck not live long?"

Perpigno spoke again to the man.

"He says they last about three moons. They are burnt in the high sun and shiver at night, and are the first to provide Spalda with entertainment."

"Entertainment?"

"When the Galley Master gets bored, he kills them for fun. The Moor says you can sometimes hear their screams. Then the Corsairs ram another trader, take their cargo and ship, and replace the dead with the strongest of the crews they capture."

Alec bent and stared out of the oar hole. They were not more than an arm's length above the sea, which stretched out, an unbroken, untroubled, blanket of blue. A gull landed on the water and flew off again, out of view. He jumped as a single drum beat echoed throughout the galley. Men ran around on the deck above them. Bolts snapped open, the iron grille rose and the muscular frame of Konini came down the ladder.

"Hold your oar," warned Perpigno, "and only push it out of the hole when he tells you. Until the Slave Master goes back on deck, put all your strength into it. Remember, he needs the strong to stay strong and does not beat them, but he shows no mercy to the weak."

Konini stood, legs wide apart, in the central aisle and slowly uncoiled a leather whip. For a moment, his eyes met Alec's eyes. That single glance was enough. The Slave Master had made it clear he would be watching him and it struck terror into the Scotsman's heart.

"But what if I do not row?" whispered Alec to Perpigno, with false bravery.

They felt the ship drift and turn, as it broke its moorings. All the beams of light moved in the same direction and the beam from Alec's oar hole came to rest on the back of a bald slave directly in front of him. The slave winced as the heat of the morning sun caught his scars. Alec stared, wide-eyed, at the long, red lines of agony. Half of the man's skin was gone.

"No need to answer, my friend. I already know."

***

At high sun, the lower deck was like an oven and the smell of human waste was truly terrible.

Alec felt sick in his stomach as the drum kept time. The bald slave with the scars, in front of him, began to tire, sweat pouring from every pore, and his partner cursed his lack of effort. They missed some strokes and then got back into the rhythm again. Even though Konini wasn't there, they could not afford to slow. The drum thudded inside Alec's head, making him think of nothing except his fatigue and mind-numbing boredom.

"Will they not stop, rest us, give us water?" asked Alec.

"No. Not until sundown or the wind changes, and not even then if they have a pressing need to keep going."

The drum stopped and every slave fell forward onto their

oars, utterly exhausted. Shouts came from the Corsairs who ran around up on deck.

"Something has happened," said Perpigno.

The iron grille was lifted and Konini descended quickly. He flexed his whip and fear showed on the wide-eyed faces of his prisoners. Alec glanced out of the thin gap above the top of his oar. Just sea and nothing else. The drum sounded again and Konini walked up and down, checking the work of the slaves, but not harming them. The pace of the beat quickened and Alec used all his reserves of energy just to keep up. The pace quickened again and the slave in front of him missed his stroke. There was a sharp *crack* as Konini's whip cut into his back. The bald man screamed in agony. The speed of the drum increased once more, to an unbearable pace and Alec felt as though his head would explode with the pain.

"Keep going," said Perpigno. "It will not last long. Keep going."

The drum kept beating.

"We must be moving at an incredible speed," gasped Alec.

Sweat dripped from his hair into his eyes, blinding him, and he felt his wet hands begin to slip off their oar. There was a huge *crash* at the front of the ship and all the slaves were thrown violently forward. Someone screamed. Alec helped his friend back onto their bench and glanced up at the Slave Master. He stood like a rock in the centre aisle and hadn't moved a hair's width during the collision. Konini stretched out his whip, shouted something, and moved both hands across his chest, sideways.

"Pull the oar into the ship," said Perpigno.

They pulled, everyone pulled and the cutting, oval beams of sunlight returned. Then Konini ran to the ladder, climbed up and the iron grille was bolted shut. The slaves talked in excited whispers.

"They must have rammed another trader," said Perpigno.

"Poor devils."

The slaves on the other side of the galley peered out of their oar holes. Some shook their heads.

"What's happening?" asked Alec.

The muffled sound of fighting came to them through the wooden hull. Their boat seemed to move quickly sideways towards the trader. Everything shook as the two hulls thumped together. Outside, men cried out in anger and fear. Swords clanged. Screams, awful screams. Then there was silence.

Alec tried to take his mind away from whatever was happening and held his hands inside the beam of light that now cut downwards from the oar hole to his chained ankles. Most of the skin on his palms had been rubbed away. Blisters formed on the joints of his fingers. They stung and he dreaded having to put them back to work again.

After a while, they heard loud bangs and the sound of heavy things being stored up on the deck. Two terrified, dark skinned men were forced down the ladder by Konini. He pushed past them and stood in the aisle in front of Perpigno. He pulled up a pin and gestured at the bald man with scars, and his partner, to get up. Both men shook with fear. Konini shouted at them to hurry and everyone jumped. The slaves got up and shuffled sideways along their bench, and were replaced by new, stronger rowers. Before the Slave Master reached the ladder, he turned and spoke to Perpigno, who bowed his head. Then Konini disappeared up on deck to deal with those who had not fully done his bidding.

The slaves in front of Alec glanced around fearfully, their eyes adjusting to their new dark world. One held his nose.

"What did the Slave Master say to you?" asked Alec.

Perpigno rested his body against their oar.

"He said to tell you that when one slave fails, his partner dies too. He realises we are friends and wants you to know that my life is in your hands."

Screams came from the deck directly above their heads. Something banged against the hull next to Alec. Blood dripped down outside his oar hole. Alec bent, stared out and looked straight into the upside down face of the dead bald man. The face swayed from side to side as waves hit the galley, and Konini's message was rammed home.

"I am watching you."

***

"We must have fair winds," said Perpigno. "A whole day without rowing."

Alec blew onto his hands, trying to take the heat and itch out of his blisters.

"Perpigno, have you ever wondered?"

"Wondered what?"

"Who sat on this bench before us?"

"No."

"How many men have died on this oar?"

"I try not to think about it."

The Moor behind Alec tapped him on the shoulder and pointed at his oar hole. Alec looked out at a sandy shoreline, backed by date and fig trees that grew amongst the taller palms.

"Can you ask the slaves on the other side what they see."

Perpigno spoke to them and turned back to his friend.

"They see trees."

"Then we are in a river. Perhaps the Corsairs are returning to their village."

"Two days' sail, east of Melillia."

The iron grille at the front of the ship opened and they saw Konini's powerful legs coming down the ladder. He walked straight towards Perpigno and Alec, and pulled up the pin, which held their chains. His finger curled at them and they pulled the chain through their ankle irons and stepped onto the aisle. Konini pulled out another pin and ordered the new slaves, who sat on the bench in front of them, to do the same. Utter dread swept through Alec's body and he began to shake. Had he not pulled hard enough on his oar? Had he done something to upset the Slave Master? What punishment would follow? Konini shouted new orders and the two pairs of slaves changed places. They

32

pulled chains back through their leg irons and Konini checked them, before securing the wooden pins. Then he was gone. Alec counted the shadowy heads of the slaves in front of them.

"Only twenty seven benches to go."

When Perpigno's words came, they were spoken with a deep sadness.

"If we live that long."

Alec peered out of his new oar hole. The riverbank was closer now and he tried to guess how far inland the pirate village was. He didn't have to wait long to find out. A semi-circular cluster of about thirty white, square houses soon came into view. All the houses had flat roofs and stood on a small hill overlooking the sandy riverbank. The galley turned, Alec's view changed and he felt the floor scrape over sand. Lines were thrown ashore and pirates jumped down into the shallows, pulling the boat in and securing lines around huge stones. The Scotsman watched a crowd of old men, women and children make their way down towards the galley. Then Konini was there, wading out of the water and dropping a wine barrel onto the sand. Four young children ran to him and he bent down, hugged them and lifted a small girl up to kiss her.

"Konini has children."

Perpigno raised his eyebrows.

"I hope he treats them better than us."

Alec watched the Slave Master lift the girl onto his broad shoulders and carry her to a house, the other children laughing and skipping behind them.

"He could not treat them any worse. How long do you think we will stay here?"

"Forever, I hope. Even a few days without the drum would be like gold to me now."

The slave in front of Perpigno slid forward on his bench and relieved himself of yesterday's meal. Alec's nose twitched.

"How long until the wash-out at sundown?"

"A while yet."

"Do you know what I fear most?"

"No."

"Drowning. Unable to escape. Trapped below deck."

"Try not to think about it, Brown Eyes."

"Can we try something?"

"What?"

Alec rattled his chains.

"You see the pin?"

"Of course."

"Can you ask the slaves in front of us if we can borrow their oar?"

"Why?"

"Just ask them."

Perpigno asked them and they passed their oar over their heads.

"You take it and put the end against one side of the pin."

He did it and Alec did the same with the end of his oar, but on the opposite side of the pin.

"Squeeze the oars together, then lift the pin."

They pushed their oars together, hard, and the pin rose up and out of the hole. Alec glanced out of his oar hole. Konini was returning to the galley.

"Now is not our time. Get the pin back in," warned Alec.

Working together, they tried to get the pin back into its hole, but it kept slipping on the end of their oars and no matter what they tried, they couldn't do it.

"What do we do now?" asked Alec, fear in his voice.

Perpigno quickly passed his oar forward and the slaves took it.

"Sleep."

Bolts were drawn back, the iron grille lifted and Konini walked down the aisle, two loaves of bread in one great hand. He stopped beside Perpigno and shouted. Perpigno sat bolt upright, pretending to have woken with a start. The Slave Master gave him the bread and saw the pin on its side. He stared at it, trying to remember if he had forgotten to replace it when the slaves had changed places. He cursed himself and put it back. As he left the lower deck, Alec let out a long breath of relief.

"We must not do that again until we are sure the way is clear to the deck."

His friend nodded and handed him the food.

***

Alec wondered why the Corsairs had not unloaded most of the wine barrels. The other trader, the one they had rammed, must have had a cargo too and he hadn't seen anything else carried ashore, so it was still up on deck.

"Why haven't they unloaded all the cargo?"

Perpigno opened his eyes and lifted himself off their oar.

"They need a big market to sell them. From what you have said, their village is small. At some time we will sail to a trading port, but not Almeria or Melillia."

"Why not?"

"We have been there many times. Have you ever seen pirates there?"

"No."

"I think they wait until the ship is full and then sail east. Maybe as far as Rome, or Carthage on the North African coast."

"Those places really exist?"

"They do, although I have never sailed to them. Carthage is said to be one hundred times bigger than Almeria."

"So many people?"

"So many more traders who will buy pirate goods. The pirates and those traders must be very wealthy."

Alec jumped as the drum was hit five times. He looked out of his oval oar hole. Corsairs were leaving their homes and walking back to the ship. Alec blew onto his sore, rough hands and picked at the loose skin around a blister.

"Well, we are going somewhere."

***

Two days' hard rowing later, Alec felt his arms. They were thinner, but harder to the touch, the muscles more defined. The drum had stopped as the sail picked up a strong tail wind and the word amongst the slaves was that they headed east towards Corsica and then, maybe, on to Rome.

Everyone was hungry and exhausted, and Perpigno breathed slowly, his shoulders hunched over their oar. Alec sniffed the foul air and for some reason it did not seem as bad as it had when he woke from Konini's blow.

In spite of rowing for days, he was not as utterly weary as on the first morning aboard the galley when he had collapsed with exhaustion. Was he getting used to things? Toughening up? He thought about Perpigno's translation of the Moor's words, the Moor who now sat two rows behind him.

"Three hundred and ten nights, so almost a year."

A year here, chained below decks in a stinking, brutal, hell-hole. Alec found it difficult to imagine what the man must have suffered, and began to believe that he too would not walk in sunshine, a free man, again. Then he pictured his twin and the lands around their farm. They were clear pictures and, for a short time, Alec escaped slavery by walking the high pastures in his mind.

"You do not sleep," whispered Perpigno.

"No. I dream with my eyes open."

"That is the only escape Konini cannot prevent."

"Our time *will* come. Be patient and remember how we lifted the pin. We cannot wait for the Slave Master to move us to the front, and I do not intend to stay here and rot for as long as the Moor."

"I have never asked you, Brown Eyes. Can you swim?"

"A little. I am not strong in the water."

"We will need to be close to the shore then."

"The closer the better."

"What do you see out of the oar hole?"

"A black sky, a black sea and growing waves."

"You think a storm is coming?"

"Don't know."

"Get some sleep, Brown Eyes. The drum could start at any time."

Alec lowered himself down on to their oar and shut his eyes.

"One day, Perpigno. I will show you the lands around my home."

***

Alec dreamt about walking with Dougie down to the loch on a summer's day. Lissy had told them to return home before darkness came and, of course, Dougie had faithfully promised to do so, but Alec wanted to stay out for as long as he could, without upsetting his grandmother too much. By the loch, the twins undressed and waded out into the cool water, the sand squashing up between their toes. The water felt so good.

"Alec, wake up."

"Hmmm."

"Wake up." Perpigno's voice.

"Go away. I am dreaming."

"Wake."

Alec opened his eyes. The galley lurched downwards and then rose up violently. It fell again and sea water shot in through the oar holes. A slave on the other side of the aisle was sick as the ship rose again, the water stopped coming in and Alec peered out. The blackness was cut apart by a brilliant white bolt of lightning that, in an instant, showed him a vast, angry sea. Cold water lapped at his ankles.

"Are we near to land?" asked Perpigno.

Alec stared out, waiting for lightning to help him see. The flash came and he blinked, but there was no shore to be seen. He shut his eyes and listened to the screaming wind blowing through the hole. The galley lurched downwards and the scream was replaced by a jet of water.

"No. I saw only sea. What about the other side?"

37

Perpigno called across to the slaves. One man shook his head.

There was a loud crash above their heads, Corsairs shouted and ran around, which meant some of the cargo had broken loose and was being lashed down again. Another, louder crash. The roof above them shook. The slaves jumped.

"What was that?" asked Alec.

The front of the galley rose up, the closed iron grille almost directly above their heads now, and they were forced back on their benches, leg irons digging into their ankles, using their leg muscles to stop themselves falling backwards. The prow hovered at the height of its climb, then the mighty wave subsided and they crashed down. Timbers creaked, men moaned in fear and water gushed in through the oar holes. Some of the slaves jumped up, pulling madly at their chains. The grille was yanked open and the dripping figure of Konini climbed down, The drum sounded and the Slave Master called out new orders.

"What did he say?" asked Alec.

"The mast has snapped. If we want to live, we must row to keep the galley facing into the wind. If we are struck by a wave on the side of the ship, we will be lost."

Alec twisted their oar so that it could be pushed through the oval hole. Konini shouted out, but louder this time, trying to be heard above the storm and the screams of the slaves up on deck.

"Oars out," said Perpigno. "Watch his arms."

A face appeared at the trap door and yelled. The drum beat quickened. Konini held out his left arm and all the slaves on Alec's side rowed for all they were worth. After twenty strokes, the face yelled again and the Slave Master lowered his arm and raised his right arm. Alec and Perpigno pushed their oar down, lifting the other end up and out of the sea. The slaves across the aisle took over.

Another crash up on deck. Water spilled in bucket-loads down through the trap door and, for a moment, the face disappeared. Konini called up and Alec sensed the fear in his voice. The face returned with scared white eyes below dripping hair. The man called out new instructions and Konini raised both arms. Everyone rowed and felt the ship lurch, before rising up and dropping down with a bang, like a giant hammer striking the hull. The water-jets returned, more slaves were sick, but everyone put their full weight behind their oars.

The galley rolled sideways, dropping down on Alec's side and his oar became completely submerged. The ship shot forward and the oar thumped backwards into his chest. Perpigno took the worst of the strike and gasped for air. The slaves in front of them were knocked completely off their bench and one stayed down, struck senseless by the blow.

Above their heads, the deck rumbled as barrels rolled around. Lightning lit the sky behind the face at the trap door and a monstrous wave washed over him. Then the face was gone. The drum stopped beating. Konini ran back down the rocking aisle and scrambled up the ladder.

Panic swept through the lower deck. Slaves yanked helplessly at their chains and some cried out the Slave Master's name. Another wave and water rushed through the trap door. The galley lurched, as though the hand of a god had clasped it and twisted it onto its side. Alec felt his friend's body slide across their wet bench, pinning him against the hull. The slaves who stood, tugging at their chains, were thrown down. The sea flooded in.

A blinding flash came from the back of the lower deck and Alec's body was racked with unimaginable pain. Perpigno shook as their chain sparked and glowed blue. The smell of burnt flesh wafted forward and attacked their senses. Alec snapped himself out of his pain and felt under the water at his burning ankle irons. The metal was red hot, but the iron unbroken.

"Perpigno, get an oar."

No answer and Alec pulled back his friend's face and slapped it.

"Get an oar."

Perpigno stirred.

"We are lost."

"We are not lost. Take this."

Alec pulled in their oar and shoved it into Perpigno's hands. Then he was up, the ship rising and falling below his feet. He twisted around, trying to grab the oar from the slaves behind him. Their still smouldering bodies were slumped across it. He put his palms under their foreheads and pushed them backwards off the oar.

"You know what to do."

Another wave hit the galley sideways on and they were thrown off their bench into the rising water. The slaves on the other side of the aisle, above Perpigno and Alec now, screamed as they dangled from their leg irons. The ship lurched and the dangling slaves swayed backwards and forwards. Alec scrambled back onto his bench and stuck his head up above the water.

"Up, Perpigno." He pulled him up onto the bench too. "Do you have your oar?"

"Yes."

The ship righted itself, the water subsided and they rested their oars upon their knees, aiming the ends at the sides of the pin.

"Squeeze and lift," yelled Alec.

Their oars slipped off the wet pin.

"Again."

Their bodies were thrown against the side of the hull. The galley rolled onto its side again. More screams, more dangling slaves above their heads. The sea rushed in and some of the slaves on Alec's side began to fight each other, as though the blows might save them. There was terror everywhere.

"Again," yelled Alec, but now the pin was hidden under water.

They gripped their oars and tried to feel for it, sometimes missing it completely and sometimes getting a weak grip.

"Squeeze and lift."

They lifted and the pin refused to move. The sea rose up to their necks.

"Harder."

"It will not move," gasped Perpigno.

The back of the galley began to sink and the prow rose up.

Oars fell down through the lower deck like spears and splashed into the rising sea behind them. Most of the slaves in front and above Alec fell backwards, their bodies arched, held taught by their chains. He held the bench and leant forward to keep his balance. Perpigno did the same, his oar resting across his lap.

"Again!"

They bent their knees and used their leg muscles to stay upright. The ends of their oars wavered around the pin and they struggled to hold the ends still, as the ship lurched one way and then another.

"Squeeze and lift."

Behind them, one oar hole after another became a jet of water as the galley slipped backwards into the sea. Below them, at the stern, the slaves not killed by the lightning strike felt their lungs fill with water. Alec glanced up at the trap door, high above his head. An orange glow flickered around it, which meant that part of the deck was on fire.

A face appeared, and then Konini was lowering himself down on a rope into the lower deck, his powerful legs holding him away from the vertical aisle. He stopped by Perpigno and Alec, and pointed down behind them. All the slaves at the back of the ship were drowned and the sea was rushing up to claim them too. Holding the rope with one hand, he used the other to pull out the two pins that held the chains. Then he pulled himself up to the next row of benches and did the same. He continued all the way up to the trap door. Alec and Perpigno frantically pulled the long chain through their ankle irons. Then it was a mad scramble as the slaves climbed up, from bench to bench, following the Slave Master.

As the legs of the slave in front of Perpigno disappeared through the hatch and out into the storm, Alec found a good footing on the side of a bench and placed his hands under Perpigno's dangling feet. He heaved his friend up. Then a dark muscular arm came down and Alec grabbed it, and he found himself rising up into the open air. Konini sat on the side of the trap door, his

41

back pressed against the deck, which rose high above him. The Slave Master peered down into the blackness of the lower deck, making one final check that the last of his slaves were free. The ship lurched and its descent into the cold sea quickened.

Perpigno held onto the ship's rail.

"Come on."

For a moment, the two men stared at each other, trying to keep their balance. Then Konini pointed at the ocean and dived in. Alec and Perpigno dived too, and swam away from the wreck of the battered galley. The waves tossed them and Alec struggled to stop himself from being dragged under. Perpigno's face surfaced beside him, and they rose and fell together in the angry sea, lightning flashing and thunder booming in the heavens above them. Another flash and his friend was pointing madly. They swam towards a barrel, Perpigno reaching it first, then holding out his hand and pulling Alec towards him. They stared at each other across the barrel and Perpigno yelled at him above the screaming wind.

"If we live through this night to tell our children stories, I swear I will never, ever, step on board a ship again."

Alec smiled, relieved and feeling stronger inside because he was not alone.

A monstrous wave shot forward, rising up, growing, its crest towering above their barrel, water curving into a deadly arc. It crashed down and Alec lost his hold as the boiling sea exploded all around him. He was driven down, the roar of rushing water in his ears, his body rolling over and over, so that he did not know which way was up or down. Panic took him. He opened his eyes, trying to see anything that showed the way up to safety. Nothing. Nothing, but murky black. Salt stung his eyes. He couldn't breathe and his chest heaved as he kept his mouth clamped shut. Arms wrapped themselves around him and then, with both men kicking out, they burst onto the surface, Perpigno swimming on his back and pulling his friend back to the barrel.

Alec held the barrel as tightly as he had ever held anything.

"How long till dawn?"

"Long enough, Brown Eyes."

"Why did Konini save us?" spluttered Alec.

"We may never know."

"And what did he say to me?"

Perpigno spat water from his mouth and took a long breath. They rose and fell some more, the cold numbing their bodies. Perpigno smiled back at his friend.

"He said, 'Good fortune on your journey.'"

***

Alec was dreaming that he was lying on a bed of turmeric, coriander, cumin and cloves. The smell calmed him, took away his fears, making him drowse and imagine the street-sellers of Almeria who called out, gesturing at passers-by to come and buy their aromatic spices.

He opened his eyes in bright sunshine and wondered if he was still alive. A thin, dark-skinned man, dressed only in white half-trousers, was shouting encouragement at Perpigno, who was bent over a ship's rail, holding out a pole and cursing. He glanced back from what he was doing.

"Good morning, Brown Eyes. You slept well."

"We live?"

Perpigno laughed.

"We live and have to earn our passage. Come and help."

Alec threw aside a blanket, got up from his bed of sacks of spices, and walked across the deck of the small trader. The thin man smiled at him, closed his fingers together and moved them to and from his lips. Suddenly Alec felt as though he could eat forever and nodded eagerly.

"Get a pole," said Perpigno crossly.

Alec joined him and looked down at a barrel that floated close to the ship.

"It is the Shipmaster's now. His name is Ali. You owe your life to him, by the way."

43

"I thought you said you would not set foot on a ship ever again."
Perpigno shrugged his shoulders.

"I lied."

Ali came back with a plate of bread, hot fish and sliced fruits. Alec tried to shake the man's hand, but Ali placed the plate into his outstretched hand and said something before going to the stern to take the tiller. Perpigno reached out with his pole again, trying to manoeuvre the barrel closer to the rail.

"He says, 'A well fed crew is a happy crew.'"

Alec picked up a large piece of fish, smelled it and put it into his mouth. The taste was intense. He had almost forgotten what real food tasted like and he ate the rest of the fish greedily, staring around the trader. One mast, a single sail, no shelter and not longer than twenty paces. It looked new.

Between mouthfuls of bread, he spoke to his friend.

"Does Ali sail alone?"

"He likes it that way. Says people complicate things. He trades from Massilia in Gaul, where his brother sells spices in the market square. That's where we are going."

"Is it far from Massilia to Almeria?"

"Three days' sail with a kind wind."

"His boat looks new."

"I think our friend, Ali, does rather well out of his trade. He buys at a low price in North Africa and sells at a high price in Massilia, and smiles as he crosses the sea."

"Does he not fear the pirates?"

"Maybe some of his family are pirates. He says he isn't worried about them anyway."

Alec put down his plate. The sliced fruits still on it.

"Like you said, I owe my life to him."

He climbed up onto the rail and dived into the sea, surfacing behind the barrel and pushing it towards the ship.

"Don't forget, Brown Eyes. I saved you too."

Alec ignored him.

"Throw down a line."

Perpigno disappeared and then the end of a rope was thrown down. Alec tied it around the barrel and climbed back up. They pulled the barrel onboard.

"Recognise it?"

Alec nodded and picked up his plate.

"Of course."

"You know, I don't think I will ever look at barrels in the same way."

"And if I ever hear the beat of a drum again, I …"

Perpigno raised his hands.

"Let's not talk about that. Just be glad we are out here, in the sunshine."

"I can't forget being a slave."

"We won't forget it. We are scarred forever. But, please, let's not talk about it."

"Do you think Konini lives?"

"Who knows?"

"We survived. I wonder how many of the pirates survived."

"Who cares?"

"I care. Spalda will get another galley, capture more slaves and work them until they die."

"Let's not count the days by the number of times we are given stale bread. Forget it, Brown Eyes."

"No."

"There have always been pirates. There will always be pirates. What can we do anyway?"

The Scotsman's face hardened. Water dripped off his body onto the deck, the sun making his skin itch as he dried. He pictured the missing skin on a bald man's back. Remembered the screams he had heard from the deck above his head. Alec bent down and touched an ankle iron.

"I don't know, but I am going to do something."

CHAPTER THREE

CEOL THE TRULY MAGNIFICENT

Tegonini the Galley Maker felt dwarfed by Konini, but did not feel the same fear in the pit of his stomach that he did whenever he spoke with Spalda. The three men walked beside the skeleton of a galley, hammers working constantly, driving in oak pins to add another rib to the growing hull. There was wood everywhere.

"How long until it is ready?" asked Spalda.

"Two moons. We have never built a boat so quickly."

The Corsair's dark eyes flashed, a hint of danger in them.

"I want it ready in one moon."

"We will need to get more carpenters from Carthage. It will be expensive."

"How much more expensive?"

"I do not know. I will find out and send a message to you."

"But you can do it."

"Yes, with more skilled hands."

"And I want it longer."

Tegonini stopped walking and lifted up the palms of his hands, as though surrendering to an enemy.

"But it is planned to be like your old ship. Two hundred and forty slaves on two decks. It was the fastest galley on any sea."

A group of tanned and smiling workers walked past them, carrying coils of rope. Two held a long metal saw between them.

"Why do they not run?" asked Spalda.

"They are not slaves. They are craftsmen who work long and hard for you."

Spalda nodded at his Slave Master and Konini threw a knife into the back of one of the men who carried the saw. He sank slowly to his knees and Tegonini watched as Spalda walked over to him, pulling the knife from the dead man's body and speaking in a soft, menacing voice to the others. They ran off to do his bidding.

"The galley will hold two hundred and eighty slaves, one hundred and forty on each deck. It will be ready in one moon, or I will kill you and everyone in your family, Tegonini."

Spalda glanced at Konini, who untied a leather purse from his belt and handed it to him.

"The price we agreed is doubled. Sail to Carthage, get the carpenters you need and complete your work. Send a messenger to my village every three days. I want to know if you are ahead of schedule, or behind it. When the galley is ready, my people will join you here and I shall bring more gold coins."

"Yes, Spalda."

"Do not fail me."

"I have not failed you before."

Konini went to stand behind the Galley Maker and cold sweat ran down the man's back. Spalda's eyes flashed again.

"And that is why you still live."

***

Alec of Dunfermline stood at the prow of the small trader, eyes shut, feeling the wind on his face and breathing in the pure morning air through his nose. As the ship cut through the low waves, its new timbers creaked and Alec rose and fell, thinking about his brother, his home and how being here, in the sunshine, had once been a dream.

"Are you going to stand there all day, or help with the sail?" asked Perpigno.

Alec smiled, opened his eyes and looked at the busy quay of Massilia, no more than five hundred paces away. Thirty traders of different sizes were crammed together in a horseshoe harbour. Above them, on a tree covered hill, stood a tall, round watchtower. A thin tail of smoke rose up from the tower, its power spent now, but until dawn that pinprick of light had been their guide, with Ali steering a steady course towards it, before waking his passengers and asking for breakfast.

Ali shouted something at Alec and Perpigno translated.

"Half sail."

Alec joined his friend and they reduced the area of sail and immediately the ship slowed, and Ali stared ahead, picking out a gap between the traders and a lucky free berth beside the quayside.

"That has to be Ali's brother," said Perpigno.

Alec looked at the thin, dark-skinned man who patiently waited for them. He held the reins of two donkeys, which were harnessed to a cart that looked far too big for them to pull.

"As Lissy would say, *like two peas in a pod.*"

"Anyway, Brown Eyes, what do we do now?"

"Work our passage to Almeria."

"What then?"

"Who rules those lands?"

"The tribes of southern Celt Iberia are ruled by Ceol the Magnificent."

"Is he powerful?"

"Not as powerful as his name suggests, but he does command a small fleet."

"What is he like?"

"What do you mean?"

Alec gripped the sail rope and spoke with determined words.

"Will he help us fight Spalda?"

"I thought you wanted to go home."

"I do, but not until the sea is made safe."

Perpigno shuddered.

"You may have to fight Konini."

"Aye, and I cannot do that alone."

"You will need an army to defeat him."

"If Ceol has a fleet, then he has warriors who serve him. So, what is he like?"

"I am a Tongue Speaker not a friend of kings."

"What do the stories say?"

"That he rules justly, that he likes to dress well, that his children are numbered in hundreds and not tens."

Alec's eyebrows rose.

"He must be a busy man."

"Busy and hard to see."

"In Scotland, Malcolm the Younger holds a Court of Grievance. Anyone, even a shepherd, can go to his palace and have their problems recorded by a scribe. The big disputes are settled by the king himself. Does Ceol do this?"

Perpigno picked up a coil of rope and threw an end to Ali's brother. The ship bumped against the wall of the quay.

"No idea. But I think we are mad enough to go to Almeria and find out."

They helped unload the trader and soon the cart was piled high with sacks of spices. Ali told Perpigno to leave the barrel of wine onboard and, after he and his brother had argued about who should take it, Ali came over to them, smiling, and gave Perpigno and Alec two coins each. Stamped on both sides of the coins was a fish, which meant they were from Massilia, Ali's home port.

"He does not want us to leave his ship without money. Mind you, he will sell the wine barrel for ten coins, so not a bad profit for taking on a new crew."

Alec held out his hand and this time the Shipmaster shook it.

"Tell him I will never forget that he saved us."

Perpigno told Ali and they shook hands as well. Then Ali spoke and pointed at Alec's ankle irons and then up a lane, which was lined with market stalls. Some stalls sold the brightly-coloured blankets found everywhere along this stretch of coast. Some sold sandals, candles, fruit and nuts, fish or wine. One sold slaves.

"Ali says there is an ironworker close by. He can remove our ankle chains."

Alec stared at the market stall, at six black slaves who sat in pairs on a raised tier of three benches; saw the look of fear on their faces, as they wondered who their new master would be.

"Tell him I hope he enjoys better fortune than us, trading across the sea. Tell him I keep my ankle irons."

"Saving your coins, Brown Eyes?"

"No. Saving my memories."

***

The journey from Massilia along the coastline of southern Gaul to Almeria in Celt Iberia was hard work but uneventful. They each now had a coin with fish on, three coins with the grapes of Gaul stamped on both sides, and two coins decorated with the bull of Celt Iberia. Perpigno moaned about the Shipmaster they had served on the final leg of voyage.

"He wasn't very generous, was he? Think of all the work we did."

Alec ignored him and walked up and away from the quay towards the grand, white palace, which dominated everything in Almeria.

"Is that where Ceol lives?"

"Yes."

"Well there is no reason to delay speaking with him."

"I can think of many reasons to delay."

"Perpigno, you know we have to do this."

"But I am hungry. Can we not eat first and get the sway of the sea out of our legs?"

"Buy bread and eat whilst you walk."

"You know, Brown Eyes, I think becoming a Shipmaster has gone to your head."

***

Sowelli the Coin Counter sighed, put his quill down and stared around his room. Twenty two bulging leather bags had been carefully placed around the walls, each bag containing one hundred coins. Added to the ninety four coins, in piles on his plain wooden desk, this made a total of nearly two thousand three hundred coins. It wasn't enough. He picked up a parchment which listed his master's outgoings. It was a long list that included the costs of the feasts, presents for the royal

52

family, repair of the fleet, pay for the bodyguards and, of course, clothes. He sighed again and knew it wasn't going to be an easy conversation. Sowelli rolled up the parchment, left the Counting Room and walked down a long corridor with white and blue tiles on the floor and walls, and a painting of traders at sea along the entire length of the ceiling. No matter how many times he made this journey, he was always struck by the beauty of the corridor and how it contrasted so completely with his own quarters, and the rooms occupied by the many servants in the palace.

"I must remember I am paid well and risk little."

It was a well used phrase that he spoke whenever he prepared himself to give his master bad news. He approached two guards who nodded at him and opened the huge wooden and brass doors to Ceol's court. He walked upon luxurious, brightly-coloured rugs, their patterns sometimes interrupted by thick purple and green cushions. Sowelli stopped beside a fountain where a smiling Ceol was being measured by a tailor.

"Ah, Sowelli, I am glad you are here. What do you think?"

Sowelli watched as his master turned on the spot, arms held out to show off the wide sleeves of a bright yellow shirt.

"It is, er, very yellow."

"Isn't it a great colour. Best silk too."

"It's very bright."

"Oh, you don't think it's too bright, do you?"

"No, not at all, it's very you. Magnificent."

The tailor knelt to measure Ceol's inside leg and Ceol tapped him on the shoulder.

"Fetch the trousers."

The man smiled and brought over an armful of brightly-coloured trousers. Ceol took the purple ones and held them against the yellow shirt.

"Do you think they go?"

Sowelli stared at him. Tall, thin, dark-skinned, his face divided in two by a long thin moustache. Even the most expensive clothes couldn't hide that Ceol was getting old; couldn't hide the wrinkles and lines around his dark eyes as he smiled. The Coin Counter decided to lie.

"They go together very well."

Ceol turned to face the tailor.

"I'll take two yellow shirts and three pairs of trousers, one of each colour."

Sowelli's conscience came into play.

"Before we order any more clothes, I would like to suggest that we talk about money."

Ceol's face changed.

"Money, money, money. That's all you ever want to talk about."

"It's what you pay me to do."

The tailor sensed a storm brewing and, gathering the clothes together, he left them. Sowelli handed his master the parchment.

"The coins we receive from the traders are less than the number spent on the upkeep of the palace and fleet. In three moons the treasury will be empty."

"But I have bags and bags of coins."

"You do, but not as many as you once had."

A suspicious look ran across Ceol's face.

"So what has happened to them?"

Sowelli folded his arms.

"You have spent them."

Ceol folded his arms too.

"I have hardly spent anything."

"I think you should read the parchment."

Ceol read it.

"I did not spend one hundred and twenty five coins on shoes."

"You did. You bought five pairs, all the same, the ones with the silver stars on."

"Oh, yes. They were cheap for that quality."

"They were one hundred and twenty five coins and the money *is* running out."

"Then get more money."

"How do I do that?"

"Raise the levy on the traders."

"They already complain about the levy. If it becomes too high they will stop trading here and go somewhere else to sell their wares."

"But what is the problem? Lots of coins have been coming into the treasury."

Sowelli unfolded his arms and sighed.

"Not as many coins as we used to earn. More coins are being spent than we receive from the traders."

"Why aren't we receiving as many as we used to?"

"You know why."

Ceol angrily tore up the parchment.

"It's the Corsairs, isn't it."

"For two moons, six fully laden traders docked every week at your quay. Last moon, only three traders made it here, to Almeria. The merchants are becoming afraid to sail these waters. No trade, no coins, no clothes."

"I thought the raids had stopped."

"They did, for a while. Something must have happened to the pirates. Maybe they chose to plunder ships in different waters, but they are back now."

"What are the merchants saying?"

"That Spalda is back with an even bigger ship. Nothing can outrun him."

"Spalda, Spalda, Spalda. That name is all I hear about, curse him."

"Curse him."

"But what do we do?"

"Spend less, or make the waters safe for trade."

Ceol picked up the pair of purple trousers left for him by the tailor. He really liked them.

"How do we catch Spalda if his galley is so fast?"

"I do not know."

"What if we build an even bigger ship?"

"We can't afford it, not at the moment, anyway."

"And I cannot afford these trousers?"

"No."

"Sure?"

"In three moons the treasury will be empty."

The reality of his finances finally sank home and Ceol the Magnificent went to sit beside the fountain, ignoring the attentions of hundreds of children who suddenly appeared in the courtyard, laughing and skipping around in brightly-coloured clothes. Sowelli picked his way through the children and stood before his master.

"What do I do?" asked Ceol.

"Spend less, or kill Spalda."

"If only we knew where he lives."

***

"They will not let us in, Brown Eyes," said Perpigno.

"They will not let us in if we do not try."

They stared nervously at the main gate of Almeria palace. Two guards stared back at them, fingering the hilts of their long curved swords. Alec plucked up his courage and walked over.

"I seek an audience with Ceol the Magnificent."

The guards glanced at each other and Perpigno joined them to interpret. The guards shook their heads and one said something.

"They say no, so let's go."

"I am not going. Try again."

Perpigno tried again. The guards shook their heads again.

"Ask them if we may speak to someone who speaks with Ceol."

The Tongue Speaker asked them. More shaking heads.

"They say they are all busy."

"This isn't getting us anywhere."

"It isn't. Let's go to Scotland."

Anger gripped Alec and he pointed at his ankle irons.

"I was taken as a slave by Konini and we know the location of his village."

One of the guards lifted his sword so that the tip rested against Alec's chest.

"We should go," warned Perpigno.

"We are not going until Spalda has been stopped."

At the word, "Spalda," the guards glanced at each other and one went inside the palace.

"What did I say?"

Perpigno shrugged his shoulders.

"Maybe the word *Spalda* carries some weight in Almeria."

The guard returned and spoke in an agitated voice to Perpigno.

"He says everyone is busy and to come back at nightfall."

Alec tried to walk past them.

"I am not waiting."

A guard picked him up, held Alec above his head and threw him onto the street. Alec stared up at his friend's smiling face.

"Tell them we will come back at nightfall."

***

Spalda stared at the rows and rows of slaves who sweated under the burning sun, pulling steadily on their oars. He called forward to a Corsair who stood beside a huge drum.

"More speed."

Konini left Spalda, pulled up an iron grille and disappeared down into the lower deck. The beat of the drum quickened and Spalda felt his new galley accelerate forward. The small trader they chased would be taken in no time, its crew enslaved and its cargo loaded onboard. Forty rows in front of the tiller, a pair of slaves missed a beat, their oar flailing above the water. The Shipmaster roared in anger and ran down the central aisle to whip them.

***

At nightfall, a slave ran with his master's message up the narrow streets from the quayside to Almeria Palace. Two men argued with the guards by the gate and he pushed past them, demanding to speak with Sowelli.

"The Coin Counter has asked to be informed immediately of problems with Corsairs. Another trader is two days late from Melillia and we fear it is lost."

Immediately the guards broke away from their argument and one went inside to fetch Sowelli.

***

"They will not let us in," said Perpigno.

"But they told us to return at nightfall."

"That is what they said, but they now say everyone is still busy."

"Tell them we know where Spalda lives."

"I've already told them."

"Tell them again."

Perpigno told them and a guard shouted at him.

"What did he say?" asked Alec.

"Let's just say his words were not very polite."

Alec stared up at the palace walls, the height of three men.

"Shall we get a ladder?"

"If they catch us they will think we are no more than thieves and cut our hands off."

Alec began to argue with a guard and a slave pushed past him.

"That is good fortune," said Perpigno.

"Why was his message taken inside?"

"He knows someone named Sowelli who counts coins."

"Can Sowelli speak with Ceol?"

"No idea, but we will not have to wait long to find out."

The guard and Coin Counter came out of the gate and talked urgently to the slave about the lost cargo and crew. As Sowelli went back inside the palace, Perpigno shouted after him.

58

"We are escaped slaves and know where Spalda hides."

A guard pushed him away, shut the gate and Alec glanced anxiously at his friend. The gate burst open and Sowelli marched out.

"What did you say?"

***

"Nice shirt, by the way," said Perpigno and Ceol the Magnificent smiled.

They stood with Alec at the stern of the leading ship in a fleet of five. All were bigger than the traders they were supposed to protect, but nothing like as long or as powerful as Spalda's galley. Worse still, they all relied solely upon the mood of the winds and carried no slaves. Alec liked them.

"Tell Ceol his fleet is as fine as any I have ever seen."

Perpigno told him and Ceol puffed his chest out and spoke quickly.

"He says we will reach Melillia at sundown tomorrow."

"And from there it is only two days' sail east to the Corsair village."

Perpigno shuddered.

"Are you sure you still want to face Konini?"

"Aye."

"By the way, Brown Eyes, I think Ceol got a good deal. Free passage home to Scotland for you and twenty five coins for me. He will earn many times more than that if we are successful."

"But we all win."

"We all win."

"Ask Ceol if he has four men who can help me when we fight the Slave Master."

Perpigno asked him.

"He wants to know why you need four men when he has a hundred at his command."

"You know the reason. I am afraid to stand before Konini without skilled swords around me. Ask him again."

Perpigno asked him again and Ceol barked out some orders and four warriors joined them.

"He says they are all brave and skilled with the sword."

"Tell him they will need to be."

***

"Well, where is the river?" asked Ceol.

"It is here, somewhere," said Perpigno.

"And are you sure the other river was not the one we seek?"

"I am sure. It wasn't wide enough and there were no trees along its banks."

"But we are three days' sail east of Melillia."

"Be patient, my friend. It is here."

"But how do you know this? You were held on the lower deck."

"We were, but we had an oar hole and we spoke to the slaves on the other side of the aisle."

"You are sure."

"Sure."

"What is he saying?" asked Alec.

"I think Ceol is losing heart. I am a little as well, although I am trying not to show it. We should be there by now."

Alec pointed at the small bulge in their sail.

"In light winds, two days' sail can easily become three. Ask Ceol what he plans to do with Spalda's treasure."

Moments later, Ceol's face lit up.

"He asks *what treasure*?"

"Spalda has been troubling these waters for an age. How many coins did he take from us, from just one small trader? What do the Corsairs do with all the coins they capture from the bigger, richer traders?"

Perpigno spoke with Ceol whose face beamed.

"He will buy a whole new wardrobe of silk robes. Apparently they are very *him*."

Alec nodded and looked back at the fleet that followed them.

"We may need to send a scout ship ahead when we reach the river. We need to know if the pirate galley is there, or not. All our ships sailing together would be easily seen by the villagers and they would guess our intentions, and somehow send a warning message to Spalda."

With Perpigno interpreting, they worked out a plan until interrupted by a shout from the prow. They ran to stand beside the lookout.

"That's it," said Alec.

The river looked too narrow at first, but as they sailed closer, they saw how wide it really was from one sandy shore to the other. Both banks were lined with fig and date trees amongst the taller palms, and they searched for a beach where the trees were thickest and closest to the water. Ceol pointed beyond a bend.

"There," he said.

The helmsman threw the tiller over and, with the wind fully in their sail, they raced forward and heard the hull scrape and rise up onto the soft sand. Then everyone was out, splashing ashore with ropes and the ship was quickly secured. The other ships beached close by. Aboard the smallest boat, anything that gave away its true intentions was carried ashore and stored under the cover of the trees. Then barrels and boxes were taken from the other ships and put onboard. In a short time, it was transformed from a small warship into a large, well provisioned trader. Alec and Perpigno boarded and felt it slide, as strong hands pushed it back into the river. Perpigno ran and began to pull on the sail rope.

"Raise the sail," ordered Alec.

Perpigno stopped pulling and stared at his grinning friend at the tiller.

"So, a shipmaster once more, Brown Eyes."

"Aye. Now get the sail up and let's see if Spalda is at home."

***

Picturing his new clothes, Ceol clapped his hands and called to his men. The four remaining ships were completely emptied, single lines fed out to them and each line secured to a strong palm tree. One by one, the ships were pushed back into the water and their crews unrigged the masts, lifting them out of their blocks and securing them along the length of the decks. Ceol watched his fleet drift slowly seaward, as the current caught them, until the lines took the strain.

"Sink them," he yelled.

All the crews scrambled up onto the deck of one ship and stood on the starboard rail. With their weight forcing the rail down, water lapped onboard. It listed slowly at first, but then the water rushed in and swamped the deck, and it sank without trace, except for the line which ran up to the trees.

"Cover the line with sand and then sink the others." Ceol turned to walk into the shade of the trees and spoke to himself. "Spalda will never know we are here."

***

"It wasn't this far up the river, was it?" asked Perpigno.

It was a beautiful late afternoon, with the sun bright but not as burning as it had been at noon. They heard strange bird calls from the trees on both banks, and a heron lazily flapped its wings and passed in front of them. Alec stood at the tiller and called forward.

"The village is here. Be patient."

Alec pictured Dougie's face and tried to sense what his twin was doing, and sensed nothing bad or as deeply sad as he had felt in the dream.

"I wager Dougie is up on the High Pastures, tending the sheep and daydreaming. That's what he always does," Alec said to himself. "Maybe he is over the worst of his grief, or met another girl and found the simple life he always wanted."

Alec hoped so.

"We are there."

"Huh."

"Alec, that is close enough. Take us in to the bank."

The Scotsman's mind left the High Pastures and he saw Perpigno pointing at the bank off the port bow. He pushed the tiller over and their ship glided into a tree-lined channel, cut out by a small stream. Perpigno jumped overboard with a line and Alec lowered the sail.

"What have you seen?"

"Up river, the water narrows and on a low hill the same square white houses with the flat roofs."

Alec shuddered and jumped ashore.

"Show me."

They walked, cautiously, in and out of the trees, in and out of the cool shade, and crawled the last few paces where the sand led down to the main river. About nine hundred paces away, smoke rose up from a bread oven beside one of the houses and children played on the long beach where the pirate galley had berthed. It wasn't there now.

"Come on," said Alec. "We cannot stay here and that is all we need to know."

They crept backwards, then ran to their ship and sailed back to Ceol, moving more quickly now that the current was aiding them, but alert and fearful of running straight into Spalda. Just after sunset, they made the sandy shore where the fleet was hidden below water and men ran from the trees to help them submerge their ship too. In darkness, deep within the palms, they rested and ate dates and bread, and talked about the best way to attack the Corsairs. Alec reached down and touched his ankle irons.

"So, all we have to do now is wait."

***

With a strong wind full in the sail, the slaves rested and the Galley Master talked in a worried voice to Konini. Spalda shivered and not because of the falling sun.

"What is it?"

"A sickness."

"How many?"

"Sixty slaves unable to row out of the two hundred and eighty."

"And it is getting worse."

Konini nodded and stared down the ranks of slaves on the upper deck. One slave vomited, gasping for breath, sweating and shivering at the same time.

"And you feel it too."

Spalda turned his head away from the helmsman and lowered his voice, trying to hide his fear of losing authority.

"I do. I feel weak."

"I feel that too."

"What shall we do?"

"The sickness will spread more quickly now amongst the slaves. It passes from row to row and each day more fall ill. We have to feed the well with more food, to help them stay strong, and get rid of the sick, or abandon the galley. Whatever you choose, we must act now. The old women of the village know of cures and they can tend us."

Spalda called out to his Corsairs, gave them orders and they ran down the central aisle, pulling up the holding pins and dragging the sick slaves over to the ship's rail. Despite their cries for mercy, sixty men were thrown into the emptiness of the vast sea. The Corsairs returned to their master.

"At the first sign of fever, throw them overboard." Spalda turned to the helmsman. "Set a course for home."

***

"Wake, Brown Eyes."

"Huh."

"Wake up. The lookouts have seen the galley and it is even bigger than the one where we enjoyed Konini's hospitality."

Immediately, Alec was wide awake and ran with his friend through the palms, to join Ceol who peered out across the river

64

from his place of hiding. Under full sail and without drum or oar, a long galley with a great battering ram at the prow, headed slowly up river. It was a menacing sight.

"This is stupid," said Perpigno.

"Why?"

"Because we risk being taken again as slaves. I fear that more than anything. Do you remember what life was like in that wretched galley? The fear we felt every moment of every day."

"I am scared too."

"Right now we could be looking at the green hills of your home, in the land of the Scots. But no, we are here, waiting to fight the Corsairs, waiting to stand before one of the greatest warriors who has ever lifted a sword. This is stupid."

Alec stared at the galley, sharing his friend's fear and dreading the attack.

"Why do they not use their oars?"

"I do not know. I thought they would use them against the flow of the river. Perhaps they are not in a hurry."

"Not like Spalda to spare the slaves."

"No."

As a bright sun rose in the east, they could clearly see Konini join his master at the stern. The two men spoke for a while and then Konini disappeared down into the lower deck. A short while later, he returned with two slaves whom he cut down with his sword and tossed overboard.

"This is stupid," whispered Alec.

"It is."

Alec took a deep breath and rolled onto his back to look up at the top of the palms.

"Don't ever forget why we are here."

Perpigno nodded and spoke with Ceol, who also nodded and smiled and pulled proudly at his shirt. The galley disappeared around a bend in the river and everyone ran down to the shore, took hold of a single line and began pulling one of their ships up onto the sand. By high sun the fleet was afloat again, safely anchored, rigged and loaded with food. Ceol gave orders for torches to be made and every warrior was armed with a sword, a torch and slave chains. They marched up river, staying hidden in the shade and watching out for any sign of the enemy.

"Is it far?" asked Ceol.

Perpigno shook his head.

"No. We will arrive well before sunset and can hide up in the trees close to the village. When sleep takes them, we attack."

Alec guessed what they spoke about.

"Please ask Ceol to spare the women and children."

Perpigno asked him and Ceol laughed.

"He says the last thing he needs is more women and children. He will spare as many of them as he can, and even spare the Corsairs. He wants them to be slaves on his new galley."

"But he *will* free the slaves who are held now?"

"He will."

"But he will not spare Spalda."

Perpigno interpreted and Ceol spat on the ground.

"Well, that is clear then," said Alec.

***

Konini felt so weak, but despite his thumping head, sticky, stained clothes and the need to vomit, he gave orders to Corsairs to go to the ovens and take bread down to his slaves. His words lacked power, but would not be ignored.

"Feed them well."

He lowered himself down onto the sand, waved away his children and staggered up to the village. He couldn't go home. He would pass on his fever to his family, and so he headed with five other pirates up to a white, square house at the very centre of the village. Stooping he went through a small, strong-looking wooden door and entered a bare, dark room, lit by four candles on an iron stand in one corner. He shivered and walked down stairs and along a sloping, stone-lined passage, stooping all the way, feeling more and more sick, then entering an arched underground chamber. This chamber was the height of two men, the width of four men laid head to toe, and was lined with rough stones and mortar. Large stones made up the lower part of the arch and became smaller higher up so that above Konini's head the stones were no bigger than the width of his hand. He ignored the barrels stored here and opened another small door at the far end of the chamber. He stooped again and went down another passage into a lower chamber, which was just like the wine store. It was full of gold and silver, jewels and coins, and guarded by a single armed Corsair who backed away as Konini approached. But treasure was of no value to Konini now. He needed medicine, care and rest.

Konini staggered down a passageway to another small door and at last stood upright in the deepest chamber, which was longer and lined on one side with ten beds, six of which were already taken by his shipmates. An old lady came over and took his arm.

"So even the mighty can be claimed by fever."

Konini's head swam from the effort of travelling down into the Chamber of the Sick.

"How is Spalda?" he whispered.

"He says that any fever he had is gone. I think he lies."

But the Slave Master did not hear her words and swayed on his feet. More old women came to help him, leading him to a bed and covering his hot sweating body with brightly-coloured blankets. Someone lifted his head and raised a tumbler to his lips, and he drank but did not taste. As sleep took him, Konini knew he would dream bad dreams and, for some reason, he sensed a close and unknown evil, and feared for the safety of his children.

***

Alec, Perpigno, Ceol and one hundred warriors crouched down in darkness, watching the lights in the village go out, one by one. Ceol spoke.

"He asks if we have enough men," said Perpigno.

"We do, if surprise remains our ally. Tell him that we must move silently from house to house, taking any Corsairs who sleep there and chaining them. They are to be led back here in groups of five, to be guarded by ten of Ceol's warriors. If any of the enemy cry out, then we fight and may good fortune be with us."

Perpigno confirmed the plan they had already agreed with Ceol, who ran his finger and thumb along his long moustache, deep in thought. The last light in the village went out and Alec stood.

"Light the torches. Let's go."

***

Spalda twisted and turned in his bed, regretting lying to the old women about how he really felt. He pulled a blanket up under his chin, eyes wide, senses alert. Someone in another house was violently sick and he felt the food that was left in his stomach rise up. He twisted over and was sick into a bowl. Then he collapsed onto his back, shut his eyes and wondered how many of his people would survive the fever.

***

Alec and Perpigno ran with the others out of the trees and into the Corsair village. They stopped with their backs pressed against a cottage wall and Alec gently pushed at a door. It didn't budge. He laid his sword and torch upon the ground and carefully lifted himself up onto a window ledge and slid inside. It was as black as pitch, but he walked quickly to where he thought the door would be, fearing tripping over something and making a noise. He felt the door, found a wooden beam wedged across it, lifted the beam, opened the door and stepped out. Perpigno and three other men dashed in with torch, sword and chains. As Alec picked up his own sword, Perpigno placed his under the chin of a sleeping Corsair and put his finger to his lips. Then slave chains were placed around the enemy's wrists. Alec watched the torches of Ceol's men move from house to house, leading

68

tired men, who staggered on their feet, and led in groups of five towards the palms. Konini and Spalda did not seem to be amongst them.

With just ten cottages left to take, a woman cried out a warning and iron clashed against iron. Fierce fighting broke out on the far side of the village, and women and children began to run away to safety. Ceol's warriors ignored them and hunted for pirates, keeping their eyes open for Spalda, the man they had seen on the stern of the galley, the man they had been told to kill. A warrior ran to Ceol.

"Master, he is taken and without a struggle."

"Show me."

Ceol followed him, their torches flickering and lighting the white walls of the cottages.

"He is here."

Ceol bent and entered a house that smelled of sickness, and he held his nose and stared at the sleeping man who tossed and turned in a land of nightmares. Spalda's face was deathly white.

"Kill him now."

His warriors obeyed his orders. Alec and Perpigno came in, panting heavily, saw Spalda's blood-stained body and Perpigno gave Ceol a warning.

"We need help. One house in the centre of the village is not like the others. Inside there are stairs going down and a narrow, steep passage that is heavily guarded. Whatever is below the ground is denied to us."

Ceol smiled.

"Could it be Spalda's treasure?"

"It may be, but Konini is not yet found. If he guards it many will die."

Ceol turned to his warriors, who wiped blood from their swords.

"Gather every man who does not guard a prisoner. Tell them to join us at the centre of the village."

His men ran off and Alec led them out, dreading what he

knew would follow. A face to face fight with the mighty Slave Master. They stooped and entered the house and stood in a bare room lit by four candles and the torches held by the men who were crammed inside. Stairs led downwards into a passageway, which flickered yellow and orange. Muffled shouts came from deep down. A wounded and bloody warrior was passed from arm to arm out of the passage and up the stairs. Ceol spoke to him and the man coughed out some words.

"There is a long narrow passage leading to a chamber, but three Corsairs guard the way," interpreted Perpigno.

"Is Konini one of them?" asked Alec.

"Don't know."

Perpigno watched as a corpse with no head was passed back and up the stairs. Another warrior replaced him.

"Probably."

Someone called back from the passageway.

Perpigno smiled at Alec.

"Two Corsairs left now and one of them is wounded."

Alec glanced at his friend and lifted his sword.

"Come on. We must finish this tonight."

"I am not going down there."

Alec grabbed his arm and forced him forward.

"Oh yes you are."

They moved past the warriors on the stairs and stooped inside the tunnel. Ahead of them torches waved around, men cried out and blades sang. They joined the queue of warriors and were passed a man with a curved knife sticking out of his chest. They carried him up the stairs before going back. Someone cried out and Perpigno put his hand on Alec's shoulder and shouted back towards Ceol.

"Only one of the enemy left now."

They moved three paces forward, torches held up, swords ready and staring past the shoulders of the men in front of them at the fighting. Suddenly everyone was able to charge forward and they stood in a stone-lined, arched chamber that was full of barrels. Three Corsairs lay still on the floor. A man cried out, and Alec and Perpigno ran to join him at the far end by another door. Alec pushed it open.

"Come on, Perpigno."

The other warriors followed them, their torches lighting up another long, low tunnel, but none of the enemy were anywhere to be seen. Another door, another chamber and Ceol's men gasped and stood like statues, staring at mounds of treasure. One ran back to fetch his master, but Alec completely ignored the haul, and searched for an entrance to another chamber.

"Here."

Perpigno came over, a bag of coins in his hand. The others picked up gold cups, silver crosses, staring at them in the torchlight, fingering precious stones.

"Ask them to follow us."

Perpigno asked them, but no help came. Alec gathered together all of his courage, expecting Konini to be waiting on the other side of the last door. He kicked it open and the vile stench of vomit came up and out of yet another black passage, which ran down into the earth. Perpigno heard words from behind them.

"Konini has not been found."

"Then he is here."

"Wait. Wait for the others to join us."

Alec held his torch out in front of him and moved cautiously down the tunnel.

"Wait, Brown Eyes."

"No."

In front of another door, Alec hesitated before kicking it open. He held his sword up to protect his face from an enemy blade, but no attack came and he threw his torch inside the chamber. It was lined with beds and tortured, sleeping men.

"Fetch torches."

Perpigno left him and Alec walked in, picked up his torch and glanced around, searching for guards who might be hiding behind the beds. He looked into the sweat covered faces of the Corsairs and did not recognise any of them. Suddenly, his senses became alert to danger. On the other side of the chamber, two shadowy shapes bent over a sleeping man. He swung round and held his torch out. One man was dressed in a dark cloak, like the one the Watcher on the hill always wore. The other had clothes, the likes of which he had never seen before and this man had his hands inside a Corsair's mouth. The cloaked figure saw Alec and spoke softly in a strong and kind voice.

"Alec of Dunfermline. Do not fear the Slave Master."

"What are you doing?"

"Borrowing something from the past."

The other man turned, his face completely covered by some kind of magic mask. Bright yellow letters shot across the mask. The two men held each other tightly and Alec's mouth fell open as they disappeared down into the floor. He stood there for some time, trying to make sense of what he had witnessed and, as he came back to the dark of the House of the Sick, he found himself standing at the foot of Konini's bed. What sickness had laid him so low? How lucky they had been to attack the village on this night. Someone shouted out behind him and Perpigno, Ceol and armed guards raced in, holding their arms across their mouths in a hopeless gesture to keep the smell away.

"Is that Konini?" asked Ceol.

Perpigno nodded.

"That is him."

"He does not look like a great warrior."

Perpigno looked at the white faces of the other Corsairs.

"None of them do now."

Ceol pointed at the Slave Master.

"Kill him."

His men raised their swords and walked to the bed. Alec raised his own sword and stepped in front of them.

"Ask Ceol to spare Konini."

"What? Are you mad?"

"No. Perpigno, please ask him."

Perpigno asked him and spoke to Alec.

"He asks why he should spare him. I ask myself the same question."

Alec remembered how Konini had lifted his daughter onto his shoulders, how he had come back to the sinking galley to release his slaves during the storm, and how a ghost had told him not to fear him.

"We owe our lives to this man and Ceol will never, ever, have a stronger slave to pull on the oar. If Konini lives, that is."

Perpigno talked to Ceol, who shrugged his shoulders.

"He says the Corsair is spared and will become his slave. If he does survive the fever, Ceol promises to tell him that he owes his life to you, Alec of Dunfermline, from the land of the Scots, and may the gods help you if he ever gets free."

"Tell Ceol he can now buy ten wardrobes of new clothes and that he is now Ceol the Truly Magnificent."

Perpigno told him and Ceol's face beamed as he pointed with pride at his bright, expensive shirt.

Alec smiled.

"Come on, Perpigno, let's go."

"Go where?"

"Go and free the slaves on the galley."

Perpigno stared at his friend.

"You know something?"

"I know I want to go home."

"Do you know something?"

"What?"

"There are times when you do not behave like a slave, a shepherd or a Shipmaster."

"I don't?"

"No, Brown Eyes. There are times when you behave like a king."

CHAPTER FOUR

THE WINTER SOLSTICE : 21 DECEMBER 2007

Thorgood Firebrand slept, but did not dream. It was as though his mind was now full, so full after all of his experiences stretching out across the long centuries, that there was no room left for idle thoughts, dreams or pictures of things that might be. He opened his eyes and felt weak, and knew he would need to visit the Heart Stone soon. Like a thief, he quietly pulled back his furs, got out of bed, dressed, and tiptoed across to his daughter's bed. He knelt down and, as he did every morning, kissed her forehead and gently rubbed the side of her soft cheek with the back of his hand.

"Praise be to Odin the Creator," he whispered.

All of his love and tenderness were in those gentle strokes and, as he stared at her beautiful sleeping face, he pictured losing her to the fever, grieving at her loss and how empty he had felt until his own death.

"Sleep now."

He stood and left Ulrika, the sound of her breathing becoming quieter as he stepped outside their longhouse to see the sun rise above the calm and blue waters of Oslo fjord. Four longships bobbed up and down against the wall of the quay, and a few of the Valkyrie were already up, busying themselves with nets, and loading boxes onto the ships. He stared up at the high mountains that framed the fjord. Up there was the ancient Seat of Kings where he had once made his decision to sail south and attack foreign lands to help his people escape famine. Thorgood had not been back there for an age. Had not needed to go back. Everything he could possibly want was here, provided by his master. Crops grew well, the animals were strong and the ocean gifted them fish whenever they chose to raise a sail and cast a net. It was an idyllic life, made complete by Ulrika's return. But peace and tranquillity had a price.

Thorgood walked past the other white longhouses, down a cobbled lane, and headed for the Hall of the Gods. It was the biggest building along the coast, the most magnificent, and held the secret of his eternal life. Two tall oak doors, covered with brass studs the size of a hand, barred his way and he pushed with all his might against one. The door opened slowly to reveal a huge, secret dark space, and he breathed in smoky air. One thousand paces long and half that wide, the hall spoke of one thing. Odin's power. Great curved beams of oak held up a wooden roof with a single beam forming a long back-bone high above him. It was just like standing under a massive upturned longship.

Orange, red and yellow tongues of flame danced up from a fire at this end of the hall, the fire contained by a circle of rocks and twelve swords, each the height of five men, with their hilts partially buried into the earth. Their gleaming blades formed a full circle, like the hearth stones, and leaned back slightly, their tall shadows dancing upon the walls.

He passed a long table with hundreds of places set and ready for the next feast, the sound of lapping waves growing in his ears. He stopped to look at the Heart Stone. Thorgood had been coming to this place for over one thousand years and yet he never tired of seeing it, or feeling its energy. A circular pool, with a standing stone at its centre. Beneath the water, the base of the stone glowed red and the entire stone rose up, before slowly falling back to send low waves radiating out to a stone wall where he would sit and recharge his body. It was a quiet place, a sanctuary, and a place to think and dream of glory. But dreaming had escaped him for centuries.

Thorgood unbuckled his sword belt and dropped it onto the floor. He pulled off his leather tunic and the rest of his clothes, submersed his naked body in sea water and heard the deep heartbeat of the rising and falling stone, felt the cold and the power of the sea enter his arms, head and chest. Now he was strong again and rose to sit upon the wall with his legs dangling down into the pool.

The stories told how Odin and Thor had found an underground chamber when the ice retreated from the land. They took many magic, pulsing crystals and used some to make a single ruby of incredible power. The rest of the crystals were here, buried below the Heart Stone, beating, pulsing and fuelling the Valkyrie, the warriors who did not die, with life itself.

Thorgood put his head into his hands and heard his grandfather's screams of agony as Odin had returned the man's body to dust. Then Thorgood remembered how he had found a deep, inner courage to pull an arrow from his shoulder, and crawl to a river and float away from war. That had been an age ago, but these memories remained clear and he knew that one day his master would destroy him too. It would just take one disloyal thought, one mistake or show of cowardice. He looked at the rising and falling stone, and the red glow which pulsed at its base, and chose his words carefully.

"Praise be to Odin, that the Heart Stone's secret is safe from the enemy."

***

Three o'clock in the morning and the city was quiet. Olaf Adanson adjusted a strap on his heavy rucksack and stared up the River Tyne at the blue and red decorative lights shining onto the bridges, and at the dark silhouettes of the offices, apartments and restaurants of the new quayside development. A chilling wind blew in from the coast and he turned to place his hands upon the round, shiny metal rail of the Millennium Bridge. Off to his right, the old flour mill, now the Baltic Art Gallery, loomed up with a huge poster covering one of its huge walls. The poster read, "*You Cannot Take Your Eyes Off This.*" His phone bleeped, announcing the arrival of Thorgood's text, and Olaf took his eyes off the poster.

Confirmed. The bi-annual company meeting will be in Newcastle Upon Tyne.
Sunrise on 21.12.07. Everything ready?

Olaf replied – **Nearly** – and put his phone back into the pocket of his brown leather jacket.

His senses became alert. A swaying, unsteady figure emerged

from the gloom of the Gateshead embankment, to the right of the Baltic. Olaf watched, holding his nerve and thinking it would be almost impossible for the Keepers to know that he was here, or know of his master's orders. Almost impossible, unless something had gone wrong in Berlin, during the transfer of the Senator from Africa to the North East of England.

The figure stopped and a flickering light lit up the face. It was a pretty woman, with long black hair hanging down beneath a hat. Quicker footsteps now, her boots coming down heavily onto the curved metal bridge, and getting louder as she walked towards him at the very centre. He glanced casually at her clothes. High dark brown leather boots, which looked too big for her short body, and an old, long brown corduroy coat with orange woollen cuffs. Her hat was corduroy too. She looked like a fashion designer or someone who sold the *Big Issue* and he wondered how someone so small could make so much noise. The woman staggered as she sucked on her cigarette and, passing Olaf, she muttered a single word in German that she thought he would not hear.

"Scheisse."

Then the woman was gone, half walking, half staggering, off the bridge on the Newcastle side and disappearing into the half light of the city. Olaf unshouldered his heavy rucksack. He knelt down, pretending to tie a lace and, after checking both ways along the walkway of the bridge, quickly opened the top flap, pulled out the end of a chain and fixed it securely to a strong-looking metal upright. He tossed the rucksack over the side and watched it spin around and around, as inside the chain uncoiled, until plopping into the fast-flowing river. Olaf peered down, trying to make out the shape of a *Black Slug*, or the diver who waited below, but there was only a thin trail of bubbles rising up from the inky blackness.

Olaf took his phone, the screen lighting up his face as he slid the cover back. He typed one word into the keypad – **Ready** – and pushed send.

Standing in shadow, beside the Pig and Piano bar-restaurant on the quayside, a woman in a long brown corduroy coat lifted her mobile.

***

Holly Anderson took a call in the SKEPERE room on lower level five of the MI5 building in Vauxhall, London.

"Kristin, you are a long way from home."

"Following a lead."

"And working late."

"Ja. Olaf Adanson is standing on the Millennium Bridge in Newcastle."

"Do you think it is linked to our missing friend?"

"Don't know."

"Any other Seekers around?"

"Nein."

"Nine?"

Kristin's voice became agitated.

"No, none."

"OK. Keep me posted and thank you for your report."

Holly scrolled down her address book to Bernard's mobile number, remembered the time and decided not to wake him. She walked to the other side of the office and stared at the mountains, craters and shadows on a wall-mounted photograph of the moon. The answer was there, in front of her. Had to be there, if Myroy's words were true. Every Keeper knew the history of the stone, and Holly remembered a cloaked figure rising up through the floor of her bedroom as a child. Being scared, but safe and excited, and proud when she had received her pebble from Bernard. But most of all she remembered the very beginning of Myroy's story.

"Exhausted, Gora paused to look at the moon. It was full, silver and bright, the kind of moon that would signal the last days for a Stone Keeper."

One day Odin would hold the stone and become the new

Keeper. That could only mean one thing. He *could* be killed under a Gora moon. But how? Every Keeper through history had asked themselves that question, and the day it was answered would be the day when they could gift Amera's stone to the Seekers and end the eternal struggle. Holly sighed and put her mobile back into her pocket.

"The call can wait until tomorrow."

Miss Dickson, Head of Research for the Keepers, backed into the SKEPERE Office holding two cartons of coffee.

"Working late, then?"

"And I'm not the only one. Just had a call from Kristin, our agent in Berlin."

"Anything important?"

"No, just routine."

"And staring at the moon again."

"The answer is here, somewhere."

Miss Dickson handed Holly a coffee.

"Every Keeper has been told the story and, of course, it isn't just a story. It is Myroy's way of preparing them for the final battle and, OK, most of the Keepers didn't need it. They lived peaceful and untroubled lives. All the tactics of war are in those words, but the way to kill Odin is still a mystery. Not even Bernard has found a single clue to that."

"But we can still try."

Behind Miss Dickson's huge glasses, her huge eyes twinkled.

"We must stop trying and succeed. Peter will be the last Keeper, whether we like it or not."

"And Peter hasn't even heard the whole story yet."

"Oh, he will. The Winged Guardian is waiting for him in the Realm of the Dead."

Holly smiled and took a sip from her carton.

"Shall we do one last check?"

"OK."

"Screen down."

A screen came down to cover the photograph of the moon.

"Seekers within five kilometres of the Keeper."

A map of the area around Bernard's villa on the slopes of Pantokrator came on screen. A single number flashed at the centre –

0

"Seekers on the island of Corfu."

Another number –

1

"That's fine," said Miss Dickson. "Let's get some rest."

***

Kristin stared at Olaf as he left the bridge. He wasn't carrying the rucksack anymore, which worried her, and she wondered if he had thrown it into the river. If he had, the contents would already be with Odin in Oslo. The Seeker moved past the concrete pit that housed the huge hydraulic cylinders, which tilted the bridge to let ships pass through. Then he was climbing over an iron rail and standing on the lip of the quayside. Kristin saw his brown leather jacket dissolve and reform into the clothes of a Norse warrior; clothes that she had only ever seen in a story. A splash in the Tyne told her he was gone and she walked across to stand beside the river, shivering in the cold, and watching a ring of bubbles disappear and dissolve, like Olaf's clothes had done.

***

Thorgood dressed and headed away from the Heart Stone towards a round oak door, the height of two men, at the back of the Hall of the Gods. He pictured a different place in his mind, a place of healing in a different time, and walked straight through the door without bothering to open it. In less than a second, the fire-lit hall and its smoky air were replaced by bright strip lights and the smell of disinfectant. As he walked down a long corridor, his clothes dissolved and reformed into an expensive dark blue suit, and he felt the odd tingling sensation as his fur boots were replaced by socks and leather brogues. Another round door, but made of steel this time, and a round sign at its centre.

O.A.S.V. Medical Centre and Cloning Research Institute.

He stopped three metres from the door and gave a polite cough. The floor ahead of him slid away to reveal a glass floor, which stretched out from his toes to the door, and from one wall to the other. The glass lit up and Odin's face was projected onto it. The intense blue eyes flashed at Thorgood, sensing his intentions, and the floor returned as the door to the Institute swung silently open on a single hinge.

Inside, Thorgood felt the warm air and looked around. Thirty beds were neatly arranged against the outer wall of a huge, round and sterile hospital ward. A single, flat-screen monitor beeped above each bed. Black tubes rose up out of the thighs of the patients and each tube went up to the ceiling, then along the ceiling to a central pillar where they came together and disappeared down into the floor. A doctor was moving slowly, circling around the central pillar, his seat on a metal rail, allowing him to observe the console of each patient without getting up. He pushed a button on the arm of the seat and his speed increased, and Doctor Van Heussen lifted his head.

"Welcome, Thorgood. Just doing my rounds."

"Please report."

"After the battle at Cleopatra's Needle, sixty-two Seekers joined the fallen. Here we will lose another nine and save twenty-one."

"And Mick Roberts?"

The chair circled away and the doctor tapped something into Mick's monitor.

"He will wield the sword again and is conscious. Do you want to speak to him?"

Thorgood walked over to a bed opposite Van Heussen and smiled at Mick. A long sword cut ran from his shoulder to his hip. It was healing now, but he had been dealt a blow, by a member of the High Table, that would have killed most men.

"How do you feel?"

"Weak and foolish."

"Why foolish?"

Mick raised a hand and pointed at his long red scar.

"I wasn't quick enough. I should have killed more of the enemy."

"You were brave."

"I was slow."

"We were taken by surprise."

"Where did the riders come from?"

Thorgood pointed his thumb back over his shoulder.

"The past."

"And the Keeper can do that?"

"He can."

"Then how can we take back our master's stone?"

"Myroy has chosen a boy to hold the stone in keeping. That is a mistake. We will reclaim it soon."

"And the search in Australia?"

"Australia is a big land."

Mick saw something in Thorgood's eyes.

"You don't think it's there, do you?"

"No."

"Why?"

"The enemy have given us many false trails to follow. We believed we were close in Africa, but Senator Dan Donald Junior did not hold the stone. He was just like the other Keepers and refuses to speak. He will be punished."

"Still think it's in Scotland?"

"That is the home of the Donald clan."

At the central control panel, the doctor saw the speed of Mick's heart beat increase. He pushed a yellow button on his screen and a cocktail of drugs was fed into his patient's thigh. Mick felt sleep call to him.

"I will be at your side soon," he mumbled.

Thorgood smiled.

"When you are strong again."

Van Heussen joined them.

"When do you leave for Newcastle?" asked Thorgood.

"Our helicopter leaves in one hour. We join the others aboard the *Maid of Norway*, fifteen miles east of Tynemouth. Everything is ready for the bi-annual meeting."

"I want to see the boy."

The doctor nodded and led him out of the hospital ward into another, identical, round chamber. They stood before one of the beds, looking at a boy of eight summers, with long brown hair spread out across his pillow.

"Condition?"

The Doctor glanced at the flat-screen monitor up on the wall.

"Good."

"DNA?"

"A ninety-nine point eight percent match. The best we have ever achieved."

"So all we have to do is wait for him to grow."

"We do."

"And you are sure the cloning project will succeed."

"Quite sure."

"Praise be to Odin."

"Praise be to Odin," repeated the doctor.

As they left the Cloning Research Institute, the boy opened his eyes and sat up. Carefully, he twisted the tube and pulled it out of his thigh socket and his monitor, in the central control area, quietly beeped. He looked at the small plastic ring, which had been implanted into his skin, and at the fat and muscle inside his leg. The beeping became louder and he clicked a round plastic cover onto the hole, and skipped towards the central console, pushing a button to silence the alarm. Then he was skipping again and, as a cold wind blew through the Institute, his face, hair and body changed, and a grinning Tirani the Wise, the cuckoo in the nest, disappeared into another place.

***

85

Olaf Adanson stood by the quayside, the Millennium Bridge upstream and to his right, and a tall iron monument behind him. A brass plaque on the monument celebrated the river's industrial past. Written on it were the words –

Dedicated to the Glow of the Forge.

The *Maid Of Norway* berthed beside the quay, dwarfing the *River Princess* and the other cruise ships which took day trippers up and down the Tyne. Men in black T-shirts and black shorts secured lines, and extending walkways came out automatically from the side of Deck One and rested on the concrete.

As the morning sun fully rose, the meeting delegates followed Olaf across a newly paved walkway and into a modern office, to stand in front of a reception desk. The security guard's chair swivelled around. Niels Magnusson was still efficient, neat as a pin and utterly ruthless and, as he got ready to ask his test questions, Olaf left through a fire exit and bounded up stairs to the roof. He joined Thorgood who stood in silence watching one delegate after another enter the meeting room and take a seat around a long table, which was shaped like a fish. The eye of the fish was an ancient Egyptian gold bowl and every delegate would have been able to guess its value; ten million US dollars. A square glass panel, set into the roof, allowed Olaf and Thorgood to look down on the meeting, unseen. A delegate glanced up at them and nervously adjusted his tie in the square ceiling mirror.

Thorgood had never seen the big penthouse suite before, but he knew why Olaf had chosen it. The layout and view would please their master. The fish-shaped table filled most of it, but the waters of a fountain rose and fell at one end. Opposite that, on the far side, the wall was completely covered by a fitted metal cabinet. One of the long sides of the suite was decorated by a mural of a Norse longship with Thor standing at the prow. The other side was entirely glass, giving everyone inside a panoramic view of the river, the opposite quay and the Baltic Art Gallery.

"Our master will like it," said Olaf.

Thorgood ignored him and lifted his mobile.

"Niels, are the delegates cleared?"

"The test questions were answered correctly."

"Their belongings were searched aboard the *Maid Of Norway*?"

"They were. Nothing suspicious."

"You have no concerns?"

"No."

"Disarm the device."

"I obey."

At the reception desk, Niels Magnusson lifted a small metal box off his desk, collapsed its aerial and flicked a switch into the off position. A red light, which flashed on the explosive device under the fish-shaped table, went out. Thorgood spoke inside his mind.

"Master, the security check is complete. It is safe for you to proceed."

Thorgood glanced down at the fountain. Its water grew in size and Odin's body formed inside, before stepping out, his suit and blond hair dry and immaculate.

"Let us join the meeting," said Olaf.

They entered the penthouse suite, passing the fountain, and sat beside their master at the tail end of the fish. Odin glanced at the mural of his brother, at the prow of the longship.

"Begin the meeting."

The doors of the metal cabinet at the far end of the room slid open two metres, to reveal a flat TV screen which filled the space from floor to ceiling. An agenda appeared –

O.A.S.V. Bi-Annual Meeting

1. **Search for the Stone.**
2. **Arms Movements North.**
3. **Infiltration Plan.**
4. **Pebble Analysis and Cloning Project.**
5. **Abduction and Elimination Targets.**
6. **O.A.S.V. Income and Expenditure Report (2007) and Bonus Allocation.**
7. **Any Other Business.**

Thorgood rose and went to stand beside the television screen. The first agenda point flashed, blood-red.

"As you know, our attempt to capture Peter of the Line of Donald, failed earlier this year in London."

Behind him, the metal doors opened another metre to reveal three glass shelves, which held Peter's Berghaus rucksack, Tirani's calling pipe and the torn-out page from *Early Celtic Writings and Their Meanings*.

"We have evidence that points to Australia and our forces continue to search there."

Odin sensed something in Thorgood's heart.

"But you doubt that evidence."

"I do. Throughout history, the Keepers have sent us along many false trails."

"Like Africa."

"Like the Senator in Africa."

"And yet I took the Keeper's rucksack myself."

"You did, Master, which tells me something. To dare to place the Keeper before you, to place him in such danger, means we were getting close. It was a high-risk plan for them and could only have been the brainchild of one man. Bernard."

A tough-looking Turk in an ill-fitting black suit, who sat close to the gold bowl, shook his head.

"Are you completely sure that the parchment is genuine?"

Olaf answered him.

"We are. It has been analysed thoroughly and contains the old magic used by Myroy."

"But it could be a trick."

"It could, but I doubt it. I saw the look of fear on the Keeper's face as he stood beside the Thames. He was *not* acting. I do not believe that Myroy would risk placing the stone in danger like that."

Odin's blue eyes flashed. "The search in Australia will continue."

The Turk swivelled around in his seat to face Odin.

88

"Master, what is the other object you found in the bag?" Thorgood answered.

"It is old, very old. A wooden pipe which makes two notes."

"Does it contain the old magic?"

"It has not been analysed."

Odin stared at the pipe.

"Have it analysed. Next item."

Point one stopped glowing and point two flashed red, and Olaf replaced Thorgood by the screen. The metal cabinet silently slid open some more to reveal a rack of Computer Aided Rifles.

"The balance of power is roughly equal. The Keepers have strengthened their arms capability in South Africa and Australia. As we speak, all the components required to manufacture our C.A.R.s, *Slugs*, long-wave communication systems and long-range missile systems lie within the boundary of the Red Empire. The greatest single manufacturing power-base outside of this boundary is China and I will cover that in my Infiltration Report."

"Recommendations?" asked Odin.

"Keeper technology is ten years behind ours, but they do have a team of good people researching new weapons capabilities. They work for the US military and are based in Boston, Massachusetts."

"Let them join the fallen."

"I obey, Master."

As the next agenda item, Infiltration Plan, flashed blood-red, the cabinet doors slid sideways to reveal live pictures from a web-cam inside the MIR space-station. Olaf began his report as an astronaut floated by carrying a heating unit.

"We have three important projects underway. First, one of our agents has established himself as a member of the MIR team. There is some suspicion aboard the space station, but components essential to the operation of the enemy's Stone Tracking Device have been sabotaged. Their project has been set back many months."

The delegates around the table nodded.

"Secondly, we have five Seekers who have risen up the political ladder to become senior members of the Chinese Government. When the stone is taken, we are confident that the Chinese will ally with us and ship the arms we need north."

A man beside the Turk leaned forward and spoke in an American accent.

"And what does the Chinese Government get out of it?"

"Incredible wealth," said Thorgood.

More nods around the table.

"Thirdly," continued Olaf, "we have failed."

A wave of fear ran around the room.

"Once again, we have failed to infiltrate the Keeper organisation inside MI5 in London. The security system they use is thorough and effective. Thorgood will now show you how we plan to deal with this situation."

The fourth agenda item, Pebble Analysis and Cloning Project, pulsed red. Thorgood remained seated next to Odin and placed a pebble on the table.

"The Keepers identify themselves with these. This pebble belongs to Senator Dan Donald Junior of Denver in Colorado, who was used to divert our search away from America and Scotland to Africa. Each pebble is completely unique, like a person's DNA. They are impossible to copy or reproduce due to the pebbles' complex underlying crystal and mineral structure. This conclusion has forced us to look at the problem in a different way."

As Thorgood stopped speaking, Doctor Van Heussen and a young boy with long brown hair joined the meeting.

"Welcome, Michael. Welcome, Doctor. Please update us."

Van Heussen smiled and walked over to the metal cabinet, which slid open to reveal a sleeping man with long brown hair. Above the man, on a glass shelf, was a white bowl piled high with pebbles. He looked at the boy.

"This is Michael. He is a clone. His appearance, even his speech and mannerisms, are exactly the same as a senior Keeper who we caught and executed eight years ago." The Doctor pointed at the body in the cabinet. "This man is long dead and yet he still lives. Previous clones have had a maximum DNA match of only ninety-four point three percent. That is not enough to deceive the SKEPERE security system. These versions of Michael have been terminated."

The doctor went to stand beside the boy and put a reassuring arm around him.

"This is Michael too. His DNA is ninety-nine point eight percent identical to the dead Keeper's. When he is twenty years old he can be used to infiltrate the enemy's headquarters."

Olaf looked at the boy and his forehead creased.

"But this boy is eight years old. We have to wait another twelve years before using him. The real Keeper would be forty years old when returned to them and not twenty years. They are sure to ask many questions about his long absence. How do we explain that he is half the age he should be?"

The doctor smiled again.

"What you say is true. The plan I have discussed with our Master, is to allow Michael to grow up in another time, under the supervision and care of the Magnusson family."

"Niels Magnusson, the Head of Security in Oslo, a father?" asked the American.

"Niels and his forefathers have loyally served us for over seven hundred years. We can trust him absolutely to ensure the boy is schooled with a single purpose."

The Turk asked what everyone was thinking.

"Can you do the maths for me again?"

Van Heussen sighed.

"Eight years ago we killed a twenty year old Keeper, so today he would be twenty-eight years old. If we want this boy to replace him in the next two weeks, he must be also be twenty-eight years old. The solution is simple. Our Master will take him back in time twenty years. He is trained by Niels and made ready for the operation. In two weeks' time, the boy you see before you will be exactly the same age as the man who is posted as missing by the enemy."

"They will still be suspicious about his absence," said Olaf.

"MI5 rely completely on the match between the pebble and the person's DNA. When that match is made and the story we prepare is checked, even double checked, all other details will become irrelevant to them."

"How have you managed to achieve such a close DNA match?" asked the American.

"The subject, the Keeper we cloned, was young. The younger they are, the better the results. This is why we plan a second project, which is even more ambitious than this one. I will cover that next."

Odin tried to sense the cloned boy's thoughts, access his memory and dreams, but sensed nothing.

"Will Michael obey me?"

Van Heussen nodded.

"Your will is his will and after twenty years of schooling by Niels, I think we can be confident of his loyalty."

"Yet I cannot reach inside his mind."

"This may be a side effect of the cloning process. I will look into this and report back."

Olaf stared at the doctor.

"How can you be sure that this project has a future?"

Van Heussen pointed at the white bowl.

"Each year we kill between eighty and ninety Keepers. These are some of their pebbles. We only need one clone to slip through the SKEPERE security net and then the balance of power will shift our way. I believe Michael will succeed, but if he does not, we try again."

Odin's patience deserted him.

"Next."

The flashing blood-red script highlighted the next agenda point –

5. Abduction and Elimination Targets.

Van Heussen continued as the cabinet slid back to reveal the picture of a schoolgirl, stolen from the records of Pinner High School.

"This is fifteen year old Kylie, the Keeper's girlfriend. No one is closer to him. No one could do more damage to their cause than her. The second part of our Cloning Project is more difficult. We must locate and kidnap her, and take her DNA. On her death a new Kylie will be born and sent back fifteen years into the past. To Peter, there will be no visible difference. One day he is talking to his girl, then she disappears, and then a day later she reappears. Because of her age, we may even get a DNA match of ninety-nine point nine percent. Nobody could tell the difference, but there is a problem."

"Memory," said Thorgood.

The doctor nodded.

"The cloning process can give her Kylie's skin, eyes, hair, teeth. But, if Peter asks her about what they had for lunch, who they talked to and what they said, she will be completely lost. She will have no memory of her past with her boyfriend."

"Solution?" asked Odin.

"We cannot give her everything, so there is an element of bluffing her way through things. During her years of training, she must see pictures of her family, study their faces, and learn about their likes and dislikes. More importantly, we must record the days before her abduction. We need a video diary of everything the real Peter and Kylie did together. As the clone grows, this will be watched many, many times and the knowledge assimilated."

Everyone waited for Odin's orders.

"From this day and until I give new orders, all abduction and elimination targets are suspended. Issue that photograph. All Seekers are to locate Kylie and report to Thorgood. Thorgood."

"Yes, Master."

"When the girl is located, film her movements. Then take her to Van Heussen in Oslo."

"I obey, Master."

"Next item. You may leave now, Doctor."

The seven agenda items disappeared on the TV screen and

were replaced by a Profit and Loss Account. Olaf read it out as the door closed behind Van Heussen.

"This year, total income was two point seven billion US dollars. The total costs for running the global Seeker organisation, and acquiring new works of art, was two point one billion dollars. The financial results are satisfactory and we would like to thank you for the contribution you have made."

The long cabinet slid open another metre to reveal a neat stack of metal briefcases.

"Please take one when you leave. They each contain five million US dollars in five thousand dollar bills."

Thorgood looked at the smiling delegates.

"Is there any other business?" No one said anything. "Please hold the summer solstice free in your diaries for the next bi-annual meeting. The venue will be announced twenty-four hours in advance."

Odin stared out of the panoramic window at the Millennium Bridge. It was slowly rising, winking, its long curved walkway tilting and lifting out of the river a man, dressed in a diving suit, on a chain. This chain was tied tightly under his arms, around his chest, and another chain ran down and was tied around his waist. Thorgood spoke.

"May I introduce you to Senator Dan Donald. He deceived us. Made us believe he held the stone, and our people followed him from America to Africa. It was a false trail. He was captured and sent here via Berlin."

The eyes of the delegates followed Odin's and they watched in silence as the Senator frantically tore off his mask and air supply, and tried to free himself from the chains which tightened now. Odin smiled as the bridge seemed to pause in its ascent, the man's body stretching before being ripped in two. The god stood and walked into the fountain. As his body dissolved, he spoke again.

"Death to the Keepers."

"Death to the Keepers," everyone repeated.

Olaf, Thorgood and Niels Magnusson escorted the delegates and their briefcases back to the *Maid Of Norway*. A few minutes later, at the stern on Deck One, Van Heussen stared up at a chain dangling down from the bridge, still holding half of the Senator's torn body. He talked with Olaf.

"So that is one less Keeper to worry about."

As the ship broke its lines and left the quayside, Olaf pointed across the Tyne at a crowd of people who had gathered below the Baltic Art Gallery. Two men were pulling a woman's body out of the water, manhandling the dripping, lifeless figure ashore. The woman had long black hair and was dressed in a brown corduroy coat.

"Make that two," said Olaf

CHAPTER FIVE

BREAKFAST BESIDE THE POOL

Peter opened an eye, licked his dry lips and rolled onto his side. Bright, warming sunshine flooded through his open picture-windows and, outside, swifts darted above Bernard's garden, hunting for breakfast and showing off their incredible speed and agility. A tray with freshly-squeezed orange juice and a large bowl of ice-cream, topped with halved strawberries, rested on his bedside table. He poked an arm out from under his sheet, took a spoon and stuck it into the ice-cream. It was soft, which meant that Mrs Agnedes had put it there a while ago. Peter ate it anyway, smiling, thinking of Kylie and listening to the sounds around his new home. Water sprinklers tinkled, a distant horn piped, a lawnmower droned and someone whistled, repeating the same four notes over and over again.

Thirstily, Peter drank his orange, wrapped a towel around his waist and went to stand by the window. Old Mr Agnedes was pushing a lawnmower, walking methodically up and down, making neat lines and occasionally stopping to pick up leaves that invaded his private world. A boy about the same age as Peter, dressed in yellow swim shorts, dragged a net on a long pole up and down the length of the pool, before emptying leaves into a black bin liner. Peter dressed quickly to go and meet the friend he had only ever met in a story.

Stefanos beamed a friendly smile and thumped his bronzed chest.

"Herete. Me Stefanos."

"Hi, I'm Peter. You free for a swim later on?"

The boy tilted his head and repeated one of the words he had understood.

"Peter?"

Peter banged his chest, smiling.

"Peter."

Mrs Agnedes called out from inside the villa.

"Stefanos. Katerina's Kitchen."

The boy dropped the net and bin liner and ran off, waving at Peter with his hand beside an ear.

"Down the hill," said Peter and he made up his mind to read his new Greek dictionary and phrase book immediately after breakfast.

It was only two days since the battle at Cleopatra's Needle in London, but he felt safe and happy. The story, Amera's stone, Odin, Odin's Valkyrie and being a Keeper could all be forgotten, for a short time at least.

***

Spiros Theopoulis, Commissioner of Police, stared at the pebble that destroyed the symmetry of his neat desk.

"You want coffee?"

Bernard shook his head.

"Having breakfast when I get back."

"You need help?"

"No. This is just a courtesy call. The Keeper and his girlfriend are going to stay with me for a while. We flew in yesterday."

"Staying long?"

"Hope so, it just depends if anything crops up at the office."

"Security levels?"

"You can keep them low key. The Seekers are on the other side of the world. Any of the enemy on the island?"

"Just one. An American tourist who sticks out like a sore thumb and he wasn't anywhere near the airport when you arrived."

"Keep an eye on him and please text me if he leaves Corfu Town."

"I will. Are you going to the dinner?"

Bernard picked up his pebble, stood and smiled.

"Wouldn't miss it for the world. Love reunions."

Spiros's stern face became lined and sad, and he looked the age he really was.

"Two empty chairs?"

99

Bernard opened the door of the Commissioner's office and spoke without looking back.

"Two empty chairs."

***

Grandma's voice called out, "Breakfast," and Peter walked onto the veranda and over to the table and chairs, which stood outside the large patio doors. The table was already covered in jugs of fresh orange juice, coffee, croissants and jam, and a large bowl of colourful chopped fruits. Mrs Agnedes bustled over, a tray of home-made pastries and biscuits in her hands.

"How many are you feeding?" asked Peter.

The old lady smiled.

"You swim today?"

"Love to. Thought I might take Kylie snorkelling at Secret Cove."

She smiled back at him, shrugging her shoulders and offering him a cake from her tray. Grandma joined them, carrying another tray.

"Good morning, Peter. You sleep well?"

"Like a log. Isn't this just a fantastic place."

Grandma unloaded her tray onto the breakfast table and squinted in the bright sunshine.

"When I left Glenbowmond it was raining. Pouring. Isn't it lovely to be able to eat outside. I think food tastes better in the open air."

"When did you arrive on Corfu?"

"Last night. Mr Minolas collected me in his taxi."

"Best cab on the island?"

Grandma smiled.

"Smells of sweat and Mr Minolas kept looking at me in a funny way."

"Perhaps he fancies you?"

A deep booming voice came down from the air above them.

"That is enough of that kind of talk."

"Hmmm." Grandma sighed. "Is that you again, Duncan? What did we say about you respecting my privacy?"

"We are married."

"We are *not* married. You are dead."

Grandpa's voice rose.

"I am *not* dead. I am in the Realm of the Dead."

Grandma glanced at Peter.

"And Bernard is taking us all there tomorrow. Can't wait to meet The Twelve. How exciting is that? How many people get to meet all the Keepers who have ever held the stone?"

Bernard and Kylie joined them on the patio, Kylie dressed in a blue dress and sandals, her swimming costume just showing beneath her dress. She kissed Peter and sat beside him.

"And what are we going to do today?" asked Bernard.

Grandpa's cross voice cut in.

"*We* aren't going to do anything."

Bernard sighed like Grandma had done.

"Maggie, is that Duncan again? I thought that after he dumped us on the island he agreed to give us some space."

"He did."

The voice from above again.

"Not on Corfu I didn't."

Bernard sipped his coffee.

"Anyway, I was asking Peter and Kylie. So what are you two going to do today?"

They replied at exactly the same time.

"Shopping," said Kylie.

"Swimming," said Peter.

"Well, I'll leave you to argue that one out."

Kylie smiled at Peter and made up her mind to buy some new shoes.

"Oh, there'll be no arguing about it."

Peter bit into a large croissant filled with warm chocolate.

"If we aren't going to the Realm of the Dead until tomorrow, we've got time to do both," he mumbled.

101

"It gets very hot between twelve and two, so if you are going swimming, do that first thing or later in the day. We don't want you getting sunburned so early in your holiday," warned Bernard.

Peter nodded and picked up a tub of natural Greek yoghurt.

"And having to use remedies from the war in the desert."

Bernard stared at him.

"How did you know about that old trick?"

"Heard it in a story."

"But I never told you about using yoghurt."

"Yes you did. You were in one of Myroy's stories. They can be so real."

Bernard's face creased with concern.

"Was that story a part of your test as a stone Keeper?"

"It was."

"Was it terrible?"

Peter remembered how he had felt when he lost Kylie and his family, and how Myroy had tortured him with his words. He took Kylie's hand and held it tight.

"Yep."

Grandma spoke in a soft voice.

"But that's all over now. You are on holiday, so relax and enjoy the sunshine."

"Who's looking after Dog?" asked Kylie.

Grandma poured out a large orange juice and handed it to Bernard.

"Miss McKiely at the post office in Easter Malgeddie. She spoils him rotten."

Grandpa's booming voice again.

"Just like you are spoiling Bernard."

Grandma's lips tightened.

"Leave it, Maggie," said Bernard.

"I won't leave it."

Grandma grabbed the back of Bernard's head, pulled him close and kissed him on the lips. A spoon, piled high with fresh fruit, hovered in front of Peter's open mouth.

"There, I've wanted to do that for a long time."

"Steady, girl," said Bernard.

Grandpa's voice became hard, slow and threatening.

"You are still my wife."

"I am not. I'm a widow and I can do what I want to do."

"You can't."

"I can."

Bernard took a serviette and wiped lipstick off his mouth.

"Come on, Duncan. Be reasonable." Bernard's chair rose up and fell back down with a *bang*, orange juice spilling onto the tiled veranda floor. "Was that really necessary, old boy?"

"Aye, it was."

Peter grabbed another chocolate croissant, nudged Kylie and pointed down the mountainside towards the sea.

"Come on," he whispered.

As they walked, side by side, through the garden, there was another bang. They stopped and turned. Mrs Agnedes had just walked through the patio doors, holding a tray, her mouth wide open as Bernard's and Maggie's chairs, the breakfast table and a pot of flowers rose up and shot at great speed to hover three metres above the swimming pool. They both still sat around the floating table and Bernard calmly glanced back at the trail of croissants, bowls, pots and cutlery that showed their flight-path above the garden. He picked up a biscuit, which remained on the table, and bit it. Grandma shook her fist up at the clear blue sky and shouted something. Mrs Agnedes dropped her tray.

"Oh, no," said Kylie.

Bernard, Maggie, their chairs and table, and flower pot, dropped like a stone into the pool. Kylie took Peter's hand and squeezed it gently.

"You know, Peter, you've got the weirdest family."

***

Christos Dalmedes Theopoulis walked into the entrance and

lounge of the Corfu Town House Hotel, and placed a pebble onto the reception desk.

"Good morning, Mrs Veldinis. How are you today?"

The old receptionist gave him a big, warm smile, her brown eyes twinkling.

"I am well, and our friend from America still sleeps."

"How long is he booked in for?" asked Christos.

"Ten days. All paid for in advance by his company in Oslo."

"I see. I think I will go and get myself a coffee at the café over the road. Will you text me when he leaves?"

"I will."

Christos smiled and picked up his pebble.

"I bet it is the same routine as yesterday. A few hours watching people arrive at the airport, lunch in town, shopping and sight-seeing in the afternoon. Not the most exciting job I've been given."

"No."

"Do you think he knows we are following him?"

"No."

"And he is still wearing that stupid hat?"

Mrs Veldinis smiled too.

"You won't lose him, even in a crowd."

He walked out of the hotel and stepped into brilliant early-morning sunshine, crossing the busy street and sitting at a pavement café. He took out his mobile phone and sent a text –

Father, Theodore Stanton plans to stay ten days. Expect him to be in town this afternoon. Will confirm. C.

As a waiter came over to take his order, Christos's phone beeped. A text –

Our American friend leaves now. MV.

Christos spoke to the waiter.

"I'll come back for coffee later."

He looked across the road, past the speeding mopeds and yellow taxis. A tall man with a red shirt, blue jeans and a large white cowboy hat, stepped out of the hotel. A black camera hung around his neck and, around his waist, he wore a leather bum-bag that you could have hidden a suitcase in. The American raised a hand and shouted at a taxi. Christos stood.

"Here we go again."

***

Katerina's Kitchen was two hundred metres from the sea, surrounded by plastic tables and chairs, and exactly how Peter knew it would be. As they reached the sand, Peter and Kylie took their sandals off and walked down towards Stefanos, who danced to a loud pop song, whilst placing wire baskets of olive oil, salt, pepper, mustard and ketchup onto the tables. A voice called out from inside the small taverna.

"Stefanos! Music!"

The boy grinned and danced over to a radio and turned it down. He saw Peter and Kylie.

"Herete."

Peter thumped his chest.

"Herete, Stefanos." He pointed at Kylie. "Kylie."

"Kylie," repeated Stefanos.

"When you've finished, would you like to go swimming?"

The boy's nose wrinkled.

"No understand," he said slowly.

Kylie did the breast-stroke with her arms.

"Swimming?"

"Ah, sweemming."

He pointed along the beach towards a line of rocks, beyond a shabby looking store with a shabby sign above it –

Super Super Market

Peter tapped his watch and Stefanos held up all his fingers.

"Ten minutes?" asked Kylie.

Stefanos nodded and ran off.

"I must read my Greek dictionary," said Peter.

They sat on the beach, listening to the waves and waiting for Stefanos to finish his jobs. Kylie smiled at Peter.

"Now would be a good time."

"A good time for what?"

"For you to tell me the rest of the story."

"I'm on holiday."

"Oh, come on. When you read that book under the sea, *Early Celtic Writings and Their Meanings*, you learned more about your grandfather, didn't you. Here, on Corfu, in the war."

"I did, but not all of it. Some of the story was missing and I don't think we will hear the ending until we go to the Realm of the Dead."

"You said that the Winged Guardian will tell us the rest of the story about the stone's history, the High Table and the coming of civil war to Scotland."

"Myroy said that," corrected Peter.

Kylie crossed her arms.

"Well, tell me about Duncan and Bernard, and the attack on the Italian airbase."

"No. I'm on holiday."

Kylie cuddled next to him and kissed his cheek.

"Tell me."

"No."

She stroked his cheek and kissed him on the lips.

"Do you love me?"

"Yep. You know I do."

"Then tell me, please."

"No."

She stared into his eyes and ran a hand through her long black hair.

"Tell me."

"Stop it. Whenever you want something, you do that hair thing."

"Works though, doesn't it."

Peter sighed and lay back on the sand, closing his eyes and feeling the sun warm his body.

"I promise I will tell you today."

Kylie lay next to him.

"You better, Peter of the line of Donald, you better."

A shadow fell over them.

"Herete. Sweemming?"

Stefanos was carrying a plastic bag with old masks, snorkels and flippers sticking out of it.

"Swimming," agreed Kylie.

They walked along the beach, past the store, to a line of rocks where the sand ended suddenly and they climbed up, following a narrow path and smelling speedwell, mallow and orchids. Higher up the wild flowers gave way to broom and gorse. The climb ended as abruptly as it had begun and they walked out onto a flat limestone pavement, the warm sea breeze blowing in their faces. Stefanos gave a whoop of delight and ran forward, disappearing, falling, and Kylie gasped.

"Stefanos!"

Peter smiled.

"Don't worry. He always does that."

"Does what?"

"Jumps down into the cove."

They walked, hand in hand, to the edge of the cliff and stared down at a circle of bubbles in a blue horse-shoe bay. At one side was a small, sandy beach with waves lapping at it. Their friend's head popped up inside the ring of bubbles.

"Coming in?" asked Peter.

"I've got a dress on."

"It will dry, soon enough." He released her hand and jumped out, calling back. "Come on."

Kylie looked down nervously, blew air out of her cheeks, took a few steps to one side and launched herself out into space. The shock of the cold water made her feel alive. The boys were racing each other to the small beach and when she joined them Kylie placed her dress on a rock to dry, and copied the others, pulling flippers on and fixing the mask and snorkel onto her head. Then they were all back in the water, staring down at a new world. The sandy bed of the cove was brightly lit and shoals of small fish darted around, with bigger grey fish moving lazily lower down. Stefanos chased the bigger fish, but with a single shake of their tails, they were immediately out of his range. The sun warmed their backs and the sea cooled their arms and legs. It was wonderful.

Peter wondered why Stefanos didn't swim over to the cave and he kicked out with his flippers to tread water above where the black entrance should be. He adjusted his mask and sucked in a huge lungful of air before diving, hoping to swim up the long narrow passage to the secret place where, in a story, he had hidden Amera's stone. The shapes of the sun on the waves above him rippled upon the surface of the rock face, but no cave.

Later, they lay on the small beach and Stefanos gave them chocolate bars from a sealed plastic bag, which he pulled out of the sea on a length of string.

"Isn't this a great place?" said Peter, lazily.

Kylie swallowed the last of her chocolate.

"The kind of place they put in holiday brochures."

"Yep."

"And the only thing we need to worry about is how long it will take for our clothes to dry."

"Yep."

"Will you stop saying, 'Yep.'"

"Yep."

"Peeeter!"

"Yep."

"That is so annoying."

"I'm on holiday. Chill out."

"Will you buy me some new shoes?"

"No."

"I'll kiss you again if you do."

"You should kiss me because you want to. Not because you want new shoes."

"You're mean."

"Yep."

"Stop it. Stop it. Stop it."

Stefanos got up, slowly, and pointed at a path cut into the face of the cliff.

"Katerina's Kitchen."

"Oh, no. Not time to go," said Kylie.

"Yep."

"You are doing that to annoy me, aren't you."

"Yep."

"I am going to choose the most expensive shoes in Corfu Town and *you* are going to buy them for me."

Peter sighed and got up too.

"I don't get any pay as a stone keeper. Buy them yourself. You still want me to tell you the next part of the story later?"

"Yep."

***

Like a switch being thrown, old Mr Agnedes abandoned his wheelbarrow and went to sit on a bench, hands on knees, in the shade of a lime tree. He would sit like that, like a man who has found peace and complete joy, for a little while yet, until after the nice lady had gone away. He stared around his kingdom and thought about his flowers. The vines along the back wall would need to be pruned back soon, and the herbs in pots outside the kitchen needed a good watering. It was going to be a hot day again, like yesterday and the day before yesterday, but Mr Agnedes's thoughts did not wander that far back in time.

***

"Is it time for his morning snack?" asked Grandma.

Mrs Agnedes lifted a kettle off her stove and poured boiling water onto green beans in a saucepan. She nodded.

"Time is now."

She banged the kettle back onto the stove, and grabbed a lunchbox and Thermos mug. Grandma smiled.

"Shall I come too?"

Mrs Agnedes had already reached the kitchen door, and stepped out beside the pots of herbs on the sunny veranda. She called back.

"No. Upsets his, um, routine."

She walked quickly past the geranium beds and more beds full of beautiful, brightly-coloured flowers, and sat on the bench in cool shade. Carefully, she pulled the lid off the mug and placed it into her husband's hand. He sipped the coffee and held out his other hand to receive the lunchbox full of Greek salad. Mrs Agnedes repeated the words she had said in Greek, every day since the end of the war.

"Now you eat that up, Aris."

She took back the mug and placed a fork into his large hand. He began to eat up.

"The garden is looking lovely today."

Mr Agnedes speared a sliced tomato, but did not reply.

"I thought I might take you down to Katerina's Kitchen later on. Would you like a walk by the sea?"

"Sea," he repeated.

"I think business is picking up for our girl, visitor numbers are up and more people are coming to this part of the island now."

She looked across the garden towards an open window, Bernard's office.

"And we have been invited to the reunion dinner. You know how you enjoy seeing your old friends again."

"Bernard."

"Yes, Bernard will be there."

"Empty chairs."

Mrs Agnedes ran her hand through his hair and felt the scar. She moved the conversation on.

"I'll tell you all about it on our walk."

Mr Agnedes finished his salad and she took back the lunchbox and fork, and replaced them with the mug of coffee.

"Now you make sure you put your hat on before going back to work."

"Hat."

"And bring the mug back to the kitchen," she said, knowing that he never did.

"Water herbs."

"Yes, they look very dry at the moment."

She kissed him lovingly on the cheek and went back to her kitchen. Mr Agnedes watched the nice lady go, sipped his coffee and thought about pruning his vines.

***

Bernard glanced at the small television beside his computer and saw Peter and Kylie walking up to the large black gates at the front of his villa. He turned the TV off and pushed a button to open the automatic gates. A few minutes later they all sat beside the pool armed with pineapple juice, cakes and ice-cream provided by Mrs Agnedes.

"We had a lovely swim," said Kylie.

"In Horse-Shoe Cove?" asked Bernard.

Peter put his empty glass down.

"Yep, great place for snorkelling."

"What are you two going to do for the rest of the day?" asked Bernard.

They both replied at the same time.

"Shopping," said Kylie.

"Picnic," said Peter.

Bernard grinned.

"Well, it's not long to noon. You should keep out of the sun if you can. Why don't you go shopping first. It's quite cool in Corfu Town. Ask Mrs Agnedes to make you up a picnic. I've got an old rucksack I can lend you, so take it with you and I'll call Mr Minolas for his taxi. After shopping he can drop you wherever you want."

"I thought we would walk up to the cave," said Peter. "He knows where it is."

Bernard nodded.

"He does."

"Will you show me the entrance to the Realm of the Dead?" asked Kylie.

"Yep."

Bernard cut in quickly.

"But do not go inside. You are both expected by The Twelve tomorrow. Not today."

Peter and Kylie went off to the kitchen to order their picnic and Bernard sent a text message –

The Keeper is going shopping.
Please take the normal precautions. B.

***

In a street café in Corfu Town, Theodore Stanton burped, wiped his mouth with a napkin and studied the remains of his early lunch.

"Check," he shouted.

A waiter came over.

"You would like your bill, Sir?"

"That's right, Buddy."

The waiter wrote it out on a small notepad and handed it to him. Theodore felt in his jeans for his wallet. It wasn't there. He searched his other pockets and the cavernous bum-bag. It wasn't there either.

"My wallet's gone."

The waiter shrugged his shoulders and his guest's voice became angry.

"You hear me, boy? Someone's stolen my wallet."

Another waiter came over.

"Is there a problem?"

The first waiter pointed an accusing finger at the American.

"He doesn't have any money to pay for his meal."

"No money?"

"No money."

Theodore tried to explain again, reinforcing the message by increasing the volume.

"Someone has stolen my wallet."

"That is not our problem."

"It is your problem, because I can't pay."

"Can't pay, or won't pay?"

"My wallet's gone."

The waiters shook their heads knowingly.

"Then this is a matter for the police."

Theodore Stanton stood, aggressively.

"Hey guys. What kind of a racket is this?"

The customers at the other tables fell silent and watched them argue. Three policemen arrived from nowhere.

"Is there a problem?" asked one.

The waiters pointed at their guest.

"He refuses to pay his bill."

Theodore pulled the white pocket linings out of his jeans.

"Someone has stolen my wallet and you guys had better find it."

The policemen marched him to their waiting car and the café returned to normal.

***

Mr Minolas's taxi smelled of sweat and lurched to avoid oncoming cars. Peter and Kylie stared nervously at the back of his bald head.

"You Scots? Like the nice lady?"

"English," corrected Kylie.

"Ah, English, like Bernard."

"Like Bernard," repeated Peter.

The taxi slowed as it entered the busy, narrow streets of Corfu Town and they passed a huge poster showing a photograph of a pot of vanilla yoghurt. Peter read the words in the bottom left-hand corner of the advert –

Constantis and Andreous Advertising

The taxi stopped, violently, throwing its passengers forward.

"Best taxi on the island," said Mr Minolas. "Pick you up, here, at two."

Kylie smiled.

"Plenty of time. Come on. Let's shop."

In minutes her radar had located a shoe shop. They walked inside, feeling the cool air-conditioning, and she picked up a pair of open-toed, red sandals with a hemp heel and sole.

"Ooh, they're nice."

Peter tried to show interest.

"How much are they?"

"They are in the sale."

"How much?"

"Half price."

"How much?"

"Only thirty Euros."

"That's a lot."

"Not for shoes like these."

A lady came over.

"They're nice, aren't they."

Kylie beamed.

"I really like them. Do you have a UK size six?"

The assistant disappeared through a bead curtain at the back of the shop and Peter went to look at the men's shoes. There wasn't anything he liked. Kylie pointed at a pair of leather ankle boots.

"Ooh. Could you pass me those, please."

Peter passed them to her as Kylie's eyes pin-pointed another treasure.

"And those."

Peter felt his mind wither. The lady returned with a box and Kylie tried on the red sandals.

"They're a good fit."

She stood, wiggled her toes and walked around the shop, pausing in front of a tall mirror where she wiggled her toes again.

"I'm not sure."

Peter groaned. Kylie tried on the others, walking around in them and wiggling her toes in front of the mirror, and saying, "I'm not sure," again. The routine was repeated in the next shop. Six shoe shops later and the last Keeper of Amera's stone had lost his will to live.

"I should have bought the red sandals," said Kylie.

"You mean the ones we saw first."

"That's right. Come on, let's try another store."

"Can't we go and get an ice-cream?"

"When we have finished shopping."

"I'm not shopping. You are shopping. All I am doing is hanging around."

Kylie smiled, grabbed his arm and led him inside another shoe shop.

"That's what you're for."

Peter sat on a stool with his head in his hands, waiting for his girlfriend's inevitable words.

"Ooh, they're nice."

"Lovely," said Peter.

"I haven't asked you yet."

"Ask."

"What do you think?"

"Lovely."

"You're not even looking."

Peter lifted his head and saw another pair of leather ankle boots, but with very high heels.

"Lovely," he repeated.

"You are just saying that."

"No I'm not."

"Say what you think. Do I look nice in them?"

Peter made a mistake.

"Alright, you look stupid."

Kylie's face reddened.

"Right, that's it."

She pulled the boots off, put her own shoes back on and stormed out. Peter ran to catch up with her.

"What have I done?" he asked.

Kylie's pace increased. She didn't speak.

"Oh, come on. Not the silent treatment. Kylie, please speak to me, it's been a lovely day, so far."

She stopped in her tracks.

"You're mean."

"No I'm not. I just don't get this shopping thing."

Kylie shot him a hard look that could kill a man at two hundred metres.

"Everyone needs shoes. Does your mother buy your shoes?"

"Yep."

Kylie stared at his shoes.

"Doesn't surprise me."

"What's wrong with them?"

"Not cool."

"Not cool?"

"No."

Peter gave in.

"Ok. Let's go back to the shop and try those boots on again."

"I don't like them."

"Then why did you try them on?"

"I wanted to know if they fit."

"But you *don't* like them."

"I liked them then, I don't like them now."

Peter let out a long breath.

"Ice-cream?"

"No. Follow me."

She marched him down a narrow lane, made narrower by a long row of parked scooters. Peter felt himself dragged left at the end and they stood in front of the first shoe shop they had visited. Kylie nodded purposefully at the door.

"Come on."

"My pleasure," said Peter, through his teeth.

116

The lady came over.

"Red sandals. UK size six?"

"Yes please," said Kylie.

She tried them on again and took them to the till. The lady put the sandals inside a box and the box inside a plastic bag.

"That will be thirty Euros please."

Kylie rummaged around in her purse.

"Peter, do you have any money on you?"

***

Spiros Theopoulis, Commissioner of Police, heard his mobile beep. A text –

Have collected Peter and Kylie.
Leaving town now. Minolas.

He picked up a bulging brown envelope, left his neat office and took a lift down to Lower Level Two. The doors opened onto a brightly lit corridor with evenly-spaced cell doors along both sides and an untidy desk close to the lift. Spiros flinched as he watched an untidy, overweight Police Officer add a scrunched-up chocolate wrapper to a pile of wrappers and empty Fanta Zero cans on the desk. Somewhere under that mess were the prisoner files, an "In and Out" tray and a pebble. Pinned to a notice-board behind the desk were the photos of Corfu's top ten most wanted men. It was at least five years out of date.

"Officer Stavros, your desk is a disgrace to the force."

Stavros yawned and made no attempt to tidy his desk. He spoke in a tough, gravelly voice.

"I'm bored. I want to go back on street duty and see the sunshine again, like Christos."

"Why are you here?"

"I crashed a police car."

"Since joining us, Officer Stavros, you have written-off three police cars, lost two prisoners and then there was the incident with Mr Constantis."

"A simple misunderstanding."

"Mr Constantis is one of the most respected businessmen on the island and you arrested him for burglary."

"He was acting suspiciously, Loading furniture into a stolen car." Spiros sighed.

"He was taking furniture, that he had bought, out of *his* own car and carrying it into *his* own house."

"Oh, you heard about that."

"I heard about it from Mr Constantis's lawyer who, after much persuasion, agreed not to prosecute us for damaging his client's reputation."

"A simple misunderstanding."

"Take me to see the American, then tidy your desk."

Stavros took a big set of keys out of a drawer.

"You are the bossiest grandfather in the world."

The Police Commissioner ignored the comment.

"Any problems with Mr Stanton?"

"Keeps shouting. Says we are violating his human rights and wants to call the American Embassy."

Outside the cell door, they smiled at each other.

"OK. Open it."

Theodore leapt up off a bench at the back of his bare, square cell.

"Hey, you guys can't keep me here. What's the charge?"

Spiros handed him the envelope.

"One of the waiters at the restaurant just dropped this in. He told me it must have fallen out of your pocket. Please check the contents."

Theodore tore the envelope open and checked his wallet, thumbing through dollar bills, euros and credit cards.

"Everything seems to be there."

"And you are free to go. I suggest you return to the restaurant and thank the waiters for their honesty. You also have a bill to settle."

Theodore put his hat on.

"And the rest of my things?"

"Waiting for you in a tray at the reception desk."

"You haven't heard the last of this."

Spiros stared into the Seeker's eyes and suppressed his deep desire to shoot him.

"I believe you Americans have a saying. Have a nice day."

***

Peter and Kylie sat in the back of a taxi with an old, green, army rucksack between them; their packed lunch from Mrs Agnedes.

"Where I take you?" asked Mr Minolas.

Peter took a plastic water bottle out of the rucksack and handed it to his girlfriend.

"As close as you can get to the cave in the ravine. I'm dying to see where you hid out during the war."

"No problem. How shopping go?"

Twenty minutes later, they drove up the steep north eastern slopes of Pantokrator with the port of Kassiopi behind them. Mr Minolas turned his taxi into a small car park that looked as though it had been carved out of the rock face with explosives. A new, white sign with blue letters stood to one side and, despite braking hard, the taxi hit the sign and knocked it over.

"Damn sign," said Mr Minolas.

Peter got out and read what was left of it.

Tourist Viewpoint
Kassiopi and the hills of Albania
Please respect the countryside and drive carefully

Mr Minolas stuck his arm out of his open window and pointed at a path, which disappeared upwards, its steps cut into the face of the rock.

"That way. One kilometre. Keep going up."

"Thank you," said Peter and Kylie together.

As the best taxi on the island accelerated out of the car park, Peter shouldered the rucksack and led the way up the steps, the sun hot now, grasshoppers rasping out and hopping away from where they trod.

119

"Hang on a minute, Peter."

"But I'm hungry."

"Hang on."

They stopped at the top of the steps to look back down the slopes of Pantokrator. The sea stretched out like an ironed tablecloth, a brilliant sparkly blue. Small, puffy white clouds drifted above the horizon and a heat haze distorted the barren, distant hills of Albania.

"Wow," said Kylie. "That's gorgeous. Will you tell me the story now?"

"No."

"You're mean."

Peter sighed.

"Come on. Let's put our hats on."

They followed a rocky path upwards before entering the shade of a forest of ancient, gnarled olive trees. The path twisted and turned, going in and out of the trees for a long time and then they were out, walking in bright sunshine, puffing and sweating with the effort of the climb.

"Do you think your grandfather came this way?" asked Kylie.

"I'm sure of it. We should see the ravine soon and then it's not far to the cave."

They went on, passing dark, stubby volcanic rocks that had cooled millions of years ago.

"Where is it?" asked Peter. "I'm absolutely starving now."

"Hold on."

Kylie took her pebble out of her pocket and placed it on the ground. It rolled back down the slope and veered right.

"Come on, it knows where to go."

They followed and the stone sometimes stopped to let them catch up, and they rose up again to climb a small shoulder of the mountain, before dropping down into a dry river-bed with large round boulders littered around. The pebble shot up the dry river and, after two hundred metres, the sides of the valley became steep, and they followed the pebble up the ravine to the cave. Peter unshouldered the rucksack and walked inside.

"Compared to outside it actually feels cold," said Kylie.

"Lovely." Peter sat on a rock and unpacked the biggest picnic he had ever seen, even bigger than one of grandma's. "Lovely," he said again.

"Now would be a good time."

Peter handed her an air-tight container filled with chopped fruits, honey and Greek yoghurt.

"They lived here, for a while, before the attack on the Italian airbase."

"Did they destroy the planes? Did the invasion of Corfu take place? Did the Greek resistance win that part of the war?"

"Yes and no. The whole thing was a disaster."

"Are you going to tell me?"

"No."

"Tell me, or I'll never kiss you again."

"After the picnic and don't try that hair thing. It won't work."

"Tell me, or I'll take you shopping."

Peter put a foil parcel down onto the rock beside him, smiled and raised both hands.

"I surrender. It began like this ..."

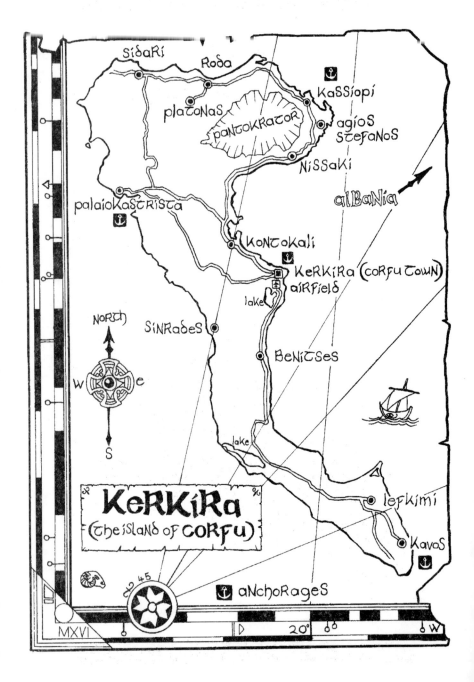

CHAPTER SIX

HELL AT 0100 HOURS

Aris Agnedes blinked in the bright sunshine and stared down the ravine. A heat-haze danced above the narrow tarmac road which joined Lefkimi and Kavos, twisting and turning through high cliffs on both sides. Minolas had chosen the place well. The Italian convoy, which patrolled the southern part of the island, was due to arrive in the next few hours. That is what Aris's informers had told him and it meant very little. The enemy didn't seem to stick to any of their planned schedules, making them unpredictable and dangerous. More often than not, they were late, preferring to take their time to drive around to show who really ruled Corfu. He hated them.

This was an arid and lonely place. No trees anywhere and only straggly, broken scrub clinging to the sides of the ravine, giving a rare burst of green against the light-coloured limestone walls. Aris shook his head disapprovingly at the earth. Not a flower anywhere.

He raised an arm, his signal to say, "Is everything ready?" To his right, six hundred metres along the Kavos road, he saw Spiros and Minolas raise their arms, but there was no trace of the cable that ran from their hiding place up to the explosives, packed into holes and cracks on the rock-face. Aris looked left, arm still raised. A small group of Andartes, recruited from Sinrades and Benitses, acknowledged his signal and then they were gone, crawling back, their Russian rifles ready, to hide behind the crest of the cliff. All they had to do now was wait, attack the convoy and give the enemy time to send a radio signal back to their airbase. Everything depended on that call for help, if the British soldiers were to have any chance of destroying the planes. A relief column rushing south would not leave the airbase undefended, but its strength would be greatly reduced.

Aris sat down behind a rock, placed his rifle across his legs, took a cloth from his pocket, wiped sweat from his eyes and wondered if the British soldiers had managed to steal the trucks they needed.

The road was deserted in both directions, and this gave Bernard and his men their best chance of stealing the two trucks they would use on the raid and in the escape afterwards. The friends stared at the concrete guard-post, which controlled the main road between Corfu Town and the airbase.

"What a ruddy caper this is," whispered Chalky.

With no cover and in brilliant sunshine, Sandy ran across the road and poured sand from a canvas bag into the diesel tank of one of three parked Italian trucks. Then he disappeared underneath the lorry. His friends held their breath as he taped sticks of dynamite around the drive shaft. A small spark was bright for a moment and then a glow, barely discernible in the dark shadow beneath the truck. That glow told them the fuse was lit and Sandy came sprinting back, jumping the wall and crouching down beside Lofty. Duncan counted to ten in his mind. At *five* he saw four Italians walk out of the guard-post. At *eight* the guards were only twenty metres from the bomb, talking, laughing at some joke. At *ten* an incredible explosion shot the truck high into the air and the Italians were thrown back, shrapnel cutting into their bodies. But the petrol tank didn't go up in flames, the sand was doing its job, preventing a black cloud that would bring every Italian on Corfu to the guard-post. The loud explosion was something they had decided to risk.

Bernard shouted.

"Let's go."

Lofty reached the guard-post first, grenade in hand, as a rifle barrel appeared in the long, narrow slit in the concrete, followed almost immediately by a loud *crack* as a bullet whipped past his shoulder. He slammed his back against the outer wall, pulled out the pin and tossed the grenade inside. He dropped onto his belly as an explosion shook the walls and a fire-flash came out of the slit. A rifle clattered beside Lofty's body. Duncan saw Bernard kick open the guard-post door and heard three shots from his revolver. Then Bernard was back outside.

"All clear. Hide the dead and start the trucks." He pointed at the twisted carcass of the lorry they had blown up. "Tow it behind the guard-post."

They drove towards the airbase, taking care not to speed or do anything that might draw attention to themselves. They saw no one and after ten minutes the two lorries turned inland up a dusty track, passing walled fields full of aubergines, tomatoes, carrots and lettuces laid out in neat rows like soldiers on a parade ground. They slowed as they approached a white farmhouse with a large barn nearby and, as they had planned with Aris, Duncan and SS leapt out, pulled open the barn's large double doors and the trucks were driven inside. SS closed the doors behind the last truck and Duncan joined Bernard, who was jumping down from the cab of the first lorry.

"I've got something for you, Duncan. A present from the Andartes."

"What is it?"

Bernard handed him a book that looked like some kind of manual. It smelled new and was written in Italian. They sat down on a pile of old tyres. Two rucksacks full of explosives lay at their feet, left for them by Aris's men who had carried them overland from the cave. One of them, someone with the strength of an ox, had brought a heavy Vickers machine gun. Duncan's forehead creased.

"I can't understand a word it says."

Bernard handed him a pocket-sized book.

Italian Dictionary
Includes One Hundred Useful Phrases

"Read it and knowledge shall be yours."

"But what is it? Some kind of military manual?"

"Aris says it is the instructions for how to drive a tank."

An hour later, Duncan had read the dictionary, learned every word as only a stone keeper can do, and now sat in a clear space in the barn with the manual on his lap. Four old tyres marked the corners of his pretend tank and Duncan was surrounded by broom handles in terracotta pots, pushing and pulling them, and turning a bucket in his hands like it was a steering wheel. He practised changing gear and everyone else grinned as Sandy and Lofty made engine noises to emphasise the different gear speeds. Bernard sat beside Duncan, the ends of two pieces of rope in his hands, the other ends tied around his boots. He pulled up his right foot and obediently Chalky moved the long drainpipe he was holding, so it pointed at the barn doors. Bernard shouted at him in a cross voice.

"You're moving the gun around the wrong way."

Chalky dropped the drainpipe onto the floor and put his hands on his hips.

"What a way to fight a ruddy war."

***

A cloud of dust and the distant rumbling of diesel engines signalled the slow approach of the Italian convoy. Aris Agnedes felt a trickle of cold sweat run down his back and he tried to work out why he felt so afraid, why some unknown instinct warned him that something was very wrong. There was no sign of Spiros and Minolas, who were completely hidden behind rocks, or of the others either. Everyone waited patiently for his signal to attack, so everything was as they had planned.

It was only an hour until nightfall and parts of the ravine were already in shadow, the dark cloaks hiding the north-south sections of the road and contrasting completely with the bright east-west stretches. The convoy drove out of one dark cloak, into sunshine, and Aris watched two men in smart uniforms in an armoured car that led the way. He counted the trucks that followed. Four trucks, two covered with tarpaulin and two open to the elements, with rows of soldiers, sitting and facing each other. The convoy was manned by at least twenty-four Italians, which was the same as the last time when Minolas had secretly shown him the ravine.

Aris shut his eyes and thought about his flowers, his village where his beautiful Anna would be cooking and getting ready for her father to return home from the school where he taught. His eyes opened wide. A wave of fear shot through his body.

"Children, school, going home time," he said.

He stared down the ravine towards Kavos. Three figures on bicycles, just visible now as they came around a bend in the ravine. One an adult, probably an old man from the way his bicycle wobbled as it laboured up the slope. Two school children. They would all reach the road below the explosives at about the same time as the convoy. He cursed his luck. Cursed his own stupidity. He should have put a soldier down the ravine to stop anyone wandering into the ambush. Straining his eyes, he could now see the old man clearly and the blue dresses of the small girls who cycled with him.

Aris grabbed his rifle, broke cover and ran towards them, shouting orders at Spiros and Minolas to begin the attack. He jumped down onto the tarmac, heard engines stop and someone yell out a warning, and he ran away from the convoy now only eight hundred metres away. Aris shouted at the old man and the children, and they stopped pedalling. They saw the running man, heard a rifle *crack* behind him and watched in horror as blood and bone exploded from the side of the runner's head, his body spinning with the impact before crashing down onto the hot road. With a flash and a thunderous *boom*, the side of the ravine above the convoy became a waterfall of rock.

With the sound of gunfire echoing around the ravine, the old man shouted at his granddaughters, and they rode quickly away from the resistance fighter who they believed had sacrificed his life for his people.

*****

At nightfall and with no moon to throw even the weakest of shadows, Duncan started the truck's engine and began the journey to the section of the airfield's perimeter fence, which lay on the far side of the main entrance. The lorry driven by Sergeant

Sturgess followed him, but stopped, and Duncan saw, in his side mirror, a shadow jump out and run back to close the barn doors. Then the black outline of the truck was moving again, catching up, with no headlights on and lurching with every pot-hole in the track that wound down to the main road. Duncan changed gear noisily and glanced at Bernard.

"Do you think the Italians know about our attack on the guard-post?"

They stopped at the junction with the main road, staring left and right, searching for vehicle lights or soldiers on foot. There weren't any.

"No. This road would be alive if they did. Come on, you know where to go."

Duncan switched the headlights on and turned right towards the airbase, resisting the temptation to drive quickly and, occasionally, glancing in the mirror at the other truck. Its lights were on too and soon, when he and Bernard turned off the main road, their truck would continue before hiding up behind a ruined cottage close to the main entrance. Their job was to get Sandy and Lofty on their way, and then set up the machine gun to stop any of the enemy leaving the base. Bernard held the barrel of a rifle between his legs and spoke in his calm voice.

"Like Cuthbert at Stirling Castle."

Duncan nodded.

"A fortress can be made a prison. One of Myroy's many tactical lessons taken from history."

"And you Keepers have to learn each one."

"We do. If the war with Odin comes, we will need that knowledge. All of it."

Bernard tapped the dashboard.

"Right. This is the turn-off."

It was just as Aris had described it. Above a narrow dirt lane with a low wall on either side were two ancient olive trees, partially lit by the bright lights of the perimeter fence. The trees rose up like gnarled guardians. You could have hidden a house under their shadows. Duncan guided the truck under the trees, slowed, braked and turned the engine off. They sat in silence on the western edge of the airbase, watching in their mirrors as their friends drove past. They waited ten minutes, the time SS and Chalky needed to set up their machine gun on a wall opposite the main entrance, and for Sandy and Lofty to begin their long crawl around the fence on the eastern side, to hide close by another gun emplacement, the nearest to the aircraft hangars. Duncan glanced at Bernard. A bead of sweat trickled down his cheek.

"What's up?"

"Just nerves, that's all."

Duncan smiled.

"We've all got those."

"Everything depends on Aris attacking the enemy convoy near Kavos and drawing a bigger convoy away from here. For all we know the airbase is still full of Italians."

"And we don't have any way of knowing."

Bernard shone his torch onto the face of his watch, cupping his hands around it so that it could not be seen from a distance.

"No."

"How long before we attack?"

"An hour."

"And you are sure they won't take their tank?"

"Quite sure. It's too slow and would hold them up."

"Do you want to run through things again?"

Bernard chuckled to himself.

"Ha. With your memory?"

"Even so."

"Alright. At 0100 hours, SS and Chalky machine-gun the entrance, draw the Italians there. At 0103, Sandy and Lofty blow up the gun emplacement by the hangars. At the same time, we blow up the gun emplacement on this side and ram the fence with the truck. If we get through, we drive to the tank, get in and use it to destroy the planes on the runway. Sandy and Lofty dynamite the fence on their side and destroy the generator in the hangars and throw the base into darkness. They then blow up any planes in the hangars. They run out onto the airfield and follow the tank that you drive through the fence four hundred yards from the entrance. SS and Chalky give us covering fire, and then they collect their truck and pick us up on the main road. We hide the lorry in the barn and walk overland back to the cave. We should be safe there."

Duncan nodded and thought about the stone he had thrown into the loch, in the Realm of the Dead. Glancing out of the window he tried to see the moon, but it wasn't there. He felt weak.

"It stinks, doesn't it."

"Yes."

"Too many ifs and buts."

"Too many."

"We need a lot of luck."

"We were lucky in the desert."

"The desert seems a long way away."

They sat in silence for a long while, feeling the warm night air blow through the open windows of their cab. Duncan broke the silence.

"We are guessing that we can get through the double fence with this lorry. Guessing the generator, or *generators*, are housed in the hangars, and we don't know which one. We are guessing that Sandy and Lofty can get past the dogs at the fence. Guessing that the tank will stay unmanned in the three minutes after SS opens fire."

Bernard sighed.

"Come on, let's not list the things that might go wrong. Let's think about how our boys are getting on."

***

Sergeant Sturgess, or SS as he was generally known, gently lowered the tripod of his Vickers machine gun onto the top of

131

a stone wall just one hundred paces across the road from the bright airbase entrance. He ran a hand along the long, wide cylinder barrel. It was a heavy beast of a weapon, but had never jammed, or let him down. It was worth lugging around for times like this.

"Easy does it," he whispered.

Chalky joined him, carrying SS's green rucksack full of ammunition.

"Blimey, it's like the Blackpool illuminations over there."

They stared across the main road. Floodlights around the double perimeter fence bathed the defensive concrete blocks, and towers at the entrance. Everything was clear as day; the planes on the runway, hangars, gun emplacements, trucks, soldiers and the tank. One soldier opened a wire gate in the fence to the right of the entrance and was immediately surrounded by a pack of tail-wagging Alsatians, barking and jumping up at the wooden box he carried. The man pulled large chunks of meat from the box, tossed them to the dogs and watched as they snarled and squabbled to decide who ate first.

"How many?" asked SS.

"Gotta be twenty of the brutes at least." Chalky fed the ammunition into the Vickers. "OK. Two hundred and fifty rounds loaded."

SS flicked up the safety catch above the spade-like handle grips and tilted his watch to face the floodlights.

"We're ready to go and there's plenty of time. Chalky, you made up your mind what you are going to do after the war?"

"Thought I might join the police."

"We wouldn't have you, not with your record."

"I'd make a good copper."

"Poacher turned gamekeeper, you mean."

"Somefin' like that."

"You've got no intention of doing anything, except stealing, have you?"

"Nope."

"Ever thought about getting a proper job?"

"Why?"

"Because it's a *proper* job."

"No."

"Too much like hard work?"

"That's right."

The Italian feeding the dogs inside the double perimeter fence backed away and left through the wire gate. Two guards, in a tower overlooking the staggered concrete blocks at the entrance, called down to him and he gave them a lazy salute, before leaning the box against a wall and lighting a cigarette. Chalky grinned.

"Still fink we should have nicked their pilots."

"But they never seem to leave the airbase. That was a stupid idea."

"Not as stupid as this one."

The Italian dropped his cigarette, stood on it and went into a hut with a long radio aerial on the roof.

"What about you?" asked Chalky.

"What about me?"

"What you gonna do after the war."

"Go back to the station. Catch wrong-uns like you. Collect my pension and buy a cottage by the sea."

"Sounds like a plan."

SS turned his head to look at Chalky. Half of his face was in shadow, half was lit by floodlight.

"It's what I've always wanted."

"A man of simple pleasures?"

"Something like that. By the way, can I have my wallet back?"

Chalky gave him his wallet back.

"There are times when I really don't like you, Private Chalk."

"What, with my charm?"

They sat in silence for what seemed like an age. A long way to their right two men, dressed like Greek resistance fighters, ran across the main road. Five minutes later, a truck drew up at the entrance.

"Keep yer eyes peeled," warned Chalky.

The guards up in the tower shouldered their guns and more guards ran up steps to stand on the walkway above the lorry, checking its roof. One Italian walked around the lorry with a mirror on the end of a stick, checking underneath.

"Fink they smell a rat?"

SS ran the sleeve of his woollen, peasant-style jumper across his forehead to take away the sweat and checked his watch again.

"Five to one. If Aris and his men attacked the convoy, they are going to be more wary than normal."

"Five minutes to go. What you gonna hit first?"

"I'll take out the towers, then shoot at anything that moves."

"Sounds like another plan."

"Just have more ammo ready."

"You think Sandy and Lofty are in position?"

"No idea. Now come on, let's make sure we do *our* bit."

***

Sandy and Lofty leapt out of the back of the lorry and, from the corners of their eyes, saw SS and Chalky putting a Vickers on top of a low stone wall. They ignored them and crawled on all fours to follow the line of the wall north. One side of the wall was bathed in floodlight, but their side was protected by shadow. Sandy stared ahead at the lanky outline of his friend and checked that the top of Lofty's rucksack did not show above the top of the wall. It was a close thing and he hissed out a warning.

"Keep your back low."

No reply, but the rucksack went down. It was a hot night. Not as hot as the nights they had sweated through in the desert, but with the weight of their weapons and explosives on their backs progress was slow. It was hard going. Lofty stopped crawling and twisted around.

"Sandy, I think that's far enough. Do you want to check, or shall I?"

"You check."

Lofty popped his head above the wall. Then he quickly dropped back down.

"The main road is about twenty-five paces wide and brightly lit. Beyond it is the double perimeter fence, curving away from the road towards a gun emplacement. No dogs that I can see and no sign of the ditch that Aris says runs parallel to the fence."

"Then we just have to trust it is there."

"This is the place alright and it's the most dangerous part of the plan. I've been dreading it. When we run across the road, we could be seen by anyone."

Sandy's white teeth showed his grin.

"Then fingers crossed. Go on. Make one last check."

Lofty raised his head, looking carefully for dogs, looking both ways down the road for sentries, cars or lorries. Nothing. He came back to Sandy.

"All clear. On the count of three. One, two, three."

They jumped the wall and sprinted across the tarmac, their fast, jerky shadows thrown behind them, the explosives on their backs bouncing dangerously up and down. Time stood still. At last, they dived into a ditch and lay there panting, waiting for gunfire or dogs barking, but it was deathly quiet and they knew they had made it.

"Right," whispered Lofty. "Let's go."

They crawled on for ages, sometimes glancing up and to their left to catch a glimpse of the gun emplacement, but could only see the relentless and impenetrable line of the double fence, with its evenly spaced lights, which pointed into and out of the airbase. Still no dogs.

Lofty called back in a soft voice.

"It didn't look this far when we saw it through Bernard's binoculars."

"Shut up. Keep going."

The base of the ditch that concealed them was littered with sharp stones that hurt their knees. Sandy heard his friend's soft voice again

"Mind your hands. There's a load of rubbish here. Bottles, opened cans, old newspapers, the lot."

"Then we are where we need to be. Let's have a quick peek."

They took off their rucksacks, lay on their bellies and wriggled up the side of the ditch. Just five paces away, the barrel of a machine gun stuck out of a thin concrete slit. The gun emplacement towered above them. They heard noises from inside; Italian voices, a chair being pushed back, glasses clinking, more voices. Only twenty paces to their left, between the two fences, lay four big dogs. The men wriggled back. Lofty pulled a large set of wire cutters from his rucksack and Sandy cupped his hand around his torch and watch, and whispered.

"Eight minutes. How the hell do we get past the dogs? As soon as you make the first cut, they'll be on us."

***

Spiros sat next to Minolas under an olive tree, both staring down at the farmhouse, its white walls appearing dark dirty grey in the blackness. They heard the front door open and a shadowy figure walked out holding what they knew to be a medical bag. They didn't move; the threat of capture was still all around them, making their minds alert and their stomachs churn.

"Is he a good doctor?" whispered Minolas.

"He is a village doctor. I doubt if he has seen many bullet wounds and never one like that."

"The girl will tend Aris?"

"Anna loves him and comes from a good family. She will not betray him, or us."

"And you are sure we cannot risk moving him to a surgeon in Corfu Town?"

"No. How we got him here alive, I don't know."

"Then God help him."

Minolas pushed bullets into the breech of his Russian rifle.

"We had to save him. Lose the ambush, but save him like he saved the children."

"Yes."

"How did we escape the bullets as we lifted him from the road?"

Spiros remembered the gun-fire singing around them, thudding into the tarmac, as the other Andartes tried to draw the shots away by throwing grenades onto the convoy.

"I don't know. I don't think we will ever know."

"Do you think the enemy sent a radio message back to the airbase, asking for help?"

As Minolas pushed his last bullet into the breech of his rifle, Spiros stood.

"Come on. We can't do anything here. Let's go back to the cave."

"Do you think the Italians have sent reinforcements to the south of the island?"

"No."

"Then Bernard's men are in for a bad surprise."

"It was a huge gamble, even with the base half empty."

Above them, the deep drone of plane engines grew louder. Minolas stood too.

"So, the CANTs are on night patrol. The British really are in for a bad surprise. Some, if not all, of the planes they plan to blow up are here now, searching for us. Do you think they will get out alive?"

Spiros shook his head.

"No."

***

Lofty smiled and gave Sandy the wire cutters, and tapped his pockets.

"I've always been good with dogs. Stay here until the dogs are

137

well away. Cut through the wire and sit like a statue below the machine gun. I'll meet you there."

Then he rose, calm as anything, walking out of the ditch to stand by the fence, both hands held open. He looked relaxed and unconcerned by any fear of capture, or death. Sandy gulped as he heard Lofty speak to the dogs in a soft, reassuring voice. Their ears pricked up and Lofty kept reassuring them with his body and voice. They got up, lazily, and wandered over, more curious than aggressive. He kept speaking, reassuring them that he meant them no harm and, one by one, they sniffed his open hands, taking the new scent and not disliking it. He undid a pocket and gave them each a custard cream. They wagged their tails and Lofty walked slowly along the line of the brightly lit fence, stopping sometimes to give them another biscuit and always talking softly, encouraging them to follow.

After five minutes they were halfway between the gun emplacement and the next one. Sandy crawled forward, placed the wire cutter against the lowest part of the fence and eased the handles together. *Snap.* The sound cut through the warm, still night air like a knife and he glanced up at the slit. The voices continued as before. To his right, Lofty gave out more custard creams. Sandy used his sleeve to wipe sweat from his eyes and moved the cutters up to the next strand of wire. *Snap.*

Lofty emptied all the biscuits from his pockets and threw them over the fence, and the dogs jumped up at them. He stopped talking and walked casually back to where he had left Sandy. A three-foot cut in the fence told him where to crawl through and he crossed to another cut, this time in the inner fence, to join his friend and sit below the concrete slit. Italian voices chattered away above their heads.

Lofty pointed at the back of his wrist and mouthed, "How long?"

Sandy took two grenades from their rucksack and passed one over. Then he held up two fingers. Lofty nodded to show he understood that there was only two minutes to go. He found half of a custard cream in his top pocket, smiled and ate it.

***

Under the dark cathedral roof of olive branches, Bernard whispered to Duncan.

"OK. Listen up. It's nearly time."

"How long?"

"Thirty seconds."

Those thirty seconds, before the short, loud bursts from SS's Vickers over at the airbase entrance, were the longest they had ever lived through. Bernard picked up his rifle and opened his door.

"Three minutes then drive through the fence. I'll cover you and, for God's sake, keep your head down."

Duncan nodded and watched Bernard run past the thick trunk of an ancient olive tree and head towards the perimeter fence. He didn't look at his watch, didn't need to. At 01.03 Sandy and Lofty would grenade the gun emplacement on the far side of the airfield. Those explosions would ring out on the still night air. A continuous, deafening siren began to sound around the airbase. Duncan cursed and started to count to one hundred and eighty in his mind.

***

Bernard crawled the last few yards up to the fence, his rifle laid across his elbows, staying low and never taking his eyes off of the slit in the gun emplacement. Shouts came from inside, barely discernible above the siren, and the long barrel of a machine gun moved quickly from side to side searching for an enemy. Two Italian rifles appeared on either side of the machine gun. Bernard breathed deeply and waited for his eyes to adjust to the blinding floodlights. He placed the barrel of his rifle onto the lowest strand of wire, steadied it and lined the sights up with the centre of the slit.

"Get the machine gunner first," he whispered to himself. "Or he'll get Duncan as he drives through the fence."

He flicked up the safety catch and another thought struck him.

"What the hell are we doing?"

***

"One hundred and eighty," said Duncan. "Three minutes."

He turned the ignition key, put his foot to the floor and the engine roared into life. He crunched the lorry into gear and it leapt forward, the engine stalling and cutting out.

"Damn. Less haste, more speed."

He turned the key again and drove away more slowly, turning out from under the olive trees and accelerating at the fence with his headlights off. Duncan felt a strange sense of relief that no dogs lay in his path and he snapped himself out of these thoughts as bullets ripped into the side of the truck. He picked his spot, a section of wire fence stretched out between two metal uprights. For a moment the enemy fire stopped and he wondered if Bernard had scored a hit, but the bullets came thudding back and he fell on to his side, still holding the steering wheel and keeping his head and shoulders below the top of the dashboard. The lorry thundered forward, then with an almighty crash the front wheels rose up, the truck lurching, the steering wheel spinning away from Duncan's grip, the front drive wheels screaming without traction before falling back down. The lorry picked up speed again and Duncan saw that the inner fence was only feet away. He slammed the accelerator down, but knew he lacked speed. Another crash and the bonnet rose forcing the fence back and down. Duncan willed the lorry through.

"Come on."

***

In the Realm of the Dead, Tirani the Wise and Myroy stood on the shore of the loch. It pulsed blood-red.

"The stone aids the Keeper," said Tirani. "Will Odin feel its power?"

Myroy stared at the calm waters, now returning to light blue, the colour of the sky.

"No, not whilst the stone is hidden here."

"Why did you allow a Keeper to go to war?"

Myroy's face became fierce.

"Let them have their foolish wars."

"And he doesn't know he is protected?"

"No."

Tirani bent down, picked up a pebble and threw it into the loch.

"Better leave it like that."

His brother nodded.

"He must not come to rely on the stone. Now, that *would* be dangerous."

***

The lorry seemed to pause at a forty-five degree angle, front wheels screaming as the engine forced them to spin with only air around them.

"Come on. Come on," willed Duncan.

The truck crashed back down and raced forward, bangs and scrapes coming from under the floor-boards as it tore over the fence. Duncan threw the wheel to his left, wheels bumping up and down, suspension groaning on the uneven ground, heading straight for the back of the gun emplacement. An Italian guard jumped out of the rear door, rifle raised. Duncan aimed the truck at him and dropped on to his side. A bullet ripped into the cab, the windscreen exploding and showering him with glass. *Crash.* The lorry hit the concrete wall, hitting the guard who was thrown back through the door like a bullet.

Duncan was out in a flash, taking a grenade from his pocket, pulling out the pin as he ran, then diving forward and throwing it inside in one movement. He rolled away and lay with his body and face pressed against the wall. It shook. A loud *bang*. Smoke poured out of the door and there was silence, apart from the continuous drone of the siren. Someone kicked him in the back.

"Right," said Bernard. "Let's go and steal a tank."

They ran across a wide expanse of short, scorched brown grass and counted three CANT bombers on a runway, all in a neat line and the tank only one hundred paces from the nearest plane. Two men were running to the tank from the hangars on the far side and they were about the same distance away from it as Bernard and Duncan. Bernard held his rifle at waist height and fired a wild shot above the enemies' heads. They dropped like stones onto the grass.

But now they saw it. Saw what they had most dreaded. As clear as day under the bright lights, the road in front of the hangars was full of trucks, jeeps, armoured cars, guards and pilots, who were jumping quickly into jeeps to reach their planes and escape to the sky.

"Bloody hell," shouted Duncan. "The place is full of them."

Bernard threw his heavy rifle away. It wasn't going to be of any use now.

"Shut up. Get to the tank."

Under heavy fire they made it and scrambled up onto the metal plates, bullets pinging off the body armour, sparks highlighting each strike. Duncan lifted the round turret lid. Bernard dropped down behind him, slamming the lid shut, their ears popping at the sudden increase in air pressure. The inside of the tank sang with the *ping* of lead on iron. They slid past a rack of shells and slumped into two seats. It was like a tomb, except for the noise. *Ping, ping, ping.* Duncan scanned the controls.

"M13. No problem."

Heavier gunfire. *Ping, ping, ping. Ping, ping, ping.* Bernard yelled an order.

"Drive straight at the planes."

Duncan searched for the red starter button. It wasn't where it had been in the manual.

"Where the hell is it?"

Bernard's fear made him snap.

"Just push every damn button there is."

Duncan pushed every button and switch. A light came on, but nothing else. *Ping, ping, ping.*

"Damn."

"Think through the manual. Where were the starter buttons in the other tanks?"

Duncan glanced above his head. A red button. He pushed it and the engines roared into life, black acrid smoke belching out of the exhausts. Bernard snapped an eye-level metal grille aside and their tiny window on the world was open.

"Turn left."

Duncan steered left and took the M13 up to full speed, a CANT Z506 sea plane directly ahead.

"Don't even think of winging it," said Bernard.

Duncan hit it full on and the tank smashed through the fuselage as though it was made of paper. Behind them the CANT's fuel tanks exploded, shaking them but not slowing them in any way.

"One down. Fifteen to go. Turn right."

Ping, ping, ping. Despite the gunfire they left the grille open. A pilot was closing the cockpit cover of the next plane.

"Faster."

"I'm flat out," said Duncan.

The propellers of the plane began to spin.

"Aim just ahead of it."

Duncan aimed ten feet ahead of the plane, which rolled forward gathering speed.

"Come on, Duncan."

The CANT shot forward and looked as though it would be too quick for them, but the tank's off-side wing took its tail off. The plane careered off the runway and began to circle across the grass, the pilot trying desperately to bring it under control.

"I'll get it," said Bernard.

He pushed a pedal down and the gun barrel rotated round.

"Is it loaded?"

Bernard waited for the plane to come around to his firing position, finger ready on the fire button.

"One way to find out."

He squeezed the trigger and the CANT exploded in a fireball.

Bernard yelled out, "Go left."

Duncan turned sharply left, the tank's tracks tearing up the hard grass. Through the slit, they watched the last bomber taxi down the runway. Bernard saw a wind-sock, saw that the plane was going in the same direction as the wind.

"Stop on the runway. It's got to come back this way."

Bernard pushed himself out of his seat, went back, pulled back the spring on the breech and a hot, smoking shell dropped onto the floor. He reloaded the gun and went back to Duncan. They watched the plane turn at the far end of the runway, ready for take-off into the wind. They waited for it to come. Bernard used his pedals to turn the gun and spun an iron wheel to raise the barrel. He took a deep breath.

"We will only get one chance at this."

Duncan turned off the engine and the tank stopped vibrating. *Ping, ping, ping.*

"That is so annoying," whispered Bernard. "One shot, that's all. Come on, baby, come on."

More *ping, ping, pings* on the metal hull. They sat without speaking, staring out of the grille at the plane that hurtled towards them. Another *ping* made them jump. The CANT's wheels left the runway and Bernard waited, his finger ready on the trigger. He squeezed and snapped the grille shut. They still caught the flash and felt chunks of metal shower their tank. Everything shook. Duncan reopened the grille. The outside of the tank was black and burning. He pushed the red button above his head and the engines roared again.

"Sandy and Lofty?"

"Yes. Go and get the boys."

144

As the tank turned to face the hangars, they saw hundreds of men charging the tank, and felt mortar bombs explode all around them. One side of the tank rose up violently as a track was blown off the wheels. Their heads hit the ceiling. Fire gushed in through the grille, burning their hair.

"Load up," said Duncan.

Bernard went back quickly and ejected a smoking shell from the breech. He slid a new shell in.

"Loaded."

"Come and see this."

Bernard joined him.

"Drive straight at them."

Duncan wrestled with the controls.

"Damn. We must have lost a track. I can't hold this thing in a straight line."

"You must. Sandy and Lofty are somewhere over there."

Duncan put his foot down, and a motorcyclist swerved and fell off. They stared through the grille. Behind the Italians, the hangars blew up in an almighty explosion, oil drums shooting up like rockets. The Italians fell over in the shock wave, the floodlights went out and the siren stopped. Bernard grinned.

"Go and give the boys a lift, Duncan."

The tank rumbled and clanked towards the orange glow and the towering black cloud above it all. One of two figures threw a grenade and a jeep burst into flames. Duncan aimed the tank at a truck and ran straight over it. Bernard aimed the gun at another truck and squeezed the trigger. *Ping, ping, ping.* The bullet strikes on the hull were like rain now. Duncan shut the grille.

"Better fight blind."

He turned left and right, and hit three unseen things, the tank shaking each time, but continuing relentlessly.

"I think we are going the right way."

Bernard snapped the grille open.

"Better check."

A bullet whistled in, ricocheting off the walls, sparks everywhere as it struck metal. Bernard slumped forward.

"Oh, God. Bernard, are you alright?"

His friend didn't move, wasn't breathing. Duncan placed his hand over a red hole in Bernard's woolly jumper. In the Realm of the Dead, the stone pulsed and the bullet came out of Bernard's back. The wound healed.

"What?" asked Bernard.

"A bit of trouble, that's all."

Suddenly, Duncan realised he was being protected by the stone and sensed no danger from Odin. He opened the grille, pressed the accelerator down and rammed an armoured car, the soldiers around it scattering away. He thought about the story.

"Stone. I need a hand now."

The *ping, ping, pings* stopped, as an orange bubble encased their tank. It was as if time was standing still. Bernard cried out a warning.

"Don't use the stone!"

"But I feel no danger."

"There is too much to lose. Stop it."

Duncan spoke to Amera's stone.

"Take away the bubble."

Immediately the *pings* started again, bullets beating like rain against the metal hull. Bernard searched for Sandy and Lofty. Lit by the hangar fire, they crouched behind the blown-up jeep, firing and throwing grenades at hundreds of Italians who advanced on them.

"Straight ahead," he yelled.

Their engine roared and they trundled forward.

"Stop now, Duncan."

The sound of men climbing up onto the tank over their heads. *Ping, ping, ping.* Bernard shut the grille and left his seat to open the hatch. Lofty's long legs came down.

"No CANTs."

"What?"

Lofty pointed towards the hangars.

"We didn't see a single plane. Not a single one. How many did you get?"

"Three."

"Damn."

"Load up," yelled Duncan.

Bernard loaded the gun.

"Where's Sandy?"

Lofty stared up through the hatch.

"He was right behind me."

Duncan put his foot down and the tank leapt forward, the hatch slamming closed with the jerk. He opened the grille and aimed at the perimeter fence four hundred yards from the main entrance. Bernard came back to sit beside him, and used the pedals to rotate the turret. The gun barrel swung round, hitting Sandy in the stomach and he grabbed it. Duncan looked out of the slit and saw his friend hanging onto the barrel for dear life. *Ping, ping.* He shouted at Sandy through the grille.

"I can't stop. Hang on."

Sandy shouted something back, but no one could hear him. The tank rumbled away from the enemy and smashed through the fence.

***

Chalky fed more ammunition into the Vickers and SS shot a long burst of fire at the Italians, who fired back from behind the huge concrete blocks at the airbase entrance. No one had fired at them from the two towers for a while now. Both had been ripped to pieces by the Vickers at 0100 hours.

"There's ruddy 'undreds of 'em."

SS ignored him and glanced up the main road. A tank with Sandy clinging to the gun barrel tore through the fence.

"Right, Private Chalk. Off you go. Take my rucksack and get the truck. Pick up the lads."

"What about you?"

"I've got a job to finish."

"You're ruddy barmy."

"You have no chance of getting away." He nodded at the Italians. "Unless someone stops them getting out. Want to volunteer?"

"No ruddy way."

SS tapped the barrel of the Vickers.

"It's never let me down. Off you go. That's an order."

Chalky shouldered the rucksack and ran back to the lorry behind the ruined cottage. It started first time and he drove at full speed, up the main road, the enemy not firing at him. He screeched to a halt beside the tank, his friends jumped into the back, and they were away.

Duncan stared back at the entrance. A lone machine gunner was holding back an army.

"We aren't going to see him again, are we?"

"No," said Bernard.

CHAPTER SEVEN

CHALKY AND THE TRAVEL TUNNEL

In the Realm of the Dead, Laura sat on her bed, a sheepdog puppy lying across her lap, talking to her mother who was filleting fish.

"I hope we are getting chips with them."

Julie sighed and put her knife down on the wooden table, and looked around the white walls of their plain cottage, with bedrooms going off from the central kitchen.

"No chips."

"But we've had bloomin' fish for lunch every day. I want a change."

"But how do you feel?"

Laura couldn't remember when she had ever felt so well, so full of energy, and lied.

"Lousy. Need chips."

James came in with Kylie's brother, Darren, and instantly Laura brushed her hair back with her hand. They had both gone to Pinner High School, but she hadn't really known Darren until being evacuated from Pinner to escape Odin's forces. James ran his hand through his hair, copying her exactly.

"Eyes off, dipstick. He's my mate, not yours."

Darren smiled at Laura.

"I think I'd like to make my own mind up about that."

James pulled a face.

"Hmmm. What's for lunch?"

Julie picked up her knife and began filleting again.

"Fried fish."

"Not bloody fish again."

"James! Language. Fish is good for you."

"Do we get chips with it?"

"No."

"Think I'll skip lunch. Coming, Darren?"

Darren smiled at Laura.

"Well, er."

"Right, come on then."

150

Julie stuck her knife into the table and it rocked from side to side.

"And where do you two think you're going?"

James winked at her from the cottage door.

"I've had this brilliant idea. We are going to change the world and have an adventure."

The door slammed shut. Laura and Julie folded their arms and spoke a single word.

"Boys."

Then Julie smiled.

"You like Darren, don't you?"

Laura's face lit up.

"Oh, Mum, I think he's really nice."

"I'm really looking forward to seeing Peter at the feast."

"Yeah, I've not seen him for ages"

"Did your father say when he'd be back?"

"No. You know what *he's* like. He used the Travel Tunnel to go to work in London. I thought we were supposed to be on holiday."

Julie pulled the spine out of a fish.

"I thought so too."

"What does he do, anyway?"

"Marketing," lied Julie.

"And what is that?"

"Getting people to buy things."

"But he's rubbish at shopping."

"Most men are, dear. Most men are."

***

Darren and James hid behind a cottage, a short way from the rowing boat.

"Quay's deserted," said James.

"But they told us not to go to the chamber under the tower."

James cupped his hands around his friend's ear and whispered.

"Exactly."

"I think we should stay here."

"Alright, be a girl. I'm going anyway."

James ran across and jumped into the boat. He waved at Darren who reluctantly followed and they pushed off with the oars.

"See. It's easy. Everyone's busy preparing the feast for bloody Peter. Even the Twelve aren't around. They're checking that Keeper Security System thingy and Dad's doing his stupid marketing stuff. The Ancient Ones haven't been around for days and that big, stupid bird is asleep at the bottom of the loch."

"My mum says Tirani is coming back today to welcome Peter and Kylie."

"Ha. Won't be here for ages. Come on, row faster."

Half way to the island, Darren stopped rowing and stared at the sheep on the high pastures, the old tower, and back at the cottages that clustered around the Great Hall.

"The Realm of the Dead is so beautiful."

James pulled a face.

"What?"

Darren pointed up at the clouds.

"The companions of the sky."

"Who are?"

"When Myroy brought us to the Realm of the Dead, he told my family we were in danger of being kidnapped as a way of getting at Kylie. The enemy knows she is the Keeper's girlfriend."

"So?"

"Myroy made us listen to the story and said that Thorgood Firebrand called clouds the *companions of the sky*."

"What of it?"

"I like that name."

"Just row, you dipstick."

They moved on and the loch pulsed, blood-red. The water around their boat boiled and a giant osprey shot up, sending out a huge wave that capsized them. On the quayside Myroy pointed his staff at Darren and James who rose and flew at great speed to land at the Ancient One's feet. They looked up through wide eyes, dripping wet and frightened. Beside Myroy stood the Twelve, all the Keepers of the stone before Peter. Dougie of Dunfermline held a sword. Grandpa was dressed in his desert uniform and pointed a rifle at the boys. The other Keepers held weapons that had been the best in their lifetimes. Their clothes showed the evolution of fashion through the ages. All of them looked angry. Tirani appeared from nowhere to stand next to his brother.

"Did someone try to steal the stone?"

Myroy nodded at the boys who cowered before him and asked them a question to which he already knew the answer.

"What were you doing?"

James thought about using one of his *who me?* looks, but decided that honesty was the best policy.

"We were bored and you told us not to look under the tower, so we decided to give it a go. Only got half way across the loch though."

Darren didn't much like the word *we*, but was too scared to say anything.

The ground beneath them disappeared and they fell and fell, before slowing and landing hard at the bottom of a tiny bottle-shaped cell. A thousand paces above their heads, a pin-prick of light showed the surface of the Realm of the Dead. The cell was cold, pitch black and utterly silent. James turned to where he thought his friend lay.

"You know, Darren, the next time you come up with a stupid plan like that, I'm not going to listen to you."

"But it was your idea, not mine."

A faraway *boom* came from high above them and the pin-prick of light vanished.

"That's the trouble with the Ancient Ones. They've got more power than they deserve."

Myroy's voice echoed around their cell.

"For once, James, I completely agree with you."

A shower of horse manure followed the words. James stared up

"That's nice."

More loose, damp, stinking manure rained down on them, then bucket-loads of putrid cat wee.

"Don't say anything else," warned Darren.

"Why? Can't get any worse."

Another voice began to speak, but from a person with them in the bottle cell.

"Anyway, I had just decided to visit the Younger's palace and see the tapestries on the walls. Do you like tapestries, young sirs? Of course you do, there isn't anything not to like about a nice tapestry. I wager the king has got the best tapestries in the whole of Scotland and I wondered if there might be better ones, you know, with bright colours and hunting scenes, over at Mountjoy. That's where Patrick Three Eggs lives. Ooh, I could tell you some stories about him, a man who doesn't do anything in small measures. Do you do things in small measures, young sirs?" The boring man didn't even stop to take breath. "I know I do. Why only the other day ..."

James couldn't stop himself yawning and sat up.

"Who the hell are you?"

The man used one of the shortest sentences he had ever used.

"My name's Holke. Merchant, trader, passenger carrier and adventurer around the seas of Scotland. Who are you?"

The boys remembered the story about Alistair's troubled voyage to Ireland and their hearts sank.

"Thought you said it couldn't get any worse," said Darren.

Another voice, a Scottish accent, but sounding slightly mad and with a wheezy chest.

"This isn't a bad cell, Nice to get a bit of a change. Best I've had for ages. Quite spacious too. Could be a lot worse. When we're fed, can I have your bread? Might be extra maggots today. By the way, I stole this pig once and ..."

James groaned.

"Not Bob the Pig Stealer." He glanced up again. "Myroy, you can't do this."

More manure and cat wee fell onto his face.

***

Peter began to demolish some of the giant picnic.

"The story ended there in *Early Celtic Writings and their Meanings*, but I got the impression something bad was going to happen when they got back to the cave."

"You think the Italians found the cave?" asked Kylie.

"Don't know. Maybe the CANTs they didn't destroy bombed them. Anyway, I think they had to go and shelter in the Realm of the Dead for a while, maybe even until the end of the war on Corfu."

Kylie put her arm around him.

"It's not an easy story to tell, is it?"

"Some of it's OK. Dougie got his family back and is safe for a while."

"But civil war is coming. Clan will fight clan. Will he be alright?"

Peter shrugged his shoulders.

"Don't know. I mean I guess so. He did pass the stone on to his granddaughter, Eilidh the Runner. We'll just have to wait until we meet the Winged Guardian. Myroy said *he* would tell us the rest."

They sat in silence, eating and thinking about Grandpa's adventures in the war. Someone called from outside the cave.

"Peter, Kylie. Are you there?"

Kylie called back.

"In here."

Bernard came in, his eyes adjusting slowly to the dark and looking around the cave.

"It's a long time since I was in here."

Peter smiled.

"Not since the war?"

"No, not since the war. Anyway, it is time. Let's go and meet the Twelve in the Realm of the Dead."

***

Thorgood Firebrand walked quickly through the Hall of the Gods, smelling its smoky air and ignoring the tongues of dancing flame inside the circle of rocks and tall swords. He passed a long table, with hundreds of places set for another feast, the sound of lapping waves growing in his ears. He even ignored the Heart Stone, but felt its energy as the base of the standing stone glowed red before rising up and slowly falling back again to send low waves radiating out in the pool. He paused at the giant door at the far end of the hall, took a deep breath and stepped through.

Odin sat, staring at his bank of television screens, remote control in hand and, as Thorgood approached, all the screens except one went dead. Olaf Adanson's face appeared on this screen.

"Master. There is no trace of the Keeper in Melbourne. We have no clues to follow, except one which points to Perth in Western Australia."

Odin pointed his control at the screen.

"Order our people there."

"I obey, Master."

"Any news of the girl, Kylie?"

"No, Master."

The screen went blank and Odin turned to face Thorgood, who spoke in a strong voice which masked his fear.

"Master. I believe our approach is wrong."

"Explain."

"I do not believe your stone is in Australia."

The god sensed something else in Thorgood's mind and his blue eyes flashed.

"I already possess this knowledge and it is not why you are here. Tell me what I need to know."

156

"The space station. We have one of our best people on board and their orders are to sabotage the enemy's Stone Tracking Device." Thorgood paused. "I have been asking myself why."

"You know why."

"So that when you hold the stone they will not be able to locate your presence."

Odin's eyes flashed again, showing his agitation.

"Continue."

"But we do not hold the stone. I think we should instruct our Seeker on MIR to do everything in their power to make the Stone Tracking Device operational. The priority must be to use the device to locate the stone. Once we have that knowledge, the space station has no value to us and should be destroyed."

Odin pushed a button on his remote and all the screens came alive, showing a web-cam inside MIR. The crew were eating dinner, the Seeker passing silver foil cartons across the table. Odin spoke without any emotion.

"Locate what is mine. Then kill them all."

***

"It's like a switch has been thrown," said Bernard. "All the reports from MIR told us it was like walking through glue, trying to get the thing to work, and now Colin Donald tells me the Stone Tracking Device will be operational in three days."

"My dad's been involved with this for a long time, hasn't he?"

Bernard nodded at Peter.

"Yes."

"And he's not in marketing at all."

"No."

Kylie slid her hand into Peter's and they stepped out of the cave into brilliant sunshine.

"Do you think we were wrong? That a Seeker was on board I mean."

Bernard's face became stern.

"No, I am sure there is at least one."

Peter took his pebble from his pocket.

"Well, that's one less thing to worry about. Shall I?"

"Please," said Bernard.

Peter knelt, placed the pebble on the ground and watched it roll up the ravine.

They all followed it, walking quickly.

"Excited?"

"Very," said Kylie. "I wonder how our families are getting on?"

"Probably at each other's throats," said Peter, even though he didn't really mean it.

After a while, the pebble began to jump up and down excitedly.

"Ready?" asked Kylie.

Bernard groaned.

"You two go on. I'll go the other way and meet you in the Great Hall for supper."

"I didn't know there was another way into the Realm of the Dead. Never heard it in the story," said Peter.

"You still have a lot to learn. Listen to the Winged Guardian's words. You know where to go?"

"To the tower on the island."

"And don't use the Travel Tunnel until you have been trained."

"We won't," they promised.

"Right, I'll see you later."

Bernard walked away, and Peter caught his pebble and placed it into the empty hole, in the middle of a stone carving of a brooch, where the ruby should be. The oval gateway to the Realm of the Dead appeared, framed by large blocks of dark stones and its blue and silver face shimmering like moonlight on water.

"It's a long way down, so best foot forward."

They walked into the stone-lined tunnel, two persons high

and three persons wide, felt a blast of cold air and the gateway closed behind them, plunging everything into darkness.

"Lights," said Peter.

Orange lights, set into the roof at regular intervals, came on and gave off a warm glow. They followed the slope down and met a round, hovering red bubble, which completely filled the tunnel. Words appeared inside the bubble.

Please use the safety harnesses provided.
Keep your hands inside at all times.

The bubble shrank to nothing.

"That wasn't in Grandpa's story either."

Kylie pointed down the tunnel.

"What is it?"

They ran to stand beside a double seat, suspended on a single metal arm hanging down from the roof. A small wheel at the top of the arm rested in the tray of a metal rail, which disappeared down a long, straight section of tunnel. The orange lights now ran along the sides of the walls and not on the roof.

"Why do I get the feeling Bernard made the best choice?" asked Kylie.

Peter shrugged his shoulders and lifted a safety bar that swung up from the seats.

"After you."

They sat and pulled the bar down to rest tightly across their waists. A loud bang from behind made them jump and they moved off, legs dangling freely, their seat accelerating quickly forward and orange lights flashing past. Ahead, the lights curved around a bend and disappeared. Peter grabbed Kylie's hand.

"Hold on."

The rushing air cooled their bodies and blew back their hair, and pinned them to the backs of their seats. The speed was incredible. The metal arm tilted as they turned the bend, the sides of their seats perilously close to the lights on the wall. Kylie screamed and Peter shouted.

"You OK?"

"It's ... fantastic!"

A right bend was followed quickly by a sharp left turn and they were thrown higher up the sides of the walls. More sharp bends, like a toboggan run, and their seat turned upside down, corkscrewing along the tunnel, Kylie screaming again with fear and delight, and Peter screaming too. Ahead, the lights disappeared into the floor and they plunged down into a black pit. More screams. They levelled out and left the tunnel like a bullet, out into sunshine, their feet dangling inches above the waters of a loch framed by distant hills. The small wheel above their heads gave off an almighty complaining shriek, as brake pads clamped themselves against its revolving surface, and they slowed before coming to rest beside a rowing boat tied to a small quay. Tirani the Wise grinned at them from the quay.

"Isn't it great?"

Automatically, the safety bar rose up and they stepped onto the quay, legs trembling, panting, unable to speak. Tirani spoke for them.

"Yes, it is great. Myroy took me to Disneyworld in Florida. Got the idea there."

Peter felt his body, checking that everything was still there. Kylie swayed a little.

"Peter, your brother caused a bit of excitement this afternoon."

"What did he do?"

"No doubt you will hear about it later." Tirani pointed down at the boat. "You have an hour until supper. Off you go."

Kylie managed one word.

"Go?"

"Over to the island. Your Guardian awaits you. The story awaits you."

Peter's legs stopped trembling and his breathing became easier.

"Can we have a minute?"

"No. Off you go."

Peter took Kylie's hand, helping her into the boat, and as he stepped down he wobbled and fell into the water. Tirani shook his head.

"The last Keeper of Amera's stone. May the power of the land protect us."

The loch pulsed, blood-red, and Peter rose up, bone dry, and was lowered down by invisible hands onto the seat next to his girlfriend. The oars rose up as well and swung around in the rowlocks to rest in their hands. Tirani skipped off the quay and called back.

"Good. Ready to go. Don't go down to the chamber under the tower."

Then a cold wind blew along the side of the loch and the Ancient One was gone. Peter glanced at Kylie.

"Welcome to the Realm of the Dead."

***

"Shut up, shut up, shut up," yelled James.

Their cell went blissfully quiet.

"Thank god for that," whispered Darren. "How long we been here?"

James whispered back.

"Days."

A minute passed and Holke couldn't stop himself talking again.

"Like peace and quiet do you, young Sirs? I remember this voyage to Belfast and my only passenger, Alistair of Cadbol...."

Bob the Pig Stealer eagerly joined in.

"Do you mean Alistair the Tadpole. He was in my cell once."

"Did he say much?"

"No."

"That's the same warrior. Anyway, he liked peace and quiet, hardly said a word the whole way over. He was going to Mountjoy. Now that's a palace that is. Wonderful gardens. My wife does like the gardening, young Sirs, just not very good at it, if you know what I mean. Do you like gardening, young Sirs?"

Darren put his head in his hands.

"I can't breathe. It stinks down here."

"Bloody hell," said James.

Bob the Pig Stealer wheezed.

"I like gardening. Of course there isn't much to work with in a cell. Not much at all, but I remember the summer before the Winter Feast, when the Younger came to the throne ..."

James stood up and screamed up at where the pin-prick of light had been.

"Let me out. These guys won't shut up and it stinks."

The floor of the cell began to shimmer and everything became bathed in a silvery light.

Myroy rose up and his nose twitched.

"Yes. It does smell a bit."

He went back down and complete darkness returned. James shouted up again.

"I hate you."

He was covered by an avalanche of rotten eggs.

"I hate you," whispered James.

A rasher of bacon landed on his head and Myroy's voice resounded around the cell.

"Enjoy your breakfast."

***

"Out the way, land-lubber."

Kylie took both oars and rowed expertly.

"Where did you learn to row like that?"

"I used to live on Skye. All the kids on the island learned to row, swim and fish."

"You never told me you come from Skye. You're not descended from the Black Kilts are you?"

"Ha, ha. Very funny. Not that I know of anyway."

Over Kylie's shoulder, Peter had a clear view of the island. No giant osprey on the tower.

"I wonder where Gora is?" he said.

Dressed in sandals and furs that reeked of sweat, Gora sat cross-legged beside Amera's stone. Eyes closed, his breathing shallow, he looked as though he was meditating and had no need for company or contact with anything in the wider world. Once he had sat this way in darkness for over a thousand years, talking to the stone, learning about its powers and wishing only to feel the wind on his face.

The stone pulsed and Gora opened his eyes. He stroked the ruby, stood, and ran past a cylinder of ice with the dark shape of a man entombed inside. Twitching fingers stuck out of the ice and he spat on them. Bounding up narrow stairs, his speed increased as the staircase spiralled and widened. With every step his chest expanded and Gora glanced at his arms. Like every other part of his body, the skin was transforming into feathers. The corkscrew stairs grew even wider to allow for his growing body, head and wings. He saw light up ahead and shrieked a warning, and drove himself out into warm afternoon sunshine. At great speed Gora opened his wings and launched himself up from the roof of the tower towards the ceiling of the Realm of the Dead.

***

"Wow!" gasped Peter.

Kylie turned her head and saw a giant osprey explode from the tower on the island. The bird circled their boat, pin-pointing them with black, keen, penetrating eyes, before shrieking again to make Kylie drop the oars and hold her ears.

"I think Gora's going back now."

Kylie nodded and watched the osprey make a perfect landing on the tower, and felt her boyfriend take an oar from her.

"Come on. Let's go and hear the rest of the story," he said.

They rowed to a small quay, that was an exact copy of the quay by the village, and walked over to the base of the tower. They stared up at the thick, roughly hewn stones which made up the wall.

"We'll never climb that," said Kylie. "Seems to go up forever."

They walked right around the wall and came back to the small quay.

"No door."

Gora's piercing screech followed Peter's words.

"OK, Gora, we're coming," yelled Kylie. She placed her pebble on to the ground. "Take us to Gora."

The pebble jumped back into her hand. "Try yours."

Peter tried his and the same thing happened. Another deafening screech from high above.

"Right. I get it. Kylie, hold the pebble as tightly as you can and don't let go of it."

She gripped it and her arm began to rise.

"Pebble, you won't let me fall, will you?" Kylie felt the muscles in her arm tighten and the pebble lifted her off the ground. "Come on, Peter. It's easy."

He rose too, passing one rough stone after another until they were both floating over the lip at the top and dropping down in front of Gora's perch. Like bookends, two stone ospreys held a long, gnarled oak trunk in their beaks and Gora's talons gripped the trunk and dwarfed it. He lowered his head to take a close look at his visitors and a blast of cold air came from his beak. The head went back up and the wings extended fully, beyond the bounds of the tower, flapping once, the wind knocking the children off their feet. Gora transformed himself from bird to man and jumped down to stand between them, and spoke in a deep, slow, purposeful voice.

"I am Gora. Welcome, Keeper."

Peter picked himself up.

"I am Peter of the line of Donald and it is a great pleasure to meet you, Winged Guardian."

Gora held out a thin arm and pulled Kylie up.

"You are the one they call Kylie."

"I am. Nice to meet you, Gora."

"You are both here for one reason. Listen to my words before

164

you feast with the Twelve. Something happened here and not long ago. A blink of an eye ago, in a time of war when Duncan Donald kept the stone." Gora ran his bony fingers through his beard. "You have been warned not to go to the chamber beneath this tower."

"Yes," said Kylie.

"Do you know why?"

"No. No idea."

"And where are you in the story?"

Peter took Kylie's hand and squeezed it.

"The last part was in *Early Celtic Writings and their Meanings*. Grandpa, Bernard, Lofty, Sandy and Chalky have driven away from the fighting at the airbase. Sergeant Sturgess, I mean SS, stayed behind to help them escape. He joined the fallen, didn't he?"

"He did. He became an empty chair at the reunion."

"Did they hide up here afterwards?" asked Kylie.

"Yes and that is when the problem began."

"Was the invasion of Corfu called off?"

Gora nodded.

"They did not destroy enough planes and it was a good thing. An invasion would have been a disaster."

"And did General Montgomery lose face with Aris, the leader of the Greek resistance over on the mainland?"

"No. Spiros spoke to him and explained that it was their failure to draw a convoy to the south of the island that made the plan fail. But that was not the reason of course."

Peter nodded.

"They had no way of checking how many planes were there and most of the bombers were out on flight patrol."

"Sometimes in war, good intelligence is the difference between success and failure."

"And the other Aris, Aris Agnedes, the leader of the Andartes on Corfu, who now looks after Bernard's garden. He never recovered?"

165

"No."

"He was very brave."

"He was. But was he as brave as Mrs Agnedes? She married him anyway, knowing she was giving her love to a man who could not even remember her name."

There was a sad silence for a while until Kylie spoke.

"I can't answer that question. I guess there are just different kinds of courage."

Gora pointed at her and smiled.

"You should remember that."

A recurring thought came into Peter's mind.

"I am being trained. That's why Myroy told me about Grandpa's adventures."

"There are some useful lessons from North Africa and Corfu."

"Like how to plan a raid on an enemy base and how not to," said Kylie.

"But that is not the only reason why you must listen to the story. The Second World War, on Corfu, was the only time, since Dougie's time as a Keeper, that Odin came close to holding the ruby." Gora held up his palm and ran a finger across it. "He came this close. The width of a hand. Now make yourselves comfortable and listen to the story."

As the sun began to fall in the Realm of the Dead, Peter and Kylie sat on one of the feet of a stone osprey, holding hands and completely unaware of anything in the world except the pictures painted by Gora's words. But he began with a sentence they could not understand.

"Of course, if Myroy had been here, he would have sensed the greed immediately."

***

"Cor Blimey," said Chalky.

Tirani had skipped along and led the friends out of the village and up the hill, past three standing stones, to a small cairn.

Sheep scattered as they approached the cairn and Lofty stared back towards the drover's road and the calm blue waters of the loch. The Realm of the Dead was beautiful.

"Cor blimey is right, Chalky. It really is just how I imagined it when Myroy told us about Dougie."

Duncan saw the island.

"Except for that tower. There's never been a tower on my loch."

The boy interrupted them with a warning.

"Do not go to the island." Tirani pointed at Bernard. "Please lift up a stone from the cairn. Any stone will do."

Bernard did so and, up the slope, a long, straight crack appeared in the grass, slowly growing wider as a wall of rock rose up.

"What is that?" asked Sandy.

The rock face stopped rising. Cut into the rock was a line of six oval caves, each cave identical, two persons high and three persons wide, and edged with roughly hewn stone blocks. The entrance to each cave a glassy flat mirror made of falling water.

"I made them," said Tirani proudly. "Follow me."

He skipped over to the first oval and spoke to it.

"Seeker Viewer on."

The glassy water changed and became a map of the world covered in thousands of red dots.

"It's very handy," said Tirani. "We can keep an eye on all of Odin's people from here."

He skipped to the next oval.

"Keeper Viewer on."

More red dots on a map of the world.

"This shows where all our people are. Bet Odin would like to see this."

Tirani skipped on.

"This is my favourite. The Travel Tunnel. Just imagine a place in your mind, any place in the world and at any time in the past or future, and you can go there. Great fun, but don't use it until you've been shown how to use it properly. Could be dangerous."

"Can we see?" asked Chalky.

"Don't see why not. Activate Travel Tunnel."

"Nothing's 'appening."

"It has. Just imagine where you want to be and when, and walk into the water. You will step out where you desire, well, nearly always. Deactivate Travel Tunnel."

The glassy face of the oval didn't seem to change again and the boy skipped further along the rock face.

"This is the Stone Locator. I put it in just in case Odin get's his hands on the stone. Trouble is, it doesn't seem to work anywhere. Might have to make it smaller and send it up into space."

Duncan glanced at Bernard.

"Space?"

Tirani pointed at the sky.

"Space."

"Blimey," said Sandy.

Tirani grinned and went to the next oval.

"What does this do?" asked Duncan.

"It's the washroom and sauna. Later on, you can go in and change out of those clothes." He pointed at their sheepskin waistcoats and woollen jumpers, the choice of the Andartes. "Your normal uniforms have all been washed and ironed for you. Look in the lockers next to the sauna."

Tirani pointed at the last oval.

"And this is the Talk Tunnel. Duncan, you have spoken to your dead grandfather."

"Aye."

"This is where he speaks from."

"How does it work?" asked Bernard.

"Just imagine the person you want to talk to and speak into the watery mirror."

Duncan thought about Maggie.

"Can I try?"

"Go ahead."

Duncan stepped in front of the mirror of falling water.

"Maggie, it's Duncan. I just wanted you to know that Bernard and I are safe and well."

A picture appeared on the face of the mirror. A young lady was working in a packed army canteen. She screamed and dropped the plates she was holding.

Tirani shrugged his shoulders.

"Hmm. Does tend to have that kind of effect on people who aren't used to it."

The picture returned to a mirror.

"Right, off you go to the washroom and get cleaned up. See you in the Great Hall for supper."

They all turned and saw Chalky. He hadn't heard a thing, hadn't moved an inch, since Tirani had explained about the Travel Tunnel, and he was standing like a statue, still staring at it.

***

Private Chalk couldn't sleep, his mind full of the possibilities and he couldn't remember anything about the feast or meeting the eleven dead stone Keepers. The Time Tunnel consumed his thoughts. He rolled on to his side and checked on Sandy and Lofty. They were still sleeping, out like lights, and Chalky knew that, after the attack on the airbase, Bernard and Duncan in the next room would be sound asleep too. He tried to measure the distance to the cottage door. No more than eight paces and a clear run with no tables or chairs to bump into. He had deliberately gone to bed with his clothes on and now felt the same thrill that he did before a burglary. It was a good feeling. A sense of danger, but not too much. He had done this hundreds of times before. Chalky made his move and tip-toed across the room, boots in one hand. No lock on the door. He smiled. They didn't need locks in the Realm of the Dead.

The walk up to the cairn seemed further in the darkness, and once he stumbled and cursed, but he never slowed to rub his sore knees. At the cairn he picked up a stone and watched the crack widen and turn into a rock face with the six ovals. Their oval watery faces, edged by roughly hewn rocks, looked grey in the dark. He dropped the stone and ran to stand before the Travel Tunnel.

"Activate Travel Tunnel."

Nothing seemed to happen, like before, and he remembered some of Tirani's words.

"*Just imagine where you want to be and when, and walk into the water. You will step out where you desire.*"

He thought about the vault beneath the Bank of England, but he had never been there and couldn't picture it.

"Better start small."

He pictured the inside of Barclays Bank near his home in Pimlico, East London.

"But when? Shut on a Sunday, so no one around. That'll do. I'll just nick an 'andful of fivers. Call it a trial run."

He stepped up to the grey flowing mirror of the entrance and gingerly put a hand into it.

***

In his eternal chamber, Odin's eyes flashed blue as he sensed a travelling man with greed in his heart. This man was of value. He had been close to his ruby.

***

Chalky's greed overcame his fear and he stepped through the watery wall of the travel tunnel. On the far side, in Odin's chamber, he felt his body picked up and thrown forward. He stared at an immaculate pair of highly polished, black leather shoes. A voice entered his mind and it felt as though someone was searching around in his head.

"What is your name?"

170

"Chalky."

His body became wracked in dreadful pain.

"Your real name?"

"Richard Chalk."

"You are a thief."

"I am a thief."

"Where is my stone?"

"What stone?"

More pain. More intense pain and Chalky's back arched on the floor.

"Please stop. Please stop."

The pain grew worse and he rolled around the floor, holding his head, blood pouring from his ears.

"Myroy has told you a story about the history of the stone. He told it to you in the desert in North Africa. You know it as *Amera's* stone. Where is it?"

"Please stop."

"Tell me."

Chalky didn't know that Duncan had thrown the ruby into the loch in the Realm of the Dead.

"I don't know."

Odin searched his mind and knew he was telling the truth.

"Who is the Keeper?"

"Duncan of the Line of Donald."

"Where is he?"

"The Realm of the Dead."

"How did you get here?"

"The Travel Tunnel. I was using it to rob a bank."

Thorgood and Olaf, who had stood unseen behind him, kicked his ribs.

"Answer only the question," said Olaf.

Odin took full control of Chalky's mind.

"You and I will go back into the Travel Tunnel, find the stone and bring it here."

"I obey, Master."

Without any control over his mind or body, Chalky got up and stepped into an oval wall of water that was still in the centre of a carving of a long-ship on one side of Odin's sanctuary. Odin saw through Chalky's eyes, saw the dark outline of far hills and turned to see the six ovals. He smelled heather and searched inside his victim's mind. There was a memory of being given a warning by a boy.

"Do not go to the chamber under the tower on the island."

Odin memorised the shape of the loch, the tower and the outline of the hills, and believed that the Realm of the Dead was in Scotland. He ran in Chalky's body down to the quay and jumped into the loch, expecting his body to travel at great speed through the water. But he came up, gasping for air and realised his powers did not work here. He crawled out, shook his wet hair, climbed into the boat and began to row. He made it to the island unseen and, at the base of the tower, gave Chalky new orders.

"Be a thief. Get me inside."

Without fear, Chalky went over to the nearest corner and began to climb the wall, using his fingers and the edges of his army boots to get a grip. Twice his feet slipped, but his strong fingers were wedged between the gaps in the stones and they saved him, and he made the top without a fall. At the lip, Chalky paused and stared at a huge winged creature on a perch. The bird's breathing was shallow and Chalky lifted himself up to sit on the top stones of the wall, unlaced his boots and laid them gently down. He moved quickly and silently to a large, dark hole that he guessed was some kind of entrance to the lower chambers, and stared at a spiral staircase with only blackness down beyond the first few steps.

Feeling with his toes, he found the edge of each step and slowly wound his way down. It was pitch black where the steps finally ended and he now felt far enough away from the bird to light a match. Its glow showed very little of the chamber, but there was a torch in a holder on the wall to his left. He took the torch, lit it and felt a sharp pain as Odin re-conquered his mind. Then Chalky thought no more.

The god thrust the torch out and yellow and orange shapes danced around the circular chamber. The same roughly hewn rocks of the outer walls had been used to line the chamber and in the centre a ruby of great size hovered in mid air. He smiled and walked towards it and held out his free hand. Odin suddenly became aware of dark shapes all around the chamber and stabbed his torch out at one shape, and saw his brother's ancient face. Myroy spoke in a soft voice.

"I have no sense of the man they call Chalky. My eyes see his body, but his mind is not his own."

Odin used Chalky's body to dive at the stone. The Twelve stepped out from the shadows and pointed at him and Odin felt his will challenged by a powerful force. Chalky's body froze. Odin's stone was there, just the width of a hand away from his own hand and Odin tried to push his arm out further. But, like the rest of Chalky's body, it didn't move. Eilidh the Runner, the second Keeper, spoke in her young, gentle voice.

"Do we kill him?"

Duncan stepped out of the shadows.

"If we kill him, we become like the enemy. Forgiveness has a power."

Myroy looked at Duncan.

"I chose the line of Donald well."

The circle of the Twelve closed in silently, still pointing at Chalky's still body and outstretched arm. The stone hovered inches from the fingertips that had tried to take it.

Dougie of Dunfermline spoke.

"We cannot stay here forever, holding Odin back."

Myroy asked Amera's stone a question.

"Will you protect Chalky, like you protected me for over one thousand and two hundred summers?"

The stone pulsed once, blood-red, and snowflakes fell onto Chalky. The flakes became bigger and swirled around his body, then the flakes gave way to an avalanche of snow that compacted from the ground up in a tube without sides. Chalky became frozen in a cylinder of ice, which ran from floor to ceiling, and the Keepers stopped pointing, and knew how close they had been to complete disaster. Odin's determination to reach the stone was clear. Chalky's outstretched fingers remained outside the wall of ice and twitched.

Myroy turned to look at Gora, who had sat in human form, unnoticed on the steps.

"Well done. No one else in the world would have heard the match."

"I slept as a thief came for the stone. I will learn from that."

Tirani stepped out of the shadows.

"Do you think he saw me?"

"No," said Myroy.

"And did Chalky tell Odin about the location of the Realm of the Dead?"

"If Odin asked the right question, then he knows. If he didn't then the Keeper is safe here."

Tirani skipped over to Duncan.

"Come on. We had better go and break the news to your friends."

**

Kylie let out a long breath.

"So he is still there, encased in ice. How horrible."

"And Odin's will still drives him. Every moment of every day the fingers twitch and try to touch the stone."

Peter shuddered at Gora's words.

"Any problems since then?"

"Not really. We tightened up all the warning systems and the defences around the island. In fact, your brother caused a bit of a scare today and I should go and release him."

"Release James?"

"From his cell. He will need time to clean himself up before the feast. I like him though, he is a bit like me when I was young; foolish and cursed with an adventurous spirit."

"Is that why you went down into Amera's cairn?"

"I am ashamed to say I was driven by greed too."

Kylie stared at Gora's scrawny body.

"Myroy told me you were punished terribly."

The man stared at the veins on the back of his hands and seemed to choose his words carefully.

"I was trapped inside the stone for so long. I went mad towards the end and it has taken me an age to recover, and even if I have another age of freedom, I will *never* be the same again."

"And you know the stone better than anyone."

"I do and it is not enough. I want you to see something before you go. This is the world I hope never to see."

A globe of the world, ten metres across, hovered in front of them. The blues and greens of the northern hemisphere, and the ice packs of the Arctic, changing to red as the boundary of Odin's empire crept out from Oslo. The globe tilted so that Oslo was at the centre.

"It *will* be a different world."

The earth tilted again and this time with China at its centre.

"Through history, the Keepers and Seekers have penetrated governments all around the world. Some are controlled by us. Some are controlled by the enemy. Our goal was always to have complete control of any country that would be outside of the Red Empire. There is no point controlling lands that are inside the Orange Band, they would fall as soon as Odin touched the stone. So, for example, Australia, South Africa and Japan are all with us. But, there is an exception."

Gora pointed at the hovering globe.

"China," said Kylie. "Why?"

"We have never been able to answer that question. Certainly they are not going to help the Seekers. China remains absolutely independent, which is why it remains a priority for us. It would be terrible if they helped Odin. If we were attacked by Odin's forces and the Chinese army at the same time, we would be lost."

Gora stood to show the conversation was over and the globe disappeared.

"Be here at sunrise tomorrow, both of you. Your first lesson starts then."

CHAPTER EIGHT

THE FEAST

"Get out. You stink!" shrieked Laura.

Julie Donald picked up a broom and prodded her son, forcing him out of the cottage door.

"Go and swim in the loch and be quick about it."

On the garden path a plastic bottle of shower gel hit the back of James's head.

"Use that," yelled Julie.

He picked it up.

"Charming."

Peter and Kylie passed him by the quay.

"Heard you caused a bit of a stir," said Kylie.

"Hmm."

"Where did Myroy send you?"

James peeled off his shirt and threw it on the ground.

"Deep beneath the earth. Some kind of cell. Felt as though I was there for weeks, but it was only a few hours."

"And what did he do to you?"

"Dropped poo all over me."

Peter smiled and backed away a little.

"If you had made it to the chamber under the tower, he would have done worse than that."

"What's down there anyway?"

"That's not your business."

"So I get covered from head to toe in horse business and it's not my business."

"That's right."

Peter held Kylie's hand.

"We'd better go and get ready. What you wearing tonight, by the way?"

"Don't know. I haven't got anything to wear. Do you think Tirani can show us how to use the Travel Tunnel? There are some good shops on Corfu."

"Hmmm."

Peter kissed her goodbye and retreated to the cottage, calling back.

"See you later."

His mother had laid out a white shirt and a light brown, green and ochre plaid on his bed. He stripped and put them on, throwing the last length of tartan over his shoulder. The floor began to shimmer, like moonlight on water, and Myroy rose up from the underworld. Without speaking, he walked up to Peter and pinned the fabric in place with a gold brooch. The Ancient One smiled and went away again, and Peter was left feeling proud that he had been chosen to keep Amera's stone. He stood in front of the mirror, thinking he looked a little like Dougie, and felt the warmth of the brooch. Laura came to his door in a bathrobe, yelled and shattered any feelings of pride he had.

"You coming, or you gonna spend all day admiring yourself in front of the mirror?"

A few minutes later, in the cottage kitchen, Julie stared at her son.

"That's not the little boy I used to know. You look very handsome."

"Thanks, Mum. You look pretty cool too." He recognised her long white dress, her small posy of flowers, and tartan bonnet with a sprig of heather pinned to the side. "Just like Mairi dressed for the Union of Souls."

"Just so."

Laura came in, dressed like her mother, dressed like all the ladies at Hamish and Babs' wedding.

"You two wallies off a to fancy dress party later?"

Julie smiled.

"You look lovely too, my chicken."

"I look horrible. I hate wearing anything I can't choose myself. I want to die."

James joined them, but however he had put his plaid on, it wasn't the right way and it bulged out around his waist and circled his neck rather than lying neatly over his shoulder.

"Go on, Mum, say something nice about me."

Julie thought about it and Laura said what she was thinking.

"You don't stink anymore."

James puffed his chest out.

"Fair enough. Can we go and eat now?"

***

In one of the laboratories surrounding the Cloning Research Centre, Doctor Van Heussen clamped Tirani's calling pipe on to a bench, pushed a rubber hose around the mouthpiece and attached the other end of the hose to something that looked like a small vacuum cleaner. He flicked a switch and tiny red lights came on at the side of the sensors, which formed a ring around the pipe. The doctor checked them.

"All lights on. All sensors working."

Back at his computer screen, he talked to himself again.

"OK. So it's a simple problem. Two notes that must be played in the right order and blown for the right amount of time. But what does it do? That is what I am asking."

He entered numbers into a spreadsheet.

"We'll start with the tuning hole open, try a one-second blow, then a two and a three and a four, all the way to ten seconds." He pushed enter. "Off we go."

He checked different screens around his desk for the results from the sensors for the one-second blow. A little vibration, no change to the earth's magnetic field, no static electricity generated.

"Hmm. Nothing. Try again."

The two-second blow was negative too, but at three seconds the screen measuring changes to the earth's magnetic field exploded.

"Ah, interesting. So, first note, three seconds."

Van Heussen wrote it onto a yellow Post-It note and stuck it onto the side of his screen, before eagerly replacing the smoking monitor.

"Right, second sequence. Tuning hole closed and we'll start with a one-second blow."

His phone rang as he pushed enter.

"Doctor, it is Olaf. Please join me in the breeding cave immediately."

"I obey."

He left the laboratory with the sound of the pipe in his ears, trying to guess what Olaf Adanson wanted.

***

Tirani the Wise waited to greet the Donalds outside of the Great Hall.

"Ah, Keeper, you are on the High Table with me. The rest of you can sit anywhere except the High Table."

"Charming," said James.

"Enjoy the feast. Follow me."

Tirani pushed with all his might against one of the two tall oak doors. It opened slowly and they all heard the sound of excited voices from inside. Laura ignored everyone and headed straight for Darren, and Peter followed Tirani. It was like going back into ancient times when every important event was celebrated with a feast in a dark smoky hall. Peter felt nervous. All eyes seemed to watch him, or stare at the brooch on his plaid, as he walked between two long tables towards a raised platform at the far end. Tirani pointed at a chair with a high back, next to Myroy, and Peter sat between the Ancient Ones. Dougie, Alistair, Malcolm the Younger, Arkinew and Gangly, Kenneth of Blacklock, Gora, Bernard and Duncan also sat at the High Table. Peter's heart sank. He didn't deserve to be with these people. They had changed history.

Peter stared around the hall. All the ladies were dressed like Mairi and the men wore the Younger's royal tartan, even Myroy and Tirani. Kylie and her family were there, as were the past Keepers and the men of Tain. Hamish roared with laughter when he saw James's plaid. Near to the double doors sat Sandy and Lofty, Mr. and Mrs. Agnedes, Spiros and Minolas, and two empty chairs near them. One chair had an old army rucksack on it. All the warriors from the Second World War looked very old. It was the most bizarre setting and mix of people imaginable.

"This is so weird," thought Peter.

Myroy smiled at him and nodded at the Younger who stood up to speak.

"We are here to celebrate. Celebrate the safe keeping of Amera's stone. On our great journey through history, the Keepers have enjoyed mixed fortunes. Some lived a life without danger and fear. Some experienced pain and saw their friends, the brave defenders of the stone, join the fallen." He paused to look at the chair with the rucksack on it. "Overall, we have been lucky. When we made mistakes, as anyone will do, the enemy was unable to take advantage of it. I think that deep in our hearts we all know that one day our luck will run out. Odin has been saying that to Myroy for over a thousand years and he is right. But he is not right today. The stone remains safe and we can celebrate."

Everyone in the hall cheered and the Younger raised his hands.

"I want to welcome Peter of the line of Donald, and his girlfriend Kylie, to the Realm of the Dead."

A wave of panic hit Peter.

"Oh, no. He wants me to say something," he thought.

Next to him, Myroy shook his head.

"No."

The doors at the far end opened and Peter's father came in quickly, dressed in a suit and carrying a briefcase. He panted as though he had run all the way from London.

"Sorry I'm late."

Myroy spoke a single word, but in a kind voice.

"Sit."

Colin sat next to Julie and the speech continued.

"Now that we are *all* here."

The Younger glanced disapprovingly at Colin Donald's clothes, making him squirm.

"Since my death at the hands of my own son, every dawn when I have woken my first thought has always been the same. Is the stone safe in the keeping? My death had to be. Without it there could be no return of a Long Peace for my people. Some things *have* to be and some things *must* not be. Never forget that if we lose Amera's stone, the world will become divided and freedom lost until the final battle. We *must* not lose the stone."

He paused again and looked at Peter who froze.

"That battle will be in your time and we are all with you."

The hall went silent.

"Through the ages, there have been people who underestimated the enemy. They were fools and most of them were killed. The Seekers are clever and resourceful. Always respect them, but do not forgive their utter ruthlessness. There have also been people who have treated the war as some kind of game."

The Younger's eyes fixed on James, who tried to look away and couldn't.

"My words to them are always the same. Ask yourself a question. What do you value most? Their answer is often, 'Being able to do what they want to do.' The war we fight is no game. If Odin holds the stone, whichever side of the Orange Band you find yourself on, the last thing you will be able to do is what you want to do. You will either be a mindless servant, or a freedom fighter fearing for his life every single day."

The Younger turned away from James, who had gone white.

"The time for constant vigilance and deception is over. The time for my words is over. Tonight I want to forget the burden we all share in some way. Just for one night, we can be happy and celebrate with friends and food. We are bonded together by one thing, a story, and so I ask you to raise your goblets and join me in a toast."

Goblets appeared from nowhere in front of all the guests. Donald drank his and another replaced it. Everyone stood and raised their goblets.

"The story of the stone," said the Younger.

"The story of the stone," everyone repeated.

Peter drank. He had never tasted heather ale before and he liked the way it gave you a warm and relaxed feeling. He wondered if his mum would approve and glanced at her. She had already finished hers and sat down again. A slurping noise came from the end of the table. Gangly had his long pipe out, trying to drink from Archie's goblet. Peter smiled and waited for them to start arguing again. Tirani nudged him.

"Bet you can't guess the first course."

"Mairi's lamb and vegetable broth."

"Oh."

The broth appeared in front of them and Tirani adjusted himself on a cushion that helped him reach the table.

"My brother tells me you battled with Odin in London. That's good experience for you."

"I suppose so."

"Did he do that mind thing on you? You know where he tries to take over your thoughts."

Peter raised his spoon and lowered it without eating to answer the question.

"He did. Grandpa saved me. He could fight it better than I could."

"That'll come. Listen to Gora. Have you had your first lesson yet?"

"Tomorrow at dawn."

Tirani gave him a strange look.

"Ah, good. Have fun."

"Should I be worried about it?"

"No. no, no. How's Kylie?"

Peter waved at her and she waved back.

"She's well."

"And what are your first impressions of the Realm of the Dead?"

"My first impression made me scream. That ride down to the loch scared the hell out of me."

"Good, isn't it?"

"Wicked."

Tirani grinned.

"Bernard hates it. He was sick all the way down."

Slurping noises came from Archie's end of the table and as Peter turned that way he caught Bernard in the corner of his eye. He was in the middle of a heated argument with Duncan.

"I'm sure you know what that's about," said Tirani.

"Oh, yes. Sometimes three in a relationship is one too many, particularly when one is dead, but not really dead."

Everyone had finished their broth except Peter who had been answering Tirani's questions, and the bowls vanished. Tirani asked another question.

"Not like broth?"

"Love it, when I get time to eat it."

"By the way, can I have my pipe back?"

Peter shook his head.

"It's in my rucksack. Odin grabbed it before diving into the Thames."

Tirani dropped his goblet.

"What?"

"Odin's had the pipe since I fought him in London. Is there a problem?"

"That's a Calling Pipe. If he blows it correctly, the stone will go to him."

The next course materialized in front of them. A huge joint of roast lamb with peas. Tirani spoke across Peter to his brother.

"Odin has my Calling Pipe."

There was a deep trembling noise from deep down in the earth. The knives and forks rattled against the plates, Peter's mound of peas collapsed, and Gangly fell off Archie's shoulder and lay unconscious on the High Table. Myroy watched the peas dance across his plate.

"I know. I am very afraid."

The smoky hall became deadly silent.

"What is it?" asked Peter.

Tirani replied in a scared and shaky voice.

"It is the old magic and someone is using it."

***

Olaf stared out of the long, reinforced-glass window in the observation chamber. Spear-like tails pointed out from the honeycomb of small caves and the walls of the great cavern were covered in thousands of the hideous creatures. Many competed for space in the island of trees. The lake was a mass of the deadly red jelly fish. A railway line had been constructed and ran from a jetty on the edge of the lake, past the trees and through the barley to end at the steel doors, where the Keepers had entered the cave and met their deaths. Olaf pointed at a swarm of creatures that hovered above the pines and spoke to Doctor Van Heussen.

"Our master asks for an update on the breeding programme."

"The programme is going well now that we have overcome the main problem. The fish and the birds only eat live prey. In fact it's feeding time now."

The steel doors rose and a train with six wagons, all reinforced with steel plates, rolled slowly into the cave. In the centre of the barley field it stopped and the sides of half the wagons automatically lowered to become wide gangplanks from the cargo bays to the ground. Cows reluctantly walked out and it was as though something inside each truck was forcing them to leave. As the gangplanks folded up and locked back into place, the humming noise from the audio system became loud and intense, and the cows ran as a terrified herd towards the trees. The train rolled on to feed the fish.

"The target is one million of each species. What is there number now?" asked Olaf.

"Approximately twenty thousand birds and eighteen thousand fish."

"When will the target be reached?"

"The second breeding chamber will be ready in four weeks. The third chamber in twelve weeks. Twelve weeks after that we should be at the target population."

"So, twenty-four weeks."

"Yes, give or take a week or two. It's not an exact science."

They were thrown to the ground by a violent earthquake. Deep rumbling sounded from the depths of the earth, the audio system died and a crack shot across the glass of the observation room. The doctor tried to stand and was thrown back down by another tremor. The rumbling and shaking ground stopped suddenly.

Olaf helped Van Heussen to his feet.

"My experiment. Quickly Olaf, follow me to the lab."

They ran through the Cloning Research Centre, closing steel doors behind them in case the birds penetrated the observation chamber, sparks coming from some of the monitors and men in white coats tidying papers that had been thrown to the floor. The door to Van Heussen's laboratory lay flat on the ground, blown off its hinges by some incredible force, and Odin stood on it.

"After you, Doctor," he said.

Inside was a ruin, machines and sensors just twisted metal, sparks jumping as electric circuits arced. There was a hole the size of a beach ball in the bench and the pipe lay unharmed on the floor. The doctor ignored the pipe and grabbed sheets of paper from a smoking printer and tried to put them into some kind of order. He found the sheet he wanted and threw the others away. His voice became more excited as he spoke.

"The experiment terminated at five seconds with the tuning hole closed. We now have the sequence. Three seconds open, five seconds closed."

Olaf picked up the pipe and handed it to Odin.

"Master, it is the old magic. I do not know what it does, but I sense nothing bad. Do you sense any danger?"

"No."

Odin put the calling pipe to his lips and blew for three seconds. He placed a finger over the tuning hole and blew for five seconds. A gold brooch with a ruby of great size appeared in his free hand and he stroked the warm surface of the gem with his thumb. Everyone stared at it in silence, not believing what had happened. Odin smiled and tossed the pipe to the doctor.

"Destroy it. It is a calling pipe and no one shall use it against me."

"I obey, master."

Now he held the greatest power in the world in his hand. He had dreamed of this moment so many times and yet the stone had been within his reach since fighting Peter of the Line of Donald in London. It had been there, for him at any time, and only a pipe-call away.

"Ha."

Inside, Odin wanted to jump for joy, but feared losing his authority in front of others.

"Our search is finally over. Olaf, order all Seekers to join me here. Today we will begin to build our empire, the Red Empire."

"I obey, master."

The Ancient One looked deep into the blood-red ruby and pictured Thor.

"Brother, the stone is home and I will use its power to destroy Myroy and his followers. Your death will finally be avenged."

Odin's mind wandered back through the centuries and he remembered how close he had come, so many times, and how Myroy had thrown him off the scent, or led him down fruitless dead ends.

"Your luck has run out."

Odin clutched the brooch tightly in his hand.

"Take me to Myroy," he commanded.

***

Peter cut off some lamb and ate it.

"Absolutely delicious" he thought.

"I prefer beef, myself," mumbled Tirani, pulling a lump of

gristle out of his mouth. "Still, tradition is tradition."

Peter watched his grandfather point his fork at Bernard, their conversation more and more heated. Mrs. Agnedes saw it too and left her seat, picked up the old rucksack and dumped it on the table in front of them. She spoke one word in her thick Greek accent.

"Respect."

Myroy stiffened and put his knife and fork down.

"Odin comes."

Peter put a hand onto his brooch to protect it and felt it melt away. He felt sick with worry.

"Myroy, I am losing the stone. Is this *real*? I mean, is this another test for me, or is the world we know about to change?"

He looked at the hard lines on Myroy's face and knew it was real. Tirani spoke across him to Myroy.

"We are not ready for this."

"The balance of power is equal."

"But Peter is not fully trained."

Myroy's face became hard and determined.

"He will be trained."

The hall went silent as the floor over by the double oak doors began to shimmer, but not like moonlight on water. These shimmers were red. Tirani slipped off his cushion and hid.

"What are you doing?" whispered Peter.

A small voice came from under the table.

"Odin doesn't know I still live. Let's keep it that way."

The god rose up, Amera's stone in hand, and Myroy turned to Peter.

"Do not fear him. He cannot use the stone's power here."

You could have heard a pin drop as Odin walked towards his brother, smiling and without any fear for his own safety. His eyes never left Myroy's, ignoring everyone who sat at the long tables on either side of him. Then he leant forward with his hands resting on the High Table, looking up and down it, memorising the faces of everyone there. When he saw Peter again, his blue eyes flashed and, despite Myroy's words about not fearing him, the last Keeper shrank with terror, sweat dripping down his back. The god's eyes returned to Myroy.

"Your luck has run out."

Myroy did not move a muscle and Odin smiled.

"I have a message for you and your followers."

"I thought you might," said the Younger in a cold voice. "Please speak."

This threw Odin a little. He wasn't used to anyone giving him permission to do anything and he hesitated for a moment. A deep growling noise came from Hamish's chest as Odin spoke again.

"You are now *Seekers*."

Donald took his dirk from his belt and threw it at Odin's back. Myroy nodded at the knife and it shot up, and buried itself in a wooden beam, the handle vibrating from side to side. Odin glanced up at the knife and walked slowly back towards the door. Before descending into the underworld, he stopped beside Donald and his blue eyes flashed at him.

"I look forward to killing all of you."

CHAPTER NINE

THE EVACUATION OF LONDON

Holly Anderson sat with Miss Dickson in the SKEPERE office on lower level five of the MI5 building. Without any instruction from them, the large photograph of the moon rose up to reveal a map of the world. Thousands of red dots were converging on Oslo. The biggest migration of Seekers was north from Australia. Miss Dickson sipped her coffee.

"Odin has ordered all his people home. How odd."

Holly nodded.

"I wonder what it means?"

***

As soon as Odin had returned to the earth, Colin Donald ran from the Great Hall, out of the village and up the slope to the cairn. Panting again, he lifted a stone off the cairn, tossed it aside and waited for the rock-face to appear.

"Come on."

He watched the watery face of the last oval rise up.

"Activate Talk Tunnel."

He pictured the SKEPERE office in his mind and saw Holly and Miss Dickson appear on the face of the oval.

"Holly, we need to speak."

"We do. All Seekers return to Oslo."

"Odin holds the stone. Evacuate our people from London now."

Their faces went pale. Miss Dickson dropped her coffee and began to cry. Holly tried to compose herself.

"Er, yes. I mean, codeword please."

"The codeword for the evacuation is *Dunkirk*."

"Please repeat."

"*Dunkirk*."

"OK. We'll start right away."

"Every second counts now. I'll prepare the Travel Tunnel this end."

The SKEPERE office vanished on the watery screen and Colin ran to activate the Travel Tunnel. Almost immediately, a small number of men and women began to run out, all holding laptops, files and anything else they could carry. Hamish, Donald, Bernard and Duncan joined him and Bernard took out his pistol.

"Just in case we get any unwanted visitors."

The trickle of people coming out into the Realm of the Dead became a flood.

"Any sign of Miss Dickson or Holly?" asked Bernard.

Colin peered through the water and down the tunnel, and shook his head.

"Do you want me to go through and find them?"

"No. They are probably helping the evacuation."

Hundreds of people now sat on the slopes between the small cairn and the three standing stones. Most of them had only heard of this place in a story, and they stared around in awe at the loch and the far hills. Some cried and everyone looked empty, lost and shell-shocked.

"That must be nearly everyone," said Duncan.

Aiden ran out of the tunnel and Colin grabbed his arm.

"Have you seen Holly?"

He looked even scruffier than normal and spoke in his thick Irish accent.

"No and there are Seekers in the building. Even lower level five. God knows how they got in."

Bernard pointed down the tunnel.

"There they are."

Holly and Miss Dickson were running along the Travel Tunnel, but the watery face of the exit disappeared and was replaced by a grille of iron bars. Their arms poked through the bars.

"Help us," yelled Holly.

But as soon as she spoke, their arms were pulled back. Shadows dragged them away and the wall of water replaced the bars. Odin's face filled the water and stared out into the Realm of the Dead.

"Death to the Keepers," said the face.

Bernard fired at it and Odin smiled, and went away. Colin ran to the Keeper Viewer and shouted at it

"Activate Keeper Viewer."

All the red dots in Europe and North America were heading south.

"Word's got around."

Hamish pointed his claymore at two dots that broke the pattern, heading from London to Oslo at a fantastic speed.

"Oh, no," said Bernard.

**

Odin stood before the rock carving of a longship, with Thor at the prow pointing his mighty hammer forward. All the evil creatures of the deep followed his ship; sharks, giant squid and sea creatures that no longer exist in our time. He held up the ruby to show Thor.

"It is mine again and, in your name brother, I shall take revenge."

He walked past the bank of television screens, none of them working, then to the lift and up to the roof of the O.A.S.V. building in Oslo. Thorgood and Olaf waited for him there and they both fell to their knees as the lift door opened. Odin looked up at the sky. It was another cold day in Norway and the sky was featureless and grey. He raised the stone above his head.

"Seal my lands."

A beam of unimaginable power shot up and the sky, from horizon to horizon, turned the colour of blood. In the hemisphere centered on Oslo, millions of people knelt to the god's new authority. Thorgood and Olaf stood and joined their master, and stared up at the red bubble that was the Red Empire's impenetrable shield. No one spoke, but Odin sensed his servants' delight and relief that the centuries of searching were finally over.

**

Aboard space station MIR, the port side of the Long Corridor was packed with crew, floating, holding on to metal handholds, or anything else they could grip, and peering out of the round windows. Commander Gregoriev pushed himself away from a window and twisted his body to face the crew's sleeping quarters. He bumped into a lady dressed in a green jumpsuit.

"Excuse me, Lesley. I need to talk with MIR Control. Please make sure someone takes pictures."

He floated away and entered his cabin feet first, and pulled a microphone from a socket on the wall.

"This is Commander Gregoriev. Come in MIR Control, Cape Canaveral."

There was a five-second delay.

"Good evening, Ivor. I was just about to call you. All hell has broken out down here."

"I am not surprised, Mike."

"What can you see?"

"A red force field centered on Northern Europe, covering nearly half the planet and edged by an orange band approximately one hundred kilometers wide."

"Can you repeat that."

Ivor repeated it.

"Anything else?"

"I am surprised."

"We are all *surprised*."

"It is not a perfect circle. The red hemisphere stretches out to cover the north-eastern seaboard of the USA. In Europe it does not stretch as far south as it would if it were a circle."

"Does it cover Corfu?"

"Yes."

"And the Orange Band?"

"It cuts through the Mediterranean sea. Some of it touches North Africa."

"OK. Please study the phenomenon and report back."

"OK, Mike, will do."

Lesley floated into his cabin.

"And how can I help the botany department?" asked the Commander.

She took a pebble from the top pocket of her jump suit and pushed it towards him. It floated over and he caught it between two fingers.

"It's happened, hasn't it."

"Yes. Shut the door."

Gregoriev pushed a button on the microphone and spoke again.

"Bernard. Please go to the Talk Tunnel."

They waited during the five-second delay and for another two minutes after that. Then Bernard's voice came to them in the cabin.

"Hello, Ivor. Hello Lesley. You have seen the red hemisphere too. Is it as we expected?"

"Exactly the same," said the Commander.

"And it stretches out to give Odin a toehold in the United States?"

"It does."

"I'm glad you called. We must get the Stone Tracking Device working. How long?"

Lesley answered.

"Two to three days."

"That's good. Now, I have received a warning from Thorgood. He told me to look out for the *birds in the sky*. It might not be you that he has in mind, but it did cross my mind that he might try and destroy the space station."

Commander Gregoriev nodded.

"We shall be vigilant."

***

With Thorgood and Olaf on either side of him, Odin walked to the edge of the roof to meet his people. Packed into the car parks and gardens of the office complex, fifty thousand Seekers fell to their knees.

"Stand," commanded Odin.

He showed them the stone and they cheered.

"Every one of you has a new name. You are now Keepers."

The cheer was deafening this time; even Odin gave a small smile.

"And now I gift you something. You are all part of the new ruling elite. I have ultimate power, but you have controlling power. Follow my rules and together we shall conquer the world."

Olaf and Thorgood stood like statues, waiting for their master to issue the rules of the Red Empire. Odin pointed the stone at the red sky and white letters appeared, curving from one horizon to another.

Obey me without question.

Crush all resistance.

Supply men and arms for the war in the Orange Band.

Send tribute to me in Oslo.

As the crowd read the rules, Odin spoke again.

"We fight the war on two fronts. South through our lands in the north-east of the United States and Canada. South from Europe into Africa. The stone of power aids us and we shall be victorious."

The crowd began to chant his name and he silenced them by raising a hand.

"Thorgood of the line of Firebrand and Olaf Adanson are my generals. They will speak to you in the coming weeks and allocate you lands to govern in my name. Olaf will conquer the Americas. Thorgood will conquer Africa and the Middle East. You will report directly to them, or to people they nominate. I shall personally command our *Black Slugs* and rule the seas." Odin pointed at the letters in the red sky. "Obey the rules of the Red Empire. Obey me without question."

The crowd fell to their knees again and spoke like a congregation saying a prayer.

"We obey you without question. We obey you without question."

Odin pointed up at the second rule.

"Crush all resistance."

His people chanted his words.

"Crush all resistance. Crush all resistance."

Odin spoke the other rules and everyone repeated them. When they had finished, Odin left the roof and heard his name chanted continuously by his people. As he descended in the lift to his inner sanctuary, he spoke to Thorgood and Olaf.

"Kill anyone who does not obey my rules. Feed them to the birds and the fish."

"I obey, master," they said together.

"Thorgood, tell Van Heussen to cancel the human cloning experiment. It has no value now. Put every effort into the creature breeding programme."

"I obey, master."

Odin stepped out of the lift and turned to face his generals who remained inside. He smiled.

"Well done. You have each earned the right to rule half of my empire."

As the lift doors began to close, he added something else.

"And do not forget that the rules apply to you too."

***

In the underground chamber beneath the tower, on the island in the Realm of the Dead, Chalky's outstretched and twitching fingers became still. The stone he had reached out to for over fifty years was now gone. A pool of cold water grew around him on the floor, fed by a constant drip, drip, drip as the ice encasing his body melted away.

Later, Gora entered the chamber and saw Chalky's limp body on the flagstones, his Eighth Army uniform wet through, but otherwise exactly as it had been when Duncan spared his life.

"It does not matter what he does now. Odin has the stone," thought Gora.

Gora gently picked up the body and, with a strength not suggested by his thin arms and legs, he bounded up the stairs, skin changing to feathers and chest expanding as the spiral stairs widened. He exploded from the roof with Chalky gripped in his talons and saw the crowd of people near the Travel Tunnel, and flew over to join them, giant wings flapping with great power, shrieking out to Myroy. A small crowd stood in front of the renamed Seeker Viewer, watching the red dots flee from Europe and the north-east of America.

"It's slower than we planned, but most of our people are making it through the Orange Band," said Colin.

"And the Super-Bases in Washington and Al-Jaghbub?" asked Bernard.

"Fully operational. All our warriors will gather there."

Dougie turned to see the people who had arrived through the Travel Tunnel, and saw them staring up in awe at Gora, who circled and landed by Myroy. The osprey gently placed Chalky on the grass and Myroy nodded at the limp body. Chalky's eyes opened and his body shivered.

"It's ... ruddy .... cold."

Duncan hugged him.

"Welcome back," said Bernard, shaking his hand.

"Who the hell are you?" asked Chalky.

"It's me, Bernard."

"Blimey, you look old."

Bernard smiled.

"Thanks a lot."

"'Ere, I 'ad the funniest dream. I was in the Bank of England and there was this lovely gold bar, but it was just too far away for me to reach. Tried to get at it for ages."

"You certainly did," said Duncan. "Sixty-four years. You have been asleep for sixty-four years."

Chalky raised his eyebrows.

"No."

"Aye.

"I've been asleep for sixty-four years?"

"Aye."

"No, I don't believe it."

"It is true. You are standing in a different world," said Bernard.

"Blimey."

"Anyway, that doesn't matter now. You are back and safe. In this time, Odin holds the stone and the planet is dividing into two; the Red Empire and the free world. The Second World War is long over, but a new war begins."

"Blimey."

"Blimey is right. You had better get some warm clothes on and get ready to fight again."

"By the way, who won the war we fought?"

Duncan thought about SS.

"No one," he said.

Sandy and Lofty made it up the slope at last, slowed by the stiffness of their old bodies.

"I don't believe it," said Lofty. "It's Chalky."

Sandy smiled.

"Good to have you back, Private Chalk."

"Who the hell are you?"

"Your old friends, Sandy and Lofty."

Chalky began to recognise them.

"Well, I'll be. What 'appened to you two?"

Sandy took a plastic card from his wallet and waved it at Chalky.

"Got my free bus pass. Everyone gets old in the end."

Chalky glanced at Duncan. He looked older than when he had last seen him, but nothing like as old as the others.

"Except the ruddy Keepers."

"I am a Seeker now. We are all Seekers."

Myroy interrupted the reunion.

"Peter and Kylie, come to me."

***

Everyone, except Peter and Kylie, had fled the Great Hall to help the evacuees and they now sat together at the High Table holding hands.

"You OK?" asked Kylie.

"No."

"It wasn't your fault."

"My ancestors kept the stone safe for generations and I lost it."

"Any one of them could have lost it."

Peter became angry and snapped at her.

"Yeah, but they didn't, I did."

As he spoke, the walls and ceiling of the hall went black.

"Peter, what is happening?"

The blackness closed in on them, the long tables fading away, the chairs on which they sat fading away. They felt cold, but appeared in bright sunshine, still in a sitting position before falling backwards onto the grass. Tirani skipped over.

"Peter, you are now the last Seeker. Have you got a plan?"

"A plan?"

Everyone around the cairn, three standing stones and Travel Tunnel looked at him.

"Yes, a plan."

Peter shrank inside and there was a long silence, broken only by a gentle breeze and the far off bleating of sheep.

"Er, I need time to think," stammered Peter.

Next to the Younger, Dougie of Dunfermline nervously raised a hand.

"Please speak," said Myroy.

"Um, I think we should steal the stone back, but not yet. Odin will be very protective of his new powers and only time will make him drop his guard."

Myroy nodded.

"Let him enjoy the authority and riches he craves for. We steal the stone in ten years, on this day, on the anniversary of the *Taking*."

"Why ten years?" asked Donald. "I'm not waiting ten years for a fight with the enemy."

"There will be plenty of fighting to do. Peter will be a man then, trained and strong."

Tirani pointed at all the people who sat listening to them on the hillside.

"We are waiting, Peter. What is your plan?"

Peter thought back through every scene of the story.

"I haven't heard it all. I still don't know about the civil war that is coming, or if Seamus rescues Margaret from Borak One Hand. But I will tell you what I have learned and what I think it means for us."

Kylie slipped her hand into his and whispered.

"Go on."

"In the story about the *mountain*, Carn Liath, Dougie and the men of Tain fought the Black Kilts in the homeland of the Picts. The key to victory was something Myroy said. *A fox never has one way of escape*. They found another way into the Dark Fortress."

Peter looked at his brother.

"James, work with Tirani. Find a secret way into Odin's chamber. An adult couldn't do that, two children may have a chance."

"You nuts?"

"No. Find it and come back to me with that knowledge."

Peter glanced at Myroy for some sign of approval. A small nod gave him the confidence he needed to continue with his plan.

"In the story named *island*, Thorgood captured Orkney and lands along the northern coastline of Scotland. He did this by assembling the greatest fleet that had ever been seen. Alistair and Dougie were rescued by Kenneth of Blacklock off the Outer Islands. I want every available warship placed under your command, Kenneth."

Kenneth gave a small nod as Myroy had done.

"Stop the *Black Slugs* sailing through the Orange Band. Make our oceans safe for trade in the free world."

"Aye."

"In *castle*, Alistair was rescued by Dougie from the bowels of Berwick castle. I learned that together we are stronger. To win, our forces must work together. Malcolm, I would like you to lead our forces in the Americas. Grandpa, lead the defence of Africa, and both of you, work as one army. We *will* lose if we are divided."

"We shall work as one," said the Younger.

Kylie squeezed his hand.

"Go on."

"In the battle of the light iron, on the island of Man, I saw in my mind how the slaves of the foundry rose up against Tella the Mac Mar. Armed by Dougie and the men of Tain, they fought for freedom with a ferocity never seen before, or since. I would like Holly Anderson to accept a mission."

Bernard sadly shook his head.

"Miss Dickson and Holly didn't make it back."

There was silence as this news sank in to Peter's heart. He took a deep breath and summoned up the courage to continue.

"OK. Kylie and I need to work out a way to free the people Odin oppresses. One day, they will be our greatest allies."

"And how are you going to do that?" asked Tirani.

Peter smiled at the boy.

"I have no idea. But we must do it."

"Continue," said Myroy.

"In north Africa during the Second World War, a small and fast force of brave warriors destroyed an oil base at an oasis, Al-Jaghbub. Without fuel, the enemy tanks were useless and a major victory was won by the Eighth Army. Hamish and Donald."

Hamish growled and Donald nudged him in the ribs.

"I wager I kill more than you."

More growling and Peter carried on.

"Create a small army capable of lightning raids deep into enemy territory. Move in secret and destroy any fuel you find."

"What shall we call it?" asked Hamish.

"Raiders of the Orange Band," suggested Kylie.

"Ooh, I like that," said Donald, "Hear that, Hamish? We are going to be *raiders*."

"You are going to be dead if you don't shut up."

Peter cut in on their brewing argument.

"After Al-Jaghbub, a raid on an airbase on Corfu went horribly wrong." Peter's voice became sad as he thought about the sacrifice made by Aris Agnedes. "Lives were lost and, worse than that, a life was changed forever. The raid failed because of bad intelligence. To beat Odin we need two things and, Bernard, I want you take responsibility for both."

Bernard thought about the Keeper networks he had set up after the war.

"We need a network of spies inside the Red Empire and we need to make the Stone Tracking Device work," he said.

"Yes," said Peter."I also learned from a scribe named Denbara. Maps have a power. Bernard, please work with Tirani, our cuckoo in the nest, to give us a detailed plan of Odin's chambers and the O.A.S.V. offices in Oslo."

Peter stared at Bernard.

"We have detailed satellite photos of the terrain in the Orange Band?"

"We do."

Peter tried to think of anything else he would want from Bernard, but couldn't.

"When Scotland was on its knees and under the threat of invasion by Tella's dark alliance, Dougie and Alistair were sent to the court of Patrick Three eggs at Mountjoy. Through luck and courage, they brought the Irish into the war and the tide turned against the Picts. A moment came."

Peter turned to look at the first Keeper, and Dougie's heart sank as he guessed something bad was coming.

"Do it again. Go to Beijing and win the help of the Chinese government in the coming war. If you cannot win them as allies, then stop them siding with Odin. We cannot fight Odin and the Chinese army at the same time."

Peter smiled at his mother and father.

"Weapons made from the new light iron tipped the balance of power. Will you control armaments production for us and work with Arkinew? I know he cannot see the future clearly, but sometimes you need someone a little, er, eccentric, if you are going to make a difference."

Gangly whispered something in Archie's ear.

"I'm not potty," said the alchemist.

"Arkinew will be in charge of all weapons research. Mum and Dad, work with him and may good fortune be with both of you."

"We will," they promised.

"Grumf," said Gangly.

Arkinew walked backwards towards an oval with a watery face.

"Activate Stone Locator."

Nothing happened.

"I'm not potty," he said to himself.

Myroy shook his head.

"Carry on Peter."

"During the battle of Stirling Castle, I learned that a fortress can become a prison. Two hundred spearmen from the Outer Islands trapped a much larger force and made Cuthbert's army useless."

Peter stared around the hillside at the people who had fled from Odin's tyranny. He didn't know any of them and wondered if they had heard the story. But Myroy had armed every one of them.

"If you do not know the story, then hear it you must. It isn't just the history of how we protected the stone for thousands of years. It is our plan of action. If Odin builds fortresses along the Orange Band, then we know how to deal with them when the time is right."

Laura put her hands on her hips.

"And what do I do? James got something, so why don't I get bloomin' something?"

Peter smiled.

"I was just coming to you. Work with Darren."

Laura beamed at him.

"Good start."

"I want you to launch a radio station operating on long wave. When I was tested as a Keeper during the Battle of Pinner High School, nothing except long wave worked. Not television, medium wave or FM, nothing. Laura, find out the frequency Odin will use to speak to his people."

"And what do I do?"

"Play your music, really loud. Snow Patrol and the Killers should do it."

Laura still had her hands on her hips.

"Why?"

"Because, sister, it annoys the hell out of me. Just think how it will annoy Odin when his authority is completely undermined by you. He needs to appear invincible to his people and his empire will be built on that. You could make the Red Empire tumble down like a pack of cards."

"Do I get paid?"

"No."

Peter saw Chalky.

"When our moment comes, I will need the best stone stealers in history at my side. Chalky, Dougie and Alistair, be ready for that day."

The last Seeker faced Myroy, the old man who had taught him everything he knew about the stone.

"I do not know what I need from you."

"Yes you do."

Peter searched his mind and a terrible thought struck him like a freight train.

"Find out how to destroy the Ancient Ones and the old magic."

Suddenly Peter felt drained, as though a part of him had been taken away as the plan flowed from his mind. Being strong was hard. His legs buckled and Kylie put an arm around Peter, and steadied him.

"Well done," she said.

Tirani turned to Myroy.

"He's got it, hasn't he."

The Ancient One nodded, and stared at the wrinkles and veins on the back of his hands.

"The line of Donald never fails to surprise me."

Then Myroy turned to face the hundreds of people who sat on the slopes, listening to Peter's plan.

"Gather your weapons and prepare for war."

CHAPTER TEN

THE ATTACK SIMULATOR

As a weak dawn sun rose in the Realm of the Dead, Peter and Kylie climbed into the rowing boat and pushed away from the quay.

"Do you feel any different?" asked Kylie.

"What do you mean?"

"Yesterday you were the last Keeper and today you aren't. Odin holds the stone and I wondered if you felt, well, weaker."

"No, not really. Maybe that's because we're here. It's a magical place. Do you feel safe too?"

"Oh yes, and did you see that Odin couldn't use the stone when he appeared in the Great Hall. Has Myroy explained why? With all the power in Amera's stone, he couldn't use any of it, not even as a weapon. Did you see his face when he looked at Donald? He would have loved to kill him there and then."

"No, he hasn't explained that. But I think it's something to do with the Twelve. All of them have kept the stone, and Gora too, of course. Between them they have looked after it for thousands of years. Do you think the ruby actually *feels* something towards them?"

Kylie smiled.

"Wouldn't surprise me, after all it is nice and warm when you hold it."

"Oh yes, thanks for reminding me."

"Hey, Peter, don't feel bad. Why didn't they warn you before Cleopatra's Needle that you had to keep the pipe safe? All they had to do was put a warning in *Early Celtic Writings and their Meanings*. I think Myroy thought it was time to give up the stone. His brother was always going to take it at some time."

"I don't think so. Myroy was worried as hell in the Great Hall when Tirani told him I'd left the pipe in my rucksack."

"It wasn't your fault."

Peter pulled hard on his oar and their boat lurched.

"But why, why, why, did it have to be me?"

Kylie pulled harder to keep them in a straight line.

"I think Myroy has made up his mind. I think he has chosen you to fight the final battle."

"Oh, that's great. I'm just not ready. Not ready at all."

Kylie smiled again.

"But you've got ten years. Let's go and get trained. By the way, that speech you made was really cool."

"Hm. I've been thinking about that. I have no idea where all that stuff came from."

"It came from the story."

A deafening shriek made them jump when they tied up the boat to the wooden quay below the stone walls of the tower.

"Haaaaaaaa."

They quickly took their pebbles in hand and rose up to curve over the lip at the top. Gora had already transformed himself into human form and sat, legs dangling down from the oak trunk held in the beaks of the stone osprey bookends. He called down.

"This is your first lesson. Work together. You are here for a single purpose. Kill Odin. I will be watching how you get on."

Wooden doors appeared in the talons of the stone ospreys. The door to their left had a single word carved into it.

In

The door to their right had another word.

Out

Suddenly Peter felt nervous.

"But what do we do?"

Gora gave a shrieking, bird-like laugh.

"Haaa. Go in, come out and I hope you do better than your grandfather."

Kylie took Peter's hand and walked with him to the door.

"Does this thing have a name?"

"Haaaaa. Attack Simulator."

"We're not going to like this, are we?" whispered Peter.

Gora shouted down from the oak perch.

"It is not for you to like or dislike. Now go in and kill Odin."

211

Kylie entered first, still holding Peter's hand, into the base of the stone osprey. A red light came on as the door clicked shut behind them. They had stepped inside a metal cylinder and were like ants at the bottom of a tin can. A rectangular slot had been cut out of the can where the door was.

A recording of Miss Dickson's voice spoke to them.

"Please select the level of difficulty. Easy, medium or difficult."

"Easy," they said together.

"The easy level is selected. Enjoy the simulation."

They felt the cylinder revolve and make a noise like a worn out conveyor belt. Behind them, the rectangular cut-out moved sideways across the door, which seemed to get thinner and thinner, and was finally replaced by rock. The cut-out continued on its circular journey and a new door began to appear. A lighted sign began to flash above it.

Easy – Easy – Easy

They left the cylinder and hid behind moss-covered rocks, the noise of traffic not far away and the air much cooler here than in the Realm of the Dead. Peter's Berghaus rucksack lay on the ground.

"Where are we?" asked Kylie.

"If this is about killing Odin, my guess would be Oslo."

Kylie slowly moved her head to look around the side of a rock.

"Come and see this."

Peter stopped looking into his rucksack and joined her, and they stared across a busy dual carriageway with the cars driving on the right. There were a lot of Saabs and Volvos. A long approach road led off the dual carriageway and beside a section of fence, with no visible gate, was a sign.

Main Entrance
O.A.S.V. Headquarters Oslo
No Visitors Without An Appointment
All Vehicles To Stop Between The Yellow Lines

They looked at two yellow lines and at a double wire fence

surrounding the entire O.A.S.V. complex. Big dogs ran around in the gap between the fences, but stayed well away from the outer fence.

"Think the outer fence is electrified?" asked Kylie.

"Yep."

"And this is the *easy* simulation"

"Yep."

"Stop it. What's in the bag?"

"Amera's stone, Tirani's calling pipe and some sandwiches."

"That's good. We can use the stone to get in."

A lorry pulled off the main road and stopped between the yellow lines in front of the fence. A television camera on a tall pole rose up from the ground and swivelled around as someone checked the number plate and face of the driver. A section of fence sank into the ground and the camera did the same. Peter read the label and handed Kylie a sandwich pack.

"Cheese and pickle."

"Shall we follow the lorry in?" asked Kylie.

"No. Let's see what else happens."

The lorry drove away along the approach road and the section of fence rose up again. Nothing else happened for a long time and they were beginning to get hungry again when a long black limousine braked between the yellow lines. The same thing; the camera up and the fence down again.

"Now?"

Peter shook his head.

"What are you waiting for?" asked Kylie.

"Somewhere at the end of that approach road is a security guard who checks out the visitors. I'm waiting for a changing of the guard."

Peter took the brooch from his rucksack and gripped the ruby tightly.

"Please tell me when the new security guard comes on duty."

It pulsed once. An hour later an old Volvo stopped between the yellow lines and the stone pulsed again.

213

"OK that's it. Let's go."

They ran across the dual carriageway and, as the camera sank into the ground, the car moved forward and Kylie and Peter jumped into the back seats. The driver slammed the brakes on. He was dressed in a smart dark uniform and he put his hand into his breast pocket. Peter gripped the stone.

"You do not need a gun."

"I do not need a gun."

"You are happy."

The security guard smiled.

"You have done well," said Peter.

"I have done well."

"You have captured two defenceless children who your master seeks."

"You are my prisoners."

"Odin commands that you take us straight to him."

"We go to Odin immediately."

The car moved on again along the approach road and Peter sat back in his seat.

"Nicely done," said Kylie.

"Well, I don't know the way. I don't even know if the guard knows the way."

They rounded a sharp bend and the O.A.S.V. office block came into view. The sinking sun reflected in its rows and rows of windows. Kylie's jaw dropped.

"It's huge."

"Come on. Let's find out if the guard can get us in."

They walked towards the main entrance and Peter shouldered his rucksack, and spoke to the driver.

"We must be taken to Odin. It is the master's wish."

"Odin commands me."

At the reception desk, a beautiful lady with long blond hair smiled at them.

"Do you have an appointment?"

Peter gripped the stone.

"Yes we do."

"Yes you do. Who are you visiting?"

The security guard replied.

"It is the master's wish that these children are taken to him immediately."

"Odin's wish?"

"Odin's wish," repeated Peter.

"Please proceed."

They walked past a fountain and down a long corridor with hugely expensive paintings on both walls. Kylie stopped by one painting and read a name in a bottom corner.

Monet.

"You think they are real?"

Peter nodded.

"You could buy a small country with what they are worth."

At the far end of the corridor, a red light flashed on a camera above a lift door. Peter spoke to the stone in his mind.

"Please make us invisible to all who seek us."

They stepped into the lift and the guard ignored the buttons for the other floors and put a key into the panel. There was another button under the panel and he pushed it. Peter felt the lift go down and put the stone into his pocket, the guard silent and still beside him.

"Make this your last place of hiding," said Peter.

The stone pulsed and turned his pocket red.

"Expecting trouble?" asked Kylie.

"As soon as the lift doors open."

The lift slowed.

"Well, here we go."

Thorgood grabbed Peter and threw him on to the floor in front of Odin, his sword swinging down, the tip just breaking the skin between Peter's shoulder blades above his rucksack's straps. Olaf Adanson did the same to Kylie. The lift door shut on the security guard and cyanide gas filled the lift.

"Why are you here, Peter of the Line of Donald?" asked Odin.

Peter spoke with the side of his face pressed hard against the floor.

"I am here with a gift and a message from your brother."

Peter felt Odin's will enter his mind, searching around for the truth, and he fought back by picturing the stone and inventing a scene with Myroy giving him a message to take to Odin.

Odin sensed danger.

"What is the gift?"

"A ruby of great size and power."

"And the message?"

"You rule half of the world and allow the free peoples to govern their own lands."

Odin's blue eyes flashed.

"Where is the stone?"

"In my pocket."

The pressure from the sword eased off and Peter felt Thorgood go through his pockets. He took the stone and handed it to his master.

"I give it to you," said Peter.

The stone pulsed blood-red as Odin pointed it at Kylie. An intense death beam turned her body to dust. She didn't even have time to scream. Peter jumped up.

"Come back to me."

The stone returned to its last place of hiding and Peter tore it from his pocket.

"Protect me."

A red protective bubble surrounded him as Thorgood and Olaf's swords struck out. They bounced off, but Odin entered Peter's mind again.

"Give me the stone."

Peter stared at the pile of ash that had once been his girlfriend and anger entered his heart. He shot a death beam at Odin who raised his hand, reflecting the beam back, ripping through the bubble and making Peter's body explode.

Kylie woke in the giant tin can with a slot for the door. A red light showed that the whole cylinder was revolving, with rock slowly changing to a doorway. Peter stirred beside her.

"Oooh, my head hurts," he said.

"Mine too, try and get up."

They stood, shakily and watched the last line of rock disappear. A lighted sign above the door flashed.

Exit – Exit – Exit

Gora shouted at them as they stepped out of the wooden doors in the second stone osprey.

"No, no, no. How did Odin know you were there?"

Peter held his thumping head and felt sick.

"I don't know."

"How many of you stepped into the lift?"

"Er ... three."

"And how many did security see enter the lift?"

"Oh," said Kylie. "They would have only seen the guard. The stone saw to that."

"So how did they *know*?" asked Gora.

Kylie sat on the ground, still holding her head.

"The floor of the lift measures the weight of the people in it. They know the weight of the guard and realised something was wrong."

Gora smiled.

"Exactly. So why did you choose invisibility? They knew three people came to reception *because* of the camera in the waterfall, and they knew only one person got into the lift *because* of the other camera there. But they also knew there was extra weight in the lift that they could not account for."

"I didn't see a camera in the waterfall," said Peter.

"You know it now."

"How do we know all this?" asked Kylie.

"The Keepers' organisation did function whilst you were both at school. We got people in and out again. More often though, they didn't come back again, so the information we are using has come at a very high price."

217

"Do we go back into the Attack Simulator now?" asked Peter, secretly wishing he didn't have to.

"No. You will try the medium degree of difficulty tomorrow, at dawn. Peter, think about today's simulation and learn from it, and do not forget to practice the skills Myroy gave you; learning all you read and talking to your ancestors."

Gora walked away towards a wide circular staircase set in the top of the tower. As he descended down to the underground chamber, Peter turned to Kylie.

"Well, what did you learn?"

She gave him a big grin.

"I'm not that keen on cheese and pickle sandwiches."

CHAPTER ELEVEN

THE RISE OF THE RED EMPIRE

Rule 1 – Obey me without question.

Thorgood pointed a remote control at the bank of television screens. Once again, nothing happened.

"Master, no map."

Odin unfolded a map of Europe and laid it over the long meeting table, near to the carving of Thor's longship. He placed his stone in the centre.

"Show me the empire," he said.

Thorgood joined him and watched Norway, Sweden, Finland, parts of northern Russia, Poland, Germany, Holland, Belgium and Luxembourg turn red. Thorgood waited for news of the other countries under his master's control. France turned red, then Spain and Portugal. A minute later, Italy turned red too, which meant that any resistance there had been crushed. Thorgood heard a Valkyrie's voice in his mind.

"London has fallen."

He studied the map. The United Kingdom and Ireland remained green.

"Why are they not completely taken?" asked Odin.

"Pockets of resistance in outer areas. Cornwall, Wales, Scotland and Ireland. They all have more people who are not influenced by the stone."

"Forget the others. Drive Myroy's people, the Scots, towards the sea. They must obey me without question or join the fallen."

"I obey, master."

Thorgood watched his master and sensed his growing anger towards those who resisted his will. Odin took the ruby and spoke into it.

"All *Black Slugs* are to surround the eastern shores of Scotland. Sail immediately and await further instructions."

There was no reply, but all around the world, *Black Slugs* altered course.

On the map, Greece and all its islands, including Corfu, turned red. The east of Canada and the north- east of the United States turned red too, which meant that Olaf Adanson was making progress. Odin spoke to the stone.

"Show me the Orange Band."

It appeared on the map and Odin ran a finger along the band where it cut the Mediterranean in half, dividing Europe and Africa. He looked at Africa and the Middle East.

"Not yet," he thought.

Odin pointed the ruby at the longship carving. The entire rock face shimmered, red, and a picture of central London appeared, showing cars and buses, bumper to bumper around Marble Arch. The pavements were busy with shoppers, tourists and people in suits.

Odin spoke again, but in a slower, more commanding voice.

"People of the Red Empire, hear my voice."

In New York, Paris, Berlin, London and all the cities, towns and villages under the red sky, nearly all the people fell to their knees. Traffic came to a stop and there was silence.

"Obey my rules or join the fallen."

Thorgood watched the images of people on their knees in the streets of New York. But one or two remained standing, not influenced by the stone's power. These people stared around, confused, wondering what on earth was happening. The rock face changed and showed Trafalgar Square, the Champs Elysées and Saint Peter's Square, one after the other. The same thing in those cities.

Millions of people began to chant the god's name.

"Odin, Odin, Odin."

Thorgood listened to the chant echo around the eternal chamber as Odin willed his rules to appear in the red sky from horizon to horizon.

"Look up."

Everyone looked up, including those free of Odin's will.

"Obey me without question," said Odin.

Millions repeated the rule.

"We obey you without question."

"Kill all who do not kneel to my authority."

Thorgood watched the image of the scene in central Berlin. Thousands of people leapt up, punching and kicking to death anyone who had stood. Odin smiled.

"I am now your master. Obey me without question."

His followers chanted all four rules, reading the giant white letters in the sky. Odin released his grip on the ruby, his speech over, and Thorgood watched the crowd in Berlin. They were picking up the broken bodies of the fallen and tossing them aside as if they were pieces of litter.

Rule 2 – Crush all resistance.

Under a red sky, Thorgood's jeep pulled up to a toll booth on the Forth Road Bridge. A sign flashed –

£1 please

A tank drove through the booth, smashing it to pieces. Thorgood was dressed in the warrior clothes of the Valkyrie, his sword in a long sheath hanging down his back. He stood on the seat of his jeep and looked back towards Edinburgh. As far as the eye could see, the road on both carriageways was full of armoured cars, tanks and jeeps from all the British regiments who now obeyed him. Those who did not obey him, mainly refugees and some armed warriors, had been chased north through the Borders and out of Edinburgh. At the same time, another loyal army had driven the enemy from the west coast of Scotland towards Fife in the east. Thorgood took a map of Scotland from his pocket and drew two arrows on it that showed the progress made by both of his armies. He spoke to Odin in his mind.

"Master, the disloyal of Scotland are being driven east to the lands named Fife. All resistance will end there, upon the shores of the river Forth, close to the fishing villages of Crail, Pittenweem and Anstruther."

In his eternal chamber, Odin clutched his ruby.

"All *Black Slugs* are to enter the river Forth and await further orders."

Thorgood put the map away, sat, and pointed across the bridge. "Forward."

His driver started the engine and the jeep pulled away, the army following, moving quickly up the M90 motorway, before turning east to pass through Kinross, Glenrothes and Leven, and heading back towards the river Forth. So far, they had met little resistance and had easily overrun small numbers of the enemy who had not been able to join the string of cars, buses and lorries that ran before Thorgood. On the far side of Leven, an enemy tank, that had stayed behind to protect the retreat, fired on them and never missed. Thorgood's army filled the road and was an easy target. But it was only an irritation. Thorgood stood on his seat again and stared through binoculars at the tank. It hid behind a petrol station and he spoke into a long wave radio.

"Attack the enemy, one kilometre ahead of us."

Two Tornadoes with RAF markings screamed above his head and fired air-to-ground missiles. The tank and petrol station exploded, sending a black tower of acrid smoke high up into the atmosphere.

Now the good roads gave way to small country lanes and the advancing army slowed, becoming strung out over many miles. Thorgood ordered his tanks to fan out and they moved easily across farmland, smashing through hedges and fences. In half an hour, Thorgood's jeep was flanked by over three hundred tanks, on the outskirts of the fishing village of Anstruther.

Coaches, lorries, buses and abandoned cars littered the approach road and some of the buses had been parked across it to form a series of barricades. Thorgood looked through his binoculars. Thirty to forty soldiers waited for him there, their rifles sticking out of windows or poking around the sides of houses. If that was their measure then the village would fall quickly. His radio hissed.

"This is Tornado Leader. The enemy are boarding fishing boats and some already sail from Anstruther harbour. Do you want us to attack?"

"No. Return to Leuchars air base."

"We obey."

The Tornadoes circled and headed north-east, leaving white vapour trails across the red sky. Thorgood used the radio to speak to his tank commanders.

"Fire at the barricades, then drive through. Do not destroy any ships."

The turrets rotated as they picked out their targets and the tanks rocked violently backwards as round after round was fired at the enemy. Buses flew into the air. Shops and houses shattered and became rubble. Without a single shot being fired, the enemy soldiers, who survived the barrage, ran down towards the harbour. Thorgood waved at a tank.

"Forward."

His driver slammed the jeep into gear and they followed the tank, which bulldozed its way forward, and they drove between burning houses, and rose up and down over piles of brick and rubble. The other tanks followed and lined up all the way along the harbour road, their guns pointing at colourful fishing boats, which were packed with people. None of the guns fired. Thorgood counted the ships on the wide river.

"Over two hundred."

One last fishing boat was motoring through the harbour exit, its decks covered with men, women and children clutching suitcases of all sizes. They looked terrified.

Thorgood watched the grey, rippling waters, cut by the wakes from the vessels and spoke in his mind.

"Master, the enemy are driven into the river."

A Sergeant in full battle-dress ran up to him, machine gun in hand.

"Thorgood, enemy soldiers are escaping into countryside on the east of the village."

Thorgood nodded.

"Lead the army. Take this jeep. Find them all and kill them."

"I obey."

The tanks followed the Sergeant's jeep and Thorgood walked over to a metal rail, which ran all around the top of the harbour wall. He sat motionless on the rail with his sword across his knees, listening to the fading sound of tank engines and staring across the river towards a line of low hills framed by a red sky. The colourful fleet seemed to gather together and Thorgood guessed that instructions were being shouted from boat to boat. Then all ships headed east, hoping to make the open sea. Behind them, thirty *Black Slugs* rose up from the riverbed, forming an impenetrable line across the Forth. Thorgood looked towards the sea. Hundreds of the menacing submarines were surfacing and trapping the enemy. Missiles automatically rose on tripods, from panels in the hull of each *Slug*, and locked onto their targets.

Thorgood thought about his journey from London to Berwick, then through Scotland. None of his men had told jokes, or disobeyed a single order. All of them were utterly fearless and had shown no emotion, except loyalty to him. His forehead creased. After three days he had been forced to stop the journey and order his worn out army to eat and sleep. Despite the centuries of planning, this had surprised and worried him. As a commander, he got exactly what he asked for and nothing else. No initiative, no will, or ability to change course if he was not there to give the order. He decided to talk to Olaf Adanson and Mick Roberts about it.

A picture came into Thorgood's mind. The men, women and children clutching their meagre belongings, and crammed together on the decks of fishing boats. He hoped they were still unaware of the trap Odin had made for them. Being unaware meant they would not suffer fear or panic, and death would claim them quickly. Then he regretted these thoughts and, as the first missile was launched, he pointed his sword at the sky.

"Crush all resistance," he said.

Rule 3 – Supply men and arms for the war in the Orange Band.

Thorgood stepped out of a lift and smiled at Mick Roberts.

"Good to have you back. How is the wound?"

"I can walk, but I can't run yet. It's getting there."

"And how is the operation going?"

"It is on a *huge* scale. Everyday, one hundred thousand men arrive in London from all over the country." Mick pointed out of the new observation tower, two hundred metres above the entrance to the Channel Tunnel. "They arrive here by train and we issue them with uniforms and weapons, and send them through the tunnel. In less than sixteen hours, they are ready for basic training at our main base in Marseilles."

Thorgood walked along the curved observation window, staring down on a sea of tents of all shapes and colours. A long train with twenty carriages pulled slowly into a siding. A siren sounded and men in civilian clothes left the train on one side. Soldiers left the tents, like ants, and boarded from the other side. The train pulled away and entered the tunnel.

"It's a twenty four hour operation and pretty hectic, but we are overcoming most of the problems."

"Problems?"

"Oh, last week we didn't have enough ammunition. The week before we received no Computer Aided Rifles and we ran out of boots."

"What action did you take?"

"Carried on as normal and issued the men with what we had. I've ordered more of the equipment we were missing and I'll ship it down to Marseilles when it arrives. How are things across Europe?"

"The same. The biggest army the world has ever seen is gathering in the south of France. Our factories struggle to keep pace and there are shortages, but overall progress is satisfactory."

"One of the drivers told me that the factory workers are coping with one meal and only four hours' break a day. You are pushing them hard."

"Maybe too hard, but we can reduce production when the army is at full strength."

"And the problem then will be ships."

"Yes."

"How many do you need?"

"Enough to carry forty million men across the Mediterranean."

"That's vast."

"It is."

"Will they fight for us in the Orange Band?"

"I think so. The stone's power will be less there, but I am sure the master's control will hold."

"And beyond the Orange Band?"

Thorgood shrugged his shoulders.

"Wait and see."

Thorgood compared the lack of initiative shown by his warriors with the clear thinking of Mick Roberts. He pointed down at the tents.

"What do you think of the men?"

"That is a good question. They are fantastic at taking orders and bloody hopeless at giving them. If I don't tell them what to do they don't do anything, just sit around, waiting for the next instruction. Frightens me a bit."

"Why?"

"Just not used to it, that's all. Trying to get the entire population of a country to do the same thing has always been impossible. People have different beliefs and want, no, need to be different. It's not like that now."

"No."

Mick Roberts stared at another train that slowed beside the siding. The siren went again.

"So, you will soon have forty million warriors, fully armed and under your complete control. How does that feel?"

Thorgood let out a long breath.

"Terrifying."

Rule 4 – Send tribute to me in Oslo.

Thorgood stood beside Odin in the Rijksmuseum in Amsterdam, looking up at a huge painting. A sign beside it said –

The Night Watch
Rembrandt 1642
Oil on canvas

"Please report," said Odin.

Thorgood updated him on progress; the complete destruction of resistance across Europe, the holding camp by the Channel Tunnel and arms production figures.

"Send more workers and machines to the CAR factories."

"I obey, master."

"Kill any worker who does not do my bidding."

"I obey, master."

"What troubles you?"

Thorgood told him about the lack of initiative shown by his men.

"I can think of more important things for you to worry about."

"Yes, master."

At the far end of the gallery, two men with blond hair lifted an oil painting off its hooks on the wall and gently lowered it onto a laid-out white cloth. They wrapped it neatly, protecting it, and placed it on its side on a trolley with other paintings, and wheeled them away. In another gallery, a vase smashed, shattering the peace of the Rijksmuseum. Odin's eyes flashed and a lady in brown overalls flew through the air, flashing past boxed statues and laden trolleys. She landed at speed and slid across the polished floor, spinning around on her back. She looked up at Odin, her wide eyes full of terror.

"What is your name?"

She replied in a shaky voice.

"Maria van Lyndon."

"And what was broken?"

"A Chinese vase. Fifth century BC. There isn't another one like it anywhere in the world."

"Can it be repaired?"

"Yes, but it will never be the same again."

Odin sensed her passion for art and complete loyalty and honesty. He also sensed the deep agonizing fear she felt in his presence. He liked that.

"Maria van Lyndon, go back to work and be more careful."

"I obey, master."

She ran out of the gallery and Thorgood stared at his master. In all the centuries of service to him, he had never, ever, seen anyone spared when they had failed in their duties. He wondered if possession of the stone was having some kind of influence, taking the edge off his utter ruthlessness. Odin heard his thoughts.

"Thorgood of the line of Firebrand, what have I always desired?"

"The stone. Power over others. Absolute loyalty secured by fear."

"I have the stone and that girl is loyal. Why should I send her to join the fallen?"

"As an example to others."

"But my followers need no example now. They do my bidding. Their loyalty is secured by the stone."

"Yes, master."

Odin stared up at the painting.

"Update me on the tribute for Oslo."

"Our people are in all the major art galleries around Europe. Olaf Adanson is personally supervising the galleries in New York. Here, Munich, Berlin, Paris, Rome and London have the biggest prizes. Berlin alone has delivered enough works of art to fill four Boeing 747s. They took off an hour ago for Oslo."

"Total number of pieces?"

"At least twenty thousand, mainly paintings, but some of the Egyptian stone and pottery work is exceptional."

"Total value?"

Thorgood shrugged his shoulders.

"Master, I do not know, Priceless. No one in history, or in the future, will ever own such a vast collection."

Odin smiled.

"And the new gallery?"

"It is complete and may need to be extended. There is one technical problem. The paintings are from various periods of time and the artists used different paints and pigments. Each will require individual care, and different temperature and humidity settings, to preserve them. Doctor Van Heussen is working on this problem."

"And the cloned creatures?"

"You have half a million birds and four hundred thousand fish at your command. Their speed of breeding has increased dramatically since introducing live food."

Odin clutched the stone and the Night Watch rose up and off its hooks, and hovered before them.

"This is a very clever painting, it tells many stories."

"Yes, master."

"Give it pride of place in the new gallery."

"I obey, master."

"And the girl, Maria van Lyndon. Put her in charge of the collection."

"Yes, master."

"How big will the new gallery need to be?"

"We still need to collect the art in the possession of private individuals. When the rest of the world falls to your authority, there will be more works of art to store, or display. The gallery may need to be twice as big as we originally planned."

Odin smiled again and walked with Thorgood out of the main entrance to the Rijksmuseum, the huge painting by Rembrandt floating along behind them

CHAPTER TWELVE

A MEDIUM DEGREE OF DIFFICULTY

Gora's shriek shattered the peace at dawn in the Realm of the Dead, and sent a shiver of fear down Peter's spine.

"Haaaa."

Kylie gripped her pebble and began to rise up the outer face of the tower.

"Alright, Gora, we're coming."

She glanced down at Peter who was tying their rowing boat to the small quay.

"Come on."

He rose quickly and caught up.

"Peter, I'm scared this time."

"Why?"

"Well, I know it's not real, but the simulator seems real and this is it, isn't it? This is what you have to do as the last Keeper. Sorry, I mean last Seeker. You have to kill Odin and take back the stone. Gora's getting you ready for the final battle."

"Yep."

"Well?"

"Well what?"

"Don't you feel scared?"

Peter did feel scared, but tried not to show it.

"It's an *attack simulator*, not the real thing. We should be safe enough during the training."

"You are scared."

"Let's just do our best. By the way, I am really glad you're with me. I'd hate to do all this on my own and on such a special day too."

"A special day?"

Another of Gora's shrieks ended their conversation and they dropped down onto the flagstones on the top of the tower. They looked up at huge talons wrapped around the oak trunk between the tall stone ospreys. Gora lowered his head and stared at them with dark penetrating eyes.

"Haaa. What did you learn?"

Peter felt tiny in the shadow of the osprey and shrank even more at his words. He hadn't thought about the easy simulation at all and hadn't even talked to his grandfather about it. His reply was like a young child apologising for being late for school.

"I'm sorry, I didn't think about it at all last night."

Gora's beak opened inches away from his face and Gora shrieked, throwing Peter back holding his ears in agony and the sound exploding around his head.

"I'm sorry, I'm sorry."

Gora jumped down, wings full out and flapping once, the rush of wind blowing Kylie down too. The osprey's huge talons landed on either side of Peter's shaking body.

"Haaa. You know where to go."

"Yes."

"Then go."

Gora took off from the tower, circled the island and landed close to the village on the other side of the loch. Peter felt a warm hand take his and pull him up.

"He can make his point, can't he?"

Peter's knees trembled.

"He's right though. He told us the information about Odin's headquarters came at a high price. That means some of our people died getting it and they did it all to give me a chance to fight on equal terms. I feel ashamed."

Kylie put an arm around him.

"Let's go in. Keep your wits about you."

They walked over to the door, in the talons of the stone osprey, with the word, "In," carved into it. Inside, the red light came on and lit the giant tin can, which began to turn as soon as the door clicked behind them. They watched the door-slot revolve across rock and Miss Dickson's recorded voice spoke to them.

"Please select the level of difficulty, easy, medium or difficult."

"Medium," said Peter.

"Medium is selected. You will not enjoy this simulation. Good luck."

Tirani's voice followed.

"Please note that the contents of the Attack Simulator have recently been updated by a cuckoo in the nest."

The cut-out in the metal cylinder revolved slowly past the door with *Easy* above it and finally stopped at another door. A lighted sign flashed above this door –

Medium – Medium – Medium

They stepped out into darkness. No moon showed through the canopy of pine trees high above their heads, and everything was silent except for a cold, gentle wind rustling the leaves and moving the top branches. Peter bent down and lifted his Berghaus rucksack, and felt around inside. His fingers found Amera's stone.

"Stone, please light up the inside of my bag."

A dim red light showed sandwiches, a flask with "tea" written on the side, and a folded white linen cloth. They sat with their backs to a fallen pine, about twenty metres away from a double fence, and used the stone's glow to read a ground-plan of the O.A.S.V. office complex drawn onto the cloth. It showed the five upper floors, the reception area with its fountain, and the long corridor which led to the lift. But the lower levels lacked the detail of the offices above them and big areas were shaded, with red words printed across them.

Unknown Area

"And we have to find out what's in those areas," said Kylie.

Peter turned the cloth over.

"Look at this."

The back was a more detailed map of the entire O.A.S.V. site. Kylie studied the detail.

"We know more about the outside than the inside."

"That doesn't surprise me. Want a sandwich?"

"Is it cheese and pickle?"

"Yes."

"I'll just have some tea, thanks. By the way, what did you mean by a *special day*?"

Peter's forehead creased and he lied.

"Being in the Realm of the Dead. It's a special place."

They studied the new map. The double perimeter fence had TV cameras marked on it every one hundred metres and words ran along the fence.

Electric Outer Fence. Danger of Death.

The long approach road ran past a security post and then curved towards the main entrance of the office block. The fence formed a continuous rectangle around the site, but was a different colour where the complex met the sea.

"I didn't know Odin's base backs onto the sea," whispered Kylie.

"Makes sense though. He draws upon the power of the sea and travels through water. I bet he feels safer with it close by."

"Why does the fence change colour by the cliffs?"

Peter put his finger by a legend of symbols at the bottom of the cloth.

"It's still there, but underwater, with sensors to detect swimmers. Hmm, even got mines to take out boats."

Kylie poured herself some more tea.

"Nice."

"Shall we try that?"

"Enter the base by water?"

"Yep. I think we should, but it doesn't take away the big problem."

"What's that?"

"In the first simulation, I used the trick that Malcolm and Murdoch discovered when they were children. I *gave* Odin the stone and made it return to its last place of hiding. As soon as he used it, the ruby came to me and I shot a death beam at him using all the anger I had inside me. It wasn't enough. He just put his hand up and deflected it back at me, so even if we get in, I'm not sure if we can kill Odin."

"Don't say that. There must be a way. Ooh, I don't like the look of that, there by the cliffs at the back of the base."

A wide tunnel ran from the sea and opened out into a massive underground chamber, before becoming narrower and running beneath the O A S V building. The underground chamber had two ominous words printed on it –

Slug Base

Two more tunnels ran off the chamber. One coming out on to the surface next to the office complex and the other leading to an even bigger cave that was drawn with a dotted line around its boundary. More printed words –

Chamber Under Construction

It was at least twice the size of the *Slug* Base.

Kylie screwed the cup onto the top of the flask and dropped it back into the rucksack.

"And why is this *medium*? What makes this simulation more difficult than the last one?"

"I think Odin knows we are coming."

"Then it doesn't matter if you use the stone or not. I know he can't sense it when you use it a little bit, like making a guard let you through a door, but we might try something more, um, powerful. If he knows we're here anyway."

"Like a direct attack. Dougie is the only one to have ever done that."

Kylie shuddered as she remembered the story.

"That was horrible. He killed everyone in Stirling Castle. Burned them alive with lava."

"Anger drove him."

"Maybe it is your anger that's the problem. You aren't angry enough inside because Myroy returned me and your family to you. When Dougie charged the castle he thought the Angles had killed his children."

"When I was tested by Myroy, the anger I felt frightened me. But now, I don't think I am, well, naturally angry."

Kylie smiled and held his hand.

"Actually, you are kind and thoughtful. That's why I went out with you."

"Not my good looks?"

"Certainly not."

"Ouch, that hurts."

"I think the stone responds to emotion. You remember in the story when Dougie grieved for his family and cried beside *Dog's* bones. He didn't eat for days and the stone filled his purse with oats. It felt his sadness and hunger, and fed him. What other emotions did the stone respond to?"

"Anger, greed, sadness, forgiveness."

Kylie stiffened.

"That's it! Myroy always said, *forgiveness has a power.* Try that."

"How?"

"Walk in, give Odin the ruby and say that you know about the cruel and terrible things he has done, and say you forgive him."

Peter couldn't hide the disbelief in his face.

"That is the worst plan I have ever heard."

"Well, what do you suggest?" she snapped.

"Part of this simulation is to help me learn about Odin's base. We have gone through the front door. Let's try the back door."

Kylie stood.

"OK. You are obviously in charge."

Peter shouldered his rucksack and whispered.

"I see you aren't in a forgiving mood either."

"What was that?"

"Nothing."

Kylie crouched down and pointed at the pines by the fence.

"No, not you. Over there. Twenty metres."

The hairs on Peter's neck stood up and he went cold.

"Get down," hissed Kylie.

He was rooted to the spot and she pulled him down. Three guards in black uniforms moved like shadows in the dark along the outside of the fence, only visible by the glow that came from the displays on their Computer Aided Rifles. They moved towards the sea.

237

Peter smiled.

"What's up?" asked Kylie.

He remembered the words from the story.

"More good fortune."

The guards hadn't seen them and walked on.

"Let's follow and see how they get back inside."

Staying under the cover of the trees, they ran and hid, finding cover before moving on again and keeping their distance, never taking their eyes off the guards in case they turned. The distant roar of waves became louder, the air salty and fresh. Ahead, the pines gave way to coarse grass, leaving a dangerous area of open ground to cover before reaching the edge of the cliffs. The enemy still followed the line of the fence and Kylie saw a CCTV camera rise up on a pole and swivel to monitor the guards' progress.

"Think it's got night vision?" she whispered.

"Sure of it."

They stayed in the trees and watched the guards walk to the edge of the cliff, turn, take one last look around and then disappear over the edge. Peter let out a long breath.

"There must be a way down. Can't see anything though."

"I thought I heard their boots on wooden steps Shall we use our pebbles to go down? Might make less noise."

Peter watched the CCTV camera descend into the ground.

"Yep." He gripped Amera's stone. "Please make us invisible to those who seek us."

The stone pulsed, blood-red, and they ran, pebbles in hand, across the grass and jumped off the cliff. Kylie gasped when she saw the drop and the waves rushing in to battle with the beach far below. They floated down, arms stretched up, shoulders aching after a while with the strain and searching for any sign of the guards.

"Can you see them?" whispered Peter.

"No, and no lights either." She pointed with her free hand. "What's that? Looks square."

They stared through the darkness and Peter guessed it was a

sign. He remembered the linen map and guessed just in time.

"Stop," he hissed.

They hovered a metre above a shingle beach and Peter pointed the ruby at the sign. The red glow lit the sign and a high fence behind it.

Danger of Death
This Side of the Fence is Mined
Keep Out

"That was close," said Kylie.

"What about the fence?"

"Up and over?"

"OK."

They spoke to their pebbles in their minds and they rose over the fence and landed on crunching shingle at the base of the cliff. Something caught Kylie's eye.

"Look."

A curving bow wave shot away from the base of the cliff and two red lights, like eyes, shone just beneath the surface of the sea. Something big, something fast, was forcing the water to lift and curve, but no sign of any metal, skin, or scales.

"It's a *Slug*," said Kylie, "and it came from there. The tunnel must be under water beneath the cliff."

"More good fortune. Right, hug me."

"What?"

Peter put his pebble in to his pocket and gripped the stone.

"Hug me. We need to be close together."

"Is this a trick?"

"No."

She put her arms around him and Peter spoke to the stone.

"Please protect us and take us below the water."

An orange bubble formed around them, lifting them and submerging a short way from where the waves hit the land. Underwater, everything went completely black.

"The entrance to the cave must be here. Stone, please take us through."

The bubble lurched forward, throwing Peter and Kylie backwards to hit the bubble wall.

"Can we have some light?" asked Kylie.

An orange glow lit the bubble which was big enough to stand in.

"You can let go of me now," she told Peter.

A beam threw red light forward, illuminating the smooth walls of a wide tunnel. In some places the walls seemed to move.

"Hold on," said Peter, "can we see the walls?"

The bubble slowed and drifted sideways, and the beam turned on to the rock face. It was covered in huge red jellyfish, which swayed backwards and forwards with the current, but anchored by suckers on their tails to the tunnel wall. Kylie gasped.

"They are so ugly."

Peter saw the spines between their suckers.

"And deadly."

"I've never seen creatures like them."

"Me neither. Alien?"

"No idea, but they don't know we're here, so let's leave."

The bubble moved on and they were thrown backwards by the acceleration again.

Peter shook his head.

"Stone, are you doing that on purpose?"

The ruby pulsed once.

"Hm. Well please stop it," said Kylie crossly.

Beneath them, a soft orange sofa formed out of the bubble wall, lifting them up into a sitting position.

"That's better."

"Come on, everyone," warned Peter. "Keep your minds on the job."

Kylie stared ahead.

"The tunnel's getting wider now."

Suddenly, the protective bubble darted sideways and they watched the long black hull of a *Slug* motor past, the thunder from its engines growing louder as the tail came closer.

"Awesome," said Peter. "I wonder how many Odin controls?"

Grandpa's voice boomed around the bubble.

"Over two thousand and that number grows every day."

"Duncan, when you did the simulation, what went wrong?" asked Kylie.

"Lass, that's for you to find out."

Peter took a deep breath.

"Come on. Into the chamber. Lights off."

They floated forward in complete darkness, the only noise the fading sound of the *Slug's* engines, which became higher pitched as it increased speed in the open sea. Kylie remembered the killer jellyfish and put her hand into Peter's.

"I'm scared now."

Both sides of the bubble bent inwards and there was a slipping, sliding noise as the orange membrane squeezed between two curved objects.

"Is the tunnel narrowing?" asked Peter.

"Shouldn't do, not yet anyway. Can we risk a light?"

"OK, just quickly."

The red beam came on. They were moving between the hulls of two *Black Slugs* berthed close together, like two huge cucumbers laid side by side. The dents in the side membranes popped out and the beam vanished.

"We're through. What next?"

Peter clutched the ruby.

"Are we still invisible to those who seek us?"

It pulsed once.

"Surface." Peter looked at Kylie. "We need to hide up and see what's going on before we move further into the base."

The bubble surfaced under bright lights set into the ceiling of the chamber. Men in black T-shirts and shorts were loading supplies onto neatly spaced submarines, berthed beside jetties that ran off a long concrete quay. Electric cars moved quickly along the quay and a line of cranes serviced the *Slugs*. A train with many steel wagons stopped at one side of the chamber, near to a storage area with stacks of oil drums. The rails ahead of the train carried on for a short while before curving left to stop at a steel door, which guarded one of the tunnels. A single word was painted on the steel door.

Danger

Peter remembered the linen map.

"That tunnel goes off to the chamber that's under construction. Should be another tunnel entrance next to it."

There was, and a container lorry came out of it and parked beside the train. Cows were transferred from the container to the wagons. There were armed guards everywhere. The scale of the operation was massive and Kylie let out a low whistle.

"The quay must be, what, two kilometres long?"

"Yep. I'd guess there are over five hundred *Slugs* here."

"And enough fire-power to destroy every city on the planet. How come no one knows about it? You can't keep something this big a secret. You just can't."

Grandpa's voice again.

"Many senior people in governments were Seekers. Norway is no exception."

Kylie nodded.

"And Odin's got the money."

"Over the centuries he became the richest man in the world and that is a secret he did keep. No one knows the true extent of his fortune."

"So why does he want the stone?" asked Peter. "He has everything he can ever want."

Grandpa's voice became dark.

"He has not got everything he wants. His greed is without boundary."

"And his greed is greater than his anger."

"Myroy believes so."

Peter held Amera's stone on the palm of his hand and stared at it.

"Then I cannot fight him with greed. With anger I have a chance."

There was silence as the bubble dropped down behind a forest of stacked oil drums.

Kylie glanced quickly around.

"Can't see anyone. Protective bubble off."

They crouched behind a stack of drums, thinking about what to do next.

Grandpa's voice came to them like a whisper.

"Peter, the simulation really begins now and the ruby is taken from you. You can replace it with anything at any time, just ask, but you cannot use the power of the stone."

They watched as the brooch melted away in Peter's upturned palm.

"But ...."

"No buts, Peter. Odin is the Keeper now and when you go to take back the stone, you will only be armed with the story, your courage and whatever you learn from Gora."

"But I feel useless without it."

"Then you will fail and die."

Kylie tried to encourage him.

"Come on. Let's give it a try."

Peter sat down, unable to think about how he might reach Odin with all the guards around.

"Well it is *medium*. What did you expect?"

"That Odin knew we were coming."

"Then he doesn't know." She poked her head around a drum. "Look at this."

Another container lorry drove up to the side of the train. They heard the hiss of pneumatic pumps and the sides of a steel wagon were lowered down. At the same time the sides of the container dropped down and touched the side of the wagon to form a bridge. Cows began to cross and enter the train.

Peter took a deep breath.

"We can make it. OK, now."

They ran from the drums, Peter climbing up onto the metal bridge first, pulling Kylie up and both crouching and moving forward with cows all around them. Some of the cows walked a little faster when they appeared, but were not startled. Kylie patted the one beside her.

"Don't worry, we won't hurt you."

They went in to the truck and pressed their backs against the wall on either side of the door, and the cows continued to enter, packing it out and making the children wonder if they might be crushed. The sound of pumps again and the sides of the wagon rose, making the last cow on the gangplank slip inside. Peter pushed his way through the herd and stood beside Kylie, protecting her as best he could. As the train pulled away, they peered out of a long thin slit in the metal wall and watched the oil drums disappear. Kylie ran her finger along the slit as an electric car sped by in the opposite direction.

"I hope it's not a long journey. There won't be much air in here."

Ahead, the rails curved left and ended at the huge metal door with *Danger* written on it. Now they could read more words in smaller letters.

Danger of Death
Strictly No Admittance for Unauthorised Personnel

"Looks ominous," said Kylie.

The metal door rose, sliding up into a rock arch above it. The warning sign gradually disappeared. The train curved left and they heard a rhythmic bang, bang, bang as the wagons crossed a join in the rails where the train entered the tunnel and the steel door closed behind them.

"This is weird," said Peter. "Why would Odin transport cows around in an underground cave?"

"Maybe he likes cows."

"Don't be stupid."

"Anyway, I'm sure this tunnel goes to the chamber that the map said is under construction."

"The really big one."

"Bigger than the *Slug* Base."

Peter's forehead creased.

"For cows?"

"Don't be stupid."

"But what if we can't get from the next cave to Odin's chambers?"

"Then we catch the next train back."

The train stopped again.

Peter stared out of the slit, but everything was black inside the tunnel.

"What is it this time?"

A growing light came from the front of the train.

"Another door, I guess."

Kylie sniffed the air. A smell even stronger than cow.

"Ooh, that's horrid."

The cows became unsettled, moving around restlessly and pinning Peter against Kylie.

"Peter!"

"It's not me, it's the cows. Ouch."

The pressure eased as the train moved out of the tunnel into bright artificial sunshine.

Kylie gasped.

"It's like farmland. Can't be. We're so far beneath the surface. That's barley and they're pine trees. Is that a lake?"

"Looks like it."

"Do you think Odin is experimenting with underground farming because he wants to destroy the surface of the planet."

"Hope not."

Half way between the tunnel exit and the pines, the train stopped. Kylie sensed the unease of the cows.

"I don't like this. Something is scaring the cows and me."

"And me, let's stay on."

The pneumatic hiss started again and the entire side of the wagon dropped down, touching the earth and flattening the barley. The cows stared out, ears up, but didn't move.

"The smell is worse here," said Kylie.

"Sickly."

The pneumatic pump hissed and the wall behind them began to move across the inside of the truck. Peter watched as the cows edged away from the moving wall.

"Oh, no."

They were forced out onto the metal gangplank, the front cows reluctant to go down, but forced onto the barley by those behind. Peter stepped onto the side of the gangplank and jumped down.

"Come on."

Kylie jumped too as the cows joined with more cows from other wagons, and the herd bolted away to the trees. The pump stopped hissing and the back wall now filled the exit side completely.

"No way back in."

A small shudder as the metal gangplank rose up and slid horizontally into a slot beneath the wagon. They watched as the same thing happened to half the other wagons.

"Can you hear something?"

Peter did.

"Get under the train."

They dived into the gap between two wagons and slid underneath to lie between the two rows of wheels, just as they began to turn. Peter glanced up.

"Can you see anything to grab on to?"

Kylie brushed her hand along the metal plate above her head. It was perfectly smooth.

"No."

One wagon after another rolled over them, until they were left in open countryside, Peter running after the train, trying to jump onto the back, but no hand or foot holds again. He crashed on to the track and glanced at Kylie. She stood, eyes wide, staring at the sky above the train. Her body began to shake. Peter heard a high-pitched whine, like a mosquito, but so much louder. He turned and felt a spear-like tail stab through his stomach and cut through his back. He tried to scream and couldn't. He wanted to cry with pain and couldn't. The creature began to eat him.

***

Peter sat up, startled, holding his face and checking if the skin was still there. It was and he stared around the smooth walls of the high metal cylinder inside the stone osprey. The rectangular cut-out now rested around a door with a lit sign above it.

Out

The door was open and he got up, feeling his stomach, half expecting to find a hole, and walked out onto the top of the tower. Gora and Kylie sat with their backs to him, and Peter stopped to listen to their conversation.

"The stone gifts you power as you gift it emotion. The stronger the emotion you feel, the more power it releases."

Kylie nodded.

"Like Dougie's anger at Stirling Castle."

"Yes."

"Like Odin's anger and greed."

"Yes."

"Any emotion?"

Gora ran a bony hand through his long hair.

"I do not know."

"And my task is thankless. Without any hope or reward?"

"No, not without hope. Always have hope. The stone's power is linked to the moon. Like the tides, it ebbs and flows."

"Why?"

"If we could answer that, we could defeat Odin tomorrow."

Kylie shook her head.

"I am frightened."

"You must have courage."

"I'm not even sure I can do it."

"You may not. We will see."

"But there is still time."

"Some time, yes. In terms of the chapters of my life, the time for you to learn is only a short sentence."

"What can I do to prepare myself?"

Gora put an arm around her shoulder.

"You must choose your path, not I. I can only guess how it all might end."

"I am scared."

"We all are, and particularly Peter, even though he tries not to show it."

Peter joined them and sat down.

"What's all that about?"

Big tears fell down Kylie's cheeks.

"This is not your concern," said Gora. "What did you learn from the simulation?"

"Not to follow cows to find Odin."

"You mean there are areas on the map marked *unknown*, or *under construction*, that you must avoid. Sticking to the paths we actually know about, with all their twists and turns, will be hard enough."

"What were those red things that attacked us?"

"Tirani told me that Odin has cloned different creatures, made them bigger and more deadly. He breeds them in great numbers and plans to use them against us."

Kylie brushed her tears away.

"They are horrible."

Gora stood and pointed at the entrance to the simulator.

"It is not over yet. Back you go."

***

A few minutes later, they crouched behind the forest of oil drums, back in the massive chamber which housed the *Slug* base. More electric cars sped along the quay and cranes loaded missiles aboard the submarines. Kylie stared at the metal door where the railway line ended and shuddered.

"We need another way in."

A container lorry left the quayside and entered the tunnel further along. Peter unrolled the linen map.

"What about that way?"

"It seems to just go up to the surface at the side of the O.A.S.V. building. There are lifts marked here on the far side of the tunnel, shall we try one of those?"

They stared down the quay, past the two tunnels, the lines of cranes, guards with CAR's and moored *Slugs*. In the distance was a stack of containers. The three lift doors were over two hundred metres away and there was nothing to hide behind between the children and the lifts.

"How does Odin get down here?" asked Peter.

"Probably just comes up through the water. He doesn't need a lift."

"Hmm."

An electric car steered close to them and they pulled their heads back behind a drum.

"Grandpa, could you please tell me about Odin's inner sanctuary."

A deep voice replied from above.

"It is where he studies the world and regenerates his power as an Ancient One. It has a bank of television screens, a long table and a stone carving of a longship. In a separate cave is a standing stone surrounded by sea water. Odin walks into the stone and feels the power of the sea."

"Hmm."

"Do you think the water comes from this cave?" asked Kylie.

No answer from Grandpa, but Peter guessed it.

"If it does there must be another tunnel running under the quay to the foundations of the office block."

Kylie rolled the map out again.

"There is a narrow tunnel coming out of the *Slug* base. Probably full of water, but it might be the back door we've been searching for."

Peter ran his finger along the tunnel.

"It's too long to swim through, we'd drown."

Kylie smiled.

"Duncan said you can replace the stone with anything. Fancy a scuba dive?"

Peter smiled too.

"Good idea. Where does the tunnel start?"

On the map it went inland from close to where the railway curved to the steel doors. Kylie pointed at the edge of the quay.

"Must be there, by that submarine."

"But how do we get from here to the water?"

"Wait. Something will turn up."

But the activity along the quayside intensified. Cranes worked more quickly, electric cars sped around and the guards never left their positions. Peter realised that as soon as they left the safety of the oil drums, they would be seen.

"We have to cross the quay and the railway line. We won't make it."

"Wait," repeated Kylie. "Odin doesn't know we are here. Be patient."

Three hours later, they still hid behind the oil drums.

"Do they never take a break?" asked Peter.

"Must do. Everyone has to eat and sleep sometime."

"Maybe, when Odin holds the stone his people don't need to sleep. Is that one of the lessons we have to learn?"

Kylie stretched her legs.

"I'm getting stiff."

"Me too. Hang on, who's that?"

A tall man, dressed in the clothes of a Norse warrior, stepped out of a lift. He looked around and his eyes seemed to fix on the oil drums. Peter and Kylie froze with fear.

"That's Thorgood," whispered Peter.

Then the warrior walked onto the quay and raised his sword. Immediately, all work stopped. The workers, drivers and guards left whatever they were doing and followed Thorgood in a long procession along the roadway that went into the second tunnel.

"I think it's break-time," said Kylie.

"Yep. Let's go."

They ran to the edge of the quay and stood behind a crane.

"Let's get ready," said Kylie.

They began to undress to their pants and T-shirts, Peter speaking as he kicked his shoes off.

"Grandpa, can we have some sub-aqua gear?"

"Yep."

Kylie folded her arms.

"Don't you start that *yepping*, as well."

Duncan ignored her.

"Is there anything else you need?"

Peter couldn't think of anything.

"No. Don't think so."

"Are you sure?"

"Yep."

"Not waterproof torches?"

"Er, oh yes."

Flippers appeared on their feet, masks around their necks and they felt the weight of air cylinders on their backs. The torches came into their hands. Peter put his mouthpiece between his lips and sucked in air. He removed it and looked at Kylie.

"How's yours?"

"Working fine."

"Masks on, torches on, and keep a steady pace. Don't rush, it could be a long swim."

They jumped out into the cold water and took long, slow kicks with their flippers to propel themselves forward, their torch beams darting around, searching along the wall of the quay for the tunnel entrance. They were right by it, a black round hole about five metres across. They shuddered as they swam in. The water here was even colder, almost icy, and their fingers soon became numb. Gradually, the tunnel went upwards, and the bubbles from their breathing rose to the ceiling and bumped along the smooth roof ahead of them.

Peter shone his torch at Kylie and gave her a thumbs up. She put her thumb up too, which meant she was coping with the cold, but the same nagging doubt went through both of their minds.

"This is too easy."

The smooth sides of the tunnel began to change. Norse runes, as tall as a man, appeared on both sides of them, each letter carved deep into the rock. Peter shone his torch on some of them and tried to guess what these ancient letters meant. He flashed his torch at Kylie and she shrugged her shoulders. Peter checked his air supply gauge. Thirty minutes left. He swam beside Kylie and checked hers. Twenty nine minutes. A terrible thought came to him.

"This is going to be a one way trip."

They swam on, their torches lighting the tunnel, which neither narrowed nor widened, perfectly smooth except for the runes. Kylie's torch picked up something else and she grabbed Peter's arm. He shone his torch that way and they saw two white pillars, like marble, that partly blocked the way forward. They moved closer and realised there was room for them to swim through if they went one at a time. Peter went first and shone his torch around. Beyond the pillars, it didn't look any different from the rest of the tunnel and he waved Kylie on.

Their torch beams cut through the blackness like laser beams and suddenly Kylie pointed forward. Two more white pillars, ten metres ahead. They ignored their frozen limbs and bravely kicked on, but an Ancient One waited for them. A brightly lit face, with intense blue eyes, filled all the space between the pillars and Odin spoke into their minds.

"Who disturbs my peace?"

They tried to hide their names and purpose from the staring face, but Odin searched deep and spoke again.

"Peter of the Line of Donald and Kylie. You are both known to me and the reason why you are here is clear."

The face vanished and a metal door descended between the pillars to block the way forward. Fear gripped their hearts and Peter nodded desperately back down the tunnel. They swam as

252

quickly as they could towards the first pair of pillars, but before they reached them, another metal door came down, trapping them completely.

Peter used his torch to check his air supply. Only fifteen minutes left. Wildly, he shone his torch around the smooth walls with their runes. He checked the floor and roof, but no way out, not even a crack in the rock. Peter swam back to Kylie and put his hand into hers, and wondered what pain he would feel when he drowned.

***

"Haaaa. What did you learn?" shrieked the giant osprey.

Peter had crawled out of the simulator exit on his hands and knees, soaked, shivering and coughing up sea water.

"Leave me alone."

Gora flapped his wings and rose up to his perch on the oak trunk, held between the beaks of the stone ospreys.

"Haaaa. Do you think any entrance to Odin's inner sanctuary would be unguarded? Fool, fool, fool."

Kylie crawled out of the exit and collapsed beside Peter, her long black hair wrapped all around her face. Gora shrieked at them and the walls of the tower seemed to shake.

"Haaaaaa."

"How do we get in?" she whimpered.

Gora lowered his head and opened his beak wide.

"Learn. Learn. Learn."

"But we can't do it," said Peter.

"Everything you believe you cannot do, you cannot do. Learn. Learn."

Kylie's chest heaved and she vomited a river of water.

Gora took off into the skies of the Realm of the Dead and called down to them.

"Come back at dawn tomorrow. Be afraid. The next simulation awaits you."

CHAPTER THIRTEEN

EDGING CLOSER TO DESTINY

Kylie and Peter ran out of the simulator exit, screaming, hair on fire, skin blistering and their clothes almost completely burned away. Hamish and Donald threw a bucket of water into their faces, tossed the buckets away and picked up full ones, which they poured over the children's heads.

"Haaa. What did you learn?"

They fell to the ground, still smouldering, unaware of the presence of the huge osprey high above them on his perch. Gora screeched and they rolled over holding their ears.

"Haaaaaaaa."

"Leave me alone," groaned Peter.

"Leave you alone?" screeched Gora. "What then? Death to us, death to you."

Hamish and Donald threw more water over them. Kylie spluttered.

"I can't do it anymore. I can't go back in there."

"What did you learn?"

Peter sat up and smoke came out of his mouth.

"Not to try and get to Odin by going through the Cloning Research Centre. The face in the floor guards it."

"Go back. Try again. Try the *difficult level* once more."

Kylie began to sob.

"I just can't."

Gora stretched out his wings and jumped down, his body transforming from bird to man.

"Can't, or won't?"

"I'm all in," said Peter. "Can we not rest for a while?"

Donald grinned and threw more water into Peter's face.

"I like this job," he said.

Hamish growled and did the same to Kylie.

"Fire gone now," he boomed.

Peter felt the skin on his legs. The blisters had vanished. As the pain subsided, Gora sat between the children.

"Then rest, but do not be idle. The full history of the stone

256

must be told to you. In Dougie's time, clan will fight clan, and there is a destiny to fulfil."

"I like this bit," said Donald. "Can we hear it again?"

Gora pointed at Hamish and Donald, who rose up and flew through the air over the lip of the tower. Two splashes in the loch followed, then the sound of fighting.

"Rest then, but do not be idle," repeated Gora. "Listen to my words. Myroy's prophecy about the joining of the royal households, of Elder and Donald, is about to come true."

***

Dougie of Dunfermline sat on the High Pastures, counting his sheep, smiling and feeling mighty pleased with himself. He thought about Alistair, Hamish and Donald, who had brought him the huge flock of Welsh sheep, and the goodbyes they had said the day before.

"Thank you."

He lost count and started again. Unable to read or write, he used his fingers to count ten sheep and then bent a finger over to help him remember how many tens of sheep he had counted. He bent his last finger.

"One hundred."

He smiled at his bent fingers and knew he had reached the limit of his ability. For the first time in his life, Dougie had more sheep than he could count.

"I wish Alec could see this."

Two black and white sheepdogs lay, fast asleep, with their heads on his lap. They had been a gift from the Younger himself and at first had given the shepherd a problem. Calling them both *Dog* hadn't worked, it just confused them, and calling them Malcolm and Murdoch, or the Watcher and Arkinew, had seemed disrespectful to those great people. But he wanted names which helped him remember his friends from his adventures.

"Hamish and Donald does the job."

He rubbed their ears and they stirred a little, but were too comfy in the late morning sunshine to break away from their dreams about chasing hares. He watched Donald's back leg twitch, the dog dreaming about running along the drovers' road, and Dougie thought about being chased by the Angles after rescuing Alistair from the dungeons under Berwick Castle. He sighed.

"I'm glad all that's over."

He looked down the hill towards the stile and the stand of pines that marked the end of his land. Then across the waters of the loch, the drovers' road, the tiny speck that was his cottage, and up the slope to his left to the cairn and the three standing stones. It was everything he wanted or needed.

"There is no more worth having than this."

He undid the leather tie around the top of his purse and took out the brooch that Malcolm the Younger had also given him. For some reason Dougie knew the ruby was happy, just as he was. He touched the ruby at the heart of the brooch and felt its warmth. His dogs' ears pricked up, alert, and he put the brooch safely away. He followed Hamish and Donald's gaze and sensed that they were not scared, just aware that someone was approaching who offered no threat to them. Tanny was walking up the slope towards Dougie, shouting at the sheep to get out of the bloomin' way, and carrying something. He watched her get closer, smiling and remembering how the Watcher on the hill had returned her to him when he had believed that all his family had been killed. He loved them more because of that.

She sat down beside Dougie, panting, out of breath.

"Mum says the bloomin' cheese you got from Stewart of Balgedie has gone mouldy."

"Uh ha."

"What you going to do about it?"

"Are you fooling around again?"

"No. What are you going to do about the cheese?"

"What's wrong with it?"

"Gone off and mum wants to know what you are going to do about it."

"I am not going to do anything. I'm looking after the sheep."

"I saw you. You were just lazing around, daydreaming again."

"I was counting."

Tanny folded her arms, like her mother often did.

"You aren't busy, so what are you going to do about the cheese?"

Dougie sighed.

"Do you know I am a member of the High Table of Scotland?"

"Well you should have lots of coins to buy more cheese."

As he always did, the shepherd gave in.

"Tell your mother I'll buy some more cheese tomorrow."

"She wants it today."

"I'm busy today."

"You aren't busy."

Tanny looked critically at Hamish and Donald who had gone back to sleep on Dougie's lap.

"You've got two of the best sheepdogs in the kingdom. They can look after things whilst you get the cheese."

Dougie decided to go on the attack.

"Shouldn't you be cooking?"

Tanny shook her head, her golden hair swaying.

"Not without cheese."

His heart sank and Tanny handed him a parcel wrapped in cloth.

"What's this?"

"You won't know unless you open it."

He unwrapped the parcel. Oat bread, cheese and an apple.

"There's nothing wrong with this cheese."

Tanny had already jumped up, startling the dogs, her long golden hair bouncing as she ran down the slope, giggling and shouting out.

"Cheeky Black Kilt. I'm a cheeky Black Kilt."

Dougie watched her go, laughing inside and wondering why he was always fooled by his daughter.

He had stood at the end of the world, fought the Picts, the Norsemen and the Angles and yet he fell for Tanny's tricks every time. He picked up the apple, bit it and glanced at the cairn. Like a ghost, the Watcher on the hill rose up and placed a bunch of flowers on the stones. The old man nodded at Dougie and smiled.

"I am not going on another adventure."

The Watcher's reply was as clear as if he was sitting next to Dougie.

"You are not going on another adventure."

Dougie let out a long breath.

"I'm glad about that."

"I have news you will also be glad about. Your twin, Alec, returns to Scotland."

"Alec? How is he? Where is he? How ..."

The Watcher raised his hand.

"At sunrise on the day before the next full moon, stand by the waters of the Forth, at Culross. Go alone. Ride there on a horse."

"Alec comes by ship?"

"Take him to the Younger's palace. Help him until his destiny is fulfilled."

Fear gripped the shepherd.

"And it's not another war?"

"War will come to Scotland now. Clan shall fight clan, but you will play no part in it."

"Will Alec play a part in it?"

The old man ignored his question.

"Keep the stone safe, here, below the waters of the loch. If you sometimes see a giant bird, do not fear him."

"Ooh."

"Do not take the brooch with you, Dougie of Dunfermline."

"I promise."

The old man began to disappear down into the ground and Dougie called out.

"When do I gift the stone to my children?"

Myroy stopped descending, his arms, chest and head still above the grass.

"You have many summers to enjoy before you make that choice. You have more than earned that, first Keeper. Live long, my friend."

"When will we meet again?"

"After your death, in the Realm of the Dead."

The Watcher vanished and Dougie thought about the instructions he had been given. He took Amera's stone from his purse and, with little effort, threw it towards the loch. It pulsed red as it arched across the lower pastures and the drovers' road, then flying high above pines before splashing, sinking and resting. The waters boiled where it splashed and a giant bird erupted from the depths screeching out a warning.

"Haaaaaaa."

Dougie watched the osprey dive back into the loch and thought about the other instructions.

"But I don't have a horse."

Hamish and Donald barked loudly.

"What's up with you two?"

They barked again and Dougie stood and turned around. A grey Highland stallion was walking down the slope towards him and he went over to hold the rope around its strong neck, stroking the mane and talking softly.

"You are a wonderful horse."

The Highland tossed his mane and stamped a foot on the ground.

"I know," said Dougie, "I'll call you *Dog*."

***

Konini the Slave Master hardly moved as the whip came down across his wide back. He sat chained beside another Corsair who was so weak with fever that his weight on their oar was a burden, slowing their strokes and earning Konini a cruel reward.

The pace of the drum slowed and the Slave Master was able to keep time again, one long stroke after another, and waiting for this part of the voyage to end. Sometimes he got a brief look at the upper deck when the hatch and iron grille were opened. That was his only way of escape, and escape was on his mind.

The drum slowed to half pace and he glanced out of the gap at the top of the oar hole. There was a harbour wall with many feet in sandals standing on it. Konini guessed they had reached Almeria and that Ceol the Magnificent's people had turned out in great numbers to see Ceol's new ship and treasure trove. A loud cheer sounded from the open deck above, the drum stopped and Konini felt the ship move sideways, forcing his oar inside, and the sandals disappeared as the oar hole nudged closer towards stone.

The Corsair next to him had not moved for a long time and Konini pulled the man's shoulders up off the oar and looked into his eyes. There was no life left in them. A man with a whip walked down the central aisle and pointed at the Corsair. Konini released his partner's shoulders and the man fell forward like a rag doll. The new Slave Master ran off and returned quickly with four armed warriors. He lifted the pin, pulled the chain through the slaves' ankle irons, and Konini lifted the dead man up and placed him face down on the central aisle. The warriors never took their eyes off Konini and held their swords ready, but Konini sat back down and pulled the chains back through his irons, and the new Slave Master yanked it tight and secured the pin. They carried the corpse away, pushing it up through the hatch, securing the iron grille behind them and throwing the body overboard. The splash was accompanied by more cheers from above.

Konini waited. He knew the routine well; the crew would be desperate to get ashore and tell their stories, and feast well into the dark hours. An unlucky few would be ordered to remain on deck and on guard, although their friends might bring them food and drink to help them celebrate too.

"That is when I leave," he thought.

He remembered the illness and how dreams and nightmares had replaced any reality or real memory of his time deep down in the Chamber of the Sick. He half remembered an old woman laughing and helping him into bed. He half-remembered Ceol's men standing over him with swords, ready to cut him down, and how helpless he had felt.

It was only two days after he had woken up, here in the bowels of his master's slave ship, that Konini discovered the truth. He knew Ceol's warning, word for word.

"You are a lucky man, Konini. The warrior from the land of the Scots, the one they call Alec of Dunfermline, pleaded with me, asked that I spare your life. He told me you saved his life and that of his friend, Perpigno the Tongue Speaker. His words moved me, but I warn you. Try to escape and we will hunt you down and take revenge for the ships you plundered and the men you slew."

"So I owe my life to a foreigner who was once my slave."

Konini leaned over his oar, sniffed the foul air and fell asleep. As the feast in the palace came to an end, Konini's eyes opened and he took his oar, turned it upright and put one end between his bench and the chain. He leaned against the oar, pushing with all of his great strength, forcing the chain to tighten and stretch. The pin in the central aisle snapped and the chain went loose. He pulled it through his ankle irons and jumped up onto the aisle. Some of the slaves stirred and Konini whispered to them.

"Today I gift you freedom. Now, gift me silence."

No one spoke, but many wide eyes watched him climb the ladder to the iron grille. It was bolted shut, like the wooden hatch above it was bolted shut, but Konini placed his feet onto strong beams and his back under the grille. He heaved. At first, the bolts held, but one broke, the wood around it splintering. Sweat ran down into his eyes as he listened for footsteps up on deck. Silence. He continued to put pressure on the grille. The other bolts gave way and the hatch flew up on its hinges before crashing down onto the deck like a door slamming. Someone on deck shouted out a warning, but it was too late. The Slave Master was loose and he had come to reclaim the ship, and pay tribute to Spalda's spirit.

***

"Hey, Brown Eyes. The sea is colder here, and darker. Even the birds are different."

It was dusk and Alec of Dunfermline smiled, and looked up at a quarter moon.

"We sail on a different ocean, but we are still a long way from Scotland."

"It is further away than I thought."

"Much further."

Perpigno shivered with the cold.

"What do you wear at home to keep warm?"

"A plaid."

"What is a *plaid*?"

"A long length of woollen cloth. You wrap it around and around your waist and throw what's left over your shoulder. You can even sleep in it."

"Hmm. You sleep in your clothes?"

"Aye."

Perpigno's nose wrinkled.

"I can't wait to smell that."

"Any sign of the other ship?"

"Not for two days. I think we lost them."

"You still think they were pirates?"

"It looked like the ship where we were slaves. But Ceol took that and I don't think he would sail so far away from Almeria. Well, not unless he heard that someone makes good shirts around here."

Alec shrugged his shoulders.

"But their boat was so much bigger and faster than our trader.

Why did they choose only sail, and not sail with oar? Why did they break off the chase so suddenly?"

"It is a mystery, Brown Eyes, and I have no answer. Maybe their slaves are all dead?"

Alec bent down and touched his ankle iron.

"I hope not. They have a terrible life, but it is better than joining the fallen."

"Are you sure about that?"

"Aye."

As the light faded, Perpigno pointed at a rocky coastline off to their right.

"Do you know those lands?"

"I do not know their name, but I have sailed here before."

"Is it not the land of the Angles?"

"No."

"So, you're not home yet?"

Alec pictured the hills around his cottage and how as a child he had swum in the loch with Dougie.

"No."

"How long, Brown Eyes?"

Alec stared again at the quarter moon.

"With a fair wind, we should enter the mighty Forth a few days after the next full moon."

***

Ignoring rank or status, Konini shared the food equally, so that everyone on board suffered the same until fresh supplies could be stolen. For a while, he even refused to take bread himself so that the weakest crew members had something to eat, but their supplies of bread and meat ran out and he was forced to give up the pursuit of the trader and loot a small fishing village. It gifted little of value. Their total stock now stood at three barrels of water, five goats, a piglet the size of a cat, a barrel of salted fish that tasted awful and twelve chickens, which were given the lower slave deck as a new home. It wasn't enough to feed one hundred and fifty men for more than a week, even if they spread the jam thin.

No one rowed. Konini had released every slave and smiled as they came up on deck to breathe clean air. On his own he had killed every guard who opposed him and learned of Alec of Dunfermline's plans from those who escaped death by joining his crew. The Scotsman he sought was going home, and Konini knew from the stories told by traders that home for Alec was north along the coastline held by the Celtiberians, and when those lands were passed he would need to sail north-east to pass between the lands of the Gauls and Angles. It was going to be a long journey, but his mind was set and his crew were completely subservient to him. They loved Konini like a brother.

He spoke to the helmsman next to him.

"North?"

The man nodded and made a small adjustment to the tiller.

"Still north."

Konini looked up at the huge sail. It billowed out in a curve, like a wave rolling in to a horse shoe bay, and he knew that the trailing wind would give the speed he needed to run Alec down. A Corsair from Konini's village ran to him at the stern.

"A single sail. Brown like a trader's sail."

"How far?"

"Too far to overtake before dark comes."

Konini stared up at a quarter moon and spoke to the helmsman.

"Follow the sail, but keep your distance."

He smiled at the Corsair.

"Tell the crew not to light torch or fire tonight. We board just after dawn tomorrow."

***

As the sun rose above a choppy sea, Perpigno smiled at his sleeping friend who was wrapped in a colourful blanket with only his long brown hair showing. Perpigno tied the tiller with a rope, checked that their ship continued north, then baited a hook and threw it into the sea. Almost immediately, his line went tight.

"These waters provide a quick breakfast."

He pulled in the line and looked at the fish. Its flapping scales were brown with a blue-green shimmer.

"Hmm. Not seen your like before. Are you good to eat?"

Perpigno banged its head on the rail and placed the fish carefully on the deck.

"I'll ask Brown Eyes when he wakes."

He baited the hook again and threw the line overboard. As it splashed into the sea a distant thud sounded. Perpigno went cold. Another thud and another, getting quicker and each drum beat sent a shudder of fear down his spine. He turned slowly, eyes wide, legs trembling. He saw the Corsair galley bearing down on them under full sail, more than one hundred oars adding to its speed. A giant of a man stood at the prow, staring at him.

"My god, it's Konini."

As he whispered the words he knew their trader was lost and that he would soon be dead or a slave again. He called out.

"Brown Eyes. Wake up!"

"Huh."

"Wake up."

"Why?"

"Corsairs are here. Get up."

A tired face came out of the colourful blanket.

"Corsairs?"

"It's Konini. He must have escaped and taken back Ceol's ship."

Alec threw the blanket aside and ran to stand beside his friend at the rail.

"Do we fight?"

Perpigno shook his head. "Against so many?"

"I don't want to be a slave again."

"It's that or death."

"At home we used to have an old claymore. If I held it now I would fight."

"And you would lose."

"I would not lose my dignity."

They felt helpless and terrified, and even though Alec remembered the words of the ghost in the Chamber of the Sick, he felt sick in his stomach as lines were thrown from the galley. Corsairs jumped aboard and, ignoring their captives, they searched around the deck for food. Konini jumped onboard as well and strode menacingly towards Alec.

"Kneel," whispered Perpigno.

They knelt and shook with fear, absolutely terrified, as the Slave Master's long shadow fell over them. Konini spoke to Perpigno who interpreted for Alec.

"Stand up, Brown Eyes."

Konini drew his sword and Alec shut his eyes. Then he felt the hilt being pushed into his hand and he opened his eyes to see Konini kneeling before him, his massive shoulders bent over and his head placed at Alec's feet. The Corsairs aboard the trader knelt too.

"Why does he kneel before me?"

Perpigno asked Konini and gave Alec the reply.

"You spared his life and now he is your slave. The galley is yours too, and the crew have sworn an oath to serve you without question." Perpigno gave Alec a huge grin. "So you are a Shipmaster once more. What are your orders?"

"Tell Konini to stand." Alec pointed at his ankle iron. "Tell him that no man should be a slave."

"Anything else?"

"Aye, ask him if he knows the way north to the land of the Scots. On the galley we should make the Forth just before the full moon."

Perpigno spoke with Konini who stood and Alec gave him back his sword. Instantly the Slave Master threw his arms around him and hugged him, squeezing the air from Alec's chest.

"Perpigno, help!" he gasped.

"It is the way of the Corsairs. He will let you go in a little while."

Konini released him from the bear hug and Alec staggered across the deck sucking in air. Konini spoke to Perpigno.

"Brown Eyes, Konini says that if he cannot be your slave then he shall be your friend and protector."

"Tell him I am deeply honoured and that I only need help to reach the Forth. After that he can return home."

Perpigno told him and Konini bowed.

"And I have two important questions for you," said Perpigno.

"What's that?"

"What do we do with the trader?"

Alec looked at the Corsairs. They were half starved.

"Sell it for food. What's the other question?"

Perpigno picked up the fish.

"Can you eat this?"

CHAPTER FOURTEEN

CLAN AGAINST CLAN

Tirani the Wise and Myroy sat at an oak table in the Chamber of the Ancient Ones, the map of Denbara the Scribe laid out in front of them and a dull orange glow, from crystals set into rock on one wall, lighting the chamber. Tirani picked up a leather bag and took out a small toy figure, which looked like Malcolm the Younger, and placed it carefully on to the map where the palace was marked in black ink. The boy took out two more figures, Prince Ranald and Morag McCreedy, and stood them so that they both faced the Younger.

"Is the Younger ready to join the fallen?" asked Tirani.

"He knows what to do and will stand before his son on the day before the next full moon."

"So, you are allowing Ranald to rule for one day."

"The Younger will allow his son to rule for one day."

Tirani put his small hand back inside the bag and placed Borak One Hand, Margaret and Columba onto Skye, as close as he could to the small square that Denbara had drawn to show the location of the fortress at Deros.

"And Borak prepares for war."

"Borak prepares a trap for Seamus. He does not have enough warriors to fight a war."

Tirani took out two more figures and placed Seamus and Finn McCool onto a model ship, to the south of Skye. Tirani's face showed concern.

"Hmm. How are you going to make sure Alec of Dunfermline has enough followers to become king?"

Myroy ignored the question.

"Continue with the pieces."

The boy placed more toy figures on to the map. Off the coast of Berwick, Alex and Konini stood on the deck of a model Corsair galley. A gypsy caravan followed from the bag and Tirani placed this to the south of the Younger's palace.

"Interesting. You really aren't taking any chances, are you?"

272

More toy caravans came out of the bag and joined Barbarini the Traveller's caravan. Myroy's face became as hard as stone.

"If there is going to be a new Long Peace, the clans of Baxter, McCreedy and Morgan must be destroyed. The High Table will only unite again if a clear example is made."

"Do you know, you sound like Odin sometimes?"

Myroy's eyes flashed.

"Do not forget what will happen if our brother holds Amera's stone. Dougie of Dunfermline, and all the Keepers who will follow Dougie, will only be safe if the kingdom finds peace."

"War will always come, like it always has."

"Yes."

"But Ranald knows his father gifted a ruby to the shepherd. When he is king he will try to take it back."

"Ranald will not be allowed to seek it. During the second Long Peace, Dougie's family will be forgotten. As the centuries go by, the Keepers will only exist in a story. Odin will seek, but not find."

Tirani took the last two figures from the bag, placing Llewellyn at the centre of the Welsh kingdom and Thorgood Firebrand over the sea by the port of Dublin.

Myroy stared at them.

"Thorgood is the key to all this. He will invade Ireland and use it as a base to attack Llewellyn."

"You would allow centuries of war on Welsh soil to protect the Keeper?"

"Yes."

"So, Thorgood is out of the picture."

"For now."

"How long?"

"Until the last Keeper."

Tirani picked up the models of the Younger, Ranald and Morag, and laid them on their sides. He replaced them at the palace with Alec and Margaret.

"I like a nice wedding."

Myroy slowly stood, his great age showing in the way he moved. He stretched and stared up at the rock arch above his head, remembering how the ground had given way beneath his feet, falling down into this chamber and being covered in ice, but protected by the pulsing glow of the strange crystals. Myroy went over to Frey's mummified body and gently stroked his mother's arm. It was as hard as granite.

"That was so long ago," he whispered.

"Margaret won't like it."

Myroy's eyes flashed again.

"The royal houses of Donald and Elder *will* be united."

"You really are ruthless sometimes."

"I have learned to be ruthless. What choice do I have?"

Tirani tried to copy his brother's deep voice.

"You always have a choice. Always."

Myroy walked back to the table, picked up his staff and began to wave it in a circle just above the ground.

"I go now."

"To play with history?"

"To create a new peace and ensure the safety of the Keepers."

"And who are you manipulating this time?"

"Manipulating?"

"Who are you using to do your will?"

"Barbarini the Traveller."

Tirani's face became sad.

"Are you really going to make her watch?"

"I am."

"Do you want me to come with you?"

"No."

Tirani watched his brother disappear into the underworld and asked himself a painful question.

"What have we become?"

***

Barbarini the Traveller knew these were dangerous times. She could feel the tension in the air whenever she asked for coins to tell someone's fortune. Perhaps they feared her because she was different to them, an outsider, or maybe they simply feared what cards fate would deal them. The mighty castle at Berwick had yielded few coins and there had been even fewer at Melrose, and the other small towns of the border lands. The fortress at Hawick had been torn down before she arrived there; evidence that clan now fought against clan. Barbarini was poor again and did not care. She pictured her partner from the Union of Souls and smiled, wondering where Hamish of Tain was and when they would kiss again.

She listened to the rhythmic sound of her pots and pans as they swayed with each turn of the wheels. That sound, along with the *clip clop* of horse's hooves, had been with her forever. She loved those gentle rhythms and they meant she was moving on again to a new market where she could sell her dreams about the future.

This was a lonely path, sandy and narrow, and Barbarini let her horse walk at his own pace, almost hypnotised by the gentle tinkling of the pots, and completely lost in her thoughts. People had been scared in the border lands and not because of their old enemy, the Angles. Those peoples, from the villages and towns of Northumbria, were in mourning at the loss of so many of their menfolk at Stirling and, even though they hated the Scots, there was no will to attack them. In fact there was widespread relief that Cuthbert had joined the fallen and could no longer exert his cruelty. Under the rule of Grahm Deer there was hope for peace and a more just future.

When Barbarini had crossed the waters of the mighty Forth at Culross, the ferryman had eyed her suspiciously and only taken her across at a high price. The excuse he used for charging more was the danger from carrying her caravan and horse, which needed to cross separately anyway. But she knew that was not the reason from the tension in his voice. He would be punished by his master if he let an enemy cross the river, and if he was going to take the risk, he wanted to be well rewarded for it. All of her coins were now gone, but she was moving north towards the Younger's royal palace and that was where she sensed Hamish to be. She pictured Culross again. It had been deserted. Even the main path to the palace had few people on it, but there were signs everywhere of the tension and fear gripping Scotland. Strangers refused to talk to her and warriors watched her from the high places. At night, these lookouts lit fires as a warning to other clans that they were ready for an attack. Once she passed a cottage, its roof burned away and the dead bodies of a family abandoned beside the path. It was gruesome, and made her wish, more than ever, that big Hamish was by her side.

The rhythm of the pans made her eyes droop, and she pictured Hamish in her mind and, half in dream, she watched as he helped others put a roof on to a white cottage. Then they mounted Highlands and rode away from a loch. Barbarini knew that loch and the vision made her sure she would see Hamish soon. Her smile disappeared as she was jolted from her dreams by silence. The horse had stopped, ears up and alert, and the pots no longer swayed. The grass beside the path began to shimmer, like moonlight on water, and an old man in a dark cloak rose up from the underworld. Barbarini sensed no danger, no evil intent, from the man's wrinkled face.

"Do not be afraid," he said.

"I am not afraid. You are Myroy and my husband has spoken of you."

"Continue on this path towards the palace of Malcolm the Younger. You will soon be reunited with Hamish of Tain."

"I know."

"Tell him to approach the palace with care."

"I will."

"Hamish travels with Alistair of Cadbol. Tell Alistair that Ranald will become king and that he must seek out Kenneth of Blacklock for a journey across the Great Sea to find Margaret, the Protector of the Outer Islands and Queen of the Irish Peoples. Alistair must win the support of a friend and an old enemy for the coming war. Tell him to lead his new allies to the palace by the next full moon."

"A friend and an old enemy?"

"Alistair will know what to do."

"I shall tell him."

Barbarini sensed the man's great wisdom and age.

"You are tired and seek peace through death."

"I will find that peace, one day, but not until the last Keeper fights under a Gora moon."

"I hope that comes soon."

"It will not come soon, but it will come."

"My thoughts go with you, Ancient One."

Myroy's face became sad.

"When you travel to join Benita and your people, leave the path and watch them first from a lonely place. Then do whatever your heart tells you to do."

"I fear words like those."

"But you will do it."

"I will."

"Have faith, the future will be kind to you. A new Long Peace shall come to Scotland and Hamish will be the best of fathers."

Barbarini's cheeks reddened as Myroy disappeared into the grass.

***

Donald and Alistair heard a deep growling noise come from the depths of their friend's barrel chest and knew Hamish was going to speak.

"I think Dougie liked his new roof."

Donald nodded.

"Aye, and the sheep and the dogs. He must be the wealthiest shepherd in the kingdom."

"Dougie is wealthy for another reason. He is with his family

277

again," said Alistair. "I don't think he cares too much for wealth."

More growling from Hamish's chest.

"But they are reunited in a kingdom that is torn apart."

They all remembered talking with the Younger when they had returned from Iona and had expected their king to be in good spirits. Tella the Mac Mar was finally dead and wee Matina was safe. But the Younger's words and mood had been dark.

"The High Table is divided. Even now the clans loyal to me have returned home from battle and my son rides alongside the McCreedys, Baxters and Morgans, and many other clans who seek advantage from my death. Ranald has promised them all new lands to secure their loyalty to his banner. It will not be long before Ranald claims my throne."

Alistair broke the silence that followed.

"At the water's edge on Iona Sound, Matina drew pictures on the sand and helped me understand that the Picts had captured Margaret and Columba. We later heard that Seamus has gone to Deros, on Skye, to free Margaret from Borak One Hand. Is there any news?"

The king shook his head.

"No riders have arrived from Seamus."

Then the Younger's face became warm.

"There is something we must do for the Keeper. He has suffered terribly at Myroy's hands and has been tested so that anger grew in his heart. Fresh horses are ready for you in the stables. Ride now and take the Welsh flock to him."

A servant entered the Great Hall with two black and white sheepdogs.

"These are the finest sheepdogs in my kingdom. Gift them to Dougie too and return here."

"Shall we return quickly?" asked Alistair.

The Younger remembered Myroy's prophecy about how Ranald would kill him and his first thought was for the safety of his friends.

"No."

Hamish stuck his chest out.

"How many men does Ranald command?"

"Six hundred."

"And your guard at the palace?"

"Two hundred."

"Shall we raise the loyal clans?" asked Alistair.

The Younger shook his head.

"Not yet. Something has to happen first."

"What?" asked Donald.

"You will know when the time is right."

But Alistair knew the prophecy too, knew what had to happen first, and as he headed south from the palace his heart was broken and he believed that this would be the last time he would ever see his king.

"How far is it to the palace?" asked Donald.

Alistair looked up at a grey and featureless sky. The coming rain would slow their progress.

"A day."

The path back to the palace twisted upwards through a deep wooded valley with a gurgling stream to one side, and trees on both slopes turning gold, brown and yellow, but none of the leaves had fallen yet.

"It will be a cold winter," growled Hamish.

"If Ranald sits upon the throne it will be cold *and* dark," said Alistair.

Hamish's face became grim.

"Well, let's make sure he doesn't."

They rounded a bend and rose up to the head of the valley. Here they could see a wide expanse of farmland stretching out to far hills. Beyond those hills was the palace. Their path wound down to run between golden fields of barley, and close to a stand of pines rested a gypsy caravan.

Donald grinned at Alistair.

"That's Babs."

Hamish urged his steed into a gallop and they didn't catch up with him until the caravan, where Hamish already held Barbarini in his arms, her legs dangling above the ground.

"How are you, angel?"

"I am well."

"I have missed you."

"I missed you too."

They ignored Alistair and Donald's cooing, and kissed.

"Put me down," said Babs. "I have a message from Myroy for you."

Hamish lowered her down gently and the cooing stopped.

"You are to approach the palace with care."

"Aye."

She looked at Alistair.

"Ranald will be king. You must seek out Kenneth of Blacklock and journey across the Great Sea to find Margaret, the Queen of the Irish Peoples. Myroy says you must win the support of a friend and an old enemy for the coming war. Bring these new allies to the palace by the next full moon."

"My guess is that a *friend* will be Seamus and the Irish army, but who is the old enemy?"

"Myroy says you will know."

"It's not the stinking Black Kilts is it?" asked Donald.

Alistair thought about Borak One Hand. He was clever, very clever, and strong.

"Perhaps. But whoever it is, we do not have long to win their support."

"Just till the next full moon," said Babs.

Hamish wrapped his great hand around her hand.

"What do we do next?"

"Go to the palace. My path, for now, lies elsewhere."

He bent and kissed her. More cooing from his friends.

"Stay safe. These lands are no longer free of danger for the travelling people."

"We will both stay safe, whatever happens."

"How do you know?"

"Myroy told me."

"Did he tell you anything else?"

Babs winked at him, climbed up on to the seat of her caravan, and took hold of the reins.

"Oh, yes," she said.

***

At sundown, a quarter moon appeared and disappeared as fluffy white clouds scudded across the sky.

"It will rain soon," moaned Donald. "Shall we find shelter?"

Hamish growled.

"Och, we'll be at the palace before then if we press on."

"And why do we need to approach the palace with care?"

Alistair's face became hard.

"I think it will be under siege. If Ranald is to be king he must take the palace and kill his father."

"Ranald was a horrible child," said Hamish.

Donald nodded.

"Still is."

"Ambitious and dangerous. We must not underestimate him."

"Or Morag. She is horrible too. They make a nice couple don't they."

Alistair swivelled around on his Highland and stared back into the gloom.

"What's that?"

The outline of a horse and rider, moving quickly, began to take form.

"Does he wear the king's own tartan?" asked Donald.

Hamish strained his eyes.

"Can't see. Could be anyone."

They turned their horses and drew their claymores. The rider saw them and pulled back on his reins, and his horse reared up on to its hind legs, snorting and shaking its mane. The warrior called out.

"Who blocks the path of the king's rider?"

"Which king?" shouted Donald.

"Malcolm the Younger. Who are you?"

"I am Alistair of Cadbol and my friends here are Hamish of Tain and Donald of Tain."

Alistair recognised the man's voice. "Is that you, Ancevo?"

Ancevo dismounted and walked towards them.

"Aye. Greetings, Alistair."

The friends dismounted too and went over to shake hands. Alistair reached him first.

"What business makes you ride in darkness?"

"The Younger's business. I rode to Berwick Castle and met with Grahm Deer the Angle. He now leads the people of Northumbria and his followers are glad of it. He desires peace with us, but will take no side in the civil war. I can understand that. Their army was destroyed by fire from the earth and the few who returned home have told such tales that fear runs deep amongst them. The Angles have no appetite for war."

Alistair thought about Myroy's words.

"So we need to find other allies."

"We do."

"Has Margaret been freed from Deros?" asked Hamish.

It began to rain and Ancevo shrugged his shoulders.

"I do not know."

＊

Margaret remembered being pulled along into Deros, a thick rope tied around her waist, chained around the neck, and linked to Columba's neck by an iron bar. She had stumbled as the track curved through a cutting in a high earthen bank and struggled to her feet as Borak's horse entered the fortress through two great wooden doors. Women and children had stared at them, silent and hateful, looking as though they wanted to beat them. There had been no dignity then, but that soon changed when Borak dismounted and ran up the steps to the top of the outer walls.

She still didn't know what he had said when he called down to his people, but warriors in Black Kilts walked over and gently released them.

Later, a serious-looking thin youth with black hair, which hung down his back to meet the top of his kilt, gave them a warning.

"My name is Rolgin, a student of Aglan the Tongue Speaker. If you need our words changed into your tongue, come to me. Borak One Hand has ordered that you can walk within the walls of Deros without fear. Go where you wish. No one will harm you. But if you attempt to leave the fortress you will be severely punished."

The way the young man spoke the word *punished* had sent a shiver down Margaret's spine.

The next two days had been comfortable and the food was good, but they quickly became bored. Even though the Picts treated them with respect, they ignored Margaret and Columba completely when they used gestures to ask what they were doing, or to try and join in with them. Even the children walked away when they approached. It was like being a leper and Margaret and Columba spent their time eating, walking the walls to see the ocean, or talking to each other. Columba prayed four times a day.

All of that changed with the arrival of a single ship with a black sail. Only twenty warriors made it back from the fleet that had been berthed at Fionnphort. Aglan was not one of them. When they told their tales, the mood changed towards their prisoners and guards seized them and took them through the ancient inner walls, which protected the court of the king, the Mac Mar. Their chamber had one tiny window that was too small even for a child to squeeze through and the outside of their door had the biggest bolts Margaret had ever seen.

Columba begged the guards to fetch Rolgin the Tongue Speaker and, when he arrived, his serious face was angry, and the words he spoke full of hatred.

"My master, Aglan, is dead. Merik Benn is dead. Borak has

ordered that you be locked away for your own safety. There are many, including me, who desire your death. Our king is dead. Tella the Mac Mar was butchered by a Scot on Iona. His heir, Gath, has also joined the fallen."

"I shall pray for Aglan, Tella and Gath," said Columba.

"Pray for the others too. On the field of battle, at a place the Scots call Stirling, all of our brave warriors have fallen."

Margaret's face became sad.

"How many, Rolgin?"

"Two thousand."

"I shall pray for them too," said Columba.

"There is not a family on Skye who has not lost a father, a son or a husband."

"Your people must be sick of war."

Rolgin ignored Columba's comment.

"I have other news. Seamus and the Irish fleet are two days' sail from Deros. Borak One Hand waits for them and has sworn vengeance for the death of his brother, Tumora. Borak says he has no quarrel with either of you. For him it is a matter of honour now."

Margaret began to cry and Columba put an arm around her.

"Please ask Borak not to kill my husband. I will do anything he asks, but spare Seamus."

"I shall ask him, but I already know his reply. Vengeance grips his mind."

"Please don't kill him."

"Borak will set you free on Seamus's death."

"May I speak with Borak?" asked Columba.

"No."

"It does not need to be like this."

"That is not what Borak thinks and he is now the Mac Mar."

"But so many of your people are dead. You need a long peace and an ally to protect you from the Norsemen. They are not fools. When Thorgood Firebrand learns of your weakness, he will take your island."

"Let him try. No one has ever taken Deros."

Margaret stared into the Tongue Speaker's eyes.

"I am Queen of the Irish peoples. We can give you protection."

"No."

"Please let me speak with Borak," repeated Columba.

"No, he is *busy*."

Rolgin's words made Margaret shudder.

"Busy?"

"He prepares a trap for Seamus and the giant, Finn McCool."

As the door slammed shut behind Rolgin, Margaret collapsed in a corner of their chamber, sobbing, her head between her knees. Columba felt useless as he listened to the words she repeated, over and over again.

"Please don't kill him."

***

As her pots and pans swayed and played their tune, Barbarini the Traveller stared ahead at the path, searching for another patteran left by her people. The secret signs might be made from sticks or stones and would show the way the caravans had travelled. There were no wheel ruts ahead, which meant they had moved through these hills before the rain had started, but from the way the last patteran had been built, one small stone on a larger stone and an oak leaf in between, not long before the rain. She would be with her mother and father soon.

Barbarini felt worried and at the same time strengthened by Myroy's words. Now she did not fear the future. If Hamish was destined to be the father of her children then they would survive the war. But she did fear what he had said about leaving the path and watching her people from a lonely place. With the signs of battle all around the kingdom, it could mean that the Ancient One wanted to save her from some kind of evil. She drove these thoughts from her mind by thinking of Hamish again. Maybe he would not go with Alistair across the Great Sea. Maybe he would stand shoulder to shoulder with his king at the palace. But it didn't matter. Myroy had said they would be safe and *that was all that mattered*.

"I kiss you now, my wee Hami," she said.

At a fork in the path, Barbarini saw another patteran and jumped down to study it. An arrow made of birch twigs pointing left along a path, lined with tall bracken, which wound its way up to a shoulder of a hill. Further along the path, it twisted and turned before vanishing completely. The other fork curved right and followed a stream. Birch trees lined both banks and a kingfisher sat like a statue on a branch, before diving with a flash of brilliant blue and orange. She stared up at the hill. A ruined fort perched on its summit, sheep littered the higher pastures and the sun had turned the heather on the lower slopes purple. Barbarini sniffed the air. Now that the rain had stopped everything had that new and fresh smell. It was going to be a beautiful autumn day.

Barbarini climbed back on to her seat and ignored both paths at the fork. She steered her caravan off the path to trundle across grass and rose up the hillside towards the ruined fort. After a short way, she saw a smooth grassy path, cropped short by the sheep, which curved up and around the hill, making the climb longer but much easier. She closed her eyes and let the sunshine warm her face, imagining what the views would be like from the hilltop. She had never climbed this hill before, had no reason to, yet she knew these lands well. The Younger's palace would be too far away to see, but the ancient wooden Hunting Tower, the river Almond and the small village of Glenalmond would all be clearly visible. The deer forest around them all would stretch out like a green blanket.

Near to the summit, the sound of her pans changed and lost their steady rhythm as the path became awkward, rutted and with large stones sticking up. A wheel hit a rock and rose up before bumping back down again, making the pots swing violently. A crash came from inside the caravan. She slapped the reins down on to her horse's back, urging it on up the slope and out on to a grassy plateau with the lonely old fort at its centre.

Her caravan stopped beside a low fallen wall and she jumped down, and untied the horse to graze freely and enjoy a rest. Barbarini sat down with an apple and looked down towards the river Almond, searching for the gypsy encampment. It was where it normally was. On a meander in the river, she counted eleven caravans all grouped closely together and she could just make out three children swimming, splashing each other, and probably shouting but they were too far away to hear. Smoke rose up from a single fire at the centre of the camp. She bit her apple.

"So why do I need to watch?"

By high sun, the children had long stopped playing in the water and there was no movement at all in the camp. Barbarini stood and stretched her back.

"This is foolish. I should be with my family."

The grass beside her began to shimmer, like moonlight on water, and Myroy rose up so that half his body was visible and half still in the earth. He spoke a single word and disappeared down.

"Wait."

Barbarini sat again and stared hard at the camp. Close to sundown, she was numbingly bored and daydreaming about her Union of Souls, feeling a warm embrace, hearing the druid's words and Hamish's nervous but sincere promise once more.

"With love for each other and with respect for the world in which we live, I call upon you, Hamish of Tain, to make thy promise." The druid paused and smiled. "Will you care for and protect this woman, and love her for all time?"

"Aye, I will."

She didn't need any other promise.

Barbarini closed her eyes and became lost in thought, seeing pictures of Hamish and Donald aboard a ship, the sail billowing out and gulls soaring high above. Alistair was there too, and other men she did not recognise, all talking, or coiling ropes, or walking around wooden boxes stacked on the deck. Beside the boxes was a gypsy caravan, which slowly caught fire and became an inferno that the crew did not notice or care about.

Barbarini opened her eyes, her body drenched in sweat, and stared at the camp, not believing at first what she was seeing. Three caravans were on fire. Warriors in plaids ran around, their swords, spearheads and axes glinting in the late sun. A single figure, perhaps a woman, was mounted on a horse, pointing at any gypsy who tried to escape. When she pointed, warriors stopped setting fire to the caravans and made chase, cutting their enemy down. The silent massacre of Barbarini's family and friends did not take long, and her head dropped into her hands. As grief took hold of her, as tightly as any hug Hamish had ever given her, Myroy's words raced through her mind.

"Watch them from a lonely place. Then do whatever your heart tells you to do."

As tears ran down her cheeks, Barbarini searched her heart. Her mother had told her many times about the danger from Morag McCreedy and her clan. Morag wanted revenge, because Benita had stolen the man she loved, and now she had taken that revenge. Barbarini's sadness turned to anger. Revenge was what she craved, and right now she craved it as much as Morag McCreedy had ever done.

The gypsies never became involved in the wars or disputes between clans or kingdoms. But this had nothing to do with war or dispute. Barbarini remembered the ancient traditions of the travelling peoples. These traditions bound gypsies together no matter how far they were apart, and no matter how much they might like or dislike each other. Supporting a blood feud was their rock and their protection against outsiders who wronged them. Barbarini had been taught these rules since she was knee-high to her grandmother and had sworn to uphold her promise to any other gypsy who asked for her help in times of tragedy. Now, she knew there were many who would uphold their duty to her and that the blood feud would not end until she or Morag had joined the fallen.

Barbarini wiped away her tears, hitched the horse to her caravan and returned to the fork in the paths, listening to the rhythm of her pots and pans. Her red eyes stared forward and did not see. Her body shook with an uncontrollable rage.

"We shall meet soon, Morag McCreedy," she said.

***

After sundown and not far from the palace, the friends sat on their Highlands, discussing what to do next.

"Do we stay on the path?" asked Hamish.

Alistair shook his head.

"No. Once we reach the brow of the hill, we will be on open ground and easily seen."

"But under the cloak of darkness."

"Myroy told us to be cautious."

"Then where?"

"The best way to secretly approach the palace is to lead the horses through the woods on the eastern side," said Ancevo. "The trees are no more than one hundred paces from the walls there."

Donald smiled.

"And what's up with you?" asked Alistair.

"It's stopped raining."

"Hmm. Lead the way, Ancevo."

They left the path and moved slowly, under a quarter moon, so that their horses could pick out safe patches of ground to place their hooves. On grass they moved silently and on rock the horses' clatter made the friends glance around nervously for an enemy. But they saw no one, dismounted and led their Highlands into an oak and elm wood. They picked their way through the trees, with Ancevo leading and everyone feeling a growing sense of unease about what they might find.

As they approached the palace, Ancevo saw an orange glow.

The firelight grew brighter with each step and his pace slowed. Twenty paces from the edge of the wood, he tied his horse to a branch and beckoned to the others to do the same. On hands and knees he nervously crawled forward and Alistair joined him. The palace walls rose up, the height of four men and its towers nearly twice that, rising above the surrounding grassy plain like stone fingers. There was no gate on this side of the palace. The open ground between the wood and the palace walls was packed with tents, tethered horses and warriors wrapped in plaids sleeping around campfires. Everything was out of range of the Younger's archers. A few warriors stood on guard and stared up at the battlements. The encampment was like a tight menacing necklace, strangling the palace.

"It must be Ranald's army," whispered Alistair.

"Aye. How long do you think they have been here?"

"Not long. One day, maybe two."

Hamish and Donald crawled forward and watched the dancing firelight shadows on the palace walls.

"They are Baxter tartans," growled Hamish. He pointed at a campfire. "And they are McCreedys."

"What do we do?" asked Donald.

"Fulfil Myroy's wishes and give the Younger hope," said Alistair.

"Do we leave for Deros now?" asked Ancevo.

"Not *we*. Hamish, Donald and I will seek out Kenneth of Blacklock. You, Ancevo, must get inside the palace. Tell Malcolm we will return with the Irish army at the next full moon. Tell him to have hope."

"But how do I get in? The doors will be bolted and I can't climb the walls."

"We will think of a way." Alistair looked at Hamish and Donald. "Any ideas?"

"No," they said together.

"Any secret passages?"

No one replied and there was silence until Donald spoke.

"Why not steal an enemy plaid, walk through the camp and knock on the door?"

Hamish growled.

"The palace guards would put an arrow into your chest before you even got near to the gate."

Ancevo smiled.

"Are you sure I can't come with you?"

Alistair's reply was firm.

"No, you can't come."

An enemy guard with a spear walked in front of their place of hiding and they froze like statues. The man looked bored and ambled away.

"Can we use the power in Dougie's stone?" asked Donald.

"No," whispered Hamish and Alistair together.

Ancevo looked at a narrow window slit near the top of a tower. A torch must have been lit inside for a yellow beam shone out.

"We must let Malcolm know that I am coming. If we asked him to be ready at the gates at dawn, I might have a chance of riding past the enemy."

Donald shook his head.

"You would join the fallen."

"Can you think of anything better?" asked Alistair.

"No."

"What can we do?"

"Don't know."

"No. I don't mean how do we get into the palace? We have faced an enemy many times. What are we good at?"

Hamish pushed his barrel chest out.

"Throwing people around."

Donald smiled and pointed a finger at his big friend.

"I'm good at making heather ale, fighting and annoying him."

"How about you, Ancevo?" asked Alistair.

"I am a farmer. My father taught me to use a bow and I can kill a hare at thirty paces."

Alistair pointed at the tower.

"Could you shoot an arrow through that window?"

"If I was close enough to the base of the wall I could."

"And I can scribe, not well, but I can write a message to the Younger and tie it to an arrow."

"Why not just shoot it over the wall?"

"Could land anywhere and not be found. If we do not kill the guard in the tower, he is bound to see it."

Hamish nodded at Alistair and rose.

"Do you have parchment and quill?"

"Aye. In a bag on my horse."

"Write the note. Donald and I will get a bow."

"We will?" asked Donald.

"Come on."

"What do I do?" asked Ancevo.

Alistair smiled.

"Stay here. Calm your nerves and prepare your aim in your mind. You will only get one chance at this."

"Do I not help the men of Tain?"

Alistair's smile widened.

"I think you'll find they can look after themselves."

Alistair crawled back to his horse and Ancevo watched Hamish and Donald leave the wood and creep up behind the bored guard with a spear. The man slumped silently onto the ground and Hamish threw him over his shoulder and walked into the trees. Then the big man came out alone and disappeared into the enemy camp with Donald.

***

Malcolm the Younger tip-toed into a richly furnished bed chamber that was lit by a single torch in an iron holder on the wall. He moved quietly to a bed, tucked safely into a corner, and stared down. Matina was sleeping peacefully at last, a young kid on a blanket between the little girl's knees. The Younger smiled at the goat and gently pulled the blanket up to cover Matina's shoulders.

"Find peace," he whispered and silently left.

Back in the top passageway, a boy was carrying a tray of food to the door of another bed chamber. The food wasn't as good as it normally was. A goblet of water, a hunk of oat bread and a wooden bowl half full of broth. The siege would last a long time and even a king would need to tighten his belt.

"I'll take that," he said to the servant.

The boy handed him the tray, bowed politely and opened the door. Malcolm hesitated, remembering his last conversation with Arkinew. It was now hard to believe that his alchemist had once been one of the most powerful and feared men in his father's time. As children, Malcolm and Murdoch had been terrified of him and were told secretly that the Elder could not have extended his will across the kingdom without Arkinew's wisdom. His knowledge allowed the Elder to crush his enemies, for he knew when they were strong and weak, and precisely the right time to attack. In many ways, the man who walked backwards had been as ruthless as his king.

But now, the alchemist was a mere shadow of his former self and the Younger accepted some of the blame for that. Arkinew had been bonded to the Elder by the old magic and, on the Elder's death, his mind had begun to wither. It could not wither any more without death.

Malcolm entered the chamber and stared at the frail old man who sat bolt upright in a chair. Arkinew's eyes showed fear and his bony hands gripped the armrests.

"Who are you?"

"It is your friend, Malcolm."

"Do not come any closer."

"I bring you food."

"Who are you?"

"Your friend."

Arkinew stared at him suspiciously.

"Where is Gangly?"

"Returned to the forest. Many moons ago."

"He has left me?"

"You sent him away."

The alchemist shouted angrily at Malcolm.

"He abandoned me."

"He did not abandon you. Are you hungry?"

"Do not come any closer."

"You need not fear me. Do you remember schooling two children, named Malcolm and Murdoch?"

"Malcolm and Murdoch?"

"Aye. Young princes."

There was a flash of recognition on Arkinew's face.

"The old Norse."

"You taught us the old Norse language and many other things for which I am eternally grateful."

"Myroy."

"Myroy advised us both. You were his apprentice and I held Amera's stone for a while, whilst I was king."

"Where is Myroy?"

"Fighting an ancient war. Protecting a Keeper. Telling the story. Moving back and forth through time."

"Dougie?"

"Dougie of Dunfermline holds the stone and is safe. Odin believes the ruby is held by Llewellyn, the king of the Welsh peoples."

Arkinew pointed at the tray, his hand shaking out of his control.

"Food."

"Are you hungry?"

"Don't come any closer."

"I'll put the tray here for you." Malcolm placed it on to the floor. "If you want anything else, just call a servant, but I am afraid food is going to be in short supply for a while."

"Who are you?"

"Malcolm the Younger, son of the Elder."

There was no trace of any recognition on the old man's face now, and Malcolm felt lost and sad.

294

"I have to go."

"Gangly?"

"Returned to the forest."

Arkinew tried to stand and couldn't.

"But I must help the Elder."

Malcolm decided to lie.

"He sleeps. You should sleep soon too."

"But the Donald clan must be destroyed if the Elder is to rule the new kingdom."

"That was a long time ago."

Arkinew shouted at him again.

"It is now!"

"Eat and sleep, old friend."

"You are not my friend. You want to kill me."

"No."

"Who are you?"

A warrior in the king's own tartan entered the chamber and handed Malcolm an arrow. The arrow had a parchment wrapped and tied around its shaft.

Arkinew pointed his shaking hand at the king and called out.

"Who are you?"

The Younger felt completely useless, but managed a weak smile, and as he left the chamber he whispered to himself.

"Your dear friend."

***

At dawn, the Younger stood on the palace walls above the main gate. In half-light, he saw the enemy tents, smouldering fires and warriors wrapped in plaids sleeping around the fires. His son would be asleep too in one of the grander tents. Guards with spears sat talking and had not noticed him. Everything was quiet and peaceful, but it was the start of another day when an attack might begin. On the main path to the palace, behind the enemy and out of sight of them for now, sat a lone rider on a Highland, waiting for his moment to come. Malcolm signalled down to his men and silently the gates opened. Then he waved his arm at Ancevo, whose horse trotted forward.

The Younger hurried around the top of the walls towards the eastern side of the palace where the trees were closer. The morning chorus of birdsong drifted over from the wood, where three riders sat patiently on Highlands, thick ropes tied around their waists. There was not a trace of the guards on this side and the rest of Ranald's warriors slept soundly. The men of Tain had done a good night's work. He felt the wind on his face, smiled at his friends and nodded, and a sad thought went through his mind.

"At least you can remember my name."

***

Donald adjusted the rope around his waist.

"What are we waiting for?"

"The Younger's signal," said Alistair. "Be patient."

"But we've been up half the night. Can't we just get on with it?"

Alistair glanced at Hamish, who dwarfed his Highland.

"Where did you get the rope?"

"In Ranald's camp. They have brought supplies of everything. Food, heather ale, ladders, weapons."

"I am looking forward to this."

Hamish smiled.

"Aye."

They stared up at their king on the battlements. A gentle breeze blew back his long grey hair and the Younger smiled and nodded at them.

Alistair, Hamish and Donald drew their claymores and yelled as they drove their horses into the sleeping camp. Startled warriors sat up, eyes wide with terror, believing an army was upon them. Donald swung his sword and cut a man down. Hamish's charging horse knocked a Baxter clean off his feet. As they reached the gallop, the lines around their waists tightened and one tent after another flew away from the pegs the men of Tain had loosened. Morag McCreedy had just opened her eyes when the canvas above her head vanished as if by magic. Panic swept through this side of the camp. Men cried out warnings and everyone tried to find their weapons. In the confusion, the men of Tain untied the ropes around their waists, turned their horses and attacked anyone who stood in their way. Before an arrow or a spear was thrown at them, they were safely back inside the trees.

***

Ancevo reached the edge of the enemy camp, three hundred paces from the gates, as the roar of scared and angry men came from the other side of the palace. The guards here jumped up, alert, spears ready, and started shouting and running to find out what was going on. This was Ancevo's moment. The armed guards were quickly leaving and those woken by the commotion were not armed yet. He kicked his heels into his horse's flanks and the stallion thundered forward towards the open gates. He bent forward, staying as low as he could, trying to make his back as small a target as possible. His horse swerved around a campfire surrounded by startled men, and passed three more tents, with only one hundred paces to go to the gates. Ranald stepped out of a tent, saw the open gates and the rider. He called out and his warriors threw sleep aside to grab bows and spears, and chased after the rider.

"Come on, boy. Fifty paces to go," said Ancevo in a strong voice.

Spears thudded into the earth on both sides of the stallion. Behind Ancevo, archers knelt and drew arrows from their quivers and aimed.

"Kill the horse," shouted Ranald.

On top of the wall, Malcolm the Younger stared down at his son.

"Now," he said.

His own archers leapt up from behind the battlements and sent a rain of death down onto the enemy. Ancevo's horse thundered on to the Palace Green and strong hands slammed the gates shut

CHAPTER FIFTEEN

DEROS

After fleeing the chaos outside the Younger's palace, Alistair, Hamish and Donald felt safe enough to let their horses settle into a canter, and kept the high sun on their left so that they headed west towards the High Glens. Every now and then, they passed a burnt cottage or a deserted village, and all the travellers they saw on the path were scared of them. The civil war had touched everyone.

"Do you think Ancevo got in to the palace?" asked Donald.

Hamish shrugged his broad shoulders.

"He is in, or dead."

Little else was said as the scenery changed from forest, farmland and rounded hills to wild, lonely mountains. Alistair became lost in his thoughts. He had enjoyed many adventures with Dougie and the men of Tain, and now they were coming to an end. So much of the old world was coming to an end.

"So, one last adventure," he thought. "Place a new king onto the throne of Scotland and help establish a second Long Peace. What then? Go back to Cadbol and lead the clan, like my father? I'm not sure I can do it."

He glanced at his friends.

"Can they go back to making heather ale after all this?" Alistair asked himself, then smiled.

"Dougie will have no trouble at all being a shepherd again. If only he knew he could be king, but that path lies with his twin and Myroy says he will rule as justly as the Younger. I wonder what Mairi would say if she ever found out that she could have been a queen?"

Hamish and Donald rode in silence and sometimes watched the changing expressions on Alistair's face. Now it was sad, as though he was saying goodbye to an old friend. But he wasn't saying goodbye to anyone. Alistair was picturing the inside of a dark, gloomy church on Iona, and hearing himself speak in a soft, reassuring voice.

"Come here, Matina."

The little girl sat beside Tella the Mac Mar, rocking backwards and forwards, staring at the iron cross, which stuck up from the Pict's body.

"It's over. Come on."

She didn't reply, or notice Alistair at all. After what she had been through, it would be a while yet before she noticed anything. Alistair sat up on the long oak altar, felt the bruises on his legs and the deep cut on his arm. The side of his face ached and his tongue discovered a missing tooth. He still felt lightheaded from the punches.

"I feel as though I've been in a fight with Hamish," he muttered.

He lowered himself down from the altar.

"Do not look at him, Matina."

The girl kept staring at the blood dripping down the iron cross and Alistair went over, took her hand and pulled her up.

"Let's get away from here."

They stepped out into bright sunshine and walked down the grassy slope to the water's edge. Her trembling hand felt wet and sticky, and Alistair lifted it and looked at her fingers. They were caked in blood.

"I think a good wash is in order." He placed his free hand on to his cut arm to stop the bleeding. "For both of us."

No nod or shake of the head, and he led her down to the sand and sat behind her, the waves coming in and past them, soaking the lower half of their bodies. Alistair leant forward, took her left hand and waited for the next wave to roll in. He gently washed her hand, brushing the blood away from between the fingers, and tried to reassure her some more.

"It's over now. Whatever has happened to you is over. I will look after you, Matina, so stay close to me."

Another wave came in and Alistair washed her other hand, and felt the sting as he rubbed salt water into his cut. They stared across Iona Sound towards Fionnphort. A few masts stuck up out of the shallow waters of the harbour, but otherwise there was no trace at all of the Pictish fleet. Kenneth of Blacklock waved at him and Alistair stuck his thumb up. Ships with the three legs of Man on their sails headed south, and one towed the ship that Alistair had chased from Oban to Iona. There wasn't a Pict to be seen anywhere.

"Matina, did you see the man who waved at me? His name is Kenneth and he will take us across the Great Sea to the Younger's palace."

The little girl shook her head.

"There is nothing to fear now."

She shook her head again, waited for a wave to roll back and drew a crown on to the sand with her finger.

"That's right, the palace of the king."

Matina shook her head as the sea swept in to destroy the crown. When the water receded, she drew a face with long hair.

"Do you mean Margaret?"

She nodded.

"What has happened? The last time I saw you was when you sailed with Margaret and Columba. You left Seamus's fleet to hide here."

Matina waited for clean sand and drew a ship. On the sail she made an axe. Alistair shuddered.

"Is Margaret dead?"

She shook her head.

"Is Columba dead?"

Another shake of her head.

"O'Mara and the Irish guards?"

He felt her shoulders tremble and stared at the axe on the sail.

"Margaret and Columba were taken by the Picts?"

Matina nodded.

"And you want to find her?"

She grabbed his hand and squeezed it.

"I'm sorry. If Margaret has been captured, she will most likely be a prisoner on Skye and my orders are to return to the Younger. You must come with me."

She shook her head and drew an animal in the sand. Alistair thought it looked like a goat.

"How long have you been alone on the island?"

She held up five fingers.

"Five days."

A wave destroyed the goat and she drew another one.

"Are the goats your friends?"

Matina turned her head and smiled at him.

"Alright. Let's gather them together and find them a new home on the Palace Green. They will be the best fed goats in the kingdom."

She leapt up and they walked, hand in hand, towards the lower slopes of Dun I to find the little girl's companions.

"What's up with you, long face?" asked Donald.

"Hmm. Oh, sorry. I was just thinking."

"You have been thinking for hours," growled Hamish. "Smell the air."

Alistair sniffed.

"The sea is close. Come on, let's find Kenneth."

***

"Alistair says you must have hope."

Malcolm looked at Ancevo, the youngest of his secret riders and probably the best.

"You being here gives me hope. The men of Tain have a plan?"

"They seek out Kenneth of Blacklock at Oban and will sail to Skye to meet Seamus, and bring the Irish army here at the next full moon."

"A Gora moon?"

"I am sorry, Your Majesty. I do not know what that is."

Malcolm nodded and stared out of his chamber window on to the Palace Green. All the women and children, except one child, had been sent away to the lonely places and now his men carried large stones up to the top of the battlements. Ranald's forces might outnumber his, but the palace walls were thick and strong, and only starvation could defeat his people. A small herd of goats wandered freely across the Green and the Younger tried to work out how he might ask Matina for her permission to cook them. She came into the chamber with a tray, and politely, silently, offered Ancevo a goblet of water. Malcolm plucked up his courage.

"Thank you, Matina. Um, I need to speak to you about your goats."

Her face beamed with delight and she ran out of the chamber, and returned quickly with a tiny kid cradled in her arms.

"A new arrival?"

She nodded and handed it to her king. Malcolm stroked its head.

"How old?"

She held up two fingers.

"Two days. He's very sweet."

Matina took her companion back and skipped out. Malcolm glanced at Ancevo.

"We will just need to go hungry for a while longer."

"Until the next full moon."

"Aye." He paused for a moment. "It is a strange feeling."

"Strange?"

"Knowing the day of your death."

Ancevo's forehead creased.

"The next full moon?"

"No. The day before. A long time ago I decided to let my son rule for one day."

***

As Alistair talked with Kenneth at the stern of the *Leaping Salmon*, Hamish and Donald rested with their eyes closed and their backs against the ship's rail. Donald broke the silence.

"I'm bored."

A growl showed Hamish's agitation.

"Not again."

"I'm bored."

"Go and fish."

"I fished this morning."

"Go to sleep."

"I'm not tired."

"Rest your mouth. You've been using it a lot lately."

"Do you think so?"

"Aye."

"You want a fight?"

"No."

"I'm bored."

"You won't be bored when you reach Deros. I'm going to throw some Picts around again."

"Wager I kill more than you."

"No."

"Anyway, there may not be any Black Kilts left if Finn is there."

"Hmm."

"You ever been to Deros?"

"No."

"Heard any stories about it?"

Hamish took a deep breath.

"Only from traders who came to our village. The fortress has an outer earthen bank with a stone wall on the top. The only entrance is through giant wooden doors that could hold back ten armies. Inside the outer defences is a smaller circular wall, which contains the court of the Mac Mar. It is said to be very fine. There are riches to be had there."

Donald opened his eyes.

"And you said I needed to rest *my* mouth. That's the most I've heard you say in a long time."

"*Some* people do not need to say much."

"But I'm bored."

Hamish opened his eyes too.

"When that Angle cut your ear off, your head became lop-sided. Do you want me to cut the other one off?"

"You're too fat and too slow to beat me in a fight."

"Say that again."

"Too fat and too slow. Babs hasn't married a warrior. She's married a donkey."

Hamish grabbed Donald's neck and pulled his face close to his. Donald's dirk came up in a flash, its tip resting against the big man's throat. A shadow fell over them.

"Come on. Kenneth has spotted the coast of Skye. Are you ready to fight?"

Hamish and Donald stared up at Alistair and then smiled at each other.

"Aye," they said together.

***

Barbarini stared at Suni, at his bright shirt and large gold earrings, and tried to understand why he had so quickly agreed to the blood feud and the Star. No emotion showed at all on his lined and dark face. She spoke in a shaky voice, overawed by the man she had only heard of in stories.

"I had a long speech prepared in my mind about how Morag McCreedy slaughtered my family, and how I watched and cried."

When the leader of the travelling peoples spoke, his voice was grave and without a hint of pity.

"You are not the only one to have shed tears."

They walked, side by side, away from a circle of caravans, towards many men who led horses into the centre of a field.

"Was it Morag?"

Suni glanced at her and his earrings flapped against his cheeks.

"Either Morag, or others who have been poisoned by her lies. Many clans, that support Ranald, have turned against us."

"How many?"

"In all, seven families lost. It has to end now."

"By the blood feud and Star."

"Yes."

In front of them, the men mounted their horses and steered them into a tight circle with each rider facing outwards. Suni addressed them.

"It is many summers since I have called for the Star. Each of you faces a different direction. Each of you will ride along a different path. Tell our people about the blood feud. Bring them to the meander at Glenalmond on the day before the next full moon."

Like rays of light bursting from an exploding star, thirty riders galloped away to do Suni's will.

***

Alistair stood beside Seamus and Finn McCool, before the great gates of Deros. Seamus called up to a young man on the battlements.

"I demand to see Borak One Hand."

As Rolgin shouted back, many Black Kilts appeared on either side of the Tongue Speaker and they looked as though they did not need much of an excuse to throw their spears.

"The Mac Mar will speak with you when he is ready. He asked me to make two things clear. Margaret and Columba are well cared for. But, if any of your men try to enter Deros, they *will* be put to the sword."

"If Margaret is harmed in any way, there are many who shall be put to the sword. Go now, Tongue Speaker, and fetch your master."

"The Mac Mar will speak with you when *he* is ready," repeated Rolgin. "And only when he is ready."

Behind the gates, Borak listened to the voice of the man he hated more than anyone in the world. He nodded at a warrior who pushed his hand in to a bucket of goose fat and rubbed the fat into a giant hinge. Seamus's voice again.

"I will not leave this place until the Queen of the Irish peoples is safe in my arms."

Rolgin shouted back.

"Then wait. What else can you do? Attack and Margaret will join the fallen."

Unseen to Borak, Alistair stepped forward.

"When shall we return to speak with Borak?"

Rolgin disappeared from the top of the wall, but came back quickly.

"At sunset," he said.

The Tongue Speaker watched the enemy walk back to their camp, ran down the steps and crossed the grass to the gates.

"Master, it is as you commanded. They will return at sunset."

Borak ignored him and pointed at a hinge above the one the warrior had already greased.

"All of them," he said.

***

Mairi placed a bowl of lamb and barley broth in front of Dougie and gave him a wooden spoon.

"When do you go to meet Alec?"

Dougie sensed an edge in her voice and decided to be cautious.

"The day before the next full moon."

"And how do you know he comes by ship and will be at Culross then?"

"I just know."

"You are in real trouble, Douglas, if he brings any of the crew here."

He cut up a loaf of oat bread and passed thick slices to Tanny, Callum and Jock.

"Eat it all up, my chickens."

Tanny grinned at him.

"Have we got any cheese?"

Dougie frowned at her.

"We could all do with less of your teasing, lass."

Mairi sat with them.

"And don't think for one moment that Alec is staying here."

"And why not?"

"The cottage is too small. There is hardly enough room for us as it is."

Dougie looked around their only room. When the fire was lit, there wasn't a cosier cottage anywhere.

"What's wrong with it?"

"I want it longer."

"I have lived here all my life. I don't want it to change."

"Longer," said Tanny.

"You eat your bread."

Mairi continued the attack.

"Longer, or Alec goes to stay with Stewart of Balgeddie."

The shepherd plucked up his courage.

"My twin can stay here if he wants to."

Mairi shot him one of her looks.

"There is not room and it isn't that long ago that you brought Hamish and Donald round here."

"I didn't bring them. They just turned up on the king's business."

"They turned up without any notice or discussion with me."

"Och, they were no bother."

"Hamish ate most of our Winter Feast," said Callum.

"Oh, so you're on your mother's side."

Jock raised his hand.

"I'm on Ma's side too. I like an easy life."

Mairi cuffed his ear.

"Alec can't stay and I want the cottage longer."

"But I haven't seen him for many summers."

"You heard what I said."

"I heard it and do not agree with it."

As soon as he spoke, he knew he had made a mistake. The

children knew it too and grabbed their bread, and ran outside. They turned and heard a pot smash against the kitchen wall. Mairi's angry voice followed.

"And who calls a bloomin' horse '*Dog*'?"

Something else smashed against the wall and the children sat on the grass, smiling. They stared down beyond the drovers' road towards the calm waters of the loch and the setting sun, eating their supper.

Jock pointed at the centre of the loch.

"Are you sure you did not see the giant bird?"

Callum shook his head.

"You daydream as much as father," said Tanny.

✳✳✳

Later, the men of Tain, Seamus and Finn sat together in Seamus's tent, talking about the fortress and the civil war that raged across Scotland.

"Let's break in tonight and free Margaret," suggested Hamish.

Seamus shook his head.

"I can't take that risk."

"Then what do we do?" asked Donald.

"Continue the siege. Hunger will weaken their spirit."

"Not Borak's," said Alistair. "He hates you for killing Tumora."

Donald tapped his nose.

"He is up to something."

Seamus laid out his copy of Denbara's map on the floor in front of them.

"Of course he is. But what?"

"Do not be fooled by Borak's words," warned Finn. "Do not meet with him on your own."

Alistair nodded.

"Aye. That is when he will spring his trap."

"I need to know that Margaret is safe," said Seamus. "Even if I place my own life at risk."

Alistair pointed at the western edge of the map.

"Thorgood's fleet must journey past Skye and the Outer Islands when they sail from Sea People's Land for Ireland. The Younger told me that your lands are in danger. The Norsemen need this area," Alistair pointed at Dublin, "as their base to attack Llewellyn and the Welsh peoples. No one is better placed than Borak and his Black Kilts to protect Scottish soil, or your kingdom."

Seamus's face showed anger.

"I will not befriend Borak. He is no ally of mine."

"If Malcolm the Younger offered him the Outer Islands and made him the Protector, he might release Margaret."

Hamish shook his head.

"He does not want land. He wants revenge."

Finnegan joined them in the tent.

"Oh. The sun is low and Borak stands on the wall by the gates."

They stood and followed him out, and walked up to Deros.

"Do not agree to a duel, or talk with him alone," warned Alistair. "Listen to Finn's wise counsel."

"I am a king, not you," said Seamus in a hard voice. "Do not forget that Borak poisoned my father. If I can be alone with him for a moment, I shall take the chance and cut him down. Then we shall see the resolve of the Picts inside Deros."

They all stopped beside a wooden pole sticking out of the grass, marking the limit of enemy arrows. Seamus called up to Borak, who stood alone and like a statue on the battlements.

"If you harm one hair on Margaret's head, I will destroy you and *all* your people."

There was no reply and a tense silence followed.

"Is Margaret unharmed?"

Borak's answer was sharp and to the point.

"You have already been told the answer to that question."

"I was told by a Tongue Speaker and not by you."

"Then let me repeat Rolgin's words. She is unharmed, but attack us and she dies."

"Then your people will starve."

"*Everyone* in Deros will starve."

Alistair whispered to Seamus.

"This isn't getting us anywhere. May I speak with Borak?"

Reluctantly Seamus nodded.

"Borak, it is I, Alistair of Cadbol. We are enemies, but you know I tell the truth, even if my words and deeds harm your people. At Mountjoy you tried to win the Irish as your ally in the war against the Scots. I also needed Seamus as my ally and I did everything in my power to stop you. But you know I never lied to Patrick Three Eggs, or to you, to achieve my goal."

Borak gave him a small nod and Alistair continued.

"On the field of battle by Stirling Castle, your people were defeated. I am growing sick of war and the screams of the wounded. You are my enemy and yet I fear for you. Thorgood of the line of Firebrand will soon learn of Tella and Gath's deaths, and the slaughter at Stirling. He will know you are weakened, and will attack Skye and the Outer Islands. Together we are stronger. You cannot defend Skye against the Norsemen and their mighty fleet of longships. The Younger cannot defend the Outer Islands against them either. Join me. Be the Mac Mar *and* the Protector of the Outer Islands."

"Fine words, Alistair. Now hear mine. Bring me Seamus's head and I shall be your Protector."

"Seamus is my friend."

"Then you are my enemy."

"What do else do you want? You cannot win this war."

"You cannot win it either. I have Margaret and there is nothing you can do."

"Then we both lose. You want revenge for Tumora's death. Seamus wants revenge for the death of his father. Is revenge all that is left for us now?"

Borak pointed at Seamus.

"It is."

Seamus pointed at Borak.

"How do I know that Margaret still lives?"

"You have my promise."

"The promise of a murderer."

Their eyes locked and they stared at each other with utter hatred.

Alistair spoke again.

"Margaret is the heir to the line of Elder after Prince Ranald. I am here as Seamus's friend, but I am also here to speak for my king. If you do not kill Margaret, Malcolm the Younger will guarantee trade and safe passage for your people on Scottish soil."

Borak spat.

"Some of that soil belongs to the Picts. You stole our homelands around Carn Liath and now you plan to take Skye."

"We have no ambition to take Skye and it was Tella's ambition, not our aggression, that caused the loss of Carn Liath. You know that in your heart."

Borak did know that, but did not show it.

Half of the sun had fallen below the western horizon, turning the Great Sea in to a burnt orange blanket. The shadows lengthened.

"What do you want, Borak?" repeated Alistair.

"Nothing that you can gift me."

"I offer your people a future. Without the friendship of the Scots, I fear for them."

"We can look after ourselves."

Alistair smiled.

"In different circumstances, we might have been friends. Please let us in to see Margaret and Columba."

Borak stared out to sea and the setting sun.

"You ask too much. If I open the gates, how do I know that your army will not attack?"

Alistair shrugged his shoulders.

"How do we know you will not kill us?"

A gentle breeze lifted Borak's long black hair and he looked as though he was thinking things through.

"Order your army to retreat one thousand paces. I will order *all* my people inside the Court of the Mac Mar. My Tongue Speaker shall open the gates and one of you may enter to speak with Margaret and Columba. If any of your warriors charge at Deros, we will leave our inner fortress and close the gates. If that happens, Margaret will be the first to join the fallen."

"We agree," shouted Seamus. "I shall talk to my Queen."

Finn, Hamish and Donald glanced at each other. Alistair shook his head.

"*We* do not agree. It is a trap."

"I am the king, not you."

"You are the king and it is still a trap."

"Trap or not, I must know that Margaret is unharmed."

"Then why does he not just bring her to the battlements for us to see?"

"I do not care," hissed Seamus. "If Borak waits for me, I will be ready with my sword."

Finn McCool stepped forward and spoke in his deep commanding voice.

"Let me go."

"No."

"Then let me go," said Alistair. "I am the least likely to be killed. Finn threw the spear that killed Tumora, and you, Seamus, placed the body on a horse and made Borak ride away with it. He hates you both."

Seamus lifted his sword and placed the tip under Alistair's chin.

"No. I will go."

Borak disappeared from the top of the wall and they heard him call out Rolgin's name, and other instructions to his people. Seamus called out his own instructions.

"Get everyone back, even those who sleep in the tents."

Finn and the men of Tain reluctantly left and Rolgin appeared at the battlements.

"My master has told me to watch your army, Seamus. If they

314

move away I am to open the gates and let one person inside. Whom have you chosen to speak with Margaret?"

They were well-rehearsed words.

"I shall enter Deros."

Rolgin nodded and stared over at the enemy camp. Many warriors were being called together and led away towards the beach where the Irish fleet was berthed. When the last man was out of view, the Tongue Speaker walked calmly down to the gates and they silently opened.

"Please enter," he said.

Seamus drew his sword and followed, his long shadow advancing before him into the fortress, eyes darting around to catch a glimpse of an enemy. His senses were alive and immediately he saw two figures, a man and a woman, tied to posts about one hundred paces away. But his fear outweighed his desire to run to them. He stopped and spun around, and glanced up. No archer on the battlements and no one by the great doors, which were pushed back against the walls. He felt a little safer and moved on. Margaret and Columba were tied to posts, close to each other, the court of the Mac Mar behind them and the top of its defensive walls packed with Black Kilts. Seamus tried to spot Borak amongst them, but they were too far away.

Rolgin stood between the two hostages, pointing at the gags in their mouths, and speaking to Seamus without looking at him.

"Are you ready to speak with Margaret?" he asked in a loud voice.

"That is why I am here, Tongue Speaker."

Behind Seamus, the gates slowly and silently opened. Margaret and Columba were shaking their heads madly and pulling at their ropes as Rolgin delayed taking the gags from their mouths.

Seamus sensed that something was wrong and lifted his sword, and turned. An arrow hit him square in the chest and he fell on to his knees. A searing pain wracked his body and cold sweat ran off his forehead and into his eyes. Through the haze of sweat, Seamus saw an archer, standing in front of one of the gates, placing another arrow onto his bow. Borak One Hand came out from the gap behind the other gate, with an axe in his hand, and then his long shadow was darting towards him.

Seamus tried to raise his sword and couldn't. Margaret tried to scream and couldn't. As Columba prayed for Seamus's soul and Rolgin turned his head away, Borak's axe swung viciously down on to the wounded man's chest.

"Tumora, this is for you," said Borak.

***

"Tell Konini to keep the white cliffs off to port."

Perpigno wiped stinging, cold water from his eyes and took a deep breath.

"Hey, Brown Eyes, I never asked you. What kind of welcome will we receive in Scotland? They won't have seen a galley like this before and every trader we have seen in these waters has run away."

Alec smiled and looked along the deck towards the bow. Huge waves broke under the bow and sent a fountain of sea water over the crew.

"You are right, they won't have seen anything like this. Scottish ships are slower and much, much smaller."

"You do not use slaves to row them?"

Alec bent and touched his ankle iron.

"Some people use slaves. Now tell Konini about the cliffs."

Perpigno turned to face the Corsair, who held the tiller in his powerful hands, and told him. Konini said something back in a sharp voice.

"Ha. He says your weather is rubbish and asks if we can all go home now."

"When I land by the Forth he can leave."

"And what kind of welcome *will we get?*"

"Don't worry. Nothing much happens where I live."

At sunrise on the next morning, Finn, Finnegan, Hamish, Donald and Alistair stood by the arrow marker post in front of the gates of Deros. Behind them waited the ranks of the Irish army. Everyone was tense, wondering what had happened to Seamus. The Black Kilts stared down at them from the battlements with grim, determined faces. Borak's face was like granite. The gates silently opened and Margaret and Columba walked out, seemingly unharmed, although Margaret's step was unsteady. Columba pulled a long rope and a horse followed him out of Deros, a body strapped on to its back. Alistair ran forward and called back.

"Stay here."

Arrows and spears were trained on him, and Borak shouted at his men.

"Hold."

Alistair took Margaret's arm.

"Are you alright?"

Even as he spoke the words he knew she wasn't alright. Her eyes were bloodshot from crying and she walked without knowing where she was going.

"Margaret, speak to me."

She moved past him and Columba handed Alistair the rope.

"I am sorry, Alistair. I shall pray for your friend."

He saw Seamus's bloodstained clothes and stared up at Borak.

"It did not need to be like this."

"My revenge is complete and I have kept my word and released your people. Now, get off my island."

Hatred of the Black Kilts filled Alistair's heart and he drew his claymore. The ground beside him shimmered, like moonlight on water, and Myroy rose up. A Pict above the gate, threw his spear at the apparition and the Ancient One pointed his finger at it. The spear stopped in mid-flight and fell harmlessly to the ground. Myroy pointed his finger along

the line of Picts on the battlements and all their weapons flew
up into the sky, and did not come back down. Everyone stared
at the old man through wide eyes, believing him to be some
kind of demon.

"We shall talk now," said Myroy.

Alistair watched as Seamus's tent rose up and flew above
the heads of the astonished Irish army, and pitched itself by
the marker post. Borak, Finn, Hamish, Donald, Margaret and
Columba rose too and shot like an arrow through the tent flap.
Myroy nodded at the door.

"Follow me."

Inside, everyone was sitting silently around an iron table. The
Ancient One sat at the head of the table and Alistair sat opposite
him. Myroy's voice was fierce.

"Some of you have forgotten why we are here and some of
you have not yet been told the story. Where has your revenge
taken you, Borak One Hand? Where will your revenge take you,
Alistair of Cadbol? Where did Seamus's revenge take him?"

Seamus's blood-soaked body appeared on the table and
Margaret burst into tears as Columba put an arm around her.

"Are you God?" he asked.

"No."

Columba looked as though he was going to ask another
question and Myroy lifted his hand.

"I am fighting an ancient war that threatens all that we hold
dear. Now, listen to my words."

Even those who had heard the story before were gripped. No
one spoke, no one moved and no time passed as the history of
Amera's stone unfurled. When all was told, Myroy placed his
wrinkled hands on to the table.

"Finn. You are now king of all the Irish peoples. Rule justly.
Seamus is dead and Margaret renounces her crown. Go with
Alistair to aid the Younger, then return to Mountjoy and gather
your warriors. Thorgood's fleet is coming. Expect *nothing* in
return from the Scottish people, even though you helped them

in their moment of greatest need. We must establish a new Long Peace in which the Keeper is safe and lost from memory."

Finn nodded and Seamus's body disappeared.

"Borak. You are now the Protector of the Outer Islands. Keep the western border safe. Send a rider to the new king if ever Norsemen set foot on Scottish soil. Gather your warriors and aid the Younger at his palace. Go with Alistair and Finn."

"I will," said Borak.

"Columba. Bury Seamus on the island of Iona and pray for his soul. The Younger will join the fallen soon. Bury him next to Seamus."

"I will."

"Set aside your tears, Margaret. You must marry again and quickly."

"I will not. Seamus was my true love and there will never be another."

Myroy touched her shoulder.

"I shall marry again," she said in a dreamlike voice.

Alistair nearly said the words that were in his mind.

"You are just using that girl."

Myroy's eyes flashed.

"I am fighting a war."

Donald glanced at big Hamish.

"And what do we do?"

"Do what you do best. Ranald and the clans loyal to him await you outside the royal palace." Myroy gave Hamish a small smile. "Throw them around a wee bit."

"Shall we leave now?" asked Alistair.

Bright sunshine made everyone squint as the tent around them flew away. Myroy began to move his staff in a circle just above the ground and he pointed a finger at the sky. Hundreds of axes, spears and swords fell down on to the grass in front of the gates of Deros.

"Move swiftly and know this. There are other armies that go to do war with Ranald."

Malcolm woke at dawn on the day before the full moon and felt a sickening knot tie itself in the pit of his stomach. He had known for years this moment would come, and that made no difference. He felt afraid and doubt filled his mind. Could he do it? Could he give himself up to Ranald, knowing that his son would kill him? Could he show dignity to his followers, or would he shake with fear like he had done as a child in front of Arkinew? He dressed and half-expected Myroy to rise up from the underworld to give him some words of comfort, but the Ancient One did not come.

He left his chamber and went to check on Matina. She slept peacefully in her bed over by a corner, a kid asleep on her lap. He smiled and closed the door without a sound. Ancevo saw him.

"Your Majesty."

"Morning, Ancevo. My moment has come. Gather all my warriors and tell them to join me quickly on the Palace Green."

Ancevo's heart sank and he managed a weak smile.

"Aye, Your Majesty."

As the sun rose above the eastern horizon, the Green inside the high palace walls remained in twilight. Ancevo stood nervously beside Malcolm and they were completely surrounded by two hundred loyal warriors who formed a circle. The Younger spoke to them.

"Some of you fought at my side at Carn Liath. Some of you joined me in later battles. Between us, we have faced many enemies who desired our lands. Without you, our people would be slaves. Without you, my crown has no value. Without you, everything that gives a king authority to rule, has no value. Not even the value of one coin."

He paused and a breeze blew back his long grey hair.

"Courage and the loyalty of my people are the things that gave me power. I hope I repaid your trust by ruling justly."

Everyone stared at him in silence and one warrior raised his claymore to the sky. All the warriors raised their swords, but did not speak.

"Today I fulfil the prophecy of an Ancient One. Today, I offer my life to my son, Prince Ranald. Do not lose heart, or let fear enter your hearts. Be sure. Be absolutely sure. Ranald shall be king, but his authority will be taken from him by the sword after just one day."

Malcolm raised his claymore too.

"You must hold the palace from Ranald for one more day. At dawn tomorrow, look for Alistair of Cadbol and the Irish army. They will be joined by a new king who shall unite the royal houses of Donald and Elder. Only when those houses are one, can a new Long Peace be enjoyed. But that peace *will* come and our people *shall* prosper."

The Younger pointed at the gates.

"Deny Ranald the protection of these walls."

Malcolm turned to face Ancevo.

"Until the new king arrives, Ancevo shall lead you. Do his will and *believe* that help comes soon."

A small herd of goats completely ignored the emotional gathering and grazed along one side of the Palace Green. Malcolm saw them and thought about Matina. He stared up at the chamber, where she still slept, and instead saw Arkinew's window.

"Goodbye, old friend," he whispered.

Malcolm sighed.

"My time is over. Lower your swords, man the walls and do my will one last time."

The circle of warriors ran off and Ancevo found himself alone with the Younger.

"Is there anything else I should do?"

The greatest king who had ever ruled the land of the Scots put an arm around Ancevo's shoulders and tried not to show that he felt sick with fear.

"Don't let anyone eat Matina's goats."

321

Ranald slept soundly and dreamed happily about being king. He saw himself sitting upon the throne, enjoying power and great wealth, and planning attacks on Berwick and Skye to win more land and extend his authority. He would be like the Elder, that was how to be a king, not like his weak father. The Scots needed a warrior leader who was feared and respected. He would own the best of all things and tax his people to get them, the palace would become the grandest palace in the world, everyone would stand in awe before it, and pay tribute to him there.

His dream was interrupted by a picture of his father, the Younger, gifting a shepherd a gold brooch with a ruby at its heart. The shepherd's name resounded in Ranald's memory.

"Dougie of Dunfermline."

He would not be hard to find. That man had stolen part of his inheritance and Ranald wanted it back. He imagined himself wearing the crown on his head and the brooch on his shawl, and sitting at the head of the High table, displaying his finery to the heads of the loyal clans. Any clan who did not show him loyalty would be destroyed, just as the Elder had destroyed all the heirs to the line of Donald.

A noise woke him and Ranald opened an eye. A young warrior stood nervously by his bed.

"Get out, you dog."

"Master, something is happening at the palace and Morag McCreedy rides from her camp to join you by the gates."

Ranald yawned.

"Get out and let me dress."

"Yes, master."

Ranald threw a silver goblet at him.

"Yes, *Your Majesty*. Get it right, dog."

The young man fled.

Malcolm stared at two guards waiting beside the gates, dreading having to give them the order. Six hefty warriors also waited for his order and stood around the heavy, wooden throne of Scotland. He took a deep breath and thought something which gave him no comfort at all.

"The pain will not last long. Come on."

Ancevo wondered if the Younger was waiting for him to give the order and spoke in a strong voice, jolting the king from his thoughts.

"Open the gates."

The guards lifted a beam that sat in huge iron hooks across both gates. Then they lifted and tossed aside two more heavy beams.

"Goodbye, Ancevo," said Malcolm. "You risked your life to give me hope and I thank you for it."

Ancevo did not know what to say, or do, and froze, and watched his king walk out of the gates. The six warriors picked up the throne and manhandled it outside, where they placed it gently down and turned. As soon as they were safely back inside the palace, the gates closed behind them and the locking beams wedged back into place.

Ancevo ran across the grass and bounded up the stairs to the top of the wall, scared now that he was in charge and scared by what he might see. He pushed past the other warriors, who crowded the battlements, and spoke to them.

"Not an arrow is to be fired. Not a spear is to be thrown."

They stared down at the Younger, who showed no hesitation or fear. He was like a rock, standing fifty paces away, waiting for Morag and Ranald to dismount and walk over to kill him. The king unsheathed his sword and drove the blade in to the ground, watching the hilt rock back and forth. Ancevo heard him call out to Ranald.

"Tomorrow, the palace gates will open for you and without a drop of blood being spilled. Until then, the throne may rest with you. My son, come to me now and take my sword. Your day has come. Come and fulfil your ambition. Come and be king."

Without any trace of love for his father, Ranald walked towards him and picked up the Younger's sword.

Ancevo watched him draw it back and shut his eyes.

***

Later, Ranald sat upon the throne of Scotland. He was alone in his tent and running his hands along the smooth oak arms, thinking about all the kings who had ruled from his new seat. His father had said that the Palace Guard would open the gates for him tomorrow, on the day of the full moon, and he could not decide if he should make the guard his own, or kill them as an example to others. Ranald liked that dilemma. Only *he* could choose if they lived or died.

The floor in front of the throne began to shimmer, like moonlight on water, and he sat back, remembering how he had sometimes seen the Ancient One appear before the Younger. Myroy rose and spoke.

"A long time ago I took an oath. I promised to be an advisor to the kings of Scotland, if they desired my help. The Elder refused it and chose to be bonded to an alchemist, so that he could gain knowledge of what might be. Now, in your time, the last alchemist will soon join the fallen. I remember the Elder as a child, Malcolm and Murdoch as children, and you too. My promise of aid is equal to all of your line, who desire it. Do you want my help, King Ranald?"

The young man relaxed and his confidence returned in bucket loads.

"Yesterday, I was a prince. Today, I am a king and tomorrow I shall rule the land from the palace. Do you agree to do my will and no one else's will?"

"No."

Ranald smiled.

"What kind of advisor to kings are you then?"

"The kind that helps you learn. The kind who tells you the things that others will not, or cannot, tell you. An advisor who

324

shapes your destiny and the destiny of others around you."

"You speak in riddles. The days of the alchemists and the Ancient Ones is coming to an end. All around you, the old magic is dying. Kings shall be all-powerful."

"All-powerful?"

Ranald snapped back.

"I am not the Younger."

"You are Ranald, the new king."

"I do not need your help, old man. There is nothing that you, or anyone else, can do to hinder me. My will *shall* be done."

Myroy remained silent as he waved his staff in a circle above the ground. When he descended into the underworld, he broke the silence.

"I agree with you."

Ranald watched the last shimmers of moonlight.

"Agree with what?" he snapped.

A faint voice came from deep within the earth.

"You are *not* the Younger."

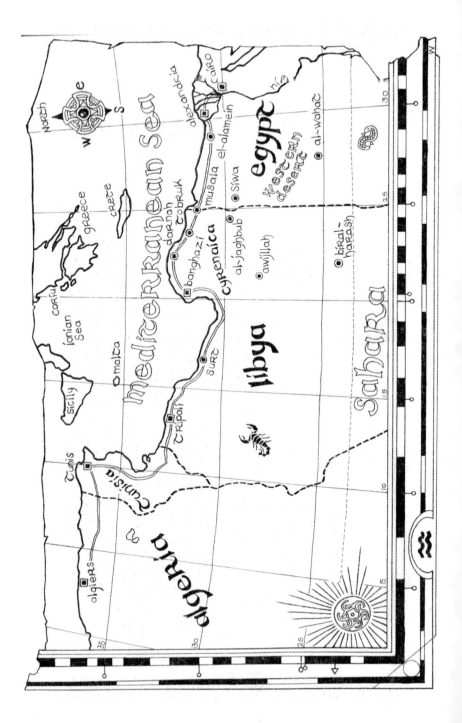

CHAPTER SIXTEEN

SUPER BASE AT AL-JAGHBUB

As Gora finished this part of the story, Peter sensed Kylie's sadness and put an arm around her.

"The Younger was such a brave man. I don't think I could ever be that brave, if I knew I was going to die."

Gora stood, transformed into a giant osprey, flapped his wings and rose between the stone osprey book-ends to stand upon his perch. He hopped and turned, and his mighty talons gripped the trunk of oak, curving all the way around it.

"Haaaa. You will need to be at least that brave. What have you learned?"

Kylie brushed a tear off her cheek.

"Ranald is a fool. Myroy offered him help, as an advisor to kings, and he turned it down because he believed that having a title, like king, made him powerful. The Younger knew that was not true. His power came from the loyalty of his followers and, when everything was said and done, that loyalty was earned by Malcolm's courage and kindness to his people."

"Haaaa. Good. Good. Peter, what did you learn?"

"That revenge makes you do stupid things. Seamus was so in love with Margaret and so desperate to kill Borak that he ignored all the warnings. Finn told him not to face Borak alone and that is exactly what he did. Seamus handed his life on a plate to Borak and it changed little."

Another ear splitting screech.

"Changed little?"

"Oh, yes, sorry. Seamus had to die if Margaret was to be free to marry again. The union of the Donalds and Elders is coming, isn't it?"

"Yes. What else did you learn?"

Peter and Kylie glanced at each other and the volume of Gora's cry went up.

"What else did you learn?"

Kylie slapped her hands over her ears, stood and stretched her back.

"Take your allies from wherever you can. The Scots and Picts had been enemies for years and yet Alistair asked Borak to become the Protector of the Outer Islands. I wouldn't want to be in Ranald's shoes. The Irish are coming, and the gypsies who want a blood feud with Morag McCreedy."

Peter nodded.

"And the Corsairs. If Alec leads them to the palace, they are going to cause quite a stir. Ranald will not have seen anything as frightening as Konini the Slave Master."

"Good, good. Go back into the War Simulator."

Their heads dropped.

"Oh, no," said Peter.

Tirani the Wise appeared from nowhere and skipped over.

"Hello, Gora. How is the training going?"

"Good. Good."

"Good. Can I borrow Peter and Kylie for a while? Malcolm the Younger says that things are quiet in the Orange Band north of our base in Washington. His number two, Jet Morrison, reports a few skirmishes and that's all. But Duncan Donald told me huge numbers of the enemy gather at Marseilles. We think Odin's first attack will be against North Africa."

"Thorgood Firebrand?"

"No reports, but he is definitely in charge of Europe. Olaf Adanson runs things from New York."

"Why? Why do you need my pupils?"

"Duncan has left for the Super Base at Al-Jaghbub and the other Keepers will stay here in the Realm of the Dead. Everyone else is helping to prepare the defence of Africa from the oasis." Tirani grinned. "Most of them have been given small jobs to do by Peter and he should be checking up on how they are getting on."

Gora flapped his wings and rose up into the sky above the loch, calling back down and watching them with his dark, penetrating eyes.

"Haaa. Bring the children back to me soon. The Simulator waits for them."

Even Tirani put his hands over his ears.

"He is so loud," said the Ancient One.

※※※

Duncan Donald sat with Bernard and Chalky, under a camouflaged net in the cigar-shaped oasis of Al-Jaghbub.

"I'd forgotten how ruddy hot this place is," said Chalky.

Duncan looked at the black sweat patches under his friend's armpits and handed him a bottle of water from a coolbox.

"Och, if you spend sixty years in a block of ice, it's going to feel a wee bit warm."

"Can we keep our minds on the job?" asked Bernard.

He rolled out the map of North Africa that he had kept safe since the Second World War. Its edges were faded and yellow, and a corner had been stuck back on with Sellotape. He pointed at Al-Jaghbub.

"OK. We are here. Odin's forces are off the map, north of Algiers and across the Med at Marseilles. Can't be more than nine hundred kilometres from one port to the other, which means Algiers is their most likely target."

Duncan nodded.

"Distance from here to Algiers?"

"Hmm. About three thousand kilometres, as the crow flies, so well within range for our fighter planes and missiles."

"What do Donald and Hamish say?" asked Chalky.

"I spoke to Donald last night on Long Wave. They are pretending to be soldiers in Thorgood's army. Donald moaned about their uniforms. They don't fit. Their weapons are short of ammo, they aren't fed often, don't sleep much and they aren't told anything. Thorgood's warriors only do what they are told to do and that is a surprising development."

"And one we can take advantage of," said Duncan.

"Yes. Kill Thorgood and Olaf and their armies are useless."

Chalky swiped at a fly by his ear.

"Until Odin takes over and there are millions of 'em, even if

330

they're uniforms don't fit. 'Ere, why aren't Hamish and Donald affected by Odin's will? They are well within the Red Empire. They should be robots like everyone else."

"Tirani thinks it's because they have Celtic blood, but no one is sure."

They stared at the map and Bernard drew two lines on it with a red felt-tip pen. One line went from Algiers to the southern tip of mainland Greece. The other joined Tripoli to Crete.

"OK, that is the Orange Band, so Algiers is half in and half out of it. God knows what will happen when we fight inside the Band, on the edge of the stone's power?"

Chalky looked around the oasis. It only felt as though he had been away from it for a few weeks and everything was the same, but different. The pillars of flies, bird song, oppressive heat even in the shade, and the tall palm trees all gave the place the same 'sanctuary' feel. But the trees had grown up in different places and the pool water was crystal clear now and not polluted by oil like it had been during the war. Also, their modified jeep was a rusting shell, abandoned long ago and decaying just a few metres away from where they now sat. As Chalky studied it, the headlights flashed and the horn gave a sad *toot*.

"'Ere, what's goin' on?"

Bernard took out his old army revolver.

"Early Warning System. We've got company."

They walked quickly through the palms to the edge of the oasis. Duncan blinked in the dazzling sunshine.

"You forget, don't you, just how hot and bright it is without shade. Can you see anything?"

Chalky shook his head and Bernard pointed at the line of distant hills, with areas of sand dunes and flat sand in the foreground. A heat haze shimmered at the base of the hills.

"Do you remember the ravine where we were captured by General Georg Grau?"

"Like it was yesterday," said Chalky.

331

"Well, look below that hill, just to the left of the tallest sand dune."

"I've got it," said Duncan, "it's the Bedouin, the wandering people of the desert. A line of them; five or six horses!"

"We still friends with 'em?" asked Chalky.

Bernard nodded.

"Good friends. After the war I stayed in contact and helped them, when I could. Now they tip us off if tourists drive out here. They played a vital role during the construction of the Super Base."

"How long did it take?"

"Twenty years, Chalky. Twenty long years."

"Crumbs. And you kept it secret all that time."

"We all did."

"And how many people work here?"

"About ten thousand."

They wandered back to the clearing by the pool and sat around the map again, beneath the camouflage netting.

"Are you sure ruddy Odin don't know about this place?"

Bernard glanced at Chalky.

"Sure of it, but he will as soon as the first shots are fired."

"Are the defences good then?"

Duncan smiled and pointed to where the far hills would be if not hidden by the palms.

"You remember the area of flat sand you saw?"

"Yeah."

"When the attack comes, that sand will become a forest."

"And where are the ruddy trees?"

"They will be there when we need them."

Another sad *toot* came from the rusting shell of the jeep, but no flash from the headlights.

"More visitors?" asked Chalky.

They watched as the jeep, and a thin strip of ground it rested on, rose up on four hydraulic metal poles. Peter, Kylie and Tirani the Wise rose up too, until the lift mechanism locked into its full open position with a *clunk*.

Bernard smiled.

"Hello, Tirani. Bringing reinforcements?"

The boy skipped over to join him with Peter and Kylie following.

"Reinforcements and news from the Realm of the Dead. I just spoke to Hamish on the Talk Tunnel. The men of Tain have been moved down to the coast. More arms and ammunition have arrived from somewhere and there are thousands of ships moored close to Marseilles."

"Then they're coming," said Chalky.

Tirani grinned.

"And I am going. Better keep an eye on things in Oslo." He skipped back to stand under the jeep and it began to sink down on the four corner poles. "Myroy says he can sense something odd going on aboard the space station. Can you check MIR out for me on the Big Screen?"

"I will," promised Bernard.

As soon as Peter had stepped through the Travel Tunnel and risen up in a lift, sweat began to drip from his forehead and into his eyes. Even here in the shade, he found it hard to breathe in the searing heat.

"Are you Ok, Kylie? I'm suffering a bit. Feel a bit faint."

"Me too. It's *soooo* hot."

Duncan handed them bottles of water from the cool box.

"Welcome to the Al-Jaghbub Super Base. You'll soon get used to it, but don't wander off outside the oasis, except at dawn or dusk. The sun is a killer out here."

Kylie took a big sip and stared around at the netting, the palms and the pool.

"This is where we fight Odin from?"

"Aye."

"Peter wiped the sweat from his eyes and tried to see any weapons, but there was only the rusty old jeep.

"Is there something we don't know?"

Bernard smiled.

"There is a lot you do not know."

"And me," said Chalky. "They keep goin' on about ruddy trees out on the sand and I can't see a single one."

***

"Clone. Where have you been?" asked Van Heussen.

The Cuckoo in the Nest skipped over and handed him a remote control handset.

"The batteries ran out and I've put new ones in. Olaf told me our master will be ready in five minutes and I didn't want anything to go wrong."

The doctor looked at his young creation.

"Odin cannot sense what you think and asked me to check it out. Do you know why that is?"

"No."

"And do you obey the rules of the Red Empire?"

"I do. Odin is my master."

"Not me?"

"No. You are my father."

Van Heussen smiled at Tirani.

"I can't keep calling you clone. What name shall we give you?"

"Arinti."

"Is it African?"

"Not sure."

"Does it mean anything?"

"It does to me."

"What?"

"The sound. *Arinti* sounds nice."

The doctor got up from his revolving seat, by the central control pillar in the Cloning Research Centre.

"Come on, there are some final checks I want to make."

They went through a massive round steel door and closed it behind them, and walked through the rest of the cloning laboratory, strands of DNA still spiraling around on computer screens, creature body parts floating in glass tanks and men in white coats talking around one tank. They ignored the men, left through another solid round door, identical to the first door, and entered a lift. Five floors down, they stepped onto the highly polished floor of the long observation room. It was in darkness and Van Heussen pointed the remote at the reinforced glass window that ran the entire length of the room. Metal shutters rose, to let artificial daylight inside, and immediately hideous mosquito-like creatures thudded against the glass. One shutter stuck half way up.

"That's a problem. It's not as if we can go outside and fix it."

Arinti smiled and took the remote.

"Let me try."

With the sound of the tinkling waters of the fountain in his ears, the boy pushed a button and the blind went back down. As it dropped, a long, thin red leg fell out from between the metal slats and Arinti pushed another button. A swarm of creatures began to eat the bird who had been trapped in the shutter. The doctor sighed.

"That's one less."

This time the shutter rose easily and the observation room was fully bathed in light.

Thorgood, Olaf Adanson and Mick Roberts joined them, Mick gasping when he saw the creatures who stared at them from the other side of the glass.

"Is everything ready?" asked Thorgood.

The doctor took back the remote from his clone, went over to two boxes mounted on the wall and pushed a button. A red light came on at the side of each counter and large numbers flashed –

1,050,206 BIRDS
1,120,891 FISH

"The final checks have been made and we can begin at any time."

Thorgood spoke to Odin in his mind.

"Master. We are ready to proceed at your command."

The tinkling grew louder as the fountain widened and Odin stepped out of the water, his light blue suit bone-dry and a gold brooch pinned to his chest.

"Proceed."

The counters both clicked over and Van Heussen pointed at them.

1,050,205 BIRDS
1,120,893 FISH

"The target has been achieved. The clone, now named Arinti, has arranged for all of the enemy prisoners to join us."

Another creature thudded against the glass and Odin stared at the boy. He still couldn't look inside his mind, or soul, but he did not feel the same unease that he had felt before holding the ruby.

"Proceed."

The doctor pushed a button and, below them in the great cavern, steel doors rose up to let a freight train enter. Once through, the doors closed quickly.

"Audio," said Odin.

The speakers came on and the observation room was filled with a low, menacing hum. The creatures on the glass flew away and all around the rock chamber the red walls began to move. Spear-like tails appeared out of the honeycomb of tunnels above the steel doors. Van Heussen pointed at the train.

"Holly Anderson and Miss Dickson are inside the rear wagon. They are the most senior Keepers, er, I mean Seekers, ever captured and will be released first."

He gave Arinti the remote control and the boy used it to stop the train. The low hum became higher pitched and deafening. Two women were forced out and down a metal gangplank, and were mobbed by a swarm of creatures. Their screams were replaced by the gruesome sound of sucking.

"Kill them all," commanded Odin.

Hundreds of people were forced from the train. Some made it

across the barley to the island of pines. None made it to the lake and Arinti smiled at his master.

"Death to the enemy."

Odin felt himself wanting to smile back, but resisted.

"Doctor, are we ready to release the creatures?"

"Yes, Master, and we now know their reproduction capacity. If we keep fifty thousand of each creature here, or in the other breeding chambers, we can create another million birds and a million fish in just twelve weeks. That is my proposal."

Odin nodded, stared at the rock chamber and placed his hand on his brooch.

"Winged creatures. Fly south through the Orange Band and kill the enemy. Creatures of the sea, swim south and let nothing pass into the Mediterranean Sea."

The stone pulsed, blood-red, and a hole appeared in the roof of the cavern. The feeding frenzy stopped and the creatures took off, circling around before shooting up and away. The red strings on the lake sank down without trace, leaving the surface smooth and blue.

Odin turned to face his generals.

"Olaf, report."

"All spare arms and men have been shipped from the northeast of the United States to Marseilles. The Red Empire is secure in America, but we cannot drive south, or east, through the Orange Band."

"Thorgood, report."

"We have forty million warriors ready. Mick Roberts has ensured we have the ships we need to move them south. The conversion of oil tankers to troop carriers helped solve some of the problem. The target is Algiers and I suggest a two step invasion."

Odin's eyes flashed.

"Two step?"

"We do not know what will happen when our forces move through the Orange Band. If we ship over one million men as an advance attack party, they can be supported by the fire power of our *Slugs* in the Med, and the creatures we have released. Once we understand how effective our forces are outside of the Red Empire, we can follow quickly with the rest of our forces. The delay is minimal and the benefits substantial."

"You still have concerns about your men?"

"Their lack of initiative."

"Solution?"

"Clear orders will be vital as they fight in the Orange Band. I must lead them through, Master."

"And the space station, MIR?"

"It has fulfilled its purpose, but should not be destroyed."

"Why?"

"The Stone Tracking Device is now operational and something unexpected has occurred."

Fear gripped Tirani as Thorgood continued.

"The stone is shown in two locations."

Odin's forehead creased.

"Two?"

"Oslo and the island of Corfu."

"Precise location?"

"The accuracy of the tracker is improving and we will know the precise location soon."

"Send one million warriors to Corfu."

"I obey, Master."

Odin walked back to the fountain and stepped inside.

"Thorgood of the line of Firebrand. Lead the advance of one million men to Algiers."

"I obey, Master."

***

Duncan watched the small patchwork of light and dappled shade dance across the ground as the palm leaves swayed high above their heads. The camouflage netting added to the strange, moving mosaic pattern and, here and there, sunbeams shone

338

down like lasers to remind everyone to be grateful of the shade in the oasis. He looked at Peter and Kylie.

"Do you want to see the base?"

"Isn't this it?" asked Kylie.

Bernard smiled and walked over to the rusty jeep.

"No. Come on, Peter's got a job to do."

They saw Bernard lean over and release the handbrake, which looked so old it might come off in the old man's hand. The jeep rose up again on its four hydraulic poles and everyone crowded underneath.

"Do you all have your pebbles?" asked Duncan.

Chalky, Peter and Kylie checked their pockets and nodded as the lift descended. It went dark and Peter counted the seconds in his mind. At thirty, the lift doors opened and they stepped out into a circular rock chamber lit by a warm red light. At the far end was an open door at the base of a tall tube that rose from floor to ceiling and stuck halfway out of the rock. A tough-looking woman, with short white hair and colourful tattoos, guarded the entrance to the Super Base. She pointed a machine gun at them.

"Pebbles please."

Bernard walked over and placed his pebble into a bowl, which rested on a table beside the tattooed lady. The bowl glowed red and Bernard took his pebble back.

"Hello, Martha. May I introduce you to Chalky, Peter and Kylie. It is their first visit."

Martha flicked off the safety catch and aimed the gun at Chalky.

"Chalky. The traitor in the tower."

Chalky put up his hands.

"'Ere, I was controlled by Odin, but I'm alright now."

Duncan smiled.

"He's back with us now, so lower the gun."

She didn't lower the gun and nodded at Chalky.

"Pebble in bowl."

Chalky put it in and the bowl glowed red. Martha lowered the machine gun.

"OK. On you go."

The others had their pebbles checked and stood in front of the open door. There was no floor inside the dark tube and a strong wind blew up from somewhere deep inside the earth. Duncan pointed at it.

"This is one of ten Air Tubes dotted around the base. You can use them for quick access to any of the different levels, but if you want to stay fit there are also stairs."

"What levels?" asked Kylie.

Bernard stared at the curved back wall of the shaft.

"Sign, please."

A sign appeared –

Surface and Emergency Exits.
Level One – Leisure
Level Two – Control room and Big Screen
Level Three – Living Quarters
Level Four – Fast Track
(to Algiers, Cairo, Siwa, Johannesburg,
Washington, Realm of the Dead)
Level Five – Armaments Store and Tree Loading Area

"Just step inside and say the level you want. Watch what I do and copy it," said Duncan. "I thought we would start by showing you the leisure facilities."

He stepped, began to fall and spoke in a clear voice.

"Level One."

Then he was gone and Bernard followed quickly.

"Level One."

Kylie stepped forward, felt herself plummet and screamed out.

"Level One!"

A massive blast of air slowed her descent and she glanced down to see Bernard twenty metres below, falling casually with his hands in his pockets. She relaxed and began to enjoy the

340

fall and the sound of wind all around. The force of the updraft increased and Kylie stepped out, through an oval door, into a brightly-lit open space. Duncan came over to her.

"Alright?"

"It's fantastic."

Duncan pointed straight ahead.

"That's the cinema. Over there is the restaurant and swimming pool. Do you like reading?"

Peter joined them, his hair sticking straight up.

"Oh yes," said Kylie.

"We have one of the best libraries in the world on this floor. Turn left at the cinema."

They looked around. It was a weird design. Everything seemed to be built around rows and rows of round metal cylinders. Each cylinder was identical to the next; painted white, twenty metres across and numbered. It was like someone had put many stacks of coins onto a piece of card and then put another card on top to form the roof. Peter went over to a cylinder, with the number seventy-eight on its face, then walked over to number seventy-nine. He counted fifty paces and guessed the distance between all of them was precisely the same. He saw a sign above an arch, which spanned the distance between two cylinders –

Swimming Pool

"Come on. I've got to see this."

As they walked under the arch they smelled chlorine and Chalky gasped.

"Ruddy Nora."

The pool was huge and had tables with parasols, and chairs along one side and grouped together in the spaces between the white cylinders. People sat at the tables in their swimming costumes and waved at them. A young girl dived off a high board at the far end and hardly made a splash.

"Hope the water's warm," said Chalky.

"Why not try it?" said Bernard.

Chalky backed away from the edge of the pool.

"I can't swim."

"What?"

"I can't swim."

"But when I recruited you at Balado, you told me you could swim like a fish."

"I meant a dead fish."

"Hm. Well, you will need to learn."

Peter slipped his hand into Kylie's.

"Let's go for a swim later. We could celebrate."

"Celebrate what?"

"You know."

"I don't know."

He released her hand.

"You think about it."

She wrinkled her nose and Duncan led them out.

"I'll show you the cinema and restaurant later. I want you to see the Big Screen now."

One by one, they stepped into the air tube, saying, "Level Two," and feeling the same powerful blast of air. Level Two was just like Level One, except that the spaces between the white cylinders were filled with office-desks, chairs and computer screens. Many of the screens were manned by people who had fled the MI5 building in London. Julie and Colin Donald stood in front of a one hundred metre long television screen.

"How quickly can we ship missiles up from Johannesburg?" asked Julie.

Colin pointed at a map in one corner of the Big Screen. Other parts of the screen showed maps of the USA, the Mediterranean and the island of Corfu. Corfu was starting to be covered in red dots. Another section showed the orbit of space station MIR. The top right of the screen contained an outline plan of the Super Base and confirmed its cigar shape. Red letters moved along the entire length of the TV –

Surface temperature 40 degrees   Base temperature 21 degrees   Base status – green

"If we Fast Track them, about an hour."

"That's good."

"That's very good. Remember we are shifting heavy equipment all the way from the south to the north of Africa, and we can do that safely and without too many delays."

"Is it fast enough?"

Colin shook his head.

"Probably not. If Odin attacks once, we might be alright, but if he attacks again quickly, we could run out of missiles."

Peter heard his parents talking and came over to study the Big Screen with them. A blue dot showed Al-Jaghbub and straight blue lines came out of the oasis to Algiers, Cairo, Siwa, Johannesburg, Washington and the Realm of the Dead.

"What is Fast Track?"

"Bullet trains in long sealed tunnels. We create a vacuum at one end and our trains are sucked towards it at an incredible speed. No need for engines."

"Who thought of that?"

Colin's face showed suffering.

"Arkinew. Apparently he saw it in the Oracle of the Ancient Ones."

Bernard, Chalky and Duncan stopped looking at another section of screen and joined them too.

"Does the Oracle still work? I thought the crystals had lost most of their power when they lifted up the mountains?" asked Bernard.

"I don't know, but he comes up with ten crazy ideas a day and we try all of them. Once in a while we hit gold."

"Any new weapons?" asked Peter.

Colin shook his head.

"No."

"But Arkinew is trying to discover some, isn't he?"

"I doubt it. He says we will need swords made of light iron to fight in the Orange Band. Even Gangly says so."

Peter smiled.

"See if you can change his mind. When Odin's warriors come through, we are going to need something even better than Computer Aided Rifles."

Julie kissed her son on the cheek and whispered in his ear.

"You've remembered, haven't you?"

Peter whispered back in her ear.

"I have, but Kylie's forgotten, I'm sure of it."

"You gave her a hint?"

"Loads."

"Maybe she's just play-acting?"

Kylie came over.

"What was that?"

Colin saved them.

"We were just saying, we can reinforce the base with missiles in sixty minutes."

"Is that good?"

Colin sighed.

"That's bloody good."

"How's Archie?"

Julie pointed at the floor.

"He is driving us mad. We gave him a laboratory in a safe corner of Level Four and no one will go near it now because of the explosions. I nearly put him on Level Five and that would have been a disaster."

"Why?"

"It's where we store all the ammunition."

"Oh."

"Oh, indeed."

Duncan spoke to the giant screen.

"Battle status?"

The TV changed to show the Med all the way across it. The Orange Band cut it in two and red dots showed the location of the enemy.

Bernard spoke to Chalky, Kylie and Peter.

"Each red dot is one million men."

One dot had broken away from the others at Marseilles and had a red ship symbol beneath it.

"I think that's going towards Corfu," said Duncan.

"So they know about the Realm of the Dead," said Bernard.

Colin shook his head.

"Before you arrived, I talked to Tirani. The spy on MIR told them about Corfu, but they do not have an exact location yet."

"What do we do?" asked Kylie.

Duncan said what some of them were thinking.

"We need the Stone Tracking Device, so we can't destroy the space station. We must find the spy and *deal* with him."

Peter felt as though everyone was looking at him, waiting for him to make the final decision.

"Oh, yes. Carry on."

Duncan smiled and gave his grandson a clipboard with a single sheet of paper on it; a hand-written checklist –

1.	Find a secret way into Odin's chamber.	James/Tirani
2.	The defence forces of America and Africa to work together.	Malcolm the Younger/Duncan Donald
3.	Stop the Black Slugs sailing through the Orange Band.	Kenneth of Blacklock
4.	Free the minds of Odin's followers.	Peter/Kylie
5.	Create a fast-attack force named the Raiders of the Orange Band and destroy enemy supply lines.	Hamish/Donald
6.	Set up a spy network inside of the Red Empire (this includes our Cuckoo in the nest) and make the STD operational.	Bernard/Tirani

345

7. Make the Chinese government our allies.	Dougie/Alistair
8. Ensure we have the armaments we need and develop new weapons.	Catlin,/Julia
9. Broadcast anti-Odin propaganda on Long Wave throughout the Red Empire.	Laura/Darren
10 Be ready to steal back the stone.	Peter/Kylie/ Chalky/Dougie/ Alistair
11. Find out how to destroy the Ancient Ones and the Old Magic.	Myroy

"Two down, nine to go," said Duncan.

"Two down?" asked Peter.

"You can put a tick against points six and eight. The cuckoo is in the nest and the Stone Tracker is working. Bernard hasn't had time to set up the spy network, but it's early days. Armament supplies are good. Who do you want to check up on next?"

Peter looked at the list.

"James?"

"OK." Duncan talked to the screen again. "Location of James Donald?"

A number flashed –

482

"He's in his room on level three," said Bernard.

Loud rock music came from James's door. Peter knocked and nothing happened, so Duncan pushed it open and stepped inside.

"What's going on?" yelled James.

Everyone came in.

"Oh, do come in."

Peter looked at his brother, lying on the bed, lad's magazines covering the floor, and pictures of beautiful ladies in bikinis on the walls. The room itself was a perfect square, without windows, and with a built-in wardrobe along one wall opposite a double bed.

"Can you turn that music off?"

James shouted at the ceiling.

"Music off."

Now, everyone could hear and think.

"Can you give me an update on the job I gave to you and Tirani?" asked Peter.

James changed the subject.

"Cool room. Isn't it? Got a great sound system."

Kylie stared at the girls in bikinis on the walls and put her hands on her hips.

"I wouldn't say it was cool at all."

"Update," said Peter.

"Do you think I've just been lying on my bed?"

"Yes."

"I've been thinking."

"Uh, huh."

"Deep thinking."

"Uh, huh."

James grinned.

"And studying Tirani's last report."

Peter pulled a pen from the side of his clipboard and got ready to put a cross against point one.

"Well?"

"Well what?"

"How do I get into Odin's chamber without being seen?"

James sighed.

"Tirani watched the release of the birds and fish. The birds got out through a hole in the cave ceiling. The fish sank down from the surface of the lake, which means there must be a tunnel that goes out to the sea. Odin is leaving fifty thousand of the creatures there, so he can breed some more, and he feeds them with cows. When that happens, they surface, form into red strings and gather to one side of the lake; the side with the railway on. That might be the best time to enter."

"And how do I get past the birds?"

"We have to find a way of getting you onto the train and I don't know yet. But, I bet there are no nasty traps in the tunnel from the lake to the sea. Odin doesn't think he needs them with those deadly creatures around."

Peter shuddered, but ticked point one.

"Thanks. Keep at it. Early days yet."

"Who do you want to see next?" asked Duncan.

Peter looked at his plan.

"Laura."

"Rooms six one seven and six one eight. The noisiest rooms on the base."

Everyone left, except Peter who hung back.

"James, do you have a rucksack?"

"Sure."

"Can I borrow it and a blanket?"

"What are you up to, dip-stick?"

Peter smiled.

"This is not your business."

Outside room six one eight, Duncan frowned.

"Completely silent. I get nothing but complaints from Laura's neighbours and she's only been here a wee while."

He knocked and Darren opened the door.

"Hi, come on in."

Laura's room was probably the same size as James's, but it seemed a fraction of the size because of the mass of equipment it stored. On the far wall was a bookcase lined with CDs and around the other walls were decks, amplifiers, flashing black metal boxes, tall speakers and a built-in desk and chair. Laura sat at the desk and spoke into a microphone, a candle in a glass lantern beside her.

"OK, Rob. Scan the next group of frequencies."

The room was filled with the sound of a radio being tuned in and out of radio stations, some loud and some faint and broken.

"Go back, Rob."

Her invisible helper tuned back and a man spoke in Japanese before playing a record.

"That's not it. Next group."

Everyone crowded around the desk, watching and listening as Laura tried to pin down the Red Empire's broadcasting frequency. A funny squeal came from the speakers, then a lady's voice.

"This is Empire News. The headlines. All our enemies under the red sky are vanquished. Today, in Oslo, hundreds of Seekers were executed under the personal supervision of our master. Thorgood Firebrand has told us that rumours of an uprising close to the Orange Band on some of the Greek islands, is completely untrue. We must all be careful about being misled by enemy propaganda. In football, Olaf Adanson announced the creation of a new cup competition between the new provinces of our glorious empire. The final will be held in Oslo next June."

"That's it," said Laura. "Darren, are you ready to broadcast?"

He nodded and put a CD into one of the flashing black boxes.

"Ready."

The lady continued with the news, her voice crystal clear on Long Wave.

"And now over to our reporter in Oslo for an exclusive interview with Odin himself. Mike are you there?"

"Thank you, Alice, and it is my great pleasure to introduce you to our master. Odin, please tell your millions of followers about today's executions."

Laura called out.

"Do it, Darren."

349

He pushed a button and lots more lights flashed on the metal boxes and a jingle came from the speakers –

Odin's not a god,
His real name's Fred.
He's got a great big bum,
And a little tiny head.

It repeated, but with a heavy rock band playing along.

Laura winked at Darren.

"Turn it off."

Alice at Empire News spoke in a flustered voice.

"Well, we seem to have a small technical problem with our link to Oslo, so over now to our Sports Correspondent, Gary Linneker, for a report on an exciting new cup competition."

Laura pushed her chair back and smiled at Peter.

"Well?"

"Odin's not a god, his real name's Fred? That's terrible."

"Is it annoying?"

"Very."

She put her hands on her hips.

"Well?"

Peter smiled too and put a tick on his checklist.

"That's great. Keep up the good work."

Once again, Peter held back when everyone left.

"Laura, can I borrow that candle and lantern?"

"Why?"

"It's a surprise."

"You'll bring it back?"

"I Promise. Do you have any matches?"

Back in front of the Big Screen, Colin and Julie Donald were staring at a map of the Mediterranean. Red dots kept appearing in the sea between Algiers and Marseilles. Ten red ship symbols showed the mooring positions of Odin's fleet at Marseilles. Colin pointed at them.

"Each red ship is one hundred real ships, so Thorgood has a thousand vessels to help him invade North Africa."

"What are the red dots?" asked Julie.

"*Black Slugs*. In the last two minutes, they have been surfacing in huge numbers."

Kylie, Bernard, Chalky and Duncan joined them and heard the comment.

"Amber alert?" asked Bernard.

Duncan nodded and spoke at the screen.

"Base to amber alert."

A new set of red words moved from left to right along the bottom of the giant TV.

Surface temperature 35 degrees
Base temperature 20 degrees
Base status – amber

A stream of people stepped out of the Air Tubes and sat down at computer screens, logging on and concentrating hard.

"What do they all do?" asked Kylie.

"They all have their own jobs," said Bernard. "But it's mainly keeping an eye on our Early Warning Systems, checking equipment and ensuring that the base is battle-ready. A lot of them operate the trees."

"What are these ruddy trees?" asked Chalky.

"Wait a while. It will not be long before you see them in action. Look, more *Slugs* are surfacing."

The Mediterranean north of Algiers was now a mass of small red dots. Duncan spoke to Peter and Kylie.

"New clothes have been put in your rooms. You can't do any more checking at the moment, not today anyway. Kylie you are in room five six zero and Peter you are in six zero two."

"Do we get room keys?" asked Kylie.

"We don't use them."

Peter looked at his checklist.

"And where is Kenneth of Blacklock?"

"Indian Ocean, gathering a fleet together. He plans to join up with the US fleet in the Caribbean, in three weeks' time."

"So he is too far away to help us."

"Yes."

The Big Screen changed to show the forward view from the cockpit of a fighter plane. Blue words appeared beneath it.

Test flight into the Orange Band. Pilot, Jet Morrison.

"Don't go just yet," said Duncan. "Jet Morrison has Fast-Tracked in from Washington. He is one of our best pilots and volunteered to check out our communications systems."

The live pictures showed the plane moving at great speed, the ground not far below flashing by. The coast and the blue of the Mediterranean was approaching fast. Bernard spoke up at the screen.

"Add Map View."

A blue plane symbol flashed and moved towards the sea to the east of Algiers. Then it turned north towards the edge of the Orange Band. Kylie watched the live pictures from the cockpit, saw a wall of orange racing towards the plane and heard an American voice.

"Five seconds to Orange Band. Get ready to switch to Long Wave."

A lady with headphones at a computer screen replied to Jet.

"Ready."

The sky around the cabin became completely orange, but it entered the band without a judder. Jet's voice again.

"I am working on fifty percent visibility, but it's still pretty good. It's a bit like being in thin orange cloud. Fantastic colour."

The lady replied.

"Receiving you loud and clear, Jet. Please send the test messages on FM, Medium Wave and digital."

"Messages sent."

Three people, at screens close to the lady, shook their heads.

"Not received, Jet. Please resend."

"Messages sent."

More shaking heads.

"Negative. How are the controls?"

The view out of the cockpit spun around as the plane was thrown into a roll.

Jet's voice on the speakers.

"No problems."

"Radar?"

"I'm picking up loads of *Slugs* about eight kilometres off-shore. Do you want me to take a shot at one?"

The lady looked at Duncan and Duncan looked at Peter.

"Well?"

Peter thought about it and smiled.

"Don't see why not."

The lady gave Jet the decision.

"Please proceed."

"OK. Missiles locked on and …away."

Two whooshing sounds came from the speakers and after a few seconds the lady spoke again.

"How is it looking?"

"Negative," said Jet. "I repeat, negative. Both missiles curved down into the sea and failed to detonate."

Bernard went over to join the lady at her screen.

"Jet, this is Bernard. Repeat the attack."

Two more whooshing sounds and a short wait.

"Negative, Bernard. The same thing; the missiles veered off course and did not explode."

"Any fault or warning lights flashing?"

"No."

"OK. Return to base."

Peter saw a red beam leave a *Slug*.

"What's that?"

Jet answered first.

"I have a trace. A *Slug* has returned fire. Impact fifteen seconds."

Everyone waited, hearts in their mouths, but the red beam

curved harmlessly away from Jet's plane. Peter thought about Arkinew and Gangly, and their prediction.

"Archie said we will need weapons made from the light iron when we fight in the Orange Band."

"Interesting," said Duncan. "Maybe weapons don't work inside the Band. Now that is interesting."

Kylie's forehead creased.

"But why? We can fly, talk on Long Wave and use radar. Why don't the missiles work?"

Bernard shook his head.

"Don't know, but if it's true, it will be a very different kind of war. Come on, I'll show you to your rooms."

Kylie kissed Peter outside room five six zero.

"See you in the restaurant in about an hour?"

Peter checked his watch.

"Six-thirty, no worries."

She went inside and Bernard led Peter past row upon row of the wide white cylinders to room six zero two.

"Thanks, Bernard. Anything else I need to do?"

"Not tonight. Just relax and enjoy the base. How about meeting for breakfast, about seven?"

"OK, goodnight."

Peter closed his door and stuck his ear against it, listening for Bernard's footsteps out in the corridor.

His bedroom was the same layout as James and Laura's, but neater and quieter, and he ignored the pile of new clothes on the bed and left to find the nearest Air Tube. He walked quickly around a white cylinder and wondered again what they were for and why they seemed to run down through all the different levels of the base. He jumped inside an Air Tube, rose to Level One and came out by the restaurant. It was deserted, except for a young man in a white apron who was putting away trays of food into a walk-in fridge. Peter snaked his way through the tables and chairs, picked up a tray and slid it along metal runners, which ran the entire length of the service counter.

"Hi, I'm Peter. Can I get some food?"

The man shot him a critical look.

"Haven't you heard? The base is on amber alert."

"Yes. I was at the Big Screen when Duncan made the decision."

"No food allowed. Everyone's got to get ready to defend the base."

Peter had to get something and spoke as if he still held Amera's stone.

"You can make an exception."

"I can make an exception."

This surprised Peter. Odin had the ruby, but he still seemed to be able to use its power, or some of it at least. Encouraged, he pushed on.

"What can I take away?"

"Sandwiches, crisps, chocolate bars, cartons of juice and fruit. Lots of things."

Peter unshouldered his rucksack and opened it up.

"Two different kinds of sandwich, but not cheese and pickle, two cartons of pineapple juice and two apples please."

The man went into his fridge, came back and placed the haul into Peter's bag.

"How much?" asked Peter.

"No one pays for anything on the base."

"Great. By the way, please don't mention I was here to anyone."

"I will not mention it to anyone."

Peter ran out and jumped into an Air Tube.

"Surface."

An incredible wind carried him upwards, the inside of the tube dark and eerie, until he hovered in front of a flashing amber sign.

Amber Alert

Miss Dickson's recorded voice came from a circle of small holes above the sign.

355

"The base is on amber alert. Do you have authorization to go out onto the surface?"

Peter imagined that he held the stone in his hand and lied.

"Yes."

A door opened and he stepped out onto a flat area of sand. It was much cooler now and the bottom of the sun kissed the western horizon and sent long shadows out from nearby dunes. The cigar shape of Al-Jaghbub was a fair distance away and the oasis looked lonely and small in the vastness of the Sahara. He knelt and quickly laid out the blanket and food, and turned a corner of the blanket over to protect the juice from the warmth of the falling sun. Peter put the rucksack into the centre of the blanket and took a last look around. It was perfect. The sand was turning orange and gold, and the ravines in the far hills were like black shadowy fingers. He stared north west. The Orange Band near Algiers was not visible from here, but in that direction, the sun made a low line of clouds shine bright red.

"Gorgeous."

He went inside the Air Tunnel, which protruded above the flat sand, and spoke.

"Level Three."

In less than two minutes he was knocking on Kylie's door. After a while it opened, Kylie brushing her hair and a toothbrush in her mouth.

"What?"

"Come on."

She waved her toothbrush at him.

"It's not six-thirty yet."

"I know, but there is something I would really like you to see."

***

Bernard and Duncan stared up at the Big Screen and thought exactly the same thing.

"They are making their move," said Bernard.

356

The people at their computer screens lifted their heads and listened to them. Duncan pointed at the red ship symbols. Some of them had begun to move south.

"It's too soon to say. Some ships are sailing south from Marseilles, but not all."

"Maybe the ships in dock are still bein' loaded," said Chalky.

Another red ship, one hundred real ships, momentarily disappeared from the screen and reappeared further south.

"Red alert?" asked Bernard.

"The *Black Slugs* are taking no action," said Duncan. "Not yet."

***

"Where are we going?" asked Kylie.

"Get in and say, 'Surface.'"

"Why?"

Peter kissed her.

"There is something I want to show you."

"Is it good?"

"It is *very* good."

She stepped inside the Air Tube.

"Surface."

Peter watched her legs rise up out of sight and followed.

"Surface."

Kylie hovered in front of the flashing sign and Peter floated up beside her just in time to answer Miss Dickson's question. He imagined himself holding the stone.

"Do you have authorization to go out on to the surface?"

"Yes," he said.

The darkness inside the tube was replaced by bright evening sunshine and, even now, it was beautifully warm.

"Are you sure we are allowed to be out here?" asked Kylie.

"Yep, it's a *special* day."

He took her arm and beckoned her to sit on their picnic blanket.

"You keep saying that."

Peter put on an innocent look.

"What?"

"A *special* day."

"How long have we been going out together?"

"About a year."

"*About* a year?"

Understanding came to Kylie.

"It isn't?"

"It is."

"Our first anniversary?"

Peter opened a pack of ham and mustard sandwiches and passed her one.

"Yep."

"Have you liked being my friend?"

"Yep."

"Stop that, right now."

"I've loved it."

Kylie looked at the sunset, the desert and far hills, the shadows behind the dunes and the red cloud to the north-west.

"Peter. This is *soooo* romantic. You're really special."

"Pineapple juice?"

"Thanks."

"I'm not special."

"Oh, come on. You were the last Keeper."

Peter frowned.

"Thanks a lot."

"And you fought Odin."

"And lost the stone."

Kylie put an arm around his shoulder.

"You won't ever lose me."

"Promise?"

She kissed him on the lips.

"I promise."

Bernard, Chalky and Duncan were rooted to the spot, staring at the red ships on the screen.

"Odin's entire fleet is sailing south from Marseilles," said Bernard.

A man at a computer called out to them.

"Algiers reports a missile bombardment on our side of the Orange Band. The *Black Slugs* are kicking things off."

"So, we can't use missiles inside the Band, but if we get them through onto the other side, then they will work fine."

"Looks like it," said Bernard.

The same man at a computer stood up and waved frantically at them.

"I've lost all contact with our forces in Algiers."

"Last communication?" asked Bernard.

"Couldn't have heard it right. Something about a humming noise and birds in the sky."

Duncan nodded.

"Get ready, everyone. This is it. Put the base onto red alert."

As he spoke, the words travelling along the base of the screen changed –

Surface temperature 26 degrees
Base temperature 19 degrees
Base status – red
All entrances to the base are being sealed

The artificial daylight was replaced by a red glow and everything fell silent. Bernard glanced at Duncan.

"The first test for Al-Jaghbub."

"And not the last."

"Are you ready, Duncan?"

Duncan nodded and turned to speak to his team who sat at their computer screens.

"Activate the trees."

***

Behind Peter and Kylie, the Air Tube sank silently into the sand.

"Want your apple?" asked Peter.

"Not Yet. Just look at the sunset on the desert. It's like something out of a fairy tale."

"Grandpa told me it gets dark quickly in the desert and that there are so many more stars out here."

"Can we stay a bit longer?"

"Don't see why not. They don't really need us in the base."

Kylie kissed him again.

"I'm glad we are here, alone and in such a peaceful place."

"You like the desert?"

"Love it."

She sat up and stared at the bright red cloud to the north west. It seemed to be moving quickly for a cloud and sometimes it darted to one side, like a huge shoal of small fish evading a predator before reforming into a shoal again.

"You ever seen a cloud like that?"

Peter shook his head.

"No. It's very red. Maybe that's how a heat haze makes clouds look. Pretty though."

He glanced at the setting sun. A thin slither of bright white light was still showing above the horizon and the sky above it was bronze and gold. He took the lantern from his rucksack and lit the candle with Laura's matches.

"You think of everything, don't you," said Kylie.

Peter grinned and shrugged his shoulders.

"It's a good job one of us has got a good memory."

"Hmm."

"Do I get another kiss?"

They put their arms around each other, closed their eyes and kissed, and felt as though they were being lifted up into the heavens.

"Wow," said Peter. "Did you feel as though you were flying too?"

He opened his eyes. They still lay on the blanket, which now rested in the centre of a flat, circular floor about twenty metres across. A gentle breeze lifted some of the sand and blew it out into space. All around them, hundreds of tall steel towers were rising as well and formed a cigar-shaped forest. Kylie crawled over to the edge and knocked sand away from the floor. Underneath was steel. She peered down.

"Come and see this. We must be over a hundred metres up."

He joined her and lay on his stomach as clunking noises sounded from inside their tower, like metal doors being slammed shut. Below them, the heads of five missiles poked out in an exact line, one above the other. They looked at the other trees. Five round holes appeared up the side of each tower and more missiles stuck out. The whole forest, the defense system of Al-Jaghbub, was exactly the same cigar shape as the real oasis and threw long, menacing finger-shadows back towards the sand dunes.

"That slamming sound. Do you think we are shut out of the base?" asked Kylie.

"Yep."

"Why?"

Peter shrugged his shoulders.

"No idea."

"So we're trapped up here. What do we do?"

Peter felt their tower revolve. All the other towers turned too as their controllers used the computers to point the missiles at Algiers.

"I don't know," he said.

Kylie stared at the fast-moving red cloud to the north-west. It was so much closer now. The hairs on the back of her neck stood up and her voice was full of terror.

"Peter. Can you hear a humming noise?"

Dougie and Peter will return in their last thrilling adventure, *The Gora Moons*.

Prince Ranald fulfils his ambition, but is king for only one day. The High Table unites once more and the royal houses, of Elder and Donald, come together to herald the second Long Peace and, at last, a shepherd can return to the quiet life he always wanted.

Dougie of Dunfermline has finished with war and adventure, but in our time his descendant, Peter, faces the most dangerous challenge of any Stone Keeper.

Odin's power grows and the forces of the free world can no longer defend themselves from the greater enemy.

The Orange Band becomes littered with death, the Red Empire expands and the world is plundered of its resources to fuel Odin's anger and greed. But an emotion held in the heart of a girl stands in the god's way, an emotion so strong that it magnifies the ruby's incredible power and awakens the Gora moons.

In the blink of an eye, Peter of the line of Donald realises the true significance of Myroy's story. The moon becomes full, silver and bright, and signals the last days for a Stone Keeper, and the final day for the planet we call earth.

If you would like to read the start of the
next book then please visit –

www.myroybooks.com

TEACHERS

If you would like to invite Colin to your school for a book reading, please contact him at the following email address –

c.foreman123@btinternet.com

The normal size of group for a reading is 30 pupils and the best age range is 9 to 12 years.
We look forward to hearing from you.